Twilight of the Gods

By Edmond Hamilton

Cover art by Robert Gibson Jones

ISBN 978-1-7358982-2-3

Cover layout by Michael Greylord

"Twilight of the Gods" originally appeared in the July 1948 issue of *Weird Tales.*

"Priestess of the Labyrinth" originally appeared in the January 1945 issue of *Weird Tales.*

"The Shining Land" originally appeared in the May 1945 issue of *Weird Tales.*

"Lost Elysium" originally appeared in the November 1945 issue of *Weird Tales.*

"The Valley of the Gods" originally appeared in the May 1946 issue of *Weird Tales.*

"The King of Shadows" originally appeared in the January 1947 issue of *Weird Tales.*

"Serpent Princess" originally appeared in the January 1948 issue of *Weird Tales.*

"The Daughter of Thor" originally appeared in the August 1942 issue of *Fantastic Adventures.*

TABLE OF CONTENTS

Twilight of the Gods

The haunting mystery that had oppressed me for eight long years had, finally, become unbearable. That June morning in New York, I readied my decision. I must try again to solve the dark riddle of my life.

Because I knew that Laughlin, my employer and my best friend, would try to talk me out of it, I bought my plane ticket first. Then I went to the office and told him.

He looked troubled. "You're going back to Norway? Eric, I wouldn't!"

"I've got to know!" I burst out. "I've got to know who I am!"

"You are Eric Wolverson," he said. "Let it go at that."

I shook my head. "I can't. Because I know that's not my real name—it's only the name they gave me."

I hurried on. "There must be *some* clue to my identity up in those mountains of northern Norway where they found me. Somewhere, I must have had family, friends, a real past."

"You found nothing, you said, in the year you lived there in the village," he reminded me.

"I gave up too easily," I muttered. "This time, I'll keep searching."

He looked at me keenly. "Eric, what about the people there? Will they have forgotten their superstitious dislike of you?"

I knew well enough that they would not have forgotten. I could hear again the children and the old crones whispering *"Troll!"* as I walked through that little hamlet in the wild, pine-clad northern mountains.

Most Norwegians, even in the remotest districts, are too well educated to harbor old superstitions. But something about me had set them against me from the first. Only the most ignorant had voiced a superstitious fear of me, but all of them—except my foster-parents—had disliked me.

"I don't care," I said grimly. "This time, I'm going to stay there until I discover who I am."

Laughlin desisted his attempt to persuade me. "I can't really blame you, Eric. It must be a maddening thing, not to remember your own past."

He laid his hand on my shoulder. "But if you fail—and I fear you will—promise that you'll come back to New York."

I shook his hand. Twelve hours later, I was in a Constellation winging eastward through the night toward my native land.

My native land? How could I be sure even that Norway was that? All I knew, all that anyone knew, was that it was where I had been found eight years ago.

Hunters had found me, up there in the wildest, forested mountains of the north. A thirty-year-old man, tall and powerful in body—but wandering almost naked in the bitter weather, and mindless as a baby.

I had known nothing, not even my own name. They had taken me back to Stortfors, their village. And there the Wolversons, that kindly old couple whose name I now bore, had taken me in.

Gradually, my strength had returned. But my memory did not. I was a victim of complete amnesia.

The Wolversons cared for me with a kindness I shall never forget. They clothed and sheltered me, and patiently taught me what I must know to live—the language, the customs of civilization, the ways of village life.

In a few months, I was to all appearances a normal man. I was taller and fairer than even those tall, fair Norwegians, but I was not unlike them in most ways. Yet they did not accept me.

I think that at first they held aloof from me because I was still a mystery. During those months, police officials had investigated without finding a single clue to my identity. No one reported a missing person of my description. My photograph was circulated, but no one knew me.

I had had no clothing or personal effects to trace. My teeth were perfect, so no dentist could provide a clue. I had old scars on my body that looked like battle-scars, but my fingerprints were not to be found in the army files.

The police gave up and registered me as Eric Wolverson, past unknown. But the people of Stortfors would not accept me as one of them.

The few ignorant folk among them muttered about me. They harked back to half-forgotten superstitions. Old women who claimed the second sight declared that I was not entirely human, that I was a troll in human guise.

I endured that silently, but it spurred me to unceasing search of my identity. I tramped to villages and lonely farmsteads, hoping always that someone someday would recognize me and call my name. But no one ever did. And the folk of Stortfors still held aloof from me.

I endured it—till the Wolversons died. With the passing of the old couple who had helped me, I lost my only friends. The suspicion and whispering of the village, the dragging loneliness, became too much for me. I left Norway, and came to America.

In the great metropolis now dropping far behind my plane, I had worked for seven years to make a new life. I had tried to put out of my mind the mystery of my past, to quit brooding about it.

I might have succeeded, had it not been for the dream. The dream that had first come to me years ago in the Wolversons' little cottage, and that had brought me out of bed sweating and crying aloud. The dream that had returned, and always a little more strongly, ever since.

It was too much for me. I felt that the mystery and the dream would end by cracking my mind, and that my only chance was to solve the riddle of myself once and for all.

Now, eight years afterward, I was on my way back to find that solution. And if I failed—

The flight-steward interrupted my brooding thoughts, by pausing at my seat.

"We will reach Oslo before midnight tonight, Mr. Wolverson," he told me.

I asked about connections, and learned I could now take a local plane to within a hundred miles of Stortfors.

The sun set, and the great plane throbbed on in the twilight above the illimitable dusky plain of the ocean.

After a few more hours, the weariness and monotony of the night flight lulled me to sleep.

And then the dream came—clearer, more real, and more overwhelming than ever before!

It began with the same voice and words as always, the same mocking, silvery voice and taunting words.

"You will not ride back from Muspelheim to Asgard! You will not ride back again!"

In my dream, I knew and hated that face. And I knew and hated—yes, and feared!—the monstrous and unhuman two creatures that crouched beside their master and menaced me.

Then I saw in the mists beyond them the other face that haunted this dream. The dark, beautiful face of a girl, framed by midnight hair, with slumbrous eyes that now were wide with alarm for me.

Hate of my taunting tormentor and his two monstrous companions flung me raging forward. Then a great hairy beast-weight crushed me and mighty jaws seized my throat.

I heard the dark girl's cry through the dream-mists.

"Loki! Loki, no!"

I struggled madly—and suddenly I was awake, with a hand shaking my shoulder.

It was the flight-steward, looking down at me anxiously. The big plane was still roaring on through the night.

"You seemed to be having a nightmare, sir!"

"Yes—a nightmare," I managed to say, wiping the perspiration from my forehead.

He looked at me strangely. Then, "We are crossing the coast now, sir. We'll reach Oslo in an hour."

I felt badly shaken. The dream had been the same as always, but never before had it been so utterly vivid and real.

What did it mean? What *could* it mean? I had asked myself that question a thousand times.

"You will not ride back again from Muspelheim to Asgard!"

I had, long ago, discovered that those names were from the ancient Norse mythology.

Asgard had been the home of the Aesir, the great Norse gods of long ago. The Vikings of the past had sworn by Odin, king of the Aesir, and by his great warriors, Thor of the Hammer and Tyr of the Sword.

And Muspelheim too was from the old Norse myths, where it was legended to be the realm of strange witch-fire where Surtr held rule.

And that frantic last cry, *"Loki, no!"*

Loki had been the devil of the Norse myths, the handsome, evil one who had turned against the Aesir and had joined their foes.

"But why should I dream of those old myths, again and again?"

I had asked myself that question, endlessly. And without ever finding an explanation.

But somehow, as the plane droned on over the dark, stark mountains of Norway, I had an eerie feeling that the explanation was near at last. That up in the wild north, waiting for me, lay the answer to the twin mysteries of my dream and of my past!

II

Nothing, I found, had changed in Stortfors. The little northern village of massive timber cottages, huddling in its narrow mountain valley, looked just the same as when I had left it seven years before.

Nor had its people changed, or forgotten me. They knew me, when I walked down the little street. Most of them spoke to me. But it was with the same reluctance, the same suspicious glances, as before.

Little children playing at a corner looked up at my tall figure with friendliness, until a wide-eyed older child whispered to them.

"Eric Wolverson," I heard. And then the whispered word. "Troll!"

No, I thought bitterly, nothing had changed in Stortfors.

But this time, I told myself, I would not let dislike and ignorant superstition drive me out until I had found the answer to my riddle.

I took up my abode in the cottage of my dead foster-parents. An old widow, whom I had given leave to live there, was still there—but she moved out within an hour of my coming.

For the next few weeks, I was too busy to mind the villagers. I had resolutely set myself to visit every farm and village within a hundred miles, until I found someone who knew me.

I found no one. It was just as before—I might have dropped out of the sky, for all that anyone knew of my past.

My hopes, that had been so high, waned day by day. And then a thing happened that set me on a strange new track.

I was tramping tiredly back into Stortfors in the soft northern twilight, after a long day of fruitless search. Passing the *stavekirk,* I bumped into an old crone coming out of the church.

She recognized me, squeaked in fear, and hastily made an ancient peasant sign against evil.

It touched me on the raw, and I suddenly flared out at her. "Why do you superstitious old fools treat me this way?"

The old crone retorted shrilly. "Because there's a look about you that people don't like, Eric Wolverson! Big and tall and strong as you are, you somehow don't look like other men!"

She wagged her head knowingly. "Trolls and changelings exist, despite what the young folk say. And you were found too close to Runestone Hill for us oldsters ever to like you!"

"Runestone Hill?" I repeated. "I never heard of it."

She cackled. "People wouldn't be likely to talk of that place to you!"

She hurried on in the dusk, leaving me standing stock still, and with a strange thrill running through me.

The name, "Runestone Hill," had for a moment, for just a second, seemed vaguely familiar to me. As though something out of my lost memory had almost come back to me.

Frantically, I tried to bring back that elusive memory. But it was already gone, whatever it had been.

That night, I felt charged by excited new hope. For the first time, a name had brought me a vague, fleeting touch of memory. I resolved to search out Runestone Hill. There, perhaps, I would remember more.

Next day found me far back in the wild, pine-clad hills. It was afternoon by the time I reached the little valley where the hunters had found me wandering, eight years before.

I gazed eagerly at the surrounding hills. Armies of dark pines, with here and there straggling birches and lindens, marched up the steep slopes everywhere. I noted one high hill whose summit was bare and decided to explore it first.

It was the hill I sought.

I knew it the moment I came out upon the bare, grassy summit, and saw the great circle of massive, ancient stones that crowned the crest.

There were twelve of the stones. They were massive oblong blocks, crumbling with age, and imbedded deeply in the earth. Some leaned drunkenly, others still stood rigidly upright.

Wonderingly, I examined them. On the inner face of each great block was carved an inscription in the rune-writing of the old Norse. I recognized the ancient writings, even though I could not read it.

I walked into the middle of the thirty-foot circle of the runestones. And immediately, dim and terrible memory assailed me.

"I've been here before! I remember—"

But it was gone as swiftly as it had come, that uncanny flash of familiarity. I remembered nothing.

It was maddening, to feel on the very verge of memory, of the solution of my life's riddle—and yet not to be able to cross that verge.

For hours, I paced feverishly around that hilltop, in my excitement paying no heed to the summer storm that was swiftly darkening over the hills.

A bright bolt of lightning searing down to strike a nearby hill, and a reverberating crash of thunder, woke me to the imminence of the storm.

Storm or no storm, I would not leave. The key to my mystery lay here, if I could only grasp it.

"What was I doing here before? What?"

The blinding bolts and the crashes came closer. Closer, until the wings of the storm were sweeping down upon Runestone Hill.

The looming stones stood out dark and massive against the lightning-lit sky. And again, I felt the tug of dim memory!

The storm-lightning and the stones—these were right, but there was something yet lacking. Something that I must make ready quickly.

I ran to the nearest clump of birches, whose graceful white trunks were rocking wildly in the wind. With my clasp-knife, I hastily cut a dozen slender birch wands.

Striding back to the runestones, I laid a wand on the ground pointing from each stone toward the center of the circle.

Why did I make these incomprehensible preparations, in the face of an oncoming lightning-storm? I did not know. I knew only that some buried memory told me that these things must be done.

And I, Eric Wolverson, gave way to that smothered impulse in the wild hope that it would waken my numbed memory completely.

I stood in the center of the runestone circle, with the birch-wands pointing from each stone toward me like white fingers.

"But there was someone else with me!" I told myself. "Someone—"

Deafening crash of thunder smote and half-stunned me at that moment, as the full fury of the storm reached my hill.

Lightning struck blindingly on the wooded slopes. Then a dazzling bolt hit one of the runestones.

The bolt seemed to hold there, like a writhing serpent of living light. And with hellish flare and reverberation, other shafts of lightning seared down to hit other stones.

Dazed and dazzled, I glimpsed the lightning dripping and flowing from the runestones, and along the birch wands into the enclosed circle in which I crouched. It flowed like liquid flame toward me.

The ground suddenly seemed to waver and dissolve into nothingness under me! I felt myself falling headlong.

III

I awakened from unconsciousness, to find myself lying on the ground. Nearby, the tall, dark runestones loomed against the twilight sky.

For a moment, I thought that the lightning had merely stunned me temporarily, and that my weird sensations had been only the result of shock. Then, as I lay looking at the tall runestones, I perceived something that sent a cold chill through me.

They were not the same stones. They were far less eroded, and they stood all rigidly erect instead of leaning drunkenly as the others had.

I scrambled to my feet, and looked wildly around. A freezing awe fell upon me.

I was not now on the summit of Runestone Hill. *I was not, from all appearances, on Earth!*

"Hysteria—delusion—" I told myself thickly. "The effect of the lightning-shock on my brain."

But I knew as I spoke that my attempt to reassure myself was false, and that I stood in the darkening twilight of another, alien world.

It was a hilltop on which I stood, at the center of the towering, brooding rune-engraved monoliths. But this hill, and the others that rose in the distance, were not the rugged, wooded hills of north Norway.

They were like small mountain-peaks stabbing the sky, stark pinnacles that had an unearthly savagery of outline. They rose out of a mighty conifer forest whose foliage was so dark green that it looked black.

Over this alien panorama arched an alien sky! The dusk was deepening, and in that sky there already blazed brilliant planets unknown to the skies of Earth, dimming the drift of stars. And meteor-moons pitted like corroded white skulls rode across the heavens in place of Luna.

And far away in the west, silhouetted for a moment against the last afterglow, I saw the distant, soaring towers and keeps of a mighty citadel.

"Another world," I whispered. "Another world, and I have somehow crossed into it from Earth."

And then I, Eric Wolverson, said an insane thing. *"But I have been here before!"*

For this unearthly scene seemed strangely familiar to me. I had the feeling that dead memory was stirring again in my brain, trying frantically to live again.

My gaze clung to that faraway citadel, until it vanished in the deepening night. Somehow, I knew that place!

"But when? How?" I asked myself hoarsely, struggling with the incredible.

I could not, even yet, waken my numbed memory to answer those questions.

As I stood there gazing wildly, I saw something else. It flew black and long and slender across the sky beneath the blazing meteor-moons.

A winged serpent-shape, like a dragon out of fable, flying fast above the forest toward the west. And it, too, seemed fantastically familiar to me.

My brain was rocking from the shock of the impossible. I took the one course of action that might preserve my sanity.

"That citadel—if I go there, I might remember!"

I had *almost* remembered, when I saw those faraway, mighty towers. And now the place was drawing me like a magnet.

I turned to go down the hill, and stumbled on something that lay at my feet within the circle of the runestones. I stooped and picked it up.

It was a sword. A long, glimmering, ancient-looking blade, whose hilt seemed to fit my hand perfectly.

The feel of it comforted me oddly. And I might need a weapon. I gripped it in my hand as I went down the hill.

The great forest closed me in. It was dark and awesome here beneath the mighty conifers, except where shafts of wild brilliance struck down between them from the hurtling meteor-moons.

As I tramped half-dazedly westward, deer crashed across my path and I heard the howl of wolves from somewhere not far away.

But beside these familiar earthly animals, other and more fantastic life was abroad in the night forest.

A half-dozen wild horses bolted down a forest aisle on my left. And they were *horned* horses, their heads having each a little upcurving tusk like that of the fabled unicorn.

Down from the blazing sky swooped two of the great winged serpents in pursuit! I heard a hissing and a frantic neighing as they all swept away from me.

"A world that is a mixture of the earthly and the unearthly!" I thought. "But how can such a world exist?"

Then the dim shape of a possible explanation entered my stunned mind. "A world distinct from Earth, yet *interpenetrating* Earth—"

The speculations of certain modern physicists, that I had read in my New York years, had recalled themselves to me.

Our Earth, those scientists had theorized, was composed of atoms which were each but a loose, tenuous swarm of infinitesimal electrons and other sub-atomic particles. It was not impossible that other swarms, other worlds, interpenetrated our own atom-swarm, just as two swarms of bees can interpenetrate each other.

This alien planet, I thought, must be such an interpenetrating world. It might occupy exactly the same space as Earth, yet would be forever separated from it by the unbridgeable difference in the rate of its atomic vibration and its time.

Unbridgeable? But I had bridged that gap, even though I knew not how! And it must have been bridged other times in the past, by design or chance, so that the flying serpents and horned horses of this world were known, if only as myths, to Earth.

And—the thought was staggering—the Earth might be interpenetrated by many other alien worlds beside this one. And chance bridging contacts with them in the past might well have supplied other and different myths to the traditions of Earth.

Abruptly, I was aroused from my bewildered speculations by the most blood-chilling sound I had ever heard. It came from only a few miles behind me—the long, swelling howl of a wolf.

But this was no ordinary wolf-cry. It had a volume and a sheer savagery that bristled the hairs on my head. I swung around, raising my sword.

"He's struck my trail!" I exclaimed. "He—"

He? *Who?* For an instant I had almost known, but then the brief flash of memory died as swiftly as it had come.

That terrible beast-howl, that seemed to throb with mad hatred, faded into echoes and died away.

But I knew, with a knowledge born of that brief flash of almost memory, that an awful danger was coming after me through the forest.

I turned around again and ran, on toward the west. I had to trust to instinct or nothing, and deep instinct told me that safety lay at the distant citadel that was my goal.

That citadel could not be far away, now. But I felt that the pursuers behind me would follow swiftly. I pressed on, stumbling through brush that ripped my thin shirt and breeches and clutched at my hair.

As I ran through the dark forest aisles and across brushy thickets open to the meteor-blazing sky, I had a fierce desire to turn and meet those who tracked me. But again a whisper from my frozen memory seemed to warn me that it would be fatal to do so here.

Great wings threshed and rattled above the tree-tops, and I glimpsed the gliding shape of a winged serpent far huger than any I yet had seen. It planed low above the forest, its snaky head turning from side to side as though it searched below.

I crouched flat against a great trunk until that nightmare dragon-shape banked around and glided back toward the east. Then I ran on.

The forest suddenly ended. I came out upon bare ground, and suddenly stopped short. I stared frozenly at what lay before me.

A few yards in front of me, there yawned the enormous emptiness of a great valley. It was like a gigantic chasm, miles deep and many miles wide, its side dropping sheerly downward from just before me.

The wild, flying light of the meteor-moons illuminated the dark immensities of the abyss. And I saw that not far along it from where I stood, there rose in that abyss a stark pinnacle whose flat summit was level with my eyes.

On the summit of that pinnacle was built the citadel I had glimpsed, a mighty stone castle with massive keeps and towers whose windows spilled ruddy light. And from the brink on which I stood, to the citadel out there on the pinnacle, arched a tremendous stone bridge painted like the rainbow.

"The old Norse myth!" I gasped. "The rainbow bridge to Asgard, the home of the gods!"

Myth had come real before my unbelieving eyes! Myth, that for years had strangely haunted my dreams.

"You will not ride home from Muspelheim to Asgard!" that hated dream-voice had always told me.

I had thought it dream only. But the Asgard of myth loomed before me in full reality.

"Have I been here too, before? *Have* I?" In my wild wonder, I had forgotten the deadly pursuit behind me. And suddenly I had terrible reminder of it.

A low, thunderous coughing from close behind me made me whirl around.

Out of the forest was creeping toward me a gray wolf of incredible size. The hairy monster instantly crouched ready to charge, its blazing green eyes hypnotically holding my gaze.

Close to it, that great winged serpent that had hunted me in the forest had just alighted. It coiled, its flat ophidian head rearing menacingly in my direction.

Then from out of the woods rode a mounted man who reined his horse in sharply beside the wolf and serpent. He wore shining mail and helmet of the old Norse pattern, and he had drawn his sword.

"So you have returned?" he cried to me, and though the tongue he spoke was strange to me, I somehow understood it. "Fool, you returned only to your death!"

I knew that haughtily handsome face, that silver, mocking voice. Yes, and I knew the two monstrous shapes that crouched at his side.

They were the face and voice and shapes of my dream. But it was no dream now!

IV

Dazed as I was by the incredible materialization of my dream, I yet recognized the deadly menace in this man and his monstrous beast-companions.

I raised my sword. And at the same time I backed toward the Rainbow Bridge. It was narrow, and on it I could face my enemies and not be taken from behind.

The mailed rider laughed. "There's no help for you from the Aesir. You'll be dead before they come. Stupid one, not to know that my arts would warn me when you opened the Way between Worlds and returned!"

He laughed again. "My pets trailed you for me, and they shall have the pleasure of killing you now. Fenris! Iormungandr!"

At those names, the huge gray wolf sprang up snarling terribly and the great winged serpent unfolded glittering wings and uncoiled for flight.

And at those names, names out of the old Norse mythology, a terrific shock ran through me. This man before me—I guessed his identity now, and yet it was impossible—

"Loki!" I whispered. "The arch-devil of old, the foe of the Aesir!"

His handsome face darkened. "So you can remember me? It's your last memory! There's no Hela here now to save you!"

Hela? That name too sent a swift shock through me, my mind flashing back to the dark, brooding-eyed girl of my dream.

And then suddenly Fenris and Iormungandr, the mighty wolf and the Midgard-serpent, were upon me!

They came with a rush, the blazing-eyed wolf charging in great bounds, the winged serpent hurtling hissing through the air.

Instinct or memory guided me in the split-second that followed. I crouched down slightly, so that the parapets that railed the bridge would protect me from the swoop of the winged serpent.

At the same moment, wielding the sword as though its use were utterly familiar to me, I stabbed with all my strength at the charging wolf.

An ordinary wolf would have spitted himself on the blade. But the wolf Fenris was too supernaturally alert for that. He—I could not think of that great beast by any other pronoun—checked himself in midspring by a marvelous effort.

Flattening his belly to the ground, green eyes and white fangs gleaming at me, Fenris inched closer. A low growl like distant thunder rumbled from his throat. It was answered by the hissing of the Midgard-serpent that was banking around in mid-air for another swoop at me.

"Dog who eats carrion! Worm of the slime!" I taunted them. "So you remember my sword?"

How did *I* remember? How did I remember the tongue in which I cried those taunts, the use of the great sword that flashed in my hand?

I cannot tell. In my overpowering rage, the strange language was as familiar to my lips as the sword to my hand.

Fenris and Iormungandr charged together! I heard the exultant laugh of Loki from the background, as I dropped to one knee.

Great wings fanned me as a dragon head snapped down at me, and missed. The wolf's green eyes blazed hellfire before me, and my sword-point found a hairy body.

Fenris recoiled, his hairy shoulder slashed. The Midgard-serpent was planing around for another swoop at me.

Then from the great citadel far behind me across the Rainbow Bridge, I heard the distant, warning blast of a horn.

"Now, quickly!" Loki cried to his beast-comrades. "The Aesir come!"

Hoofs thundered on the bridge as he spurred his mount down upon me. His upraised sword glittered, and Fenris charged beside him.

I parried and struck, with a swordsmanship that Eric Wolverson had never possessed. I beat back Loki's descending blade, and again slashed at the great wolf as he tried to leap in from the side.

Loki's eyes were raging as he reined back his plunging horse. Again he cried to wolf and serpent as though they were human.

"No time now—Heimdall and the Aesir are coming!" he shouted.

He turned his steed, galloped toward the shelter of the forest. Wolf Fenris loped beside him, and the winged serpent flew over his head.

But at the forest edge, Loki turned his head to send back a silvery cry to me.

"You have not escaped! We three will find you—when we return to Valhalla!"

Then he and his monstrous companions disappeared into the nighted forest.

I stood, sword in hand, breathing in great gasps. My mind was numbed by the shock of the incredible.

Nor was I given time to order my wild thoughts. Before I had regained breath, I heard the tramp of hurrying feet from behind me on the Rainbow Bridge.

I turned. A dozen tall, fair warriors, mailed and helmed and carrying naked swords, were running toward me from the distant citadel.

Their leader, a stalwart, commanding figure, hailed me through the twilight as they came closer.

"That was Loki and his devils' beasts! Who are you, and what do you here with *them?*"

I tried to stammer answer. "I—"

Before I could finish, they had reached me. And as they saw my face, a strange tension seemed to grip these glittering warriors.

One of them pointed to me and cried wildly to their leader. "Lord Heimdall, look at him! His clothing is strange, but it is—"

"I see him," Heimdall answered, in a steely voice. His face had set hard as he looked at me, and his eyes were bleak.

There was a little silence. The very sight of me seemed to have frozen these men for a moment. In their faces, as they stared at me, was icy hatred.

Heimdall broke the silence. "Odin and Thor must know this at once. It may portend—"

He broke off, then resumed, this time speaking grimly to me. "You are going into Valhalla castle with us. Shall it be quietly, or must some of us die to take you?"

I was too overwhelmed for a moment to answer.

An avalanche of fantastic realities had crushed me.

These were the Aesir! The Norse hero-gods of long ago, who dwelt in their great eyrie-citadel of Asgard, and who had Odin for king and Thor of the Hammer and Tyr of the Sword for captains.

They existed, real and living. Yet even more stunning than that was the fact that they seemed to *recognize* me.

They were waiting for my answer, with their swords tensely raised. I struggled to speak.

"I do not understand all this," I faltered. "But—I will go with you quietly."

Some of the tension left them, as Heimdall reached and took my sword. I did not resist.

Then I found myself tramping with them in dead silence up the sweeping ascending curve of the Rainbow Bridge.

In the deepening dusk, the abyss beneath that unearthly span seemed almost bottomless. The wild meteor-moons that rode the heavens barely illumined the depths below. Truly it was Niflheim, the gulf of nothingness that moated Asgard!

We passed through a massive gate that pierced the great wall of the mountain-citadel. Again, dim memory seemed to assail me as I looked in awe around me.

This citadel of the Aesir was far bigger than I had thought. It held a ring of stone castles that surrounded a wide-open space in the center of which rose the mighty mass of the biggest castle.

And this looming pile was Valhalla! Somehow, I knew that without question as my guard and I passed through its portals and into a huge lighted hall where many warriors were feasting and drinking.

Flashing lights of torches dazzled me. And as I stood uncertain, the rough revelry of deep voices and the clink of cups and flagons stopped dead. The warriors at the long tables, and the Valkyrie-maids who waited upon them, and the busy thralls, all stared frozenly at me.

"Lord Odin!" rang Heimdall's stentorian voice from beside me, across the hall. "One who rode to Muspelheim has—returned."

I looked across the hall. There was a high dais at its end, and a low chair in which sat a great, gray kinglike figure—a man of fifty with iron-gray hair and beard, wrapped in a gray cloak.

He rose to his feet, holding a short, heavy spear in his hand. He had but one eye, but that single ice-blue orb seemed to transfix me.

"Bring him hither, Heimdall," his deep voice commanded.

Like one in a dream, I went through the staring feasters to the dais. I saw now that another man had risen beside Odin.

A shorter man this, but a burlier and bigger, with tremendous shoulders. His shock head was bare, his red face unbelieving in expression as his small eyes stared at me. His hand clutched the helve of an enormous hammer, and I knew that this was Thor of the Hammer.

Near them on the dais stood another lordly figure, a dark-faced man of forty tall in black mail, who was glaring at me. I wondered numbly if he were the Aesir's other great captain, Tyr of the Sword.

For myth had changed to reality about me, ever since I had plunged from Earth into this neighboring world. Valhalla and the Aesir and their lords were as real around me now as I was myself!

Odin's eye brooded upon me as he spoke to Heimdall. "How came he back to Valhalla, Heimdall?"

"Lord Odin, I am not sure," the other answered. "We glimpsed Loki's beasts at the farther end of Bifrost. We hastened out but by the time we reached there, Loki and his two devils were gone. But *he* was there!"

Odin spoke harshly to me. "So it was with the arch-traitor that you returned?"

I found my voice at last. "Returned?" I cried. "I do not know what you mean! Have I been here in Valhalla before?"

A fierce laugh burst from the giant Thor. "Has he been here before?"

"But eight days have passed since you rode out from here," Odin told me accusingly. "To Muspelheim, you told us. But to join the arch-devil Loki, as we learned later!"

He drew himself to his full height. "Now you have come back, companioned by the traitor you joined, to play the spy among us. But for your crime you shall die now, Tyr!"

Tyr? Tyr of the Sword, great captain of the Aesir—was he addressing that name to *me?*

Realization stunned me. Then I myself was one of the Aesir? Then I was—Tyr?

V

For a space of minutes I stood there, too dazed by the impact of the unbelievable to speak.

Could this be the answer to the mystery of my forgotten past? Was it possible that I, Eric Wolverson, was Tyr of the Sword?

It was too incredible. On the other world of Earth, Tyr had been legend for a thousand years. How could I have lived that time?

"I cannot be Tyr!" I cried. "I have been but a few hours in this world, and before that I lived years in another, different world!"

"You are Tyr," Odin said grimly. "And until eight days ago, you were one of the most honored of the Aesir.

"Then you rode to visit Surtr of Muspelheim. You did not return. And we learned that you had joined our arch-foe, Loki."

The tall, dark-faced man in black mail who had been glaring at me now stepped forward.

"It is true," he accused. "Tyr never came to my kingdom of Muspelheim. But I, Surtr, saw him riding with Loki and his hell-crew toward Jotunland. Doubtless he has been plotting with Loki and the Jotuns."

Thor, raising his mighty hammer, strode down toward me. The burly giant's face was crimson, his voice hoarse as he raged at me.

"Tyr of the Sword, my comrade in arms who has faced the Jotuns with me a hundred times in battle, turned traitor! I could kill you myself!"

"But all that never happened, not to me!" I protested. "I remember nothing of it!"

There was an interruption. Through the glaring chieftains stepped a feminine figure in clinging white robe—a woman of fair, gentle beauty with deep blue eyes that earnestly searched my face.

"Wait, lords Odin and Thor!" she said. "It may be that Tyr tells truth when he says that he does not remember."

Thor turned angrily toward her. "What mean you, Cousin Freya?"

Freya's searching eyes had not left my face. "He has the emptiness in his eyes," she said. "The emptiness that comes from the hell-brew which kills the memory."

I looked at her, startled. "It's true that my memory of all my former life is dead. But—"

Surtr interrupted harshly. "If Tyr drank the hell-brew, it was to wipe memory of his treachery from his brain. He should die now!"

"If he must die, he must," Freya said. "But first, let him—remember. I can cleanse his brain of the hell-brew, if you allow me."

She looked up at Odin. The Aesir lord's one eye brooded upon me, and then he inclined his head slightly.

"Let him remember, then," rumbled Odin. "Let him remember, so that he may know his own black guilt before he dies."

Freya went out of the great hall, leaving us all rigid with tension. No word was spoken until she returned.

She held in her hand a little, twisted glass flagon of red liquid.

"This will wash Hela's dark hell-brew from your brain," she said. "Drink, Tyr."

Again, the name of "Hela" brought fleetingly back to my dazed mind the dream-glimpsed girl of dark beauty whom I had envisioned so often.

I took the little flagon, raised it hesitantly to my lips—and then drank.

Flame seemed to rage instantly through my brain! In the inmost fibers of my being I felt an unbinding, a loosening, a sudden releasing of chained knowledge.

Staggering beneath that wave of fiery pain, I lost all awareness of Valhalla hall and those in it. Light was bursting in upon my agonized mind—light, and *memory!*

In that dreadful moment, I, Tyr, remembered all that I had forgotten.

Yes—*I, Tyr!* For my dead memory had sprung to life at last, and I knew now who I was.

I was not Eric Wolverson of Earth. I was Tyr of the Aesir, Tyr of the Sword! And this world of the Aesir, not Earth, was *my* world!

Here I had grown to manhood among the Aesir, and here I had fought the Jotuns and our other savage foes. Here I had won my name by my swordsmanship in battle, fighting beside Thor and Odin.

Yes, all this I remembered. And I remembered too that eight days ago

I *had* ridden away from Asgard to visit our ally-kingdom of Muspelheim.

Eight days ago? But I had been eight years in that other world of Earth. Then, even as the Earth scientists had thought, time was different in this interpenetrating world, and a year there was but a day here.

Full memory flashed over me, of what had happened those eight days ago when I had ridden into Muspelheim.

I uttered a fierce shout. "I am Tyr, yes! I remember now! But I am no traitor—I never joined Loki!"

I leveled an accusing finger at Surtr, my rage against that dark-faced king exploding from the memory I had regained.

"Surtr of Muspelheim, who pretends to be ally of the Aesir, is the traitor! For in Muspelheim, I discovered Loki and his hell-brood conspiring with Surtr against us!"

It had all come back to me now, clear and terrible memory of how I had stumbled upon Loki lurking in the palace of Muspelheim.

I remembered how Loki's craft had overpowered me, and how Surtr had cried, "Kill him quickly or he will ruin our plot against the Aesir!"

And of how Loki had laughed in evil triumph and had retorted, "It will please me to have Tyr of the Sword as a mindless slave. The hell-brew of forgetfulness that Hela makes will make him that."

Yes, and I remembered that as the black drink was forced into me and my brain slowly darkened, a girl's voice had cried, *"Loki, no!"*

And that I had known it was the voice of Hela, that darkly beautiful witch whom in bygone years to my sorrow I had loved.

And vaguely, I remembered the coming of Hela to my dungeon a little later, and of how faintly her urgent words had readied my dulling mind.

"I could not stop him from giving you the hell-brew but I cannot see you his slave, Tyr! I have come to help you escape!"

Vague, vague, were my memories of riding druggedly through the night forest with her, and of her voice coming to me as though from far away.

"You cannot return to Asgard, for Surtr is to accuse you of treachery to the Aesir. But I have the art to open the Way between Worlds and send you to safety in another world!"

And then, as my mind had darkened completely, nothing but a misty dream-memory of a circle of tall stones and of lightnings amid which I seemed to sink into an abyss, and of Hela's voice calling, "Farewell, Tyr!"

Yes, it had all come back to me now, and I, Tyr, poured it forth in a raging flood.

"And *that* is why Surtr came hither to accuse me of treachery! Because I discovered that he himself conspires with Loki and the Jotuns!"

Surtr's dark face was distorted, black with blood. "Tyr lies, to cover his own guilt!"

I sprang forward fiercely. "Give us swords and we'll make trial of the issue by combat!"

Surtr recoiled and appealed to Odin. "Shall I be slain by Tyr of the Sword to make good his falsehood?"

Odin looked down at me grimly. "If you did not join Loki, how is it that he and his beasts came with you tonight to Asgard?"

"They did not come with me—they pursued me!" I exclaimed. "I fought them, on the bridge!"

"Was it so, Heimdall?" asked Odin.

Heimdall hesitated. "We could not see, in the twilight. We glimpsed Fenris and Iormungandr, but by the time we had crossed Bifrost, they and Loki were gone."

"Why should I betray the Aesir?" I asked passionately. "Have you forgotten how many times I fought for Asgard?"

"No," said Odin sternly, "nor have we forgotten that once in years past you loved that witch Hela whose magic now helps Loki's plots."

In desperation, I pointed down to my clothing, my torn khaki shirt and my breeches and boots. "Does not my strange garb prove that I have been in another world?"

Odin said slowly, "It is true that your garb is alien now. But Loki could have devised you such strange garb to support your story."

Surtr broke in. "I can bring back from Muspelheim witnesses who saw Tyr laughing and plotting in the forest with Loki and the Jotuns!"

Odin delivered his judgment. "Then you shall bring those witnesses, Surtr. I can test their truthfulness! If Tyr's guilt is proved by them, he shall die quickly. Until then, he remains prisoned."

I made a final passionate appeal. "Will you let Surtr ride out of Asgard to bring doom upon you?"

Odin answered grimly, "You are the accused, not our ally Surtr. Heimdall, see to his prisoning."

I knew him too well to make further appeals. My spirit sagged within me. Heavily, I went with Heimdall and his warriors out of Valhalla hall.

They took me down to the lowest level of the castle, to corridors and chambers cut deep in the rock of Asgard. I walked into a dark little cell, and heard the bar fall across the door outside.

For a time, I leaned my face against the cold rock of the wall. My brain seemed bursting.

I, Tyr of the Sword, prisoned as a traitor to the Aesir! A traitor who would die shameful death if Surtr brought back convincing witnesses.

But that Surtr would return, I did not believe. He would hasten back to his own fiery kingdom now, only to hurry his plot with Loki to its climax.

What it was that Surtr and Loki together were plotting against Asgard, I did not know. But words spoken when they had captured me back there in Muspelheim gave me a premonition of a terrible doom they were hatching for the Aesir.

"And I must stay helpless here until that doom breaks on Asgard!" I groaned. "It would have been better never to have regained memory!"

Yes, in my agony of spirit, I wished that I could again forget my life as Tyr of the Sword, and be again Eric Wolverson of Earth as I had been for eight years.

Eight years? Eight long years, in that neighbor world of Earth that now seemed so strange to me when I looked back on it. Eight years, that had been only eight days in this world of different time.

And a thousand years of Earth was but a thousand days of our time. I could understand now how the old Norsemen of ten Earth centuries ago had told myths of us Aesir and our world. The Way between Worlds must have opened more than once in past time, and the tale of us had somehow gone through.

As *I* had gone through to Earth, when to save me Hela had used her magic art to open the Way. So she still must love me a little, even though years ago I had parted from her in bitterness?

I paced the little dark cell feverishly, and rage against my own strange fate mounted higher in me with each passing hour.

"Tyr of the Sword, locked in a prison to die a cow's death, while war and doom gather against the Aesir!"

Finally, the door of my cell suddenly opened.

A giant figure loomed portentously in the opening, and then came in toward me.

It was Thor, and his terrible hammer glinted dully in his hand.

VI

There was mixed grief and rage in the face of the giant as he approached me. And now I saw that in his left hand he carried a long, glittering sword—my own sword.

His great voice rumbled. "Tyr, we were comrades in arms long ago. I cannot endure to see them execute you as they will do."

Hope leaped up in me. "Thor, then you believe my story? You mean to help me?"

"No!" he retorted. "But, even though a traitor, Tyr of the Sword deserves better than the shameful death they plan for you."

He handed me my sword. "You asked trial by combat, Tyr. You shall have it—against me."

I recoiled. "Thor, no! I could not fight you! We've stood shoulder to shoulder too many times against the Jotuns!"

"Why did you not remember that when you deserted us for love of Hela, and joined Loki?" roared the giant.

My own temper flashed into wrath. "You are stupid as ever, to believe Surtr's lying story! It's Surtr who plots against the Aesir, I tell you! And it's Surtr I want to meet man-to-man, not you!"

"Surtr rode homeward to Muspelheim, hours ago," the Hammerer replied. "He will be back tomorrow with the witnesses who will prove your guilt. Here, take your sword. I'd rather kill you or be killed, than have an Aesir die as you'll die."

I restrained my anger. "Thor, listen! Did ever I tell lies in all the days we two have comraded?"

"No," he admitted. "But men do strange things for love. And Hela—"

"I parted from Hela years ago, when I discovered the evil that was in her!" I insisted.

"Aye, but I have always thought that you still secretly loved that dark witch," he rumbled.

There was truth enough in that accusation to make me wince. And it must have showed in my face, for Thor's look darkened.

"Enough of this," he growled. He forced the sword-hilt into my hand. "Take it and defend yourself. I don't want to kill you unfairly."

He backed a few steps away. I raised the blade. We faced each other in the dark cell, sword against hammer.

Tyr of the Sword against Thor of the Hammer! We two famous captains of the Aesir, who together had fought the Jotuns and the Alfings and the Vanir, now seeking each other's lives.

Thor stepped sidewise, his glaring eyes fixed on me, his hammer raised only waist-high. I knew—how well I knew!—that terrible sweeping side-stroke of his that had crushed the skulls of so many of our savage enemies.

He struck! But in his rage, he forgot the cramped smallness of the cell, and the great hammer clanged and caught on the wall.

With a swiftness wonderful in so huge a man, he recovered himself. But the brief instant was time enough for my sword to drive into him.

It was time enough—but I did not stab. I stood unmoving, my sword sagging. I had known from the first that I could not fight in death-duel with my old comrade.

Thor stared at me, and then the rage slowly went out of his face and he lowered his hammer.

"Tyr, I have been a fool. I have been the greatest of fools."

"Your strength was always more in your back than in your head," I retorted.

He did not fire up as he had used to do at my chaffing. He looked shamefaced, and growled, "You know my temper. The berserk madness came over me when I thought you traitor."

Then he gripped my arm. "I should have known better! Come, we'll see Odin again. I'll convince him somehow that you're telling the truth."

I shook my head. "It's useless. Odin will not relax his decree. He'll wait for Surtr to return with the promised witnesses."

I rushed on desperately, "And Surtr and Loki will return instead with a savage Jotun army and with some mysterious and awful weapon they plan to use against Asgard!"

The Hammerer looked stunned. "But if we can't convince Odin in time, what *can* we do?"

"Thor, whatever thing of doom they are preparing against us must be at Surtr's castle in Muspelheim," I said swiftly. "For it was there that Loki was hiding when I stumbled upon him."

I went on. "I can remember the secret way by which Hela brought me out of that castle. If we two rode there and entered by that way—"

"We could kill Loki and Surtr and destroy this mystery-weapon of theirs!" Thor finished for me. His little eyes began to glitter. "That would be an adventure worthy of Tyr and Thor!"

"Can you get me out of Asgard?" I asked him tensely.

He thought a moment, then said, "Wait!" and went out.

He was back in a few minutes with a helmet and cloak. "Put them on, Tyr. And keep your sword hidden—all Asgard knows that sword."

Helmed and cloaked, I went out of the cell after the Hammerer.

The hour was late. Valhalla castle slept, and no one met us as we went up the stairs and hallways and out a postern door.

The night wind blew chill, in the open air. The towers of Asgard loomed against the flaring, splendid sky of stars and meteor-moons.

All Asgard slumbered, safe behind Bifrost Bridge and its warders.

Thor brought horses, his own great steed and a rangy, clean-limbed mount for me. We vaulted to the saddles and rode clattering through the sleeping ways to the great gate that barred the way to Bifrost Bridge.

The giant banged with his hammer on the metal bars, setting up a thunderous clangor. Heimdall, captain of the gate-guard, looked down from a window of the watch-tower.

"Open, Heimdall!" Thor rumbled. "I go forth with a companion to see if accursed Loki still lurks in the forest yonder."

"Had I not better call a company of warriors to accompany you?" Heimdall asked. I kept my helmed head bowed, as he looked down at us.

"Am I a babe that I need protection from Loki and his devil-pets?" roared the Hammerer. "One comrade is enough! Open!"

The great gates creaked open. We spurred our mounts and galloped up the great curve of the bridge, hoofs drumming loudly on the stone. Then we were across and in the shadow of the great trees.

"I know the shortest way to Muspelheim!" I called over the rush of wind. "We should reach the Fire Kingdom before dawn."

Thor laughed and swung his great hammer in the air. "It is like old days again to ride forth together, Tyr!"

Yes, it was not the first time that Thor of the Hammer and Tyr of the Sword had gone forth from Asgard into danger. But never, I knew, into such terrible danger as was gathering now.

What *was* the dreadful thing that Loki and Surtr were preparing against Asgard? I had heard only sinister hints, but enough to convince me that it was a real and awful menace.

They could bring against us the hosts of the savage Jotuns, our old foes, and the smaller army of Surtr. But these alone could never conquer Asgard. I knew Loki's evil cunning, and I felt cold apprehension.

The forest seemed dark and strange and tense, this night. By the wild rays of the meteor-moons that struck down through the trees, we saw deer and wolves and bands of the horned horses and flying serpents, all moving southward away from Muspelheim.

We had ridden but a few hours when I saw far ahead of us the strange, greenish glow in the sky that warned we were approaching the realm of Surtr.

"We are near Muspelheim!" I called. "See, yonder in the north glows the mountain of the witch-fires."

"I like not those witch-fires whose very warmth is death," Thor growled. "Only Surtr would wish to rule such a land as this."

Well-named was the Fire Kingdom of Surtr! For as we rode over a forested ridge, we had clear view of that most frightful mountain which gave the land its name.

It looked miles away from us, a great, squat crater flinging into the sky a cold, shaking green radiance from the strange witch-fires that forever churned in its mighty caldron.

Always we had known that even to approach too close those witch-fires was to die, and that only the rocks rich in lead which formed the crater walls kept these fires from inside our world from flowing outward.

But now I, Tyr, had Eric Wolverson's memories of Earth-science to give me hint of what those witch-fires really were. They were radioactive fires, *atomic* fires welling up from the depths of our world.

I told Thor, "On the world Earth where I spent eight years—or days—they have the witch-fire. It does not occur naturally there, but they have learned how to make it to use as a weapon of war."

Thor uttered an outraged roar. "Use the witch-fire as a war-weapon? That is black and shameful! Are they too craven to fight with sword and spear?"

We rode past that dreadful crater at several miles distance, and soon reached the edge of the great lake on whose farther edge was Muspelheim.

The hurtling meteor-moons poured radiance on the lake, and illumined the dark, stark citadel of Surtr that rose brutally massive amid smaller castles on the bluffs of the opposite shore.

"The secret way by which Hela brought me out of the citadel opens down at the foot of the bluff," I told Thor. "We must ride around, along the water edge."

The Hammerer glanced at me oddly. "That Jotun witch must still have some love for you, to have risked Loki's wrath to save you."

"Speak no more of that," I said harshly. "That was over for me on the day years ago when I discovered how she used her magic art."

But as we two rode down to the lake and began to circle its edge, I wondered if I spoke truth. Was it over, really? Would it ever be?

Certainly I had loved no other woman as I had that dark Jotun girl whose mastery of wizardry was surpassed only by that of Loki himself. And certainly, she had risked much to get me to safety in the other world.

Had Loki discovered her duplicity? If he had, I could guess what that arch-devil would have done to her.

And then I reproached myself bitterly for thinking of Hela when the safety of Asgard itself was at stake.

"This is the place," I told Thor in a whisper, a little later. "Tie the horses to those shrubs, and follow me silently."

We had reached the foot of the bluff directly below the citadel of Muspelheim. Here there was only a narrow strand between lake and cliff. A hundred feet above us, on the brink of the cliff, loomed Surtr's dark castle.

I led the way to an almost invisible foxhole in the rock wall. I slipped inside but Thor had to struggle to squeeze his great form through.

We crouched in a narrow tunnel that climbed upward into utter darkness.

The steep little passage was one that had been eroded naturally by water, and then enlarged by human hands. I wondered if Surtr knew this way into his citadel, or if it was one of cunning Loki's secrets.

The climbing tunnel ended in a blank stone door. I motioned Thor to silence, and then gently slid the stone slab aside.

We stepped out into one of the dank corridors beneath Muspelheim. Faint reflected torchlight filtered down into it from a stair at one end.

"Loki's lair here was on the level above this," I whispered to Thor. "It was there that I stumbled on him—and it's there that he and Surtr are most likely to be preparing their devils' work."

Thor nodded his shaggy head, and raised his hammer a little. "Just lead me close enough to reach them with Miolnir and I'll end their plots."

We went down the corridor to the stair, and listened at its foot. There was no sound from the upper levels, though dawn must be near.

"This whole place is too *quiet,*" muttered the Hammerer. "I don't like it."

I too was oppressed by the unnatural silence of the great castle. But I gripped my sword-hilt more tightly and led the way stealthily up the stair.

The corridors of the next level seemed deserted too. I went rapidly down it with Thor, and paused outside a massive door.

"This was Loki's lair," I murmured. "Be ready to strike!"

Then I suddenly pushed the door open and we two burst in with sword and hammer upraised.

The dusky stone chamber was as I had seen it before—a small room, with tables littered with the grotesque and gruesome instruments of Loki's magic art.

But Loki himself was not in the room, nor was Surtr. Its only occupant was a girl who had swung quickly around to face us.

A girl whose flowing black hair matched the jet hue of her clinging, belted robe—a girl whose wide dark eyes stared at me out of a dead-white, beautiful face.

I sprang across the room and seized her. "If you try to give the alarm I'll have to kill you, Hela! Don't make me do it!"

She looked unbelievingly up into my face. "Tyr!" She whispered. "Tyr, returned to this world and to memory! Loki told me, but I could not believe—"

I still held her tightly, my sword was still raised. But Thor spoke unexpectedly.

"Cease threatening her, Tyr," said the Hammerer. "She will never bring danger upon you, that I swear."

"No," whispered Hela, "I'll never bring danger upon you, Tyr."

She took from the silken belt-pouch that hung beside her dagger-sheath a little vial of black liquid.

"See, it is the hell-brew that destroys all memory. I have many times meant to drink it myself, because I could no longer bear to remember you."

I felt a strange emotion. I knew now that whatever had been between Hela and myself, whatever the strange pattern that the Norns had twisted of our life-threads, it was not yet ended.

And yet my dread for the Aesir drove me so strongly that I ignored the emotions that had burst in me at sight of her.

"Where is Loki?" I demanded of her. "I know that he plans disaster for the Aesir, and I am going to kill him this day."

Hela shook her dark head. "You are *too late,* Tyr! He and Surtr and their host have already gone to bear doom to Asgard!"

VII

The dim shape of the mysterious disaster that I feared seemed suddenly to become a tangible menace, with Hela's words.

"But we did not meet Loki and Surtr and their host, as we came hither!" I cried.

"They, and the army of Jotuns they lead, did not march directly toward Asgard," Hela said. "They went by way of the mountain of the witch-fires."

A possibility so awful that I could not credit it, dawned upon my mind.

"Hela, why did they go by the Fire Mountain?"

Her face was deathly pale. "Because the doom Loki bears to Asgard is the doom of the witch-fires! Yes, Tyr—he and Surtr plan to use those terrible fires against the Aesir!"

Thor uttered an unbelieving exclamation. "It is impossible! Those fires are so deadly that man cannot even approach them closely without being blasted by their rays."

"Loki found a way!" Hela replied. "He reasoned that since the lead-rich rocks of the crater had always safely confined the witch-fires, then shields of lead would protect a man from them.

"He and Surtr made such shields, and a leaden vessel to contain the captured fires. And with them and their host goes an engine that will hurl those deadly fires upon Asgard."

Fear was in her dark, wide eyes. She clutched my arm. "Tyr, I begged them not to do it! Not from love of the Aesir, who have always condemned me for my Jotun blood. But because I am afraid to see those terrible witch-fires loosed. Afraid, for our whole world!"

I felt a dread equaling hers. For I, in my Earth-years as Eric Wolverson, had learned enough of science to realize the peril of what Loki planned to do.

I whirled around to Thor. "There's but once chance. To overtake and kill Loki and Surtr before they can use that weapon!"

Thor brandished his hammer high. "Then this day comes the end of that arch-devil's life!"

We turned hastily toward the door, but again Hela caught my arm. Her dark, brilliant eyes looked up at me.

"Tyr, I have had strange visions and I think that many things end this day. Let me go with you!"

I stared haggardly down at her, and it seemed that all these past years faded away and that we were again the lovers we had been long ago.

All her bitterness against the Aesir because they would not accept a Jotun girl, all my own bitterness when I had discovered her using her wizardries to help Loki against my people—all this was gone now.

I took her in my arms. "Hela, when this peril passes—"

"Is this a time for lovemaking?" roared Thor. "Hurry!"

I released Hela and told her quickly, "Get a fast horse and ride out around the lake—we'll meet you there."

Then the Hammerer and I hurried back down the way we had come. And still we met no one. All Surtr's warriors had gone with his and Loki's host.

Day had come when we squeezed out of the tunnel onto the lake strand where our horses were tied. It was a dark, lowering day, with masses of sullen clouds brooding across the sky.

We galloped around the lake, and Hela came riding fast to meet us. Then we three rode hard through the forest toward Asgard.

The forest seemed alive with fear! As on the previous night, all its living things were moving southward in a strange, panicky stampede.

"Storm is coming, Tyr!" shouted Thor as he rode, gesturing with his great hammer toward the still-darkening sky.

"Aye, and such a storm as this world has never seen before!" called Hela, with that note of dread again in her voice.

Now, after hours of riding, our path joined the trampled track left in the forest by the passage of a great body of men.

"Loki and Surtr and their host are ahead of us!" I cried. "They must be already approaching Asgard!"

We spurred our sturdy mounts faster, their hoofs waking drumming echoes beneath the giant, solemn trees.

Lightning flared across the black sky, and flared again, and there came the crash of thunder. And the hubbub of the storm increased as we covered the last few miles.

Then, even through the tempest, we heard a different and familiar sound—the hoarse, pulsating roar of many voices, of battle.

"They're already attacking Asgard!" yelled Thor.

We had reached the last ridge of the forest, and for a moment we sat our horses on the ridge to take in that terrible scene.

Under the lowering, storm-swept sky, the abyss of Niflheim yawned black and gloomy. Out there on the lofty pinnacle that rose from the abyss, the towers of Asgard seemed to challenge the lightning.

Directly below us, on the hither side of the abyss, a great battle raged. Out across Bifrost had come the bright-mailed warriors of the Aesir, and they were pressing back a great host of dark Jotuns who had sought to win the bridge.

"Look, where lord Odin leads the Aesir!" shouted Thor. "See, there fight Heimdall and Aegir and Bragi! Come, Tyr!"

I restrained the battle-lusting giant. "Wait! Where are Loki and Surtr and their weapon?"

Hela pointed swiftly. "There, Tyr! They prepare to cast the witch-fires!"

Now I saw them, and for a moment the blood seemed to drain from my heart at what I saw.

On a hillock a little distance from the battle, ringed round by a guard of warriors, Loki and Surtr were working at a ponderous thing that I recognized as a powerful catapult.

They were fastening upon the catapult throwing-arm a huge globular flask which I divined to be the leaden container of the atomic witch-fire.

"We must kill them before they release that thing!" I cried to Thor. "Wait here, Hela!"

And then the Hammerer and I spurred our horses and galloped past the main battle in a charge for that hillock.

They saw us coming, those Jotun warriors who guarded Loki and

Surtr. They shouted warning to each other, and formed hastily on the side of the hillock to meet us.

Our charge crashed into them, and then Thor's hammer was swinging in terrible arcs of death while my own sword stabbed and stabbed.

Thor's horse was speared, but the giant leaped clear to the ground and continued to crush skulls with his awful weapon. I leaped from the saddle to his side, and we fought together up the hillock side.

There had been but a handful of Jotun guards, and half of them were dead or wounded. We had taken our own wounds, but the few men left before us could not hold us as we pressed up the hillock's side.

"It's Tyr and the Hammerer!" I heard Surtr shouting hoarsely to Loki, up there. "Cast the witch-fire, quickly!"

"A moment more!" cried Loki, busy at the big catapult. "Hold them back, slay them! Fenris! Iormungandr!"

And now through the fray I glimpsed what before I had not, that up there beside Loki were his two monstrous beasts, the great wolf and the coiled winged serpent.

And at their lord's command, Fenris and Iormungandr came down with Surtr against us! I saw the blazing green eyes of the giant wolf springing toward me, and heard the thresh of Iormungandr's wings as the mighty serpent launched through the air at Thor.

Thor struck up ragingly at the Midgard serpent that was swooping toward him. And as he did so, Surtr rushed in under his blow and stabbed his sword deep into the Hammerer's breast.

With a hoarse cry, Thor struck downward. The mighty hammer whistled and swung, and crushed Surtr's helmet and head like an eggshell.

"So much for traitors!" Thor bellowed. Then he staggered as the Midgard serpent launched upon him from the sky.

Fenris' hot breath was in my own face, his jaws closing on my throat! I recoiled, and heard the clash of his fangs meeting. My sword stabbed into that huge, hairy body that was bearing me backward.

The wolf would not die. His jaws had gripped my left shoulder, and worked nearer to my throat as I stabbed again and again.

Then the beast slumped down, his hold upon me relaxing but his green eyes still blazing hatred up at me.

"Thor!" I shouted hoarsely, as I scrambled to my feet.

The Hammerer stood, a swaying giant around whose body the Midgard serpent was wrapped in mighty coils. His face was crimson, his eyes flaming, as his hands twisted Iormungandr's dragon head in a supreme effort.

The serpent's vertebra snapped, its coils loosened and fell away from Thor.

But the last Jotun warriors, who had held back appalled from our death-duel with Loki's monstrous beasts, rushed back in upon us now.

We struck at them like madmen, fighting forward. And then suddenly came a twanging sound that struck my ears like the clang of doom.

Up on the hillock summit, Loki had fired his catapult. And the huge leaden flask of prisoned doom was hurtling across the storm-swept sky toward the towers of Asgard.

"Behold!" pealed Loki's silver voice, soaring triumphant. "Behold the doom of the Aesir!"

Frozenly, I and the staggering Hammerer and our remaining Jotun foes watched the curving flight of that deadly thing.

I saw the flask crash down upon the towers of Valhalla castle. And from it, as it smashed open, there burst in all directions an explosion of fire.

Cold green witch-fire, not red flame! Cold witch-fire that spattered and dripped in hellish, burning viridescence over the towers and walls of Asgard, spreading with nightmare rapidity.

From the Aesir battling on this side of Bifrost Bridge came a terrible cry. "Asgard burns!"

And then Odin's stern shout. "Our folk are there—back to save them or die with them, my warriors!"

The Aesir fell back across the Rainbow Bridge, back into Asgard. And after them poured the Jotun hosts, with wolfish yells of triumph.

But already, all Asgard was flaming with the witch-fires! The dread atomic blaze enwrapped towering Valhalla in a sheet of green radiance that paled the lightning of the stormy sky.

"Asgard and the Aesir are doomed!" choked Thor. He staggered, a giant, blood-covered figure, then sagged to his knees.

The hammer dropped from his hand, as I sprang to support him. He whispered, "And Surtr's stab has cut my thread. I perish with our people—"

There came a scream of terror from the Jotuns nearby. "The witch-fires spread across Niflheim! See!"

The green witch-fires now roared in infernal holocaust through all of Asgard and were sweeping across Bifrost Bridge.

I knew now what dread doom Hela had foreseen! Those awful atomic fires, feeding upon all but the most obdurate kinds of matter, could not now be stayed. For ages they had been safely prisoned in their leaden crater, but now Loki's madness had loosed them on our world.

Bifrost Bridge was burning, and the radiant green death was sweeping on from it across this battlefield. The Jotuns were fleeing with screams of terror.

I stared frozenly, and then I lowered my sword. Motionless, in an agony of despair, I waited for the blazing green death to reach me. My comrades of the Aesir were gone forever, and I would not outlive them.

But hoofs drummed, and Hela's clear cry struck my ears. She had caught my own horse and ridden to me.

"Tyr, Loki escapes!" she cried. "He has seen that this world is doomed, and seeks to flee to the Way between Worlds!"

I swung around, and fierce rage replaced my dull agony as I glimpsed Loki galloping madly into the forest on his steed.

And after him staggered a great gray shape—the Fenris wolf whom I had wounded mortally but who still followed his master with dying strength.

"Loki shall not escape!" I shouted, and leaped into the saddle. "He dies with our world and us!"

We two spurred after him, into the forest. The woods swarmed with panicky Jotuns, who yelled hoarsely in terror as they sought to flee the advancing atomic blaze.

Through the forest we rode, and behind us the sky flamed with a lurid radiance that outdazzled the lightning still darting above us.

Now, far ahead of us, we saw Loki riding fast up the side of the hill on whose summit were the runestones of the Way between Worlds.

By the time we rode up onto the summit, Loki had planted the birch-rods beside the great stones and stood in their circle as lightning struck down blindingly at them.

And Fenris, dying but still faithful, stood staggering beside his master and snarled madly at us.

I leaped from my horse and darted into that circle of awesome lightning. Loki met me, his handsome face now a hell-mask of fear and hate, his sword clashing ringing against my blade.

Hela screamed, and from the corner of my eye I glimpsed Fenris staggering with great jaws open to pull me down from the side.

"Traitress witch!" howled Loki, as Hela sprang between me and the wolf with her dagger raised.

The jaws of the dying beast closed upon Hela, dragged her down. With superhuman strength, I struck Loki's sword down and stabbed.

Lightning danced suddenly in terrific splendor about the circle of runestones that enclosed us. I felt myself sinking, falling—

Slowly, I came to myself again. I was lying on warm ground, with the sun hot upon my face and a gentle breeze rustling my hair.

I staggered up. Wildly, I looked around.

Gone were the lightnings and the lurid green blaze of the witch-fires, gone the savage hills and forests of that other world.

I stood in the sunlight in the circle of crumbling runestones upon that other hill in peaceful Norway.

The Way between Worlds had opened and I had come through to Earth.

And not I alone. Loki lay dead at my feet, and Fenris and Hela nearby.

Dead, all dead! The jaws of the dying wolf had slain Hela, as she sought to shield me.

Dead, as all the world of the Aesir now must be on the other side of the veil! A blackened, cinder planet, all its life burned out by the atomic blaze, it would remain until the end of time.

Yes, I had found my past and my people and my lost love. But I had found them only to see them perish in that twilight of the gods.

VIII

Before I left that place, I buried Loki and Fenris together on the shadowy slopes of Runestone Hill.

But Hela, I buried deep within the circle of the ancient, graven stones.

The people of Stortfors shrank from me in superstitious fear when I entered the village. A full Earth-year had passed since I left it, and now I reappeared dazed, exhausted and bleeding from my wounds.

I could not stay there long. Before a day had passed, I had left Norway by plane and was on my way back to New York.

But here in the great city where I write these words, I am now a stranger. Yes, I know that I am a stranger forever on this Earth that is not my world.

I am Tyr of the Sword, captain and warrior of the Aesir. But the Aesir and their world are gone forever now. Never again shall I ride forth with Thor to battle, never again shall we hail lord Odin in Valhalla hall.

And never again shall I see that dark witch-girl whom alone of women I have loved.

I know that memory of them all will haunt me until I go mad or kill myself. And madness and self-slaughter are no death for a warrior.

So I must forget. And there is but one way of forgetting, and that is for Tyr of the Sword to become again Eric Wolverson of Earth.

When I buried Hela, I took but two things from her body—the ring I gave her long ago and the vial of that dark hell-brew that washes away the memory.

The vial lies on my desk before me now. When I have finished writing this, I shall drink its contents. And then I shall forget.

I shall forget the world of the Aesir, and Odin and Thor and Loki—and Hela. I shall remember nothing.

My friends here will tell me that I am Eric Wolverson, and I shall believe them and take up Eric Wolverson's life again and not ever be driven to madness by the memories of Tyr.

I will read then this story that I have just written, and will think as you think that it is but a fantastic imagining.

I may doubt, in times to come. I may wonder if this story is not true, if I am not really Tyr of the lost Aesir.

But I will never, thank the fates, be sure.

Priestess of the Labyrinth

Marlin felt the Lightning buck and shudder like a wounded horse as a shell hit the right wing. The stunning shock of the explosion smacked him hard against his belt. He came groggily out of his daze to find that his plane lacked a wing and was tumbling downward through the darkness.

"I *would* have to run into flak on my last mission!" he thought sickly.

No time for further thought! The crippled plane was screaming down through the night toward the Nazi-held island of Crete at increasing speed.

Marlin ripped the cowling open, unbuckled his belt, and clawed his way up out of the seat. Then the wind caught his lanky young figure out of the plane, and he was tumbling head over heels down through the darkness.

The discipline of a Texas training field half the world away held good in Marlin's mind. Automatically, he counted, waited, and pulled his rip-cord. The white cup of the parachute unfolded over his head.

He looked down. A few thousand feet beneath him lay the moon-silvered wash of the Mediterranean. Beyond to the south stretched the northern shore of Crete, a black mass.

That dark cape down there where anti-aircraft guns were spitting viciously was Candia, he knew. He had been watching the flak only a minute before, as he helped shepherd the bombers that now were swooping toward the target of the city harbor.

Marlin's thin, dark face was grim as he waved after the roaring Liberators. "See you again someday, boys—I hope!"

He turned his attention to his own predicament. He shortened the parachute cords on one side, trying to drift toward the dark land.

Crete was still in Nazi hands, in this early spring of 1944. The ancient island, seat of the strangest and most mysterious civilization of antiquity, still warded the bastions of the Balkans against Allied invasion.

Three years before, when Brad Marlin had been an archaeological student at Harvard, it had been his dream to visit Crete someday. He had envisioned himself delving into the ruins of that enigmatic and mighty civilization, that great riddle of the past presented by the uncanny myths of Cretan science and power.

But he hadn't planned to visit Crete *this* way! Not dropping out of a night made hideous by screaming anti-aircraft shells and fiery rockets and the thunderous explosion of bombs now hitting the Candia docks.

Marlin knew that at the best, he faced a Nazi concentration camp until the war's end. And his fate might well be worse. Stories had drifted back about the treatment of captured Allied fliers. The Nazis feared coming invasion, feared it enough to make them ruthless in questioning those Allied pilots who fell into their hands.

"If I could hide out in the hills and get down to a fishing-boat some night, I could still get away," Marlin sweated.

But first he had to *reach* those hills! He was drifting down toward the huddled mass of Candia, the big seaport city.

Marlin held the chute-cords tightened until they cut his hands, and prayed for an inshore wind. He hit one at the two-thousand-foot level and it swept him beyond the bomb-rocking city.

He saw the silver thread of a river below, and knew it must be the Karaitos that ran past the ancient site of Knossos. Then those white patches of stone columns and walls below were Knossos itself, the ruins of the ancient Cretan capital?

A few minutes later, he alighted on a ridge just beyond the white forest of ruins. The chute dragged him roughly over the bumpy ground until he got it collapsed. He stood panting, a lanky young figure in his flying suit, his black hair bare, his dark, thin face strained.

In the moonlight, the white ruins that were all that was left of ancient Knossos stretched on his right. Farther inland from him, there yawned shadowy gorges that ran back into the hills.

Marlin felt the irony of it as he glanced at the pillared ruins. As a student archaeologist, he had dreamed of coming to this very spot. Its tales of magic wonders, of the cruel sea-kings, of the sorcerer-scientist Daedalus and his doomed son Icarus who had been the first men to fly, of Labyrinth and Minotaur, had puzzled the world for four thousand years.

And now he was here at ruined Knossos—but in mortal danger. He must not fall into Nazi hands. If they hadn't seen him landing, if he could hide out in these hills until he found some native fisherman to smuggle him out—

"Er ist da," shouted a sharp voice through the moonlit ruins at that moment. *"Schnell."*

Marlin's hopes shattered like a bubble. He had been seen falling. Dark figures were running toward him through the ruins.

"Stop or we fire!" cried a sharp voice, in English, as Marlin turned and ran toward the inviting darkness of the nearest gorge.

An automatic rifle let go a moment later and bullets screamed off the stone pillars around the running American.

The rattle of the rifle was drowned by the successive explosions of bombs falling, ripping the Nazi barracks between Candia and Knossos. Marlin heard the roar of the Liberators sweeping closer as he ran.

He was in the gorge. He stumbled along a dry stream-bed with the boots of the Nazi patrol pounding loudly behind him. He tripped over loose stones, collided with boulders in the deep shadows.

He could hear the Nazi officer who commanded the small patrol cursing his men and urging them to greater speed. The stone walls of the ravine, sculptured long ago by the builders of dead Knossos, held monstrous bull-headed figures who glared down at the running pilot in the moonlight.

Marlin heard the Nazi officer yelling to his men not to fire, to take the Amerikaner alive. He knew what that meant. It meant a merciless inquisition by the Germans that he would probably not survive.

Blam! Blam!

Flame and thunder rocked the gorge as a stick of bombs started falling along it from a Liberator a little south off its target.

Marlin knew the rest of the stick was coming, and dived behind a big boulder as the explosions rocked along the rest of the ravine and brought down showers of pebbles from its split rock walls.

He hoped for a moment that one of the bombs had got the patrol pursuing him, but his hopes were dashed when he heard that sharp, hateful voice a moment later.

"Schnell!"

Marlin was breathless, his heart slugging his ribs, as he stumbled on around a curve of the moon-dappled, narrow gorge.

Rock debris was still sliding from a sculptured cliff that had taken the full impact of a bomb. Marlin glimpsed a dark opening or cavity in the shattered cliff.

He stumbled toward it. It was a possible hiding-place. He could not go farther, in any case. This whole region would soon be alive with searching patrols, for now the Liberators were leaving.

He scrambled through the opening, and was surprised to find that it was no mere cavity in the rock but a high, narrow tunnel that led back into the cliff. And it was man-made, for the floor and walls were smoothly squared.

He realized instantly what it was. An ancient passageway of the Cretans, uncovered after ages by the explosion of the bombs.

Marlin grinned mirthlessly in the darkness. "Hell of a way to make an archaeological discovery," he thought.

It was pitch dark in the tunnel. He groped forward. There was an intense silence, all the clamor outside now cut off.

The tunnel curved. It curved until it was going at right angles to his former course. It went straight a little way, then wound spirally downward in what was actually another right-angle change of course, and then again it became a straight passage for a few yards.

Then it curved again until it was following a course at right angles to all *three* of the former directions. And as he went around this final turn of the quadruple curve, Marlin felt a dizzying, sinking sensation as though he were falling through infinite spaces.

Marlin stopped, suddenly startled by realization. "What the devil! I couldn't have made four turns all perpendicular to each other!"

That was impossible, for there were only three dimensions. Three spatial dimensions, that is—the only fourth dimension was the abstract one of time.

He swore to himself. "I must be getting dizzy and imagining things in this darkness." Yet Marlin knew he wasn't, that he had really turned in four mutually perpendicular directions. For he had the unerring sense of direction and orientation that a fighter-pilot must have to the last degree.

"But it's crazy! You can't make four different right-angle turns when there are only three dimensions."

Marlin groped mystifiedly onward. Other tunnels forked from the one he followed, he discovered.

He felt utterly baffled. "What the devil kind of a labyrinth is this?"

A labyrinth? No, *the* Labyrinth! He suddenly realized it. He had found the long-hidden and long-sought great secret of ancient Crete!

The very words labyrinthine and labyrinth came from this place. This was the magic maze built beneath ancient Knossos by Daedalus, legendary scientist of Crete, the man supposed to have invented artificial wings.

Marlin remembered those tales of the dread of all the ancient world for the Labyrinth in which strange magic worked, in which horror walked curving ways no man could escape once he entered. Daedalus, they said, had built the Labyrinth and made it the haunt of the Minotaur, the terrible man-bull.

"And that stick of bombs uncovered the entrance to it," Marlin thought. "Hidden all these centuries—"

Marlin found himself groping around another of the uncanny quadruple curves. Again, his head swam with strange dizziness as he rounded the fourth right angle. Something like panic came over him.

He turned around, to retrace his steps. Then he stopped and stiffened as a sharp echo came through the dark from the way he had come.

"Vorwarts—schnell!"

The Nazi patrol had seen him enter the tunnel and had come into the Labyrinth after him, he realized!

He gave up all thought of turning back and ran on gropingly through the diabolically twisting tunnels. The voices echoed louder behind and he had a dismaying sense of being hopelessly trapped in this ancient maze.

Then came something that brought the hair prickling up on Marlin's neck. It was a sound, but not a sound of voices. And it came from ahead of him, not from behind.

A distant, echoing, bellowing sound, unutterably brutish and hideous, boomed through the darkness of the curving tunnels. That blood-chilling bull-bellow stopped Marlin in his tracks.

"Good God!" he whispered. "That sounds like—"

He could not finish the sentence, even to himself. It was too insanely fantastic.

That hideous bellow had been both human and taurine in quality. It had been like the mingled voice of bull and man.

"Just an echo!" he told himself thickly. "Imagination getting the best of me, making me think of the Minotaur legend."

Yet if the Labyrinth itself was now proved a reality, might not the dreaded Minotaur be real also? The Minotaur, monstrous guardian of the magic maze, surviving centuries and still haunting this place?

The rush of feet, the flash of light from behind him, woke Marlin from his stupor of amazement and spun him around. Two Nazi soldiers, led by an *oberleutnant* with a flashlight, had come around the curve behind him.

"Stop—raise your hands or we shall cut you down!" shouted the German officer as Marlin turned to run.

Marlin had no choice. The two automatic rifles of the soldiers were trained upon him. The flashlight beam made him a perfect target.

He helplessly raised his hands. The Nazis approached. The young lieutenant searched him efficiently for weapons, and found none.

"Amerikaner, as I thought," he snapped. "Who told you about this hiding place—the Greek underground? How long have they been using it?"

The Nazi lieutenant was younger than Marlin. He was tall, stalwart, superbly muscled, with a face as cold and merciless and handsome as a panther's.

Marlin's lanky figure sagged a little from fatigue and frustration. "I never knew of the place before, and doubt if anyone did," he answered. "The bombs that hit the gorge uncovered it."

"A likely story!" sneered the Nazi. He glanced along the curving tunnel. Its floor and sides were of smooth, massive blocks. The roof was almost out of sight overhead.

"An ancient Cretan relic, without doubt," the German muttered. His eyes narrowed. "I begin to understand now. The ruins of Knossos were excavated for years by Sir Arthur Evans, the English archaeologist. He and his co-workers must have found this place and kept it secret—probably it's been used by Allied spies and the underground right along."

One of the two Nazi soldiers, who had been looking nervously along the tunnel, ventured to address the officer. Marlin knew enough German to understand.

"Lieutenant Preyder, can we not leave? This place is creepy—the giddiness we felt coming through it, and the cry that Blaun heard—"

"Blaun heard an echo!" snapped Preyder scornfully. "And the dizziness is due to the bad air in this place."

"It didn't sound like an echo," muttered the man Blaun. "It sounded like the cry of some monster."

Preyder's ice-gray eyes were fixed on the American. "You are going out with us for questioning. You must know something about the Allied plans for invading Crete."

Marlin had expected that, and he smiled crookedly. "I'm just a fighter-pilot. I rarely talk over strategy with General Wilson."

Preyder's lips tightened. "But you can give valuable information, I'm sure. Gestapo headquarters in Candia will see to that—"

The man Blaun interrupted by opening his mouth and screaming. He screamed like a man who has seen the devil rise before him.

A terrific bull-bellow shook the corridor. Marlin spun, reckless of the rifles. He stiffened, like the others, in horror.

In the shadows beyond the flashlight beam, a vague, monstrous shape towered up and was glaring at them with flaming eyes. Incredible, that monster. The eye saw it but the brain rejected it.

It was human, manlike, in bodily form. But the misshaped, massive head, the brutish jaws, the great horns of the giant skull—they were not human. Bellowing, it charged toward them.

II

Marlin was as frozen as the Nazis by the rush of the monstrous creature. That human form, that massive, taurine, horned head with its flaming eyes and gaping jaws—they *couldn't* be real!

Then the American was shocked to the reality of it by the shriek of the Nazi soldier beside Blaun. That man had been nearest the creature, and its lowered horn had caught his side as the thing charged.

"Gott!" screamed the soldier Blaun, scrambling frantically to flee.

Preyder had whipped out his revolver and was firing. The bullets ripped the shoulder of the bull-horned giant, and blood spouted.

That spurt of blood, more than anything else, convinced Marlin that it was no insane nightmare. The crashing echoes of the gunfire were followed by a terrific bellow of pain from the creature.

It turned and with incredible swiftness darted back around the curve of the tunnel. Its bellowing reached them in a hideous, brutish clamor of rage and pain.

Preyder's face was pale and glistening with sweat. "Bull-head and man's body—the Minotaur of ancient legend!" he husked. "But it can't be—"

His revolver warned Marlin back as the American started to bend over the fallen Nazi soldier. Preyder himself stooped over the man, picking up his rifle and then examining him. The man was dead, for that savage horn had ripped his heart.

"The thing was real enough to kill that man of yours," muttered Marlin, feeling an icy horripilation along his spine. "This is the ancient Labyrinth of Knossos, no doubt of that. Legend always said that it was monster-haunted."

"But that thing, monster or not, could not have lived in here for four thousand years!" exclaimed Preyder. "It was flesh and blood, monstrous as it was. And flesh and blood can't live that long."

Thunderous bawling echoes of the man-bull's bellowing rocked the vaulted tunnel again. And they seemed now to be answered from other directions in the dark, intricate maze.

"Gott, there are other of the creatures in here!" whispered the shaking man Blaun.

"If there are, we can handle them with the guns!" snapped Preyder. The Nazi officer's pale eyes had a gleam in them now. "We've found something big here—a mystery that must be investigated. But it's a job for headquarters to handle. We'll get out now with this Amerikaner and make our report."

Not for a moment had Marlin been able to make a break. Preyder's gun had covered him since the disappearance of the bull-monster, and now he motioned with the weapon back along the tunnel by which they had come.

The man Blaun seemed frantically eager to get out of the place, as they started back along the curving passage. Preyder followed them closely, the dead man's rifle in his hands.

Clamorous echoes of the hideous taurine bellowing were louder about them now, seeming to come from all directions. They came to a fork in the curving tunnel.

"To the right," ordered the Nazi officer confidently. "That is the way we came."

But the right fork wound left, as soon as they entered it. It curved and curved again in those weirdly dizzying loops and spirals, until they seemed going ever deeper into the baffling Labyrinth.

Preyder stopped and swore. "We'll have to go back and take the other turn."

But they did not seem able to find that fork when they retraced their steps. For what seemed hours, they stumbled through the dark tunnels in vain search. And ever the brutish bellowing was louder, nearer!

Marlin's head reeled. The geometry of this maze was unearthly. That was the only word for it. Time and again they would go through one of those uncanny quadruple loops which each time gave Marlin the dizzying sensation of moving through a fourth dimension.

The terror of the man Blaun was now extreme. The bellowing followed them, always behind. Flaming eyes watched from the darkness behind them. Yet when Preyder turned the beam back, they would never be in time to see anything but a flash of movement.

"There must be a dozen of the creatures," Preyder muttered. "What in hell's name are they?"

He speculated aloud. "Genetic experiments might produce such monsters. But why here, in this hidden maze? It's too cursed appropriate with the Minotaur legend."

His flashlight beam was dimming, the battery failing. Preyder forced a pace of desperate urgency. They stumbled through the curving ways with the little light growing weaker each moment. And the bull-bellowing behind grew louder, nearer, exultant.

It seemed like a crazy dream, to Marlin. He'd wake up and find himself back at Bengasi base with the morning sun pouring through the tent-flap. He'd draw a long sigh of relief to find himself awake—

The light went out! A wail of terror from the man Blaun was echoed by a savage chorus of taurine bellowing from behind.

"Keep your rifle against the Amerikaner and shoot if he tries to escape in the dark!" exclaimed Preyder to the Nazi soldier.

Flaming eyes were coming toward them through the dark. Preyder fired at them. But the crashing roar of gunfire was followed only by the whine of bullets glancing off the curved stone walls.

"Look—there's a light!" screamed Blaun.

Marlin saw. It was a dim, effulgent white glow that was dawning along the curving tunnel from behind them.

It came into view, something tiny and glowing that was advancing along the curving passageway.

"Good God!" muttered Marlin. "It's a girl!"

The figure approaching almost confirmed his belief that he was dreaming. She was as uncannily beautiful as the bull-men had been uncannily hideous.

She was tall and fair-haired, a slim figure in low-cut waist and long, flounced white skirt. Her yellow hair, falling to her shoulders, was bound around her temples by a golden circlet in the front of which was set a great crystal that emitted the soft, dim glow of light.

Marlin's skin crawled as he saw that in the shadows just behind her the flaming eyes of the man-bulls were advancing also, and that she paid no attention to them as they followed her. Her sea-blue eyes were fixed in wide amazement on the three men, her face white and startled.

"You are men from beyond!" she gasped, amazement and dawning terror in her eyes. "You have opened the Labyrinth!"

Marlin could only vaguely understand her language. It was Greek—not the ancient Attic he had learned in his Harvard classrooms but a dimly distorted dialect of that tongue.

"What do you mean? Who are you?" he husked in halting Attic.

"Gott, look at her arms!" choked Blaun.

Marlin looked, and felt a deepened sense of the uncanny. He had noticed that the girl wore golden, serpent-like ornaments twined around her arms. Now he saw that the golden serpents were alive. They were not metal, but little golden snakes which entwined each arm and raised their heads to stare at the men with wise, wide yellow eyes.

A girl out of mystery, a girl who spoke the ancient tongue and wore living serpents like the snake-goddesses of the ancient world, and who seemed to have no fear of the incredible taurine horde shuffling in the deep shadows behind her!

Preyder broke in. The Nazi officer apparently knew the classical Greek of the schoolroom also, and he spoke sharply to the girl.

"Are you of the underground?" he demanded of her. "What are those brutes behind you?"

The girl glanced only a moment back at the vague, monstrous forms of the shadowy shapes that bulked behind flaming eyes.

"The Minotaurs? Do not be afraid—they will not harm you. They obey me always."

The Minotaurs? Marlin's brain reeled. Legend was coming true before his eyes. What did it all mean?

"I am Luane, priestess of the Temple and daughter of the high priest," she was saying rapidly. The dread in her blue eyes deepened as she added, "Your opening of the Labyrinth is a disaster neither he nor I had foreseen. You must come at once with me to my father Daedalus!"

"Daedalus?" Even Preyder was stunned out of his suspicious attitude for a moment by that name.

Daedalus, legendary builder of the Labyrinth? The fabulous sorcerer-scientist of ancient Crete who was even supposed to have invented artificial human wings that had brought death to his son Icarus? This girl—the daughter of Daedalus?

Luane seemed to understand Marlin's stupefaction, the Nazi's incredulity. "My father will explain all to you. But you must come with me at once. There is terrible danger every moment that you linger here!"

Her desperate urgency, the dread of mysterious catastrophe that widened her eyes, penetrated the daze of the men.

"She's either crazy or lying but she must know a way out of this devil's maze," muttered Preyder. "We will go with her. But you'll get a bullet in the back if you try an escape, Amerikaner!"

"This way—and hurry!" Luane exclaimed, already leading the way forward along the curving tunnel, the radiant jewel on her forehead lighting the way dimly.

Marlin followed at her heels, Blaun and the officer close behind him. And in the shadows behind *them* came the shuffling, trampling footsteps of the monsters the girl had called Minotaurs.

Marlin's brain was beginning to grasp a possible unearthly explanation of this mad situation. He was remembering the uncanny quadruple curves of the twisting maze, that had given him the sensation of turning through a fourth dimension. The fourth dimension of matter was *time*. Then this incredible Labyrinth wound its maze not only through space but also through time? Had brought them into past time when ancient Crete existed?

Luane's steps were quickening, as though dread spurred her. She led the way through the insane maze without the slightest uncertainty. Finally the tunnel they followed ended in a heavy door of silvery metal.

Luane bent forward, so that the crystal upon her forehead touched an engraved boss on the door. The door clicked, and then swung open.

"Hurry, now!" she pleaded as they passed through the door. "There is no safety until we reach my father's laboratory."

They had entered a dark, vault-like room of stone. The girl was hastening toward a spiral of stone steps that climbed upward around it.

Marlin looked back wonderingly. The massive silver door had swung shut behind them. The monstrous horde of bull-men, then, had not followed them up out of the tunnels?

"They do not leave the Labyrinth," Luane said quickly, as though guessing his thought. "They do not like the upper world, those poor children of pain and darkness."

"Where are we?" demanded Preyder harshly, suspiciously, his gaze searching the dim, vaulted room.

"In the lowest level of the Temple of Wisdom," answered the girl. "Come quickly!"

They climbed after her. Daylight, sunlight, showed somewhere above them. Marlin saw that the little golden serpents twined around the girl's arms now lifted their heads eagerly toward the light, preening themselves.

They climbed up into a big oblong ball of unstained white marble whose brilliant light dazzled their eyes. The light came from a pillared window at one end, which opened on a landscape of white sunlight.

The man Blaun uttered a hoarse cry. "Where are we? This is not Crete!"

Marlin was stunned by the vista too. But not as much as the Nazis. He had been half-expecting this.

Outside lay a mighty city, one larger and far different than any town of modern Crete. Tens of thousands of unpretentious houses of sun-dried brick, a sea of flat roofs, stretched toward the blue sea and the harbor in which were a forest of masts. Far out on the sea, strange galleys with colored sails were cleaving the waves.

Through the streets of the city swirled a bewilderingly polyglot crowd. Marlin's eyes ran over them dazedly. Cretan soldiers in bronze helmets, armed with heavy swords and double-bladed axes; Greeks in short chitons; dark-faced Egyptians in linen robes; towering, skin-clad Hittites; all the ancient Mediterranean world seemed represented here.

On a low hill a mile eastward rose a structure that was colossal. It dominated the city, that massive, oblong marble bulk that crouched like a drowsing white dragon watching the sea. Those looming walls and colonnades of pillars, those giant stairways and rounded cupolas, were familiar to Marlin as though remembered from a dream.

"The palace of Minos!" he husked. "And this city is Knossos in the great age of Crete!"

Luane had an agony of apprehension in her face. "You must not linger here. If Minos learns of your coming—"

Marlin knew his guess had been right. That alien Labyrinth whose tunnels curved in time had brought them four thousand years into the past.

III

Preyder had taken the shock of realization even more than Marlin, for the Nazi had no mental preparation for it. His widened eyes turned from the incredible vista outside to glare at Luane.

"Knossos? *That's* not Knossos!" he snapped. "What kind of trick is this? Where have you brought us?"

His raised rifle menaced her. "Answer, or I'll—"

Luane made no movement. But the golden snakes that entwined her arms suddenly moved, with a swiftness beyond belief.

They shot like flying shafts of gold through the air toward the Nazi. They whipped around Preyder's neck and tightened.

The Nazi staggered, clawing the air, dropping the gun as his face went purple. The other German recoiled with a cry of horror.

"Loose the man, my daughter!" commanded a deep, urgent voice.

Marlin whirled. The man who had entered the hall was dressed in the long cloak of ancient Crete, a white garment edged with black designs.

His hair was thin and gray. The face was the withered countenance of an old man. But the eyes, black, glowing, afire with life and intelligence, were ageless.

Luane uttered a low, honeyed note of sound. The golden snakes ceased to tighten around Preyder's neck. They entwined with blurring speed and leaped back onto Luane's upraised arms, coiling lovingly around them. The old man had advanced. His deep eyes widened as they looked at Marlin and the Nazis. "Then there was someone in the Labyrinth, as the Minotaur's outcries betokened?" he said swiftly to the girl.

"Yes, but not Minos' spies as we thought," Luane answered. "These are men from across time. The Labyrinth has been opened!"

Daedalus blanched, like a man receiving a shock of terrible intelligence.

"The Labyrinth opened?" he whispered. "But if Minos learns of this, it means—"

Urgent alarm and haste flashed into his eyes. "Quick, to my laboratory! Minos' mental vision cannot see there!"

Marlin dazedly allowed himself to be hustled with the other two through a series of connecting halls and corridors, by Daedalus and his daughter. The stunned Preyder attempted no further resistance.

The American glimpsed a few white-robed men servitors of the temple, Cretans who stared at them wonderingly. Then they were led into a small, windowless room of octagonal shape, whose walls were sheets of dull lead. It was illuminated by silver lamps. The room was a laboratory; but not such a one as he had known in his own time.

Many instruments were of familiar design—crucibles, retorts and other chemical apparatus. But there were also ancient alembics, charcoal braziers, twisted glass tubes through which bubbled yellow gases, metal geometrical models of outlandish alienage that made the eye ache to look at.

"Not even Minos' mental vision can penetrate these walls of lead," muttered Daedalus. "But if he should already have learned that the Labyrinth had been opened—"

Supreme apprehension was in his face and in Luane's. Marlin recognized their dread, even though he was mystified by it.

"You built that Labyrinth?" Marlin said hoarsely to the old Cretan. "Legends for four thousand years have spoken of Daedalus as its builder."

"Four thousand years?" murmured the old man. "Then you come from that far in future time?"

Preyder was staring wildly. "Does it mean that we came in that hellish maze through *time?"* he husked to the American.

Marlin nodded shakenly. "We're in ancient Crete. How, I don't know. Except that that maze is a miracle of super-geometry that twists in four dimensions. Legend has spoken of it for forty centuries, and of the Minotaurs—"

Daedalus broke in. "The Minotaurs were not of *my* creation, stranger. Minos made those monsters out of men. And they fled to me for refuge, and I gave it to them."

Marlin's brain reeled. "I don't understand all this. In my day, it was only wild myth."

Preyder's eyes had begun to gleam. "What a secret to stumble upon! A pathway into past time!"

Luane was at her father's side, her blue eyes troubledly surveying the three men as her father rapidly spoke.

"I cannot explain everything to you," Daedalus said. "But this I must tell you—your coming has threatened Knossos and all our world with dark evil. Yes, and because you have penetrated the Labyrinth and come here, that evil danger threatens even your own far future age!"

"Danger? Danger from what?" demanded Marlin, his thin young face puzzled.

"From Minos," came the answer. "The king who is lord of Crete and who wields a dark wisdom equaling my own. And who is evil incarnate in his purposes!"

He almost spat the words. And Marlin began to remember now that the old legends spoke of Minos the king and Daedalus the scientist as deadly enemies—enemies wielding the magic of ancient wisdom.

"We have science, we of Crete," Daedalus was saying. "Perhaps not the same as your science of the future. I perceive by your dress and weapons that you have mastered many material forces. We have concentrated on other problems, on the subtle laws of time and space and life.

"Greatest of scientists in our land are Minos, hereditary king, and I, high priest of this Temple of Wisdom. But the researches of Minos have always been unholy. For he has long cherished a black, evil purpose.

"Minos has always wished to breed new, monstrous, semi-human races who would serve him and extend his power over all the earth! Years ago, he sought for the ultimate seeds of life, the tiny germs that control every aspect of a living creature's growth and formation.

"He found those controlling germs of life, and bred horrible new creatures from human stock. Men who had only a travesty of human shape, whom the experiments of Minos had caused to grow into bestial forms! Yes, the beast-headed monsters whom you saw in the Labyrinth, the poor mockeries of humanities whom Minos called his Minotaurs!

"Those creatures escaped their master and came to me. They hoped that I could make them human. But I could not. I could only give them refuge here and refuse to return them to Minos. But I resolved that Minos should make no more Cretans into such monsters!

"I told Minos that if he took any more Cretans to create unholy races, I would raise the whole Cretan people against him by telling them just what he was doing! He had to desist, but from that time forward Minos has hated me."

Marlin was horrified. So *this* was why horror had clung to the name of Minos for forty centuries!

The Cretan sorcerer-king had engaged in blackly evil genetic experiments in his efforts to create new monstrous races to buttress his power!

Daedalus was continuing urgently. "I was then engaged in a great experiment of my own. I believed that I could create a super-geometrical pattern that would enter four dimensions and thus would penetrate time, past and future. Beneath this Temple, I built the Labyrinth.

"I pierced thus into other ages. I looked forth, and saw Knossos as it will be in future ages, dead and ruined. I looked even farther and saw strange things of Earth to be that even you do not know.

"But then Minos learned of my achievement. He came to me. He wished me to let him use the Labyrinth. My threat to tell the people had prevented him from using any more Cretans for his hideous life-experiments. He proposed to use the Labyrinth to raid future ages for human subjects!

"I refused! I sealed up every outlet of the Labyrinth into future ages, so that it could not be used. Minos and Pasiphae and their evil followers, much as they wished, could not hope to find the sealed openings of the Labyrinth even had they taken possession of it by force and overcome the Minotaurs whom I let dwell in it."

Daedalus' heavy voice rang with dread foreboding as he concluded his rapid recital.

"But if Minos learns now that the Labyrinth has been opened from outside our time, then he would move at once to seize it and use it as a roadway for the raiding of future ages!"

Marlin stared incredulously. "Then what do you intend to do with us?"

I.uane answered urgently. "Father, they must go back through the Labyrinth to their own time, and the Labyrinth must be sealed again."

Daedalus nodded anxiously. "That is the only solution. But first, we must be sure that Minos is not watching—"

Preyder broke in eagerly. "Wait! I could help you to conquer Minos!"

Marlin looked at the Nazi in sharp distrust. Preyder was excitedly explaining to the old scientist and the girl.

"In my own future age," the Nazi declared, "this island of Crete is held by my countrymen, the Germans. They are defending it against a motley horde of nations who attacked us. Our soldiers could come through the Labyrinth to *this* time, and help you sweep Minos from the throne!"

Preyder added eagerly, "In return, we'd ask only the privilege of taking refuge in this time if our enemies invade the island—of taking refuge merely until we can go back and counter-attack them by surprise."

Marlin gasped at the hellish audacity of the Nazi's plan. He saw instantly its terrific menace to the Allied cause.

The Allied forces, sooner or later, would invade Crete. If the Germans could retreat through the Labyrinth to this past age, they could wait until a favorable moment and mount a sudden counter-attack of stunning surprise. An ambush from time!

"Don't believe him!" Marlin cried to the two Cretans. "His people are not defending the island—they invaded it and now oppress its inhabitants, and my country and others are seeking to liberate it!"

"A lie," said Preyder flatly. "This American is of my nation's enemies, and that is why he twists the truth."

Daedalus spoke sternly. "I know nothing of the wars in your future age, nor do I wish to know them. I do know that you three must all return through the Labyrinth to your own time as quickly as possible."

The old scientist added meaningly, "I shall use hypnotic means to wipe all memory of it from your minds before you are thrust out of the Labyrinth. And I shall seal it again, so that no others may come through. And this must be done at once, before Minos learns that it was ever opened."

"But my people can offer you riches and power for your alliance!" Preyder persisted.

Daedalus looked icily at the Nazi. "Minos offered me power and riches, and I refused. No, you go back to your own time!"

He turned toward his daughter. "We shall take them at once, Luane. But first—"

He stopped. Preyder, turning away to a little distance, had suddenly whipped out his revolver and was covering Luane with it.

"This weapon kills instantly," snapped the Nazi. "If those serpents of yours move this time, you'll die at once."

Daedalus and Luane were frozen, and so for the moment was Marlin.

"There is a secret here that can mean ultimate victory for the Reich," Preyder went on harshly to the old Cretan scientist. "You're going to help me make use of it, or your daughter will pay the penalty."

Marlin jumped! He had been tensing himself for the last few seconds and he swept toward Preyder in a low, flying tackle.

The man Blaun was too dazed by events to act quickly. But Preyder whirled with wolf-like swiftness and shot.

The gun went off almost in Marlin's face. He felt a scorching blast of flame, a terrific blow, and then nothing.

IV

Marlin came back to consciousness with the salt stickiness of dried blood on his forehead and a feeling that his skull had split apart. He opened his eyes to find that he lay on the floor of the octagonal laboratory. The silver lamps still glowed softly, but the room was silent.

He stumbled up and then saw the withered, prostrate figure of Daedalus lying nearby. The old Cretan scientist was sprawled in front of a silver cabinet of instruments, blood seeping from a bullet wound in his side.

Marlin looked wildly around. The two Nazis and the girl Luane were gone.

He bent and frantically tried to revive the old Cretan. "What happened? Where is Preyder?"

Daedalus appeared mortally wounded. Yet the old scientist's eyes opened, and he whispered faintly.

"The phial of blue liquid," he murmured hoarsely. "In the cabinet—"

Marlin stumbled to the silver cabinet and searched hastily. There were many strange-looking instruments and vessels in it. But he soon found a flat, twisted-necked glass phial of bright blue fluid.

He returned quickly with it to the Cretan. "Break the neck and pour the liquid into my wound," whispered Daedalus.

Marlin obeyed, drawing the old man's cloak aside and letting the blue drug drip into the bullet-hole in the withered flesh.

The results amazed him. The lips of the wound drew together as though from a super-clotting agent affecting tissues as well as blood. And strength and life seemed to pour back into Daedalus' pallid face.

The Cretan sat up in a few moments. There was an agony of dread in his wide eyes as he looked up at Marlin.

"Your enemy left us both for dead!" he exclaimed. "After he struck you down with his weapon, he turned it upon me also as I was rushing to call the Minotaurs against him!"

Marlin raised an unsteady hand to his head. Preyder's bullet had grazed his skull only, but the wound that had stunned him would have been interpreted by the Nazi as a fatal one.

"As consciousness left me," Daedalus was continuing hoarsely, "I heard the man you call Preyder and the other one binding and gagging Luane. They were going with her to Minos! Your enemy plans to make with Minos the bargain that he could not make with me!"

Terrible apprehension gripped Marlin at this information. He saw again all the dread possibilities if Preyder succeeded in turning the unearthly Labyrinth into a weapon of Nazi strategy.

Preyder's reasoning was clear. The Nazi must have allies in this ancient time-world if his compatriots were to use the Labyrinth. Daedalus had refused the unholy alliance. So he had gone to Minos, who also desired to use the road through time for evil purposes.

"But why would he take Luane with them?" Marlin cried.

"You forget what I told you—that only Luane and myself know the Labyrinth well enough to find the openings to other ages," Daedalus replied. "They will need Luane to be their guide."

"Then without her, they could not use the Labyrinth?" Marlin exclaimed. "Then we've got to get her out of their hands at once!"

Daedalus nodded swiftly. His eyes were solemn. "Yes, we must risk all to get Luane away from them and then close the Labyrinth again."

Rapidly, he thought aloud. "Your enemy will tell Minos that I am dead. And Minos will rejoice, and will at once send to seize this temple so that they may force Luane to guide them through the Labyrinth."

"Then, at once, we've got to get into Minos' palace and free your daughter—and there's just the two of us, without weapons!" Marlin exclaimed. He was appalled by the dire necessity facing them.

"I have weapons, of a certain kind," muttered Daedalus. He went to the silver cabinet, and hurriedly took from it some small copper instruments which he put in an inner pocket of his cloak. "Now come with me!"

The old Cretan seemed to have recovered miraculous strength from the blue drug that had closed his wound. Marlin stumbled at his heels, out of the lamplit laboratory into the marble halls of the temple.

Night had fallen upon Knossos while they lay unconscious. The porticos gave a view of the great, dark city, its streets splashed with red torchlight, the lighted windows of Minos' great palace on the distant hilltop glaring out over the nighted town and sea.

Thin, vague starlight came through the openings into the temple halls.

Marlin stumbled over something small and soft and looked down to discover that it was the dead, crushed body of one of Luane's little pet golden serpents. The other lay nearby.

Daedalus had found the bodies of two of the temple servitors across the room. The men had been shot by Preyder and Blaun. They were naked except for loincloths, their cloaks missing.

"The Nazis put their cloaks on so that their strange clothing would not be noticed going through the city," muttered Marlin.

"Listen!" Daedalus exclaimed.

A heavy tramp of feet was approaching the Temple of Wisdom. They glimpsed a long column of bronze-helmeted soldiers led by torchbearers coming through the streets toward them.

"Minos' guards, coming here to seize the temple and Labyrinth as I thought!" said the old Cretan.

"Let's get out of here then before they find us!" Marlin cried, starting toward the door.

"Wait!" Daedalus commanded. "We can do nothing that way. Minos' palace is always ringed by guards. We could not even approach it."

"But we've got to make the attempt!" Marlin exclaimed desperately.

"Yes, but not that way. Come with me."

To the American's surprise, Daedalus led him up a spiral stairway that climbed to the very top of the temple. They emerged onto its flat roof.

The Temple of Wisdom was a massive octagon building of great height. Up here in the windy darkness, they were far above the torchlit streets of Knossos.

Daedalus went to a small shed-like structure on the roof, unlocking it and entering. He returned in a moment, bringing two big and grotesque-looking devices.

"These are our only means of reaching and entering Minos' palace unobserved," he declared. "I had kept this invention secret lest Minos hear of it. Not since my son Icarus was killed making trial of them, have I used these wings."

Marlin stared dumbfoundedly at the thing which Daedalus had handed him. He suddenly remembered all those old legends that told of Daedalus' invention of a means of flight and of the death of his son in its trial. For the thing *was* a pair of big, artificial wings.

They were broad, batlike pinions six feet in length, made of a dark, skinlike substance stretched on a light interior skeleton. The wings seemed to grow like living ones out of a flat, heavy mass of muscular flesh covered by gray, lifeless skin. To it was attached a harness.

"But these wings surely can't enable you to fly!" Marlin protested incredulously. "There's no motive power, no machinery at all."

"I told you before that our Cretan science concentrates not on matter and machines but on the forces of life and space and time," reminded Daedalus. "There is pseudo-life in these wings and in the powerful muscles that operate them. It is quiescent now but it will kindle to awakening when you wear the wings against your body."

He showed Marlin by example how to buckle the strong leather harness around his shoulders, so that the flat muscle-mass between the wings was clasped tightly against his back between the shoulders.

Marlin obeyed unbelievingly. "But it's impossible! The things are just lifeless matter—"

He broke off suddenly. He had felt an uncanny twitching of that mass of pseudo-living muscle clasped against his back.

It was an almost horrible sensation, that writhing and flexing of powerful tendons which a minute before had been lax and dead.

"The wings are waking to life from the kindling aura of your own living flesh!" Daedalus warned. "When they begin to beat strongly, run with me along the roof and launch yourself into the air."

Marlin felt the flexing of the great artificial muscles against his back, swiftly increasing in power. A breeze fanned his cheeks as the great bat-like pinions behind him began to sweep to and fro.

The wings that Daedalus wore had begun to flap also. Both men staggered unsteadily as their threshing wings almost lifted them.

"Now!" exclaimed the old Cretan. "With me—we fly!"

He was darting across the roof toward its edge, his wings now flapping powerfully.

Marlin, feeling more than ever caught in a fantastic dream, mechanically ran forward after the other. He was nearly to the edge of the roof—then he flung himself forward into empty space.

He did not fall! Instead, he rocketed forward into the darkness, borne up by the powerful threshing of the great pinions at his back.

"Steer upward, like this!" Daedalus' thin call reached his ears.

Marlin looked up and saw the old Cretan against the stars, soaring upward on beating wings as he extended his upcurved arms before him like a rudder. The American imitated the action with his own arms, and rose rapidly until he was flying close beside Daedalus.

Marlin looked down. They were high above the dark streets and winking torches of Knossos. Down to the right lay the black harbor and the lanterns of gliding galleys. From below, he knew, they could not be seen except as batlike shadows against the stars.

He felt a wild thrill as the throbbing wings at his back bore him onward with Daedalus through the upper night, the chill wind roaring around him and hammering at his face.

"I've flown a lot in my own time, but this is different and better!" he called.

"Yes, but the wings have their limits," warned Daedalus. "They can fly only a few hours without rest—then their pseudo-life dies and they collapse. It was so my son Icarus died, trying too long a flight."

The massive palace of Minos loomed up on its distant hilltop, ahead of them. The old Cretan soared still higher, until at last they were a thousand feet above the flat roof of the monster marble structure.

Then he turned, using arms and legs as rudder, and Marlin imitated him. They began to glide down through the darkness toward the palace roof.

"Be ready to unharness the wings the moment we land!" cautioned Daedalus.

Marlin glimpsed bronze-armored guards stationed at every entrance of the great royal structure. But there was no one on the roof. Who would expect intruders from the sky?

His arms extended downward like the Cretan's, he planed down through the darkness until his feet touched the roof. He had the harness of the wings already unbuckled, and instantly he slipped it off.

He sprawled on his face on the roof from the shock of the alighting. When he picked himself up, he found that the wings he had hastily discarded had at once ceased their flapping. The strange pseudo-life of their artificial muscles could only operate when in close contact with real life.

Daedalus had landed more deftly. For a moment, they listened. There were dim sounds from the palace beneath them, but no sound that betokened discovery of them.

The old scientist handed Marlin a long, sharp, bronze dagger. "You may need this—I have other weapons. Now come with me."

Hiding the lax and lifeless pair of wings in the shadow of the parapet that bounded the roof, Daedalus then began a careful search along that low, massive wall.

It was constructed of huge marble blocks. The Cretan finally fixed upon one of these. He groped at it with his fingers, then pulled. The great block swung silently aside, disclosing a black opening that led down inside the great wall of the building.

Daedalus turned to the American. "I was the architect of Minos' palace," he explained in a whisper. "I thank the gods now for that, for I know every secret passageway that the tyrant had built into its walls."

He added, "This is the only road by which we can hope to find Luane. If we succeed in doing so, we shall return by this same way and then when you have gone back through the Labyrinth I shall close it forever."

The Cretan disappeared down into the black opening. Marlin, following, found that there was a narrow, steep stair inside the wall.

They went down many steps, then along a cramped passage. Daedalus stopped, applied his eye to a tiny aperture in the inner wall.

"They would not have her in the throne-room," he murmured. "We must search further."

Marlin, lingering a moment to look through the little aperture, saw a vast, torchlit hall paved with red and white gypsum slabs. Its walls were brilliantly painted with figures of wild bulls and lions, and swarthy, armored Cretan soldiers stood beside a massive, empty throne.

Daedalus led onward, seeming to know his way without hesitation through the cunning hidden passages of the walls. Presently he stopped again at a tiny loophole.

"These are Minos' apartments," he began to whisper, then suddenly stiffened. His thin hand gripped Marlin's arm. "Luane is here! And Minos and Pasiphae, and your enemy—"

Marlin almost crowded him bodily from the tiny aperture to see. He looked this time into a much smaller room, similarly paved in red and white, hung with brilliant silks, illuminated by swinging lamps.

He instantly saw Luane. The fair-haired Cretan girl sat in a high chair of carved wood, bound to it by hide thongs. Her face was very white but there was defiance and hatred in her blue eyes.

She was looking bitterly at the others in the room. Preyder, fantastically incongruous in his drab modern uniform, stood beneath the central lamp. The man Blaun, rifle in hand, was staring from the side of the room where a half-dozen watchful Cretan warriors were stationed.

"It means power unlimited for you over *your* world, and for my nation over the world of *our* time!" Preyder was saying eagerly in his halting Attic.

The Nazi officer was speaking to the Cretan man and woman who sat in massive silver chairs at the far side of the room.

"Minos and the queen Pasiphae!" Daedalus muttered in Marlin's ear. "Your enemy has made his bargain with them!"

Minos was well over middle age, but his long hair and flowing beard were raven black. His vulpine face, dead white as that of a corpse, was a fitting setting for the infinitely cunning eyes with which he looked at the enthusiastic Nazi. His attire was a rich, gold-worked silken cloak.

The woman was far different. Pasiphae looked slim as Luane, and as young. But when Marlin glanced at her bold eyes he revised estimates of her age. There were unclean depths in those eyes. Not even the lush beauty of her figure in its clinging green silks could banish that taint.

Minos, stroking his beard with jewelled fingers, asked the Nazi a question in a hoarse, thick voice.

"If your nation is so powerful in its own time, why are you so hard-pressed by enemies that you need the Labyrinth as refuge?"

"It will be only a temporary refuge," Preyder answered quickly. "We Germans will merely retreat through it to this time for a period, and then issue forth again in surprise attack to crush our enemies."

He added, "And even if our enemies should gain victory in this whole war, we can use the Labyrinth to defeat them ultimately. For we can retreat through it to this time, secretly amass forces here for another war, and issue forth to conquer our world by an attack of complete surprise."

Marlin was aghast. For the first time, he realized the full scope of Preyder's scheming. It was not merely the possession of Crete which formed the stake for which the Nazi was plotting.

It was a chance for Germany to launch a third world war upon mankind. Preyder, like most other Nazis, must realize the inevitable triumph of the Allies. But when that triumph came, the Nazis could secretly gather forces and prepare for a new assault on civilization by taking refuge through the Labyrinth in this age of the past!

V

The king Minos nodded his head indifferently at the Nazi's explanation. "Your nation and its wars in the future world mean little to me," he declared. "But I need an inexhaustible supply of human subjects to breed into the beast-races which can extend my power over all this world. And if I use people of this time as subjects, they will rise against me."

"Germany will furnish you as many human captives as you need from the races we shall conquer when our triumph is complete," Preyder promised.

"Then it is agreed between us," Minos said. "Tomorrow we will enter the Labyrinth, with sufficient warriors to slay the Minotaurs who haunt it. I bred the creatures but they hate me for it and were fanatically devoted to Daedalus, so they will have to be killed.

"Now that Daedalus is dead," he went on, "the priestess Luane is the only one who can guide us through the Labyrinth to the tunnels that open onto future ages."

Luane spoke in a low, throbbing voice. "I will never guide you, so that you may work evil on the future world and on this one."

Minos smiled tolerantly, fingering his beard. "Torture will change your mind. There are devices in my laboratories which will bring you whimpering to my feet in submission."

Marlin turned frantically from the peephole to Daedalus. The old Cretan had drawn from his cloak one of the small instruments he had brought with him, and was bending over it in the darkness.

"We've got to get in there somehow!" Marlin whispered hoarsely. "At the least, I've got to kill that devil Preyder!"

"There is a secret door beneath the loophole which can be swung open," Daedalus whispered swiftly. "But not yet! It would be useless to rush out onto the swords of Minos' guards."

He was fumbling with the little instrument. It was a circular copper frame in which four curious black prisms revolved on an axle around a larger black prism whose facets were cut in a baffling design. The old Cretan was spinning the rotating prisms rapidly around the central one.

"I told you that I was not without weapons of a certain kind," he muttered. "Wait!"

"But there's no time to wait!" Marlin protested wildly. "If we—"

His words froze on his lips. An uncanny thing was happening. The prisms were rotating so fast that they could be seen only as black blur. And that blur of blackness was *spreading.*

It was spreading outward like water flowing from a fountain—a fountain of utter darkness.

In the dim light that came through the loophole of the wall, Marlin could see that flowing darkness seeping out through the solid wall itself, expanding in all directions.

"Wait until the darkness grips the chamber, then pull open the door by the handles below the loophole!" Daedalus whispered. "You'll have a chance to snatch Luane back in here, in the dark!"

At that moment, Marlin standing by the loophole with one hand gripping the stone handles below it and the other grasping his long dagger, he heard a sharp cry from inside Minos' chamber.

A Cretan captain in plumed helmet and bronze had burst into the room from a door opposite. He ran toward Minos.

"Highness, my warriors and I seized the Temple of Wisdom as you ordered but we did not find Daedalus' body in it!" he reported.

Minos' vulpine face raged and he leaped to his feet. "Then he is not dead, as you told me!" he hissed at Preyder.

"He *must* be dead!" Preyder declared bewilderedly. "I shot him myself—"

Minos' furious face stiffened suddenly as he looked beyond the Nazi. The expanding cloud of darkness, bursting through the solid wall, had already engulfed half of the lamplit chamber.

"Daedalus' darkness-magic!" yelled the king. "He's *here!* Guards!"

Even as the bewildered Cretan guards ran forward, the darkness expanded to fill the whole chamber.

Instantly Marlin pulled hard, felt the heavy stones slide inward. He burst through the aperture into the chamber. He was in absolute, utter pitch-darkness, every ray of light blotted out by Daedalus' apparatus.

He had already taken the bearings of every object in the chamber and he plunged straight toward the chair in which Luane sat bound.

"Luane, it's your father and I!" he whispered as his dagger sliced the hide thongs that bound her to the chair.

He heard her sob of relief as he pulled her to her feet. Minos was raging in the darkness, Preyder was yelling furiously to Blaun.

Marlin, lunging back with Luane through the darkness, collided with a uniform-clad man and struck with his dagger in wild hope that it was Preyder. But it was Blaun's throaty death-cry that shuddered out.

"Daedalus or his friends are in this chamber!" bellowed Minos' voice. "Range around the walls and link hands!"

But Marlin was already thrusting Luane through the unseen door into the wall. He felt the stones slide shut as Daedalus closed them.

"Up to the roof at once!" Daedalus exclaimed urgently. "The darkness will die as the prisms stop spinning."

"There's no escape from the roof!" Luane gasped as they ran. "We'll be trapped."

"We have the wings there," answered her father swiftly. "They can carry double weight for a short distance. We must get back to the temple and close the Labyrinth."

They emerged onto the roof, beneath the stars. But now the whole great palace was alive with noises of alarm beneath them. They heard men rushing out from it, heard Minos shouting.

"They've slipped away! But they'll make for the Labyrinth. Quick, to the Temple!"

Daedalus and Marlin had grabbed up the lax wings and were buckling on the harnesses.

"You must carry Luane, for my arms are not strong enough to hold her," the Cretan said swiftly. "Now—fly!"

Their wings were already beginning to flap strongly as that weird pseudo life again awoke in their artificial muscles.

Gripping Luane's slight figure in his arms, Marlin ran with the old Cretan along the roof and then leaped wildly upward.

For a terrible moment, he felt himself falling backward. The added weight of the girl seemed pulling him down. Then his wings seemed to flap even more powerfully against the drag, and he soared heavily up and outward from the palace roof.

As he and his burden launched outward with Daedalus into the dark sky, he glimpsed mounted horsemen riding out of a torchlit court of the palace. And Minos and Preyder were in their van.

"We'll reach the Temple ahead of them!" called Daedalus' thin voice over the rush of the wind. "But Minos' guards are already in possession of it!"

The octagonal white pile of the Temple of Wisdom was looming up close ahead, now. They rushed down toward the roof, Marlin landing heavily and spilling the girl from his arms.

She was up instantly, helping him unharness the wings from his shoulders. Daedalus reached their side.

"Bring the wings with you, for we must not leave them for Minos," he warned.

He lingered a moment to peer down over the edge of the roof. "The guards posted around the Temple did not see us," he said quickly. "If there are none inside, we can get to the Labyrinth and close it forever."

Luane clung to her father in sudden horror. "But there is only one way in which the Labyrinth can be closed forever!"

"And that is the way that must be used, Luane," Daedalus said solemnly. "There's no time for argument! Come quickly!"

They went down the spiral stair, Marlin expecting every moment to hear the horsemen of Minos and Preyder gallop up to the Temple.

The dark halls of the ground level were deserted except for the dead servitors who still lay there. Daedalus rapidly led the way on down the stair, down to that underground, vault-like room in which was the silver door that was entrance to the Labyrinth.

The vault was aflare with torchlight and six Cretan warriors were on guard in it! And the Cretans instantly saw the three as they emerged from the stair.

"Daedalus! The sorcerer is alive!" yelled the first warrior to glimpse them, and ran toward them raising his double-bladed axe.

Marlin thrust the wings he carried into Luane's hand and leaped in front of her and the old scientist.

The axe came down toward him in a savage stroke. But the fine-trained reactions of a fighter-pilot saved the American. He swerved, and as the axe whistled past him he struck viciously with his long dagger.

The blade buried in the Cretan's neck between chin and breast-plate and he went down. Marlin snatched up the heavy axe to face the other Cretans who were rushing forward.

"Back onto the stair!" he yelled over his shoulder to Luane and Daedalus. On the narrow stair, he'd have a slim chance for defense.

But as his raised axe fended the weapons of the attacking warriors, Marlin glimpsed Luane darting past him and past the warriors toward the silver door of the Labyrinth.

Had the Cretan soldiers not hampered each other by the closeness of their attack, Marlin must have died in the first moment. Even as it was, his clumsy use of the axe barely parried the weapons that struck at him.

He knew this unequal battle must end swiftly, and the knowledge was made suddenly more bitter in his mind by the sound of trampling hoofs and shouts that came dimly from above. Preyder and Minos had arrived with their horsemen.

Then a weird, high call floated through the battle-noisy vault. Luane had opened the silver door and was calling that strange cry down into the dark depths of the Labyrinth.

"Gods—*the Minotaurs!*" screamed one of the Cretan warriors in the back of the attackers.

The monstrous, beast-headed creatures, the hideous things that Minos had bred from man, were pouring up out of the Labyrinth in answer to Luane's summons.

The Cretans, overcome by superstitious horror of these monsters whom all Knossos whispered of and dreaded, tried frantically to flee.

They had no chance. Seven or eight of the ghastly Minotaurs were in the room, their bull-bellows rocking the walls as they charged till horns ripped into flesh.

"They are here!" yelled a hoarse voice from high up on the stair. "After them!"

A gun cracked, a startlingly anachronistic sound, and a bullet sang off the wall close by Marlin.

The American looked up and saw Preyder, revolver in hand, racing down with Minos toward them at the head of a mass of armored warriors.

"Into the Labyrinth, quick!" panted Daedalus, dragging the American toward the silver door. Luane was calling the Minotaurs.

Then they were in the dark, winding tunnels of the great four-dimensional maze, the shaggy, monstrous horde of the Minotaurs behind them as they ran forward.

Daedalus' strength seemed failing fast. "We must—get to the heart of the Labyrinth," he gasped. "Only there can it be closed permanently."

Torchlight from behind reddened the corridors at their back, and wolf-voices shouting sent fierce echoes through the curving ways.

"Minos has brought scores of his men—they'll search every tunnel until they find us!" Marlin husked.

The Minotaurs were sounding their mind-crushing bellow, seeking fiercely to turn back and give battle to the pursuers. But Daedalus urged his monstrous followers on.

"I shall need them, to close the Labyrinth," he gasped. "We are almost at its heart."

The radiant jewel on Luane's forehead had dimly lighted their way. But now they came from the curving tunnels into a high, round room of stone that seemed the very core of the fantastic maze.

A giant pillar of cylindrical stone blocks rose at the center of this shadowy fane, supporting a curving roof. And it seemed to Marlin's dazed mind that that great, carven pillar was slowly turning.

Daedalus laid his hand upon it.

"This pillar is the keystone of the entire labyrinth," he said. And then, to the Minotaurs, "We must pull out the lowest block of the pillar!"

Obediently, those giant creatures laid hands upon the block that formed the lowest section of the giant column. This basic block was set in a wide groove in the stone floor, so that it might be slid aside to collapse the entire pillar if desired. But even the huge strength of the beast-men could only budge it imperceptibly.

Daedalus spoke hoarsely to Luane. "You must not stay here, daughter. You must guide our friend back out through the tunnels to his own time, before the Labyrinth closes."

She clung to him in an agony of weeping. "No! I stay here to die with you!"

"Die?" echoed Marlin. "What's going to happen? What are you doing?"

"I am closing the Labyrinth in the only way in which it can be permanently closed, by collapsing and destroying its whole maze!" answered the old Cretan solemnly. "When I built it, I made provision to do this should ever the need arise.

"And now the need has arisen! The Labyrinth will perish and with it will perish the plotters who seek to make use of it for evil purposes. And my poor Minotaurs will die here with me, for death will be kinder to them than life."

"And I too die here with you!" Luane repeated wildly. She told Marlin, "Go, make your escape while there is time!"

"How can he escape when he does not know his way through the tunnels?" exclaimed her father. "You must guide him and go with him, Luane."

He held her tear-wet face between his hands. "Death is almost upon me, in any case. The wound I received was truly mortal—the drug I used merely closed it but could not heal it. You must go! And you must take the wings with you, for they may help you to escape when you reach the future world."

He thrust them, by a last effort of strength and command, away from him toward one of the tunnels. Sobbingly, Luane led the way into that dark passage.

Marlin glanced back and in the shadows could just see the old Cretan scientist exhorting the giant, faithful Minotaurs who now were sliding the block farther and farther from beneath the pillar.

"There is little time!" came Luane's choked voice. "We must hurry!"

They stumbled around the dizzying quadruple curves of the mysterious maze, the girl leading the way, carrying the lax wings.

And finally, Marlin glimpsed an opening ahead and moonlight! He and the girl, a moment later, stumbled out of the tunnel into the moonlit gorge outside the ruins of Knossos.

"I'm back in my own time, my own world again!" Marlin exclaimed hoarsely to the girl. "A world in which Crete's civilization has been dead for forty centuries."

There came a sudden crashing, prolonged roar from behind them. The whole cliff from whose interior they had just emerged seemed collapsing in upon itself.

Dust rose to veil its broken face, and the roar died away to silence. Luane sobbed wildly.

"The Labyrinth—gone forever!" Marlin husked. "And dead in it, Daedalus and the Minotaurs, and Minos and Preyder!"

There was a sharp cry from somewhere in the distance—a guttural call in German that was answered by other distant voices.

"The Nazis—the collapse of the cliff has attracted their attention and they'll soon be here!" Marlin exclaimed. "We've got to get away at once. If these wings will still work—"

He and Luane buckled them on. A minute later, the pseudo-living pinions began their powerful threshing.

Marlin and the Cretan girl ran along the gorge and leaped, soaring up into the moonlight. He heard a startled exclamation from somewhere below, a wild cry that receded as he and Luane flew on.

They soared higher, and Marlin headed southward across the dark, narrow mass of Crete.

"Can we reach Africa with these?" he asked the girl flying beside him.

"I fear not," she answered. "It is too far. Nor do I care for life now. This is not my world."

"Luane, it's going to be our world *together* if we can escape," he told her, his heart in the words.

In the moonlight, the girl flying beside him looked at him and her pale, tear-stained face softened.

They soon were passing over the southern shore of Crete, winging on over the moon-silvered Mediterranean toward distant Africa. But in the next hour, as the flapping wings beat ever more slowly and tiredly, Marlin knew that they would never make that distance.

He scanned the moonlit sea desperately for a ship. And finally, when the tiring wings were letting them fall lower and lower toward the sea, he glimpsed a distant black dot on the silver water.

"If we can reach that ship we're safe, Luane! It must be an Allied craft for there are no others in these waters."

They were less than a mile from the ship and could see it as a destroyer knifing the waves westward, when Marlin's wings went dead upon his back. He shot down like a stone to the water below.

The impact stunned him. He came to himself and found he was floating, supported by Luane.

"I came down after you and dragged you to the surface," she gasped. "But I had to discard our wings before they dragged us both back under."

"Luane, we were seen falling!" Marlin cried joyfully. 'That destroyer is turning toward us!"

It was a much-puzzled British naval officer who greeted the American pilot and the strangely-clad girl whom his boat-crew had just pulled out of the sea.

"We saw you jumping," he told Marlin, "but your parachutes didn't seem to be working right and we didn't hear your plane at all."

"My plane was hit by a shell over Candia and its motor was dead," Marlin told him. "This girl is a refugee from Crete I was bringing back."

The explanation satisfied the officer. It would satisfy everyone, Marlin knew, and it was the explanation he would always have to give them about what had happened to him.

No one would believe the truth, if he tried to tell it.

Besides, he thought, the explanation was true enough. The girl whom he was holding closely and protectively in his arms was a refugee from Crete, in fact. There was no one who would guess that she came from the Crete, not of 1944, but of four thousand years ago.

The Shining Land

Brian Cullan had flown the big army amphibian plane almost halfway back across the North Atlantic to America, when he saw the sign in the sky.

Every mile that had slipped behind them had lessened a little the war-weariness that had sagged Cullan's lean shoulders and put premature lines of age in his dark, worn young face. The war was over, and they were going home, and he felt dull, tired relief.

An odd darkness was gathering in the sunlit sky around them, an increasing obscurity as of coming storm. Cullan and his co-pilot, squat, merry Jeff Lewis, had been watching it. Then suddenly, lightning flared through the obscurity—lightning that for a moment seemed to take the form of a flaming, spinning circle.

"Lugh's wheel!" exclaimed Cullan, an uncanny thrill jerking him bolt upright in his seat. "The sign of Tir Sorcha!"

"What the devil are you talking about?" demanded Lewis.

Cullan saw that freak of curving lightning vanish as he spoke. The queer thrill of eeriness left him.

He smiled a little shamefacedly. "An old Celtic superstition. My people came originally from Ulster, you know. I still have kinsfolk there, and I was talking to one of them before we left Belfast. She gave me this."

He held out his hand to show the ring he wore. It was a worn, ancient hoop of gold set with a curious prismatic crystal.

Cullan stared at it in sudden surprise. The crystal was glowing. Little flashes of light, tiny spears of radiance, scintillated in it. The tiny rays seemed to form a shining, wheel-shaped sign!

"That's funny—it didn't glow like that before," Cullan murmured, puzzledly. "Maybe electric influence of approaching storm—"

He suddenly remembered what his old kinswoman had told him when she gave him the ring, back there in her little cottage in the low green Ulster hills.

"The ring goes always to the oldest male in our family. And since my other grandnephew was killed in the war, it must be yours. It comes down in our family from Cuchulain himself."

"Cuchulain?" Cullan had smiled at mention of the great hero of Celtic antiquity. "You don't really believe that he was our ancestor, Aunt Maeve?"

"And how could I believe otherwise when the pride of our lineage has been handed down to us these two thousand years?" the old lady had retorted. "Isn't your name Cullan and wasn't the great Cuchulain the Hound of Cullan? Isn't that the very ring that he called the Unlocker, and that Cuchulain brought back with him from the Shining Land?"

Brian Cullan had grinned. "I've flown the Atlantic a good many times during the war, and I never saw any trace of Tir Sorcha."

"And how could you see the Shining Land when it's invisible to the eyes of man?" she had demanded stoutly. "Wasn't Cuchulain himself almost the only man who ever entered it, and didn't even he almost fail to come back from it to his waiting wife?"

Cullan had taken the ring. He knew his great-aunt's seriousness where the old legends were concerned.

He too had learned those stories when he was a child in faraway America—the great tales of the Ultonian cycle, of the heroes of the Red Branch and of the dark warrior among them who had blazed out in battle as Cuchulain, the Celtic Achilles.

His old kinswoman's firm belief made the tales seem almost real. The unquenchable romance and mystery in the Celtic soul gave her firm belief in even that cardinal tenet of Celtic legend—Tir Sorcha, the Shining Land, the strange, unseeable Elysium that somehow existed out in the western sea and was home of the great, pre-human race, the Tuatha De.

Cullan was abruptly snatched back from memory by the impact of shrieking winds on the flying plane. Startled, he looked around.

"We've got to get out of this mess quick!" Jeff Lewis yelled.

Cullan stared. "I never saw a storm come up like this!"

The whole sky around them had swiftly deepened in obscurity, and the dark haze was boiling up in terrifying thunderheads.

Cullan tried to swing the plane around. But howling winds hurled the ship on like a toy into the lightning-split darkness. The left aileron was suddenly crumpled by an inconceivable fist of wind.

"That does it—we're going downstairs now for sure!" cried Lewis.

Cullan's hands fought the controls, trying to keep the plane out of an instant plunge. He noticed startledly that the crystal on his finger was now glowing like a tiny, flaming sun.

Abruptly came a wrenching shock. The plane seemed to drop with sickening rapidity as though in a terrific downdraft. Yet for all their sudden nausea, the altimeter registered no change.

Darkness, lightning and howling winds were suddenly gone! They were surrounded by mists that glowed with wonderful, golden radiance, a glowing, unearthly haze.

Cullan, looking out into that golden mist through which the plane was slanting downward, gasped his incredulous amazement.

"Tir Sorcha! The Shining Land!"

"What do you mean?" Lewis demanded impatiently. "What—"

His voice trailed to silence and his broad red face was a frozen mask of incredulity as he looked downward through the window.

The golden mists were thinning as the crippled plane slanted lower. They made out beneath the tawny yellow swell of an ocean far different from the gray-green Atlantic.

There was an island below them! A big, whale-shaped green land, miles long, rimmed by surf-whipped white beaches. And in the misty distance beyond they could glimpse other islands, clustered near and far.

"There's no islands in the North Atlantic!" choked Jeff Lewis. "There just *isn't.*"

"Atlantic? That's not the Atlantic!" flashed Cullan. His black eyes flared with excitement. "It's not our world at all but Tir Sorcha, the Shining Land."

Stunned bewilderment made his co-pilot's voice savage. "Will you stop mouthing silly superstitions and—"

"I tell you, it's the Shining Land just as legend described it!" cried Cullan. "Tir Sorcha, the other world, the world of Lugh and Dagda and Mannanan and all the others of the old gods, the Tuatha De."

His voice raced on with his thoughts. "It must be an interpenetrating world, Jeff! A world congruent with Earth, on a different plane of vibration. The legends always said that Tir Sorcha was locked close to Earth but that neither world was visible or tangible to the other. Yet a few passed from world to world, and somehow we've done it too."

Lewis tried to voice disbelief and could not. The island looming up below was flat rejection of all his arguments.

Brian Cullan's mind was thrilling to wild surmise. He remembered how the crystal of his ring had pulsed with blinding radiance.

"The crystal did it somehow, Jeff! Cuchulain himself is said to have brought it back from the Shining Land, calling it the Unlocker. Somehow, it tuned our plane and us to the vibration of the other world—"

"Forget that and try to get us down without cracking up!" exclaimed the dazed co-pilot.

Instincts fostered by long discipline took over Cullan's mind to the exclusion of all else, as the crippled amphibian sagged toward the running yellow waves. He noted a little boy on the island's shore.

"It's calmer there—I'll try to make the beach."

The ship struck the water and skimmed forward like a giant surfboard toward the white beach of the whale-shaped island.

It rolled up through the yellow waters onto firm sand. Cullan cut the motors and they scrambled out, stood staring wonderingly.

The island was silent except for the distant boom of surf. The yellow sea, and the golden mists that hid the sun, and the strange scents of alien flowers that freighted the balmy air, held them transfixed.

"God, look at that!" exclaimed Lewis hoarsely, pointing.

Black, monstrous-winged shapes of size incredible were winging up from a distant part of the island. They were dragon-like birds of dimensions enormous, huge as the rocs of Arabian fable.

They flapped away in a direction away from Cullan and Lewis, vast wings shadowing the golden sky, uttering startled, squawking sounds.

"I know now what place this is," husked Cullan. "The Island of Great Birds. Maeldun touched here when *he* voyaged through the Shining Land centuries ago, says the story. And those other islands—"

Those other isles that rose vaguely through the distant golden mists were the isles of the Celtic Elysium exactly as legend described them!

The Island of Giant Flowers whose blooms towered higher than tall oaks; the Island of Silver whose beaches and rocks glittered as if of solid metal; the Island of Fire that blazed a red beacon through the golden mists; Cullan dazedly named them from legend as he stared.

"How are we going to get back—to Earth?" Jeff Lewis demanded, his broad face still wearing a stunned look.

"Others—few—entered this world in the far past and yet got back," muttered Cullan. "Cuchulain, and Maeldun, and—"

"Cullan, look what's coming!" yelled Lewis, pointing suddenly to their right.

Long, slim boats of burnished metal were racing toward them at great speed, oarless and sailless vessels that came obliquely across the yellow sea toward the beach on which they stood.

Cullan glimpsed the crews of the high-prowed metal boats as they hit the beach and tumbled ashore with a fierce, high yell. They were tall, fair-haired men in silver mail and helmets, carrying swords that were like brands of living flame as they charged toward the airmen.

"Back into the plane!" Lewis was yelling hoarsely, tugging at his arm. "We can taxi it out of here—"

Brian Cullan remained frozen for a fatal minute of delay, transfixed by the appearance of those towering silver-armored warriors.

"The Tuatha De!" he whispered. "The great race of the old gods who ruled Earth once—"

"Wake up!" yelled Lewis, his face livid. "They've cut us off now!"

The warriors were between them and the beached amphibian. They were rushing toward the two pilots with obvious murderous intent, brandishing those weird flaming swords and yelling fiercely as they came.

Cullan partly recognized the language in which they shouted! It was a language closely akin to the ancient Gaelic of the Celts, that Gaelic which he had learned from his race-proud father as a child.

Desperately, Cullan threw up his hand and shouted to the charging warriors in Gaelic. "Wait! We are friends, not enemies!"

The warriors stopped, seemingly amazed. "These men speak the tongue of us Tuatha!" exclaimed one.

"Nevertheless, they are outworlders," rang a clear, commanding voice. "They have broken the law, have somehow opened the Portal and entered Tir Sorcha. You know the penalty. Kill!"

"The Princess Fand has spoken—kill!" roared a captain.

Cullan's eyes flashed to the source of the order. It was a woman, slim in silver armor and helmet, a sheathed sword at her belt.

Fand! He knew that name! Princess of Tir Sorcha, wife of Mannanan—fairest of the Tuatha De, the old tales had said.

A white, lovely face, merciless in every chiseled feature, met his gaze. Sea-green eyes under straight dark brows flared at him and then suddenly those eyes widened, stared wildly at Cullan.

"Wait!" cried Fand. "Do *not* kill! Oh, fool—blind fool! It is he!"

They stood on the white beach, incredible group of two dazed airmen and puzzled Tuatha warriors, all looking at her.

Fand's green eyes were dark with sudden wild tears, and her gaze had not left Brian Cullan's dark, haggard face. She ran forward, swiftly as a sea-bird.

Her bare white arms flashed around his neck. Cullan, incredulous, felt her sobbing on his chest.

"Cuchulain!" she cried. "Cuchulain!"

II

Brian Cullan, his pulses thudding, found his arms around her. Dazed as he was, a wild thrill shot through him. Beneath the flexible tunic of silver chain-mail, her body was pliant and yielding. Stray strands of dark, perfumed hair brushed his face.

No elfin queen of faery legend this—but a girl, a woman, warm and living. Blood hammered in his temples as she turned her eager eyes up to him.

"I—I am not Cuchulain," he said stammeringly, in the Gaelic. "Cuchulain died two thousand years ago."

Fand's white face was stricken by a swift, terrible hopelessness as she scanned his face.

"Two thousand years?" she whispered. "Of course—I forgot, for the moment when I first saw you, that time is different on Earth."

Cullan felt a shock of discovery. This was the explanation, then, of the Shining Land—an interpenetrating world whose time even was at a different pace than Earth's?

If that were so, it explained why everything here in Tir Sorcha was still exactly as described by the few men of Earth who centuries ago had claimed to have visited here. Centuries had passed on Earth, but it had been a vastly shorter period in the time of *this* world.

Fand had stepped back a little, but her wide green eyes still searched his face. "But you are Cuchulain, in every feature!" she gasped. "And you wear the crystal that I gave him when he left here six of our years ago—the Unlocker that would enable him to return through the Portal. Where got you that?"

Cullan looked at the ring upon his finger. "It came down in my family for a hundred generations. It was supposed to come from our remote ancestor—Cuchulain."

"Then you are of his blood?" cried Fand. "I should have known it. For you are the mold of him as he was."

They were interrupted. The tall Tuatha captain had stepped forward, and now spoke with impatient fierceness.

"Shall we not kill them now, Princess?" he asked.

Little storm lightnings flared in Fand's sea-green eyes as she turned on the man. "No! These two do not die."

The Tuatha warriors looked shocked. "But the Law says that none of Earth may enter this world and live. And when the Portal opened so strangely but now, did you not summon us to follow you and slay whoever might have entered it from the outworld?"

"Will you argue my order?" flamed Fand. "I command the Portal, do I not?"

"Under Lugh and the other lords, you do," grumbled the captain. "But if Mannanan hears of this—"

She silenced them with an imperious gesture of her hand. "No more! We take them to Ethne with us."

She motioned toward the metal boats. Lewis, interpreting her gesture, looked anxiously at Cullan. "We can't leave the plane!"

Fand understood his objection when Cullan translated. "You wish to take that clumsy craft of yours along? Well, then you can follow our boats."

She gave brief orders to her Tuatha warriors. They followed her back toward the slim metal craft, while Cullan and Lewis reentered the amphibian.

The metal boats skimmed rapidly away across the yellow sea. Cullan started the motors and kept their plane taxiing over the smooth swells after them. But the plane could hardly keep up to the slim, speeding craft ahead.

He saw no sign of propulsion machinery in the boats except a square box at the stern of each, and a continuous flash of white fire or force that jetted back underwater. Startled, he realized that that and the queer force-flaming swords he had seen indicated a mastery of energies unknown to Earth science.

Jeff Lewis was pouring a torrent of questions on him. "Who is she? Why did she seem to know you? Cullan, what in the devil's name does it all mean?"

Cullan strove to order his own seething thoughts. "We've come into an interpenetrating world that men have entered before, though long ago. Cuchulain, my ancestor, was one of them. He was here—two thousand years ago by our time, six years ago by the time of this world!

"For time runs far more slowly in this world. A day here is a year in our own Earth. As to the girl, she is Fand, wife of Mannanan, one of the lords of the Tuatha De. She knew Cuchulain when he was here, it seems, and gave him this crystal so he could return. And I must look like him, for she thought for a moment that I was he."

Jeff Lewis whistled. "She must have known your ancestor pretty well, judging from the reception she gave you."

The co-pilot reasoned feverishly. "We've got to get back to our own world, and maybe she can help. If she could fix it for your ancestor Cuchulain to come and go, she can do it for us. Maybe that crystal would work both ways?"

Cullan did not answer. He didn't want to think of returning to Earth, in this moment. His blood was tingling with a heady excitement as they raced on over the yellow sea beneath the golden mists, past the dim green islands.

This was the Elysium of his race, found real and tangible by a freak of fate. Straight out of war-worn old Earth he had been plunged into the wonder and loveliness of Tir Sorcha, the Shining Land. He almost felt that he had been here before, as he drank in the haunting beauty of the weird land. But that, he knew, must be because legend had made him familiar with it for so long.

A bigger island was taking shape in the mists ahead. They could see it only dimly at first, for the sun was invisible above the radiant haze. Then they cried out in astonishment as they saw more clearly the island of Ethne, their goal.

The isle was not really large, a green hillock in the sea with a deep bay in its nearer coast. Around this bay clustered the shimmering structures of a city. But greatest wonder of Ethne was the gigantic geyser of water that sprang into the air from some pit or blow-hole on its farther shore.

That colossal waterspout sprang obliquely across the whole island like the solid jet of a stupendous hose—a glittering, solid rainbow of water that arched across the isle and fell into the sea just outside the harbor of the city.

"The Island of the Waterspout!" Cullan whispered raptly. "Maeldun was here, long ago—and Cuchulain—"

The boats ahead were racing straight toward the harbor. The plane taxiing after them breasted big waves that came from the point where the gigantic jet fell into the sea.

Like a Niagara falling from high heaven was that incredible jet! The thunder of it was deafening as they struggled past it, and the spray it flung high into the golden mist painted the air around it with dazzling, changing rainbows.

Then they were past it, following the boats into the harbor. Before them lay ancient docks of yellow stone, fringed with a row of large and small metal craft. Beyond rose the city Ethne.

The golden mists were darkening, as though the sun above the haze was now setting. In the darkening mist, Ethne stood out like the faery city that legend had made it.

Brian Cullan's eyes climbed its structures—shimmering spherical buildings massed like congeries of iridescent soap-bubbles. City unreal as a dream and as beautiful—elfin city built beneath the titan arch of that eternal rainbow of water across the sky!

Fand's warriors pulled the amphibian up onto a worn stone ramp. The Tuathan princess met them when they emerged from the plane.

"You go with me to my palace," she said. And then, noting Jeff Lewis' dazed face, "And fear nothing."

Ethne's streets were darkening, and lights were shining inside the semi-translucent spheres of the soap-bubble buildings. Tall Tuatha lords and ladies in silk and silver stared incredulously at Cullan and Lewis as they climbed the winding yellow streets behind Fand's guards.

Perfume freighted the air from gorgeous gardens that laced the city. There were many slaves or servants here, a race other than the Tuatha De, dark-faced and stocky.

Fand's palace loomed before them against the darkening haze, a piled, fragile-seeming mass of solid bubbles standing on the highest ground of the city amid the foliage of gardens. They followed her into a wonderful, pure-white hall that was like the interior of a pearl.

Fand stopped suddenly. Facing them was a Tuatha lord, a tall, fair, handsome young man. His gray eyes slitted as he stared at them.

"Then the warrior who came ahead of you to me told truth, Fand," he rasped. "You *have* spared two outworlders who came into Tir Sorcha."

He uttered an oath as his eyes lit on Cullen's face. "Now I understand! That outworld dog Cuchulain whom you loved—come back again!"

His hand went to the hilt of his sword. Fand's voice lashed like a whip of silver.

"You forget, Mannanan, that two thousand outer years have passed since Cuchulain went from here."

Her husband glared. "That is true. But why then did you spare this one who so closely resembles Cuchulain? They must be slain at once."

"*I* am keeper of the Portal, not you!" she flared. "The outworlders do not die."

"The Law—," began Mannanan.

"Do you cite the Law to me?" retorted Fand scornfully. "You who these many years have desired to break it, who have wished me to open the Portal to the outworld for your own evil schemes?"

Mannanan hissed, "If I tell Lugh and the other lords of your transgression, you'll not long be keeper of the Portal."

"Tell them," Fand answered serenely, "and I'll tell them of the plans you've long hatched to invade the outworld."

III

Mannanan's handsome face became deadly. He turned on his heel, strode out of the pearl-hall followed by a few Tuatha captains.

Cullan looked after him worriedly. "If our coming has made trouble between you and your husband—"

Fand laughed mirthlessly. "Mannanan has been my husband in but name, since Cuchulain came here six years—two thousand years!—ago."

Her vibrant green eyes softened on his face. "Go now and rest, and fear nothing from Mannanan. Soon I will talk further with you."

Dark-faced servants escorted Cullan and Lewis up a coiling, narrow stair that climbed from the rear of the pearl-hall to the upper levels of the bubble palace. They were taken into an azure chamber that seemed hollowed out of sapphire.

Windows in the curving, translucent blue wall gave outlook on the darkening gardens below the palace, on the bubble-domes of Ethne and the harbor. The golden mists had changed to silver, the hazy sunlight now replaced by the light of hidden moons above the mist. The stupendous arc of the waterspouts was like a silver sword across the sky.

"I *think* there's something to drink in this thing, and I hope to God it's strong," muttered Lewis, picking up a silver flagon. He poured and tasted a yellow liquid. "It is—and I need it!"

Then he came over and grasped Cullan's arm. "Cullan, stop staring out that window and come to life! What are we going to do!"

Brian Cullan turned reluctantly from his rapt, bemused contemplation of the otherworldly scene. "Do about what?"

"About getting out of this world and back to Earth!" Lewis exclaimed. "What were Fand and her hard-eyed boyfriend arguing about?"

Cullan related the conversation. And Jeff Lewis' broad face grew worried.

"Then there's danger here, not only for us, but for Earth. If Mannanan and his crowd are planning to go through into our world—"

He paced restlessly to and fro. "These people have powers. Those boats and shining swords imply control of atomic energy. The very fact that they can open a Portal between two interpenetrating worlds argues great science and power."

His face hardened. "We've just spent years of toil and blood to whip Earth back into decent shape. And if there's an invasion now from outside—"

Cullan spoke slowly. "Even if Mannanan and his followers represent a menace, they can't enter Earth while Fand guards the Portal. It was apparent that she has long refused to open it for him."

"But she could open it for *us,*" Lewis said eagerly. "We could get back, then." He continued urgently. "You can get her to do it, Cullan. I saw the way she looked at you. Earth or Tir Sorcha—a woman's still a woman."

Brian Cullen was troubled. "I'm not so sure that I'd want to leave here and go back to Earth."

"Not to carry a warning of possible danger?" Lewis prodded. "Not even for that?"

Cullan felt a chill. Lewis was right. The danger to Earth might be vague, potential—but it was real.

A servant interrupted his thoughts. "You are to dine with the Princess," he told Cullan deferentially. "I will conduct you."

"Cullan, now's your chance!" Lewis said when he understood the invitation. "Induce her by any means to let us go back!"

Cullan nodded silently. But as he followed the servant down the curving corridors and the coiling stair of the softly lit palace, he felt a strong inner unwillingness.

Leave this? Leave the wonder and beauty of Tir Sorcha to go back to war-exhausted Earth? Leave—Fand?

"None of that," he told himself roughly. "You're nothing to her—just someone who reminds her of Cuchulain. And she's not quite human—"

Not human? When he stepped out onto the silver-lit terrace where Fand awaited him, he had to concede that in her long, star-embroidered white gown, her elfin beauty was more than human.

"We shall dine here," she said. "I wish to talk more with you of Cuchulain."

He looked around. She interpreted his glance. "Mannanan is not here. He sulks with his captains in his own palace."

Black and silver dreamed the gardens below them, in the diffused mists of moonlights. Lights softly starred the bubble domes of Ethne, and gliding lights crossed the harbor.

From the great scimitar of the waterspout, shining across the sky overhead, came a steady whispering that could be heard even above the low, distant thunder where the cataract plunged into the sea.

Fand, slim fingers around a wine-glass, looked out over the supernally beautiful scene. "Your ancestor Cuchulain sat here thus with me the night before he left Tir Sorcha, only six years ago."

"Why did he ever go?" Cullan could not help wondering aloud.

"He said that loyalty to his king, Conor mac Nessa, demanded that he return to Earth until the wars of his people were won. Then, he said, he would come back to Tir Sorcha and to me. But he did not come back."

"He was killed fighting the foes of his king," Cullan told her. "He died, terrible in battle, tying himself upright to a tall stone so that he could strike still one more blow as he died."

Fand's green eyes flashed. "Aye, that would be the way that Cuchulain would die!"

She asked, a moment later, "What of the wife he told me of, the Earth girl Emer who had been mother of his son?"

"Legend has it that Cuchulain never loved Emer in the same way after his return from Tir Sorcha," admitted Cullan.

"It would be so," Fand said broodingly. "He would remember me, as I remembered him and kept hoping for his return even though hope died when I realized the centuries that had passed in your other world.

"Nor could I go into Earth after him," she continued somberly.

"Long ago, my people the Tuatha De first went from our world into yours through the Portal my ancestors had learned to open. They first peopled your Earth! But their subjects there in time revolted against their wise rulers and so—it seems but a few score years to us!—Lugh, greatest of the Tuatha, and Dagda, and the other great ones came back into Tir Sorcha and decreed that no one should ever pass through the Portal again.

"Yet Cuchulain and a few others of Earth took advantage of chance openings of the Portal to come into this world. Cuchulain won my love, and Mannanan's hate, and then left promising to return. And when he did not return, I could not transgress my duty as keeper of the Portal to go after him. I could only wait and hope that somehow he would return. And now he *has* returned!"

Cullan was startled. He stood up, and Fand too had risen and was swaying toward him. Her eyes burned him, her face breathless.

He was only human. He found his arms around her, his lips against the intoxicating perfume of her mouth. Then he stumbled back.

"Not me," he said thickly. "Not me you love, but Cuchulain that's dead two thousand years."

Fand's small white hands clutched his shoulders almost fiercely. "You *are* Cuchulain! Time has worked its cycle in the outworld, and you are the Hound reborn again, and come back again to me."

Crazy, impossible delusion of a brooding woman? Be it what it might, the fierce kisses of Fand were sweet!

"Tell me, have *you* an Emer waiting for you in the outworld?" she whispered, white arms still around his neck.

Cullan thought of the girl in America who had given him a half-promise, but she was faraway and unreal now as a dream.

"I'll not be loved for my chance resemblance to a long-dead man!" he said violently. "I'm not Cuchulain, I'm Brian Cullan, and—"

A servant came plunging out onto the terrace and Fand turned angrily at the interruption.

The man's swarthy face was livid. He cried, "Mannanan and his captains attack—"

Death-shriek rang eerily from inside the dreaming bubble-palace at the same moment. Wolf-fierce yells of shouting men and the rushing of feet and clashing of swords exploded in the silver silence.

Fand whirled, her face a white flame of wrath. "He dares! For years,

Mannanan and his plotters have coveted the Portal to the outworld, and now he dares attack openly—"

She grasped Cullan's wrist. "This way, and quickly! They must not reach the chamber of the Portal!"

The whole palace, all of Ethne, was now a hideous clamor as Mannanan's armored soldiers poured through the silver-lit gardens in swift onrush.

Cullan raced with the Tuathan princess, around the base of the palace and into it by another door. They entered the back of the shining pearl-hall.

Cullan glimpsed Mannanan and his men pouring in against Fand's guards. Swords were flashing—swords that flamed with charges of destroying force. The merest touch of those swords sent men falling in dead, blasted heaps!

"Retreat up the stair!" Fand's voice cried to her guards like a silver trumpet. "Guard the chamber of the Portal!"

There was a mad, scrambling confusion across the cool loveliness of the shining hall, as the outnumbered soldiers of Fand gave back toward the stair.

Cullan reached and snatched up a sword from a dead man's hand. The weapon was light as a rapier, its blade shining with that deadly force.

"Kill that outworlder!" roared Mannanan's voice through the fight. "Seize Fand!"

A sword struck like a lightning bolt toward Cullan as he swung Fand behind him to the stair.

Cullan parried and struck with the half-forgotten skill of fencing taught him at his university five years before. His blade slithered past the opposing rapier and touched his Tuathan enemy's arm.

The man dropped without a groan, his whole side blasted and withered by the destroying touch of the charged sword.

"Up the stair!" Fand cried. "Mannanan has suborned my soldiers—we have only this palace guard."

There began a crazy retreat up the coiling stairway, past level after level of the palace. Fand's few guards were holding the steps stubbornly, barring the narrow way to Mannanan's hordes.

"The Tuatha possess other and more powerful weapons than these swords, but Mannanan dares not use them lest he destroy the palace and the Portal with it," Fand was crying to Cullan. "If we can hold them—"

Jeff Lewis' wild face thrust between them. "Cullan, what is it? What's happening?"

"Mannanan and his bunch are trying to seize the controls of the Portal, whatever it is," Cullan rasped.

"My God!" exclaimed Lewis. "If that happens—"

Cullan heard no more, for one of Fand's soldiers had fallen directly below him on the stair. He leaped in to fill the gap.

Deadly, shining blades clicked and clashed on each other all across the stair. Men touched by them fell as though struck by lightning. Cullan felt old fencing skill coming back to him in the desperate fight.

But they were being forced back upward despite the blasted corpses with which they had strewed the steps. Up past level above level of the palace, until behind and above the defenders lay the end of the stair.

The stair opened up onto the roof of the topmost bubble-dome of the palace! Sunken in that roof was a round recess open to the misty moonlight, a windy, lofty enclosure containing a great mechanism which flashed and glittered.

The thing was a giant crystal similar in shape to the tiny crystal in Cullan's ring. But this one was huge, mounted in massive framework and gimbals of gold, and surrounded by an intricate pattern of similarly mounted smaller crystals.

Fand cried wildly to Cullan, as Mannanan's triumph-shouting hordes pressed them back at the narrow entrance of this chamber of the Portal.

"The Portal is lost unless I call for help! But the only ones whom I can call to aid will deal death to *you!*"

"Do anything, to save the Portal from that devil!" husked Brian Cullan.

Mannanan yelled fiercely from back in the press of the attackers. "Slay that outworlder, quickly!"

Cullan stabbed and struck. The light, deadly sword was almost exactly like the rapiers he had once used in fencing. And the supernal necessity of holding the attackers nerved him.

He parried thrusts of blades whose touch was destruction, and loosed destruction himself by the swift flash and dip and stab of his shining weapon. Blasted bodies now choked the narrow doorway.

Yet another of Fand's guards went down, and now only three of them were left to fight beside him, with Lewis standing ready behind him to replace the next who fell. He caught a glimpse of Fand, standing by the edge of the great crystal machine with her white arms raised toward the night, her face strange and masklike in the silver light.

Another of the men beside Cullan went down. Triumphant roar of voices broke from the attackers as they surged forward for a last onrush. They would break through, this time—

Something clicked in Brian Cullan's brain. Something made the sword in his hand suddenly flash with a swiftness and skill of which *he* had never been capable.

And as though from remote distances he heard his own voice roaring battle-challenge to the attackers before him. That terrible battle-cry rose raving above the din of the fight.

"Who comes against me?" Cullan heard his own voice roaring. "Who comes to kill the Hound of Cullan, the champion of the Red Branch, the slayer of Ferdia and the Calatin Clan? Who comes against *Cuchulain?"*

For he *was* Cuchulain now, as he fought. Except for one corner of his brain that watched wonderingly, he was another man—man berserk with battle, a man who took fierce delight in slaying.

"I am Cuchulain the Hound and I've killed Tuatha before! Come meet me, Mannanan!"

Never later would Cullan be able to decide whether ancestral personality had come out of the dim chambers of memory to dominate his body, or whether it was merely knowledge of the old legends that obsessed his mind in this supreme moment.

Red battle-madness was rocking his brain and he never could remember more than a glittering net of swords weaving death around him but not quite touching him, as he held Mannanan's warriors back. And then, suddenly, the warriors before him recoiled, staring wildly past him.

"The sign!" yelled a hoarse voice among his attackers. "The sign of Lugh!"

The crimson mists cleared somehow from Cullan's brain. He glanced and saw that around and above the whole palace a wheel of *silent* lightnings were playing. A wheel of fire, sign of Lugh, greatest of the Tuatha De.

The wheel narrowed, and bolts darted from it toward the roofless chamber of the Portal. And in that blaze of silent lightning suddenly stood men, tall, grave, unhumanly calm.

Men? No men could have appeared thus magically. Cullan's twentieth-century knowledge told him that he was seeing merely images projected from a distance in answer to Fand's telepathic call for help.

But dread images, these! Lugh, tall, grave, solemn, his somber, wrinkled face and his form wreathed with silent little lightnings, and giant, terrible-eyed Dagda, and a half-dozen others—gods of the old Celts, lords of the Tuatha De, the science-kings of two worlds once.

Lugh—or the projected image of Lugh—spoke in deep voice to the frozen attackers. "What evil is it ye do here, following Mannanan in lust for conquest of the outworld? Know ye not that such has been forbidden since I ordered closed the way between the worlds?"

Lightnings from the flaming wheel around the palace flashed threateningly toward the warrior hordes in the palace and gardens.

"Flee—Lugh's vengeance strikes!" went up the mad cry, and Mannanan's warriors turned frantically in flight.

But Mannanan darted forward, handsome face blind-mad with hate, his shining sword stabbing at Brian Cullan.

"At least *you* will perish, outworlder!"

Cullan turned—too late to parry that deadly blade. But a sword stabbed past him and ripped into Mannanan's throat. The Tuathan lord fell, face blackening and blasted.

Cullan whirled. Fand, shuddering, dropped the sword. "He would have slain you, Cuchulain!" she choked.

"Too much of slaying has there been because of these outworlders whom your faithlessness let enter Tir Sorcha!" rang Lugh's stern voice to her. "The men must die, before they cause more evil."

Fand swung herself in front of Cullan. "No!" she cried. "If you kill them, you must kill me also! Or I will shatter the Portal you gave me to guard, and open the way once more!"

A stir went through the Tuathan lords. Astonishment and anger rang in Lugh's voice. "Are you mad, Fand? The men are outworlders and they cannot stay here."

"Then let them go back through the Portal to their own world!" she pleaded desperately.

Lugh frowned. "It is not well for the outworld to learn of Tir Sorcha from them."

"They would not be believed if they told," she insisted. "Two thousand outworld years have passed since we Tuatha De left Earth, and all is but myth and legend now."

Lugh finally made a sign of assent. "So be it, then. But they must go at once, Fand. Open the Portal and send them forth."

Fand turned. Wide, brilliant green eyes looked up into Cullan's face as for a moment she clung to him.

"Cuchulain—twice found, twice lost," she whispered. "You must go. It is that, or death."

"I'll come back," he said hoarsely. "Someday, somehow. I'll find a way back in spite of all their Laws."

"Let the outworlders go, Fand," rolled Lugh's command, stern and urgent.

She thrust Cullan from her, with shaking hands. "Go quickly to your flying boat. When the Portal opens, the crystal on your finger will take you through."

She turned and blindly touched a control-stud by the side of the great machine. The giant crystal began slowly to turn in its gimbals, and the smaller stones around it turned also, faster and faster.

It was Lewis who urged the dazed, agonized Cullan down the death-littered stair of the palace, by main force.

"We've got to get to the plane quickly! Our only chance to get back!"

Palace and streets of Ethne were deserted as death, as the people cowered in fear from the flaming sign of Lugh over the palace.

The amphibian was still drawn up at the edge of the stone ramp. As they scrambled inside it, the ring upon Cullan's finger had begun once more to glow like a tiny, spinning sun.

Abruptly, everything dissolved in swirling mist. They felt a shattering shock. Then the plane rocked wildly, battered by big waves.

Sunlight—normal yellow afternoon sunlight streamed upon them through the cabin windows. The amphibian was floating in the gray-green Atlantic beneath blue sky. They had come back through the Portal to Earth.

Cullan looked about them, dazedly. "Tir Sorcha—and Fand—here a moment ago! Here, right beside us!"

Shining Land, lost Elysium, moon-misted Ethne and princess of the old gods, gone, gone—

"Months must have passed in the half-day we were in there!" Lewis was exclaiming excitedly. "We'll have to tell people that we've been floating all that time. They'd never believe the truth."

His eyes gripped Cullan's. "*Was* it true, Cullan? I'm beginning to doubt already that it was only a dream!"

Cullan looked down at the crystal on his finger, Fand's gift to Cuchulain of old and to him. Tears blurred his eyes.

"It was no dream. Someday, even if it means death. I'm going to find my way back to her."

Lost Elysium

Storm gathered ominously over the mid-Atlantic. Black clouds were boiling up across the western sky, and already the screaming wind was piling up great waves that battered at the little auxiliary yawl.

Brian Cullan, sole occupant of the little yawl, stood at its wheel and watched the gathering tempest in an agony of indecision and dread. Not dread for his personal safety, but fear that the storm might end the weird quest that had brought him to this lonely ocean waste.

"This storm will sink me unless I run before it," he muttered. "But if I stay, it *might* open the way to the Shining Land as it did before!"

Cullan's dark, lean young face was haggard as he looked down with tense hope at the ring on his finger. It was a strange ring, a worn, massive hoop of gold set with a curious prismatic crystal. But what he prayed for had not happened. The jewel was still dull, dead.

The storm was coming on with giant strides. Even under bare spars, the stout motor of the yawl could hardly keep it from swinging broadside to the climbing waves. He must flee at once if he were to escape the full fury of the tempest. But Cullan's agony of indecision suddenly ended in desperate resolve.

"I'll take the gamble! It's my only chance of entering Tir Sorcha again. I've tried everything else and failed."

And boldly he opened the Diesel's power and kept the little craft bucking directly into the storm, to maintain his position.

Brian Cullan had been cruising around this position in the lonely mid-Atlantic for days. Vainly he had been trying to force entrance back into the strange, alien world that by chance he had entered two years before.

That other time, just after the war ended, he had been flying back across the Atlantic to America and home. He had flown into raging thunderstorm and a strange thing had happened. The crystal of the old ring upon his finger had begun to glow weirdly with sparkling force.

The ring was an ancient heirloom in Brian Cullan's family. For his descent was supposed to be from the great Cuchulain, the legendary Celtic warrior-hero of two thousand years ago. And from Cuchulain had come down that strange ring which had always been called "The Unlocker."

The ring was a key, that under certain circumstances could unlock the gateway into an alien world. A world congruent with Earth but existing on a different plane of vibration, a world of unearthly beauty and horror that long ago Cuchulain and others had entered and had called Tir Sorcha, the Shining Land.

Flung into that weirdly different world, Brian Cullan had found that time in it was *different.* A year on Earth was but a day in the Shining Land. So that the twenty centuries since Cuchulain visited that other world seemed but a few years to those who dwelt in it.

And the dwellers in Tir Sorcha were those whom the ancient Celts had worshiped as gods! The Tuatha De, the great race whose chieftains Lugh and Dagda and others had been deified long ago by men of Earth, and who still lived and reigned in that other world of far slower time.

And among them—Cullan's heart yearned at the memory—was that princess Fand whom the great race had made guardian of the Gateway between worlds. Long ago, Fand had loved Cuchulain but had let him return to Earth. And when Brian Cullan came, to her he was Cuchulain returned, for a trick of inheritance had made him the double of his long-dead ancestor.

Cullan's eyes filled with tears that the howling wind and spray of the storm whipped from his cheeks.

"Fand, I swore to come back to you or die trying!" he cried into the roar of wind and waves. "And it's one or the other, now!"

For he had loved Fand, as he had loved no woman of Earth. In her faery-beautiful city Ethne, he had fought for her against her estranged husband Mannanan when that traitorous lord of the great race had sought to seize the Gateway to Earth for his own evil purposes.

He had fought and won, for Mannanan had died in the battle that wrecked his plot. But Cullan had lost too, had been exiled from the Shining Land and thrust back to his own world by the great Tuatha rulers who had decreed that none should come and go between the worlds.

He had come back to the drab, war-wearied Earth, but haunted by memory of that lost, golden Elysium and the love he had left there. He had sworn to return to Fand despite the stern decree of the Tuatha lords.

Now, after two years of preparation, Brian Cullan had come in the yawl to that spot in mid-ocean whence formerly his plane had been snatched into the other world. For days, he had vainly tried by the scientific means he had prepared to open that strange channel between the worlds of varying vibration. And all his attempts had failed.

This, now, was his last gamble. The way had been opened that other time by the unleashed electric forces of storm. It might happen again. If it did, the subtle scientific powers of the ancient ring upon his finger would take him through.

Cullan, clinging to the wheel of the bucking yawl, peered tensely at the crystal on his finger. "It *must* happen again!"

But the crystal of the Unlocker remained dead, mocking him. The jewel itself was not a door between worlds. It was only a talisman which could take him through if the door were opened.

The sky was now night-black, the howling gale raising mountainous waves that tossed the struggling yawl like a toy on their raving crests. Lightning had begun to spear blindingly across the heavens.

Blinded by flying spray, deafened by the roar of tempest, Brian Cullan fought fiercely to keep the yawl against the storm. Despair closed icy fingers around his heart, for now that the full power of the gale was unleashed, the little craft could not long survive.

Each time it dropped dizzyingly into the trough of the great waves, he managed miraculously to keep it from swinging broadside and foundering. But miracles could not go on forever. Cullan's hair bristled as he saw huger waves piling blackly and leaning forward to crush him.

Colossal hands seemed to snatch the yawl skyward, and as it hung for a moment on the crest with screw racing wildly, he knew this was the end. The whole heavens flared in that moment with dazzling lightning—

"The sign!" yelled Brian Cullan wildly. "The sign of the Gateway!"

The lightnings had whirled into a flaming, blinding circle in the sky over his head. A circle that seemed whirling down upon him.

And the crystal of the Unlocker on his finger was suddenly flaming! Scintillating with blazing rays of force that spun in a circle which was miniature match to the descending hoop of lightning above him.

Storm-lightning had momentarily opened the Gateway between the worlds of varying vibration, and the Unlocker's subtle aura of force would take him and his craft through if—

Crash! The yawl had dropped from the towering wave-crest to the surface of the sea, with a smashing shock that wrenched its beams to shrieking protest, and that flung Brian Cullan hard against the rail.

He was half stunned, but he struggled to his knees. Then he froze, looking around him with wild surmise on his haggard face.

Golden, glowing mists were about him, a strange, sprawling haze. The yawl floated placidly on a smooth yellow sea, amid that unearthly radiance. Black sky, howling storm, raving waves, had all vanished.

Wild joy, exultation in hope long-deferred but now at last fulfilled, hammered in Brian Cullan's heart.

"Tir Sorcha! The Shining Land!"

II

Golden, dreamy stretched the mists around him, stirred by the soft, warm wind into little twists of shining vapor that slowly swirled above the yellow sea. Forever hidden above the aureate haze was whatever sun lit this world. But through the sparkling, shrouding vapors there dimly bulked the outline of a distant island.

Brian Cullan felt a singing joy that thrilled his every nerve. He had fought fate and death and storm to return to this world, and his wild attempt had succeeded.

"Fand! Fand!" he whispered, and the name was like a jubilant prayer upon his lips.

He steered the yawl, its motor throbbing, toward the dim shape of the distant island.

This was a world of islands, he remembered. A strange, ocean world whose golden mists shrouded countless scattered isles that held wonders of beauty and terror unknown to Earth save in legend.

Cullan soon perceived that over the island ahead, vast-winged shadows hovered. Then he saw them more clearly as incredible, roc-like birds that were planing to a landing on the low green land.

"The Island of Great Birds!" he exclaimed. "I remember, now. And over there—"

Over there farther in the shining haze showed another isle that seemed covered by tall trees. But the trees were flowers, colossal blooms nodding and waving gently in the breeze.

The two remembered isles gave him his bearings. He turned the yawl and sent it throbbing away in a direction that was north by his gyrocompass. It was the way to the Isle of the Waterspout where was Fand's city Ethne, whose beauty had haunted his memory these two years.

"Two years?" thought Cullan. "But only two *days* have passed in this world, since Lugh forced me back to Earth."

Bitter had been that memory, of the hour when he had been exiled from this world and from Fand by stern decree of Lugh, lord of the Tuatha. But now the bitterness was dissolved in the joy of return.

Not even his knowledge that he was returning into Tir Sorcha in direct defiance of the warning of mighty Lugh, not even the penalty of doom he risked, could temper his joy. Somewhere here he and Fand would find chance for happiness, however brief.

Cullan could not measure the passage of time as the yawl sped north and north. It might be near nightfall but he had no means of guessing. Almost tremulously, his eyes strained into the mists ahead. Then at last, the island of his hopes took slow shape.

It was the Isle of the Waterspout, a low green hill rising from the yellow sea. A deep bay indented its southern coast, and above that bay climbed the shimmering structures of the faery city Ethne.

Most wonderful was the giant geyser of water that gave this isle its name. It was a colossal waterspout that sprang perpetually from a pit on the north shore and curved obliquely across the whole island to thunder down in a ceaseless cataract into the bay below the city.

"Ethne at last! And Fand there, hoping and waiting for me—"

Brian Cullan's pulse hammered as he sent the yawl speeding into the bay. Loud in his ears now was the unending, booming thunder of the falling waterspout, whose maelstrom of currents he gave wide berth.

The battered little yawl glided into the bay on throttled motor. Ahead lay the ancient yellow stone docks of Ethne, and from them climbed the streets and elfin buildings of Fand's city.

Cullan saw that remembered beauty through blurred eyes. Poised beneath the rushing rainbow of water that arched the sky, Ethne was a city of dream. Its buildings were shimmering spheres like iridescent bubbles, rising in breathtaking loveliness to the highest cluster of bubble-domes that was Fand's palace.

Suddenly, Cullan's wild elation checked a little. The city was strangely still, strangely *silent.* There was no sound but the distant boom of the falling waterspout, and no figure moved in the streets of shimmering spheres. He could see none of the fair-haired Tuatha lords and ladies, none of the dark slaves who had served them.

Fear grew swiftly in Brian Cullan's heart as he brought the yawl to the docks of worn yellow stone. He moored it hastily between the slim, burnished metal boats that floated here. Then he leaped quickly up onto the dock.

"Good God!" His exclamation came from lips stiffened by horror.

The dock was littered with slain men. Most of them were Tuatha warriors, tall, fair-haired men in silver mail and helmets, lying with their glittering flame-swords still shining in their hands, their bodies blasted and blackened where enemy swords had touched them.

But among them lay also many of those enemy warriors who had died fighting them. These were dark, stocky, brutal-looking men in black armor, men like the dark slaves whom the Tuatha had owned. There had been an invasion and battle here in Ethne!

"Fand!" cried Cullan agonized. He ran up the sloping streets toward the highest bubble-palace.

Lost now on him were the beauty of shimmering domes and gorgeous gardens. Faery Ethne was a silent city of the dead. There were corpses everywhere in the streets, mostly Tuatha but no small number of the dark warriors.

Cullan remembered as he ran what Fand had mentioned, that their slaves were prisoners taken in war with the dark, deadly enemies of the Tuatha, the Fomorians who dwelled far northward in this world.

The Fomorians? The mysterious, malign race whose memory lived in Celtic legend as lords of evil who struggled against the Tuatha gods? They had been here in Ethne, had slain every soul. But Fand?

Wild with dread, Brian Cullan reached the palace and burst inside. In here, in the great central hall that was like the interior of a white pearl, the dead Tuatha warriors were thickest. And out on the terrace where Fand and he had declared their love, and in the wondrous gardens below it, other dead bodies of the handsome Tuatha folk lay sprawled.

Cullan searched frantically through the silent halls of death, but could not find Fand's body. He stood, wild with doubt and dread, feeling a ghastly loneliness in this still city of death.

Cullan whispered through dry lips. "If those dark devils killed Fand—"

He stopped and whirled. A slight sound had reached his ears. Were there *still* some of the Fomorians here?

Cullan stooped quickly and snatched up a flame-sword from a dead warrior. He knew the weapon from previous use. As his fingers closed on its hilt, its slim blade glowed with shining force—force released from the condenser chamber in the hilt, that would blast any living thing touched by the blade.

He listened again, standing ready with the flaring sword in his hand, his lean, dark face taut and terrible. Then he went toward the heap of dead on the great stair. From there had come the sound.

A man in that heap of corpses was stirring feebly. It was a tall Tuatha warrior, whose face was on one side blackened and scorched by the grazing touch of a flame-sword.

Brian Cullan knew this man. It was Goban, captain of Fand's guards, a man at whose side he had fought against Mannanan's plotters two years—two days, here!—ago.

With fierce impatience, he raised Goban to sitting position and sought to revive him. The Tuathan, he saw, had been stunned by the glancing touch of a flame-sword and left for dead.

Now, he opened his eyes.

"Cuchulain!" cried Goban, looking wildly up into Cullan's face, and calling him by the name all the Tuatha had called him because of his resemblance to his long-dead ancestor. "Cuchulain, you've come back! But too late!"

He choked the last words out in a groan, looking around the corpse-littered palace.

"Goban, what has happened here?" cried Cullan hoarsely. "Where is Fand?"

He spoke in the Tuatha language, so like the ancient Gaelic, that he had learned here beforetime.

"The Fomorians have her—Tethra's dark warriors have taken her to black Mruun in the north!" groaned Goban. "They slew all here but me, and I should have died too."

Cullan's blood iced with dread. Fand a prisoner of the deadliest enemies of the Tuatha, the dark Fomorians whose evil had been legend even in Earth for ages?

"It was that traitor Mannanan's doing," said Goban thickly. "The cursed one who was once Fand's husband."

"Mannanan?" cried Cullan. "But he was killed two years ago—two days ago, by your time—when we smashed his plot to seize the Gateway."

"Aye," said Goban, "but it seems now that Mannanan's plot was not really his own. He was but a pawn in the hands of the Fomorians. Those black devils were the ones who really coveted the Gateway, so that they could go through into your Earth.

"And when Mannanan's plot failed, Tethra's black horde acted quickly. They came to seize the Gateway mechanism and Fand, who is its guardian and knows the secret of its opening. They poured into Ethne last night from hundreds of boats and slew all in the city. They pressed the last of us into the palace as we sought to defend Fand."

Goban's eyes lighted fiercely. "You should have seen her, wielding sword with us like a tigress against the swarming dark ones. And as she fought, she cried, 'If Cuchulain were but with us still!' That was all I heard before a sword grazed my face, and I fell stunned."

Brian Cullan's heart was bursting with wild emotion. And from his lips there broke a sound of rage that was almost a snarl.

That strange resurgence of ancestral personality, of ancestral memory, that once before had made him Cuchulain reborn, was waking in him again.

"We'll not stay here wailing her loss!" he cried. "We'll follow northward after them, even to Mruun!"

The red rage was creeping ever stronger across his brain, the terrible personality of the ancient Hound beginning again to dominate his maddening mind.

To have lost Fand, by merely hours! To have spent those long months of toil and danger and deadly risk to win back to the Shining Land and her, only to find himself too late!

"Wait, Cuchulain!" pleaded Goban. "We two could do nothing against all the Fomorians in black Mruun. The Tuatha of all the isles must be told of this. I must call Lugh, lord of the Tuatha."

"Why didn't you call when danger first threatened?" Cullan demanded savagely.

"There was no time!" Goban protested. "The Fomorians burst in upon Ethne like a flood, a wave of death that rolled upon us in moments."

Goban rose unsteadily to his feet with Cullan's help, and staggered unsteadily across the hall to a pedestal on which was mounted a nest of concentric crystal globes. He peered intently into the globes.

Light grew inside the concentric crystals. Cullan knew he was witnessing some of the alien science of the Tuathans, an ancient science transcending the younger one of Earth.

"My thought is reaching through now to Lugh and Dagda," Goban whispered. "They will use the shape-sending to come here at once."

Suddenly, magically, two men appeared there in the death-littered hall beside them. Two tall Tuathan lords, one of them a giant.

The older man was Lugh, king of the Tuathan race, he whom the Celts of old had deemed greatest of gods—a man grave and gray with age, with somber, wrinkled face and piercing eyes. The other man, a huge, fierce-eyed giant, was burly Dagda, warrior-lord of the race.

Cullan knew that he was not really seeing the two Tuatha lords. These were but images of them, hurled across distance by the "shape-sending" science of Lugh, images that could see and speak and wield certain powers.

"What reason for this urgent call—" Lugh began to Goban, and then checked himself as he saw Brian Cullan. His face grew stern with wrath. "You have returned, outworlder? Did I not warn you the penalty was death if you violated my decree and came back into this world?"

"Lord Lugh, look at these dead!" boomed the startled voice of giant Dagda, who had glanced across the corpse-strewn hall.

Goban spoke hastily. "The Fomorians have been here! They have taken the princess Fand and slain all others here but myself."

Lugh's face stiffened, almost as though in dread, as he heard Goban's swift tale. He cried, "What of the Gateway mechanism?"

"I do not know but I fear they have taken it also," stammered Goban. "I was struck down here, and Cuchulain revived me when he came."

Lugh and Dagda—or their images—glided swiftly up the stair to the roof of the bubble palace. Cullan followed hastily with Goban.

He had been up here before. In the recess on this roof, he remembered, was situated that strange mechanism of otherworld science which could be used to open the Gateway to Earth at will, and of which Fand was guardian.

But the mechanism was gone. That wonderful device of spinning crystals had been lifted from its bed, which now gaped empty.

"The Gateway in the hands of Tethra's Fomorians!" whispered Lugh. "It is what we have always feared and guarded against."

"They cannot operate it without knowing its secret," pointed out big Dagda. "And only Fand, beside yourself, knows that secret."

"Aye, but they have Fand," Lugh said somberly. "And Tethra's craft and tortures will surely win it from her in time."

He brooded for a moment. Then he told Goban, "Come at once to our citadel in Thandara. Great things impend, for now I think our long struggle with the dark ones of the north is rushing toward its climax."

He added, looking sternly at Brian Cullan, "Come you too, outworlder. It may be that fate itself has brought you back to this world against my decree, to play a part in our final war with darkness."

"Hell take all your wars and orders!" blazed Cullan. "I'm going after Fand!"

Lugh's eyes fixed him freezingly. "It may be that you will go, but it will be as I direct. Obey me, outworlder!"

He and Dagda, or their images, abruptly vanished. Cullan stood torn with indecision as Goban begged him to obey the order.

"Alone you could not even find black Mruun of the north," Goban insisted. "The lord Lugh's power only can recover Fand now."

That consideration was what impelled Brian Cullan finally to obey, despite his wild impatience. He followed Goban out of the palace and down through the silent, deathly city to the docks.

He was moving toward the yawl, when Goban objected. "That outworld craft of yours looks far too slow. We go in one of our own boats."

Cullan knew the tremendous speed of the slim, undecked metal boats of the Tuatha. He dropped into one after Goban, who went to the stern and touched the controls of the box-like generator of atomic power.

White fire jetted back under water from the stern, and the slim craft leaped out through the harbor like a frightened horse. Avoiding the thunderous falling waterspout by a swift turn of the tiller, Goban sent the boat skimming the yellow swells due westward through the golden mists.

The Tuathan captain seemed feverish with excitement over Lugh's promise of final war. But Cullan's mind could hold only one thought—memory of Fand in that last moment when she had clung to him and he had promised to return.

He had no eyes, in his agony of spirit, for the islands that took form in the golden mists and dropped behind them. The Isle of Silver with its argent rocks and burnished beaches, the strange Isle of Fire whose uprushing red flames glowed infernal through the haze, the other, farther isles that he vaguely recognized—he was blind now to their wonder.

The golden mists darkened as night began to fall. The slim boat rushed on and on over the smooth yellow swells. Then far ahead in the dusking mists there loomed a larger island. The bubble-like domes of its city surrounded the shimmering, lofty spires of a mighty citadel. Lights were shining there, many boats moving, in feverish activity.

"Thandara, citadel of the Tuatha lords and heartland of our race!" Goban was crying to him. "It wakes for the last war with the Fomorians."

Thandara, fabled citadel of the old Celtic gods! Cullan, crushed by his dread, could feel only a numbed wonder as they rushed toward it.

III

Tuathan warriors were already coming from other islands, as was evidenced by the many boats speeding into the harbor of the city. But Goban steered their own racing craft past the harbor, directly toward the point where the sheer, shimmering outer wall of the great citadel rose from the water edge.

There in the face of the wall was a water-gate opening directly into the citadel. In the deepening dusk, Goban deftly maneuvered their craft through the opening and down a water tunnel into a little interior harbor beneath the great structure. Here a sourceless yellow light illuminated a dozen other metal boats chained to a stone quay. On the quay waited a giant figure in silver mail and helmet. Cullan instantly recognized Dagda's craggy, massive face and fierce eyes.

"The lord Lugh awaits you," he boomed. "Already word has gone out to every island of our folk, and soon all will have gathered here."

"To go after Fand?" Cullan asked with feverish hope.

Dagda looked at him solemnly. "You may see her sooner than you think, outworlder."

They followed the burly giant up coiling silver stairs, through shining, iridescent corridors and chambers of soft, sourceless light. Everywhere in the citadel they heard running feet, babel of excited voices, stir of intense activity.

The Tuathan giant led them at last into a high chamber that was not large. Around its pale rose-tinged walls stood implements and instruments of the Tuathan science, their purpose unguessable to Cullan. And here stood Lugh, straight and spare in his mail, his somber face darker than ever as he listened to Goban's quick elaboration of his tale.

"Aye, it is plain enough," Lugh said, finally. "Tethra has long coveted the Gateway. And when his plot to gain it through Mannanan failed, he struck directly and took both it and its guardian."

"What will they do with her? They'll not kill her?" Cullan asked tensely.

"Not until they have wrung the secret of the Gateway from her," Lugh said darkly. "And then—then at last Tethra and his evil horde will be free to go through into your Earth."

His voice deepened as he continued. "It is why we Tuatha long ago closed the way between worlds. Your people would be defenseless against the dark science of the Fomorians. Once before, ages ago in your time, they broke through into Earth under Tethra and began conquering your primitive races.

"We Tuatha forced the Fomorians that time to return into this world. And soon after, when the men of Earth revolted against our own wise rule, we returned ourselves into this world and closed the Gateway so that the Fomorians could not again invade your world."

Lugh's face was heavy with memory. "Since then, for many years of our time and for many ages of yours, we have kept the Gateway closed. Only a few times, when the forces of nature happened to open the Gateway momentarily, have any from Earth come through. Your ancestor Cuchulain was one such, and it was because Fand gave him that ring you wear that you in turn were drawn into our world by such a chance opening of the way.

"But now the mechanism of the Gateway is in Tethra's hands. And when he forces its secret from Fand, he and his evil race will invade your world. I tell you that you folk of Earth will be defenseless before them! Your weapons of crude material science will be in vain, and the Fomorians will fasten an evil and hideous tyranny on all your race!"

Brian Cullan was chilled. He felt a fear such as he had not felt on that former occasion when Mannanan had plotted for the Gateway.

Mannanan's traitorous followers had been few, and whatever their powers he had not felt that so few could represent real danger to Earth. But these dark hordes of whom Lugh spoke, armed with inhuman powers and sciences, pouring through into an Earth already battered by war—

"Then the only means of averting that disaster is to get Fand away from Tethra's grasp before he can secure her secret!" he argued.

Lugh looked at him steadily. "You love Fand, do you not? It is why you returned to this world against my decree?"

Cullan answered boldly. "I do love her, and it is why I returned. You can kill me, I know, but I'll not go back again to Earth!"

Dagda, the giant, uttered booming appreciation. "This outworlder has courage, Lugh! Let him stay, we can use him in this fight."

Lugh was looking strangely at Cullan. "Yes, we can use him," he said slowly. "Fate itself has brought him back to use against Tethra. But let him not complain later when he learns all the tricks of fate."

To Brian Cullan there seemed something hidden, something ominous, in Lugh's words. But he was past caring for premonitions now.

"I'll complain at no risk or danger, if I can stay and fight my way to Fand!" he cried.

"We are going to Fand now," Lugh said unexpectedly. "In a few minutes you shall see and speak to her again, aye, and to Tethra too in his castle in dark Mruun."

Cullan was astounded. "In a few minutes? But Goban says that Mruun lies far in the cold mists of the north?"

"We shall not go by ordinary means, this time," Lugh said. "You go with me, for I have a reason. But first, put on Tuathan mail."

Mystified, Brian Cullan discarded his clothes and donned the silver mail and helmet that were ready. When he had done so, he glimpsed himself in a mirror. His helmeted, dark head and mailed figure looked strangely different to him, from his former self.

"It is well," muttered Lugh, eyeing him. "You are indeed exact counterpart of your ancestor Cuchulain."

He led Cullan toward a looming device in a corner, a hollow copper cube atop which were mounted queer, shielded instruments.

Cullan began to understand. "Then only our *images* are to go? As you and Dagda came to Ethne?"

Lugh nodded. "Yes, we go by the shape-sending. This machine can fling a simulacrum of our physical bodies far and fast across any distance, and so we shall enter Mruun. And then—we shall see."

Cullan sensed again that hidden purpose in the Tuathan king's words, that mysterious purpose that somehow concerned himself. But he was too desperately anxious to see Fand again to question.

He followed Lugh inside the hollow copper cube. The Tuathan king touched and turned a knurled knob upon the wall. Then from walls and floor and roof of the cube, blinding light seemed to explode upon them.

Brian Cullen reeled. He no longer felt the floor under his feet, but felt as though he were being hurled headlong through howling darkness. Vaguely, he felt Lugh's arm steadying him.

"We approach Mruun!" Lugh's voice reached him. "Now keep close behind me, and speak not until I have spoken."

Cullan seemed to himself to be hurtling behind Lugh swifter than thought, through cold, mist-shrouded night over heaving ocean. He knew that it was only his image that was so traveling, only a simulacrum of himself flung out by the Tuathan's deep mastery of atomic science.

Yet it seemed he, the *real* Brian Cullan, who was thus rushing at nightmare speed over the night-shrouded sea. And ahead of them, dooming up with incredible swiftness, towered a great island.

Shrouded in cold northern mists, the stupendous crags of this island rose like black battlements of giants. Up there on the heights was a squat, dark, ancient city of vast extent, dominated by the massive, ebon castle that perched on the highest diffs.

"Black Mruun, the chief isle of the Fomorian race," came Lugh's voice. "Remember, keep behind me as we enter Tethra's castle."

They were rushing up through mist and night toward the black and massive pile. Cullan glimpsed dark, mailed Fomorian warriors on its walls, warriors who cried out and pointed at them.

Then he and Lugh were rushing *through* the thick stone walls of the castle, as though they did not exist. He had flashing glimpses of a labyrinth of dusky corridors and levels, as they drove through them.

Then, suddenly, their rush slowed and stopped as he and Lugh entered a vast, vaulted black room filled with strange, ocher light.

"The throne-chamber of Tethra," whispered Lugh, from in front of Cullan. "Aye, and there is he, and Fand."

At the far end of the room upon a throne of carven black stone flanked by mailed guards, sat Tethra. He was a man past middle age, dark like all the Fomorians but handsome and with something in his mocking face that seemed vaguely familiar to Cullan.

Facing the taunting gaze of the Fomorian ruler stood a slim, erect white figure at sight of whom Brian Cullan's heart jumped.

"Fand!" he whispered chokingly.

It was Fand as he remembered her, slender in her starwoven white gown, her dark hair bare. Her green eyes were brilliant with defiance, her dynamic white face stiff with loathing, as she faced Tethra.

But a moment that tableau held for Cullan to witness, before it was interrupted.

Into the throne-chamber raced Fomorian guards.

"Lugh and another have come! Their images rushed through the wall into the castle—"

But Tethra was on his feet before they could finish, glaring swiftly around the throne-chamber. He became rigid as he glimpsed Lugh gliding forward with Cullan close behind him.

"Lugh's shape-sending science!" exclaimed the Fomorian king. "Fear not, my men! I expected it and have prepared against it."

As he spoke, Lugh was swiftly moving his hand. From a heavy bracelet-instrument on his wrist, bolts of shining force like living lightning darted toward Tethra.

But those dazzling bolts withered, faded and vanished in the strange ocher radiance that filled the room. And Tethra laughed, his dark, mocking face triumphant.

"Said I not I was prepared?" he taunted. "Not thus easily do you catch me, Lugh. The shape-sending trick will not avail you now."

"The Tuatha know other tricks," Lugh said ominously. "You hover on the brink of an abyss, Tethra. Send Fand and the Gateway back to us or it is war between Tuathans and Fomorians—that means your death."

Tethra laughed mockingly. "Will threats win that war for you? You are already defeated and you know it, Lugh. Long have you kept us barred out of that Earth from which you drove us. Now we go back there, for now we have the Gateway and soon we will have its secret."

Fand spoke swiftly in her silver voice. "They will never have it, lord Lugh! Fear not that any torture can force it from me."

"There are tortures of the mind that can transcend the terrors of the flesh," Tethra said smoothly. "And I know how to wield them, Fand."

"Aye," said Lugh darkly, "there are tortures of the mind. But two can play at using them, Tethra."

"Bring on your forces and weapons if you so dare," Tethra challenged contemptuously. "My warriors have long desired to slay you and your lords, including that hulking Dagda who now skulks behind you."

"It is not Dagda who is behind me," said Lugh quietly. "It is one who is not of the Tuatha at all."

And Lugh's image suddenly moved aside, revealing Brian Cullan's mailed figure to their gaze.

Tethra leaped up like a man stricken by appalling force. For a moment, as he stared at Cullan, his face was livid.

"Cuchulain!" he cried hoarsely. "Cuchulain, here from the outer-world!"

And from Fand came a glad, silver cry. "Cuchulain returned! I *knew* you would come back!"

She ran forward with wild gladness in her face, as Tethra still stood rigidly, stunnedly staring at Cullan's image.

Lugh made a sudden movement. To Cullan, the whole throne room seemed suddenly to vanish as he was withdrawn from it with incredible swiftness. He felt himself whirled back through darkness, and suddenly was standing again in the copper cube in Lugh's chamber at Thandara.

He stood unsteadily, still wild with emotion at his glimpse of Fand and her peril, as Lugh briefly told Dagda and the other of their glimpse of her.

Cullan interrupted, his voice hoarse. "We've got to do something to get her out of there, quickly!"

"We will," Lugh said quietly. "Tethra knows now that I have weapons against him."

"That devil didn't fear your weapons," Cullan said harshly. He added, puzzledly, "Though Tethra seemed almost to fear when he saw *me*, seemed to know me. Yet he has never seen me before."

"He mistook you for your ancestor Cuchulain—and he knew Cuchulain long ago when he and his Fomorians invaded Earth," said Lugh. The Tuatha king added, broodingly, "And seeing you made Tethra fear, indeed."

Cullan was too agonized by apprehension for Fand to ponder the dark mystery that he sensed again behind Lugh's words.

"We go to Mruun at once, physically and with weapons?" he cried tensely.

Lugh shook his head. "Not yet. The hosts of the Tuatha are not yet gathered. And I have still a weapon to use against Tethra before we join final battle. But it will take time."

"Time? There is no time!" Cullan retorted passionately. "If you and your warriors won't go, I'm going to Mruun alone!"

He turned to leave the chamber. But giant Dagda grasped him, and held him like a child despite his raging resistance.

"Lock him up," Lugh ordered curtly. "And you guard him, Goban. He is valuable to us for he is part of my plan against Tethra."

Struggling furiously, Cullan was carried bodily out of the chamber and down a corridor. Dagda tossed him into a small room, not unkindly.

"Be not so impatient, outworlder," boomed the giant as he shut and locked the door. "There'll be battle enough for all of us, soon."

Brian Cullan heard the huge Tuathan stride away, leaving Goban on guard outside the locked door. He stood in the small, yellow-lit room, trembling with frustrated rage and dread.

There was a tiny window. He went to it, looked out feverishly into the night. Diffused silver radiance now streamed down through the mists, from moons somewhere above the haze. The unreal light washed the gardens and bubble-buildings below this high citadel of Thandara.

Out in the harbor of the city he could see slim boats streaming in through the haze, in numbers. The Tuathan warriors were gathering from all their isles for war.

Cullan gained no hope from the sight. By the time this host was ready to go northward, it would be too late to save Fand from torture and death.

IV

Cullan turned back from the window, his fists clenched and his dark face savage in the soft yellow light.

"I'll not be locked here like a child while Lugh spins mysterious plots. If they won't go to Mruun, I will!"

But how? How escape from this room, from the citadel? The window was too small, the door locked. There was only one possibility.

He went to the door and called through it. "Goban, I want you to come inside. I give my word not to try to overpower you."

Goban's voice came doubtfully. "I do not doubt your word, Cuchulain. But—"

"Man, the princess Fand's life hinges on it!" Cullan cried.

That swept aside Goban's doubts, as he had known it would. The captain of Fand's guards, like all her warriors, had been fanatically devoted to her. Goban unlocked the door and entered the room.

Cullan spoke rapidly. "Lugh told you that we had seen Fand a prisoner in Mruun. But he did not tell you of all her peril."

Goban's face blanched as he listened to Cullan's tale of hearing Tethra threaten the Tuathan princess with imminent torture.

"The devils of Fomoria!" raged the captain. "If they do that before we get there—"

"They *will* have done it before your host arrives," pressed Brian Cullan. "Unless a few men, unless you and I, go ahead with all speed to Mruun and snatch Fand away from them first."

Goban gasped. "You and I go alone to black Mruun? It would be useless, mad."

"We would have a chance," Cullan insisted. "Tethra was startled, shaken, when he saw me. I think he fears me, or rather, Cuchulain. And I think we could secretly enter his castle. I saw all its interior ways as I went through it with Lugh in image."

The Tuathan captain hesitated, torn by his throbbing loyalty to Fand and his larger fealty to Lugh.

"The lord Lugh would slay me for breaking his command," Goban muttered. "But I will do it, Cuchulain! Better that than to let the princess die without attempt to save her!"

His decision made, Goban planned swiftly. "We can leave the citadel only by the way we came—the boats below. Wait, while I see if the road is clear."

Brian Cullan waited in tense impatience for minutes before Goban returned. The Tuathan captain handed him a flame-sword.

Sheathing the weapon, Cullan followed the other out of the room. Goban had chosen a way down narrow, little-used stairs and passages. As they hastened downward, they could hear from elsewhere in the citadel the echo of excited voices, of hasty preparations.

Without challenge they reached the quay of the little inner harbor beneath the citadel, in which yellow light glistened off the dozen swift metal boats moored here.

"Dagda's craft is the fastest by far, but it is chained and locked," whispered Goban. "We must take the one in which we came."

The Tuathan again took the helm, starting the atomic mechanism purring and steering the slim boat quickly out the water-tunnel.

They emerged from the citadel into the silver mists. At once, Goban swung their craft in a wide circle to avoid the entrance to the main harbor of Thandara.

Looking back toward that harbor, Brian Cullan saw in it many boats gathered along the massive docks. Under the flare of brilliant lights, Tuathan warriors were loading heavy, spouted mechanisms into the boats.

"They prepare the instruments of our science that will loose destruction," said Goban. "The battle that comes will be terrible."

Now they were clear of the island and the Tuathan swung their craft northward. At its highest speed it skimmed over the smooth swells of the sea, Cullan peering tautly from its bows.

Silver mists as of dreamlike moonlight shrouded all the world. Wisps and curls of the whitely radiant haze caught at their faces as their craft rushed on. Like dim ghostlands vaguely bulked the islands through which they were passing.

Cullan felt an ever-fiercer impatience, born of his dread for Fand. That dread, and the rage against the Fomorians it engendered, brought stronger into his mind that wild, ruthless battle-passion that he believed was inheritance from long-dead Cuchulain. He told himself desperately that he must keep his head clear, must be Brian Cullan, not Cuchulain.

Goban was feeling something of that same fierce excitement. For the Tuathan called to him above the rush of the wind, his voice high.

"I am glad, now! I was the only warrior in Ethne who did not die fighting for the princess, and now I redeem that shame."

Silver moon-mists and vague islands rushed past, as they sped on and on toward the north. Soon there were no more islands to be glimpsed, only the spectral sea over whose low wave crests the slim boat ran headlong.

Hours passed. Cullan saw the Tuathan constantly consult instruments in the stern and guessed that Goban was correcting and checking their course toward Mruun. They had already come a great distance, he knew.

The mists began to grow thicker, darker, colder. A chill that he had not before experienced on this world entered Brian Cullan's flesh from the wind. And ever darker, heavier, became the shrouding haze.

"We draw near toward Mruun!" Goban called finally. "Soon we may glimpse the cursed island."

Cullan's hopes flared up exultant. But the Tuathan added warning, "By now, they'll have missed us at the citadel. And Lugh can follow swiftly."

A bare few minutes later, there came such a sharp and startled cry from Goban, that Cullan whirled quickly around.

Tall and somber in his silver mail and helmet, staring at them in stern accusation, Lugh stood in the speeding boat with them.

Cullan suddenly understood. "Lugh's image! The shape-sending—"

"Aye, it is how I have followed you," Lugh said harshly. He threateningly raised his arm, on which glittered the bracelet-shaped weapon that could loose lightning destruction. "Turn back at once toward Thandara!"

"I'll not turn back!" flamed Brian Cullan. "You can kill me, but while I live, I'm going on to Fand!"

Lugh slowly lowered his arm. "I shall not kill you, for you are valuable in our struggle against Tethra in a way you do not know."

He added sternly, "But you shall not reach Mruun. I thought you would defy me so, and so when first we missed you I sent Dagda after you."

The image of Lugh vanished abruptly with that ominous warning, withdrawn by that shape-sending science he had used to overtake them.

Goban's voice was appalled. "Dagda and his warriors pursuing us? And their craft is far faster than this one!"

"They'll not dare pursue us into Mruun itself," Cullan encouraged. "If we can reach the Fomorian city in time—"

Their Tuathan boat could not go faster, since already it was racing over the sea at its highest speed. Anxiously each few minutes now they peered back into the darkening mists, but saw no pursuers.

Another hour passed thus, and another. Then far and high in the cold, dark mists ahead, Cullan descried gleams of dull ocher light. Beneath those lights bulked vaguely the black battlements of lofty cliffs.

"Black Mruun at last!" he exulted. "We'll steal in below the cliffs and then—"

"Dagda comes!" yelled Goban, pointing backward.

Out of the mists behind them was emerging the spectral shape of a rushing Tuathan boat larger than their own. It held half a dozen warriors, with giant Dagda himself crouched at its prow.

"Turn and try to lose them in the mists!" cried Brian Cullan, desperate at the last-minute menace to his hopes.

Goban obeyed, swerving their racing craft so sharply that its gunwale dipped up sea. But turn and twist as they might, the other craft and Dagda's angry, booming voice hung close behind them.

“No use, Cuchulain!” cried Goban hopelessly. “They’ll board us in a moment. And we cannot fight our own—”

He suddenly stopped, his face for a moment wild and startled as he peered through the mist beyond Cullan.

“The Fomorians!”

A dozen sharklike metal craft were rushing out of the mists upon them, from the direction of Mruun. Cullan glimpsed them, loaded with dark Fomorian warriors in black helmets and mail, yelling now in savage joy.

There was no chance for either Cullan’s nor Dagda’s craft to escape the ring that suddenly closed upon them. Flame-swords flared and clashed, men screamed and died in the mist, as the boats came together.

Cullan had his own sword out, triggering the deadly force into its blade as he struck across the gunwales at the wolfish, brutal figures looming through the mist. He saw Fomorian faces twist in agony as his blade touched bodies and loosed the destroying force on them.

“Slay not the outworlder Cuchulain!” yelled a captain in the Fomorian boat attacking them. “Remember Tethra’s orders!”

Take him alive to torture with Fand? Cullan struck fiercely at the dark warriors who now were piling into his boat.

He glimpsed Dagda’s craft rammed and sinking, the bellowing Tuathan giant pitched into the sea. Then, from his unguarded side, a Fomorian sword-hilt crashed against the base of his neck. And Brian Cullan felt himself sliding into blackness.

He awoke, his head aching violently, to a silence that seemed amazing transition from the roar and shock of battle.

Cullan opened his eyes. He was in a dark stone chamber, windowless but chill with icy mists, lighted by a pulsing ocher radiance.

“Goban, what happened?” he stammered to the man supporting him. Then he saw that it was not Goban but huge Dagda, his shock head bare.

“Goban died a warrior’s death in the fight,” boomed the giant. “So did my men—but the cursed Fomorians picked *me* out of the water like a helpless fish as I sank in my mail.”

Brian Cullan felt a pang at the news of the brave Tuatha captain’s death. Then he looked wonderingly around the dank room.

“We’re in the castle of Tethra?” he husked.

“Aye, that we are,” said Dagda grimly. His massive face was black with rage. "Captured like children by Tethra's dark devils! Outworlder, your crazy expedition hither has led us into a trap where I'll die without ever fighting in the last grand battle."

He strode the room furiously. "See how this ocher radiance shrouds all the castle? It is no mere light, but a shield of force that Tethra's science has flung forth to ward the lightning-loosing weapons of my people. Yes, the struggle will be bitter. And I to take no part in it!"

He was still growling curses when the door was unlocked. Black-mailed Fomorian guards with flame-swords entered the room.

"You go before Tethra now," snapped their officer. And as Dagda started ominously toward him, he added, "Resist, and you die here."

Brian Cullan made no resistance. He walked amid the alert guards with the swearing giant, with desperate hope that at least each stride might take him nearer Fand.

Dank and cold, flooded with the weird ocher radiance, were the black stone corridors of the castle Mruun. They came finally into a vast, vaulted room that Cullan well remembered—Tethra's throne room.

Tethra himself stood by his throne, amid guards and captains, but Cullan gave him no second glance. For running toward him flashed the slim, white figure of Fand.

"Cuchulain, you've thrown your life away by following me here!" she cried, in his arms.

Tears blurred her brilliant green eyes and wet her white face. As he crushed her close he felt the shiver of dread in her pliant body, and knew that it was dread for him.

But Cullan felt an incredible, soaring joy. He had won back to her through the dangers of two worlds, and somehow he would hold her.

"Fand! Fand!"

"They have us both, now," she whispered. "And they have the Gateway mechanism, down in the lowest level of this castle. And now—"

Cullan turned his head, and felt the raw red anger creep back into his mind as he met Tethra's gaze.

The Fomorian king stood, tall and dark in his black mail, eyeing Cullan's face with strange intentness. Again, it seemed to Cullan there was something vaguely familiar in Tethra's dark, strong, aging face.

"Cuchulain, in very truth!" whispered Tethra, incredulously. "But how *can* it be? Long ages have passed in the outworld since Cuchulain was born there."

Cullan answered harshly, fearlessly. "I am not the Hound. But he was my ancestor, long ago."

A strange, throbbing emotion showed in Tethra's eyes. His dark, sardonic face was not mocking now. It was yearning, glad.

"Now I understand!" he exclaimed. "Yes, you are Cuchulain reborn. In your veins flows his blood—and mine."

"Your blood?" Cullan cried, astounded. "Do you mean—"

"I was Cuchulain's father, long ago on Earth," said the Fomorian king. "Your forefather, *my son!*"

V

Cullan was stunned, numbed. He saw shock and horror in Fand's white face as she looked up at him. He strove to open his mouth to deny.

But Tethra was speaking quickly, almost eagerly, his burning eyes clinging to Cullan's face as he spoke.

"It was half my lifetime ago, centuries ago in your time, that I led my Fomorians to invasion and conquest in your Earth. There I loved an Earth maiden and to us was born a son, that Setanta who later won for himself the name Cuchulain.

"When Lugh and his Tuathans drove us back into this world, my son was left on Earth. But I yearned for him, and left command for him to seek me in this world when he reached manhood. And Cuchulain came, but he never found me. For he tarried with Fand until Lugh discovered his presence and forced him to return to Earth.

"For Lugh knew that he was my son! And Lugh knew when he saw *you* that you are the son of my blood reborn. That is why the Tuathan king showed you to me, by the shape-sending. Lugh meant to bargain with me, to exchange you to me for Fand."

Fand had shrunk out of Cullan's arms and the shade of horror and loathing on her face was stronger as she looked at him. And giant Dagda was glaring at him.

"It can't be true!" Cullan exclaimed. "I've no Fomorian blood, none of Tethra's blood, in me!"

"It *is* true!" Tethra affirmed. "Lugh returned later in image to offer me the exchange. He kept you ignorant of it all, of course."

Fatal conviction gripped Cullan, as he remembered Lugh's mysterious hints. And now, too, Brian Cullan realized why it was that Tethra's dark face was vaguely familiar. It was a mirror of his own face!

Tethra uttered a ringing laugh. "And now Lugh has been tricked for all his wily ways. I have Fand and the Gateway, and also I have you, the son I longed for."

He raised his voice. "Captains of Fomoria, hail my son Cuchulain, reborn and returned to me!"

From the black-mailed Fomorian lords came a roar of welcoming shouts. But Cullan was deaf to them as he turned wildly to the girl.

"Fand, this has not changed me! Even if I have Tethra's blood, my heart is with the Tuatha and with you!"

Clouded by the horror of a deep and ancient racial hate, Fand's white face looked up at him. Then that cloud vanished, and her green eyes flamed love and loyalty, as she stepped back toward him.

"I believe you, Cuchulain!" she whispered.

Angry murmurs rose from the Fomorian captains. And Tethra strode forward, astounded.

"You know not what you say, Chuchulain! You are my son, heir now to my power. Not only power over Fomoria's misty isles but power also soon over that Earth from which you came."

His dark eyes glowed and burned. "Once we pour through the Gateway, our science will crush all there who resist us. The battle will be great, but with a world as stakes. Surely such battle, such empire, must allure you if you have blood of mine."

Cullan, despite himself, *did* feel that tempting strike a strange, responsive chord within him. A chord of that savage ancestral personality that more than once had dominated him, he knew it to be.

Wild, dark blood of long-dead Cuchulain, blood of this ruthless king before him, running strong in his own veins—that was what he had to fight against.

"No, Tethra!" he said harshly. "My loyalty is to Earth and to the Tuatha who protects it from you."

Tethra's dark eyes blazed anger. "Has this white witch-girl made you a milksop? Will you turn against me when—"

Terrible interruption prevented him from finishing. A thunderous shock and roar shook the castle Mruun to its foundations. Outside the windows flared blinding light that dimmed the ocher radiance within to dullness.

Again and again came the flashes and rocking shocks. Cries were raised, and Tethra spun around with sword flaming in his hand as a Fomorian warrior rushed into the throne-chamber.

"The Tuatha fleet has come! Lugh's weapons loose their forces against the castle!"

Tethra's strong, undaunted voice rose to dominate the uproar. "To the defense, all! Lugh's warriors cannot enter here unless his weapons shatter our shield of force, and that they cannot do."

Answering with fierce yells, the Fomorian captains raced out of the throne room. Tethra delayed to shout an order to the guards of the room.

"Bind them to the pillars, all three of them!" he ordered, pointing to Cullan and Fand and Dagda. "But see that none harms them."

As the order was hastily obeyed, as the three were bound to three of the pillars along the wall of the vaulted chamber, the alert flame-swords of the guards prevented possibility of resistance.

Tethra lingered a moment, his powerful face dark with unguessable emotions as he looked into Cullan's eyes.

"You should be standing by my side in this battle, Cuchulain," he said. "But when we have beaten the Tuatha back, we will talk again of that."

He hastened out, a martial, mail-clad figure, followed by all but a few of the guards. Again, and again, the terrific lightning-flares of released forces blazed outside the castle and rocked it wildly.

But Cullan saw that the shielding ocher radiance now was burning stronger all through and around the castle. And other outleaping flares of force outside the windows told that the Fomorians were striking back at the Tuathan attackers.

Dagda, wild with fury, strained at his bonds. "To be tied here like a calf while the fate of all is decided!" bellowed the giant.

Fand, princess of a warrior race, cried to Cullan unafraid. "Cuchulain, if Lugh's great powers can force a way, all may yet be saved!"

Hell of other-world combat was raging now on the cliffs of Mruun, Cullan knew. Thunder and flare of titanic weapons seemed to set all the island shuddering as it reached terrible intensity.

And strongly, strongly, within him stirred that dark, wild battle-passion that was inheritance from the Hound. Why was he not out there in that mad fight?

"The shield of Mruun is failing!" Fand cried, her silver voice exultant. "See, the radiance dies!"

It was true. The other glow of subtle force that had protected the castle was dimming, going out.

Crash on crash of thunderous, blazing force now smote unopposed into the massive pile. Walls began to crack and crumble, great blocks of stone to hurtle down into the quaking throne room.

Cullan heard wild, exultant shouting somewhere out on the fringes of that stunning conflict. And Dagda's pale eyes flared.

"The Tuatha sweep into Mruun! Lugh's powers have breached a way for them!"

Into the throne room now eerily lit by the continuous flares outside, came pouring a battered, disorganized remnant of the Fomorians.

Tethra, dusty, bloody and disheveled but with lion-courage blazing in his face, strode toward Cullan.

"The battle here is lost to Lugh's secret science-weapons, my son! But our plan is not yet lost if we can escape. And the only escape now for us and our warriors is through the Gateway to Earth. The mechanism of the Gateway is below, and with it are the boats and weapons we prepared. This girl can operate it to take us through.

"Tell her to do it, Cuchulain! She loves you and will obey. Once in Earth, we can soon find way to bring through all the rest of our Fomorians, and so we will have snatched victory from Lugh."

Cullan, bound to the pillar, shook his head. "No! Do not do what they ask, Fand! They must not go through into Earth."

A Fomorian captain sprang raging forward with shining sword uplifted to strike at Cullan.

"This Cuchulain the king calls son is traitor to us!" he roared. "He dies with the other two now."

Tethra whirled and stabbed, his sword like a living brand of light. Its point ripped into the throat of the charging Fomorian and the man staggered and fell with his whole head blasted and blackened.

"No man kills the son of my blood, even though he fights against us!" flamed Tethra to the furious Fomorians.

"Then you can die with him!" howled voices, and his followers rushed with uplifted swords toward him.

Tethra's sword flashed with incredible speed, to cut through the bonds that held Cullan to the pillar. And then that terrible blade sang to blast down the two foremost of his attackers.

Brian Cullan, freed, swiftly stooped and snatched up the sword of the dead Fomorian at his feet. Triggering its force into its blade he sprang to Tethra's side to hold back the attackers from Dagda and Fand.

Tethra, striking and stabbing at the black-mailed onrush, shouted with fierce voice. "We two are match enough for these snarling wolves of mine, Cuchulain!"

Cuchulain? Yes, Cullan felt he was *all* Cuchulain in this red moment as he fought beside the tall Fomorian king. For the last and most terrible time, as he fought to protect Fand, there dominated him the wild, dark spirit of the ancient Hound.

Brutal faces went down blasted before the shining, stabbing blades of Tethra and himself. Fomorians maddened by rage tripped over their fellows' bodies and could not rise again before death smote them. Mad battle-passion of a dark and ancient blood roared out in the fierce war-shout that Cullan could not recognize as his own voice.

Tethra staggered suddenly, his whole side blasted where a sword had finally touched him. But as he toppled, the exultant wolf-cry of the maddened Fomorians changed to shouts of fear.

"The Tuatha!"

They were bursting into the throne room, silver-mailed Tuatha warriors whose flame-swords cut into the dark Fomorians.

In moments, there were no black-mailed warriors left standing in that bloody, shattered room. And a great silence seemed suddenly to descend upon captured Mruun.

Brian Cullan had stumbled to the pillars, to free Fand and Dagda. The girl clung sobbing to him. He turned, as Lugh entered the throne room with more of his silver host.

But it was toward prostrate Tethra that Cullan turned. He bent over the Fomorian king, whose strong face looked up at him dark and proud even as it stiffened with the approach of death.

Tethra whispered, "You fought beside me as I dreamed once of my son fighting. Blood answers the call of its own, Cuchulain."

He was dead, with the whisper. Queerly, Cullan felt a stinging in his eyes. And he rose to see giant Dagda make a gesture of salute toward the dead, black-mailed figure.

"Whatever else Tethra was, he was a warrior!" boomed the big Tuatha.

Lugh, his face still somber, was speaking to Cullan. "You proved this day that you were no enemy to our race despite your blood, outworlder. You can stay now in this world, if you wish."

If he wished? To stay here in this world of wonder and of beauty with Fand? Cullan took her in his arms for answer.

Golden mists, golden day, glowed warmly over the smiling yellow ocean as the fleet of Tuatha boats neared the end of its long journey homeward.

Lugh's craft drove beside that in which Brian Cullan sat with Fand.

The Tuatha lord called to them across the water.

"We go to Thandara. But you will to Ethne, for there is Fand's home as guardian of the Gateway. It has been cleared of its dead and others of my folk will re-people it."

Thus the fleet split, the smaller portion bearing Fand and Cullan and the recovered Gateway eastward through the remembered islands.

Through the golden mists, Ethne rose in all its bubble beauty beneath that eternal rainbow of water across the sky. Cullan, with Fand in his arms, looked raptly. He had found his lost Elysium, had awakened from the drab dream of Earth. He was coming home at last.

The Valley of the Gods

Garth Abbott was vividly aware of the danger for him in this night-shrouded place of the dead. He did not need the whispered warnings of his nervous companion to tell him what discovery of them here would mean.

It would mean, pretty certainly, the abrupt death of a too-bold young American archaeologist in this obscure little village on the Usumacinta River in upper Guatemala. The primitive folk here would deal swift vengeance to a foreigner whom they caught desecrating their cemetery.

Jose Yanez, the guide whom Abbott had picked up in Puerto Barrios, very obviously realized that to the full. His flat, swarthy face was pallid in the rays of their lantern.

"Senor Abbott, you don't understand," he persisted. "These people are mostly Indians, still savage. If they catch us—"

"They won't—they're all at the *baile,*" Abbott retorted. "Here, give me the lantern. You bring the crowbars."

The rays of the old-fashioned lantern vaguely illumined a jumble of ancient stone crosses. Behind them rose the dark, squat church, and farther behind was the marketplace from which rose a rhythmic dance music of marimbas, flutes and drums.

Abbott had a rough native cloak slung around his shoulders to ward off the night dew, but his tawny head was bare. And as he advanced through the solemn aisles of ancient crosses, his strong, rawboned face flared with excitement. He sensed himself on the verge of great discovery.

The somber eeriness of the ancient graveyard did not affect him. He ignored the evil-looking bush-vultures that boldly roosted on the stone markers and eyed the passing lantern like unclean spirits. Places of death were no novelty to an archaeologist, and he was immune to superstition.

"That's the mound just ahead!" he eagerly told his apprehensive companion. "Quick, bring along the tools!"

The mound rose squat and black just beyond the graveyard proper. It was a grassy hillock a dozen feet high, whose southern face had been partially washed away by recent rains.

Abbott had noticed that earlier in the day. His trained eyes had instantly fastened on the great hewn stones whose edges were exposed by the washout, and which bore chiseled Mayan glyphs.

The hillock concealed a Mayan tumulus of some sort. And Abbott had been set afire by his glimpse of one group of glyphs that spelled a magic name—the name "Xibalba."

Xibalba! That was the mythical lost birthplace of the Mayas, the legendary valley from which their strange race was fabled to have come, two thousand years before!

Did that fabled valley really exist somewhere deep within the unexplored Guatemalan mountain fastnesses? Many scholars had thought so. Stephens himself, the great pioneer of Mayan archaeology, had talked with a man who claimed to have seen Xibalba with his own eyes.

If lost Xibalba could be found, all the riddles of the mysterious Mayan civilization might be solved. The civilization that long ago had reared its mighty monuments and splendid stone cities from the lowlands of Honduras to the jungles of Yucatan, might then yield answers to the enigmas that had puzzled modern men.

The mere fact that this tomb might be a clue to Xibalba had set Garth Abbott afire to excavate it. But when he had asked permission from the priest of the nearby church, he had met a check.

"I dare not permit that, senor! Pagan superstition still runs deep in many of my primitive flock, and that mound is to them a sacred, forbidden spot. You would risk your life by digging into it."

Abbott had refused to give up. He had told Yanez, "We'll wait until tonight when they're all at the fiesta and open the mound ourselves."

"But when they find out what we have done—" the Guatemalan had objected fearfully.

"They won't find out. I'll simply make flash-photos of all the inscriptions and then close it up again till later."

He had waited with intense eagerness all that day for night and the fiesta to come, feeling himself on the brink of a tremendous archaeological discovery.

Xibalba! The legend-haunted name rang in his mind like a golden bell. If he could find that fabled shrine of the Mayan gods and heroes, what might he not find there?

It had begun to rain softly now, as he and Yanez set their lantern on the ground and studied the raw earth side of the mound. The yellow clay almost completely hid the huge stones within.

Abbott estimated that the mound contained a low, round rock vault, most of it buried beneath the present ground-level.

"Clear that soil away—that's it," he directed Yanez. "Now we'll pry out one of these stones and see if it opens a way into the vault."

The big block they attacked was inscribed with the worn Mayan glyphs. Again, Abbott felt a leap of the pulse as he recognized the symbol for Xibalba—and also the one for "Kukulcan."

Kukulcan was the Mayan god of light and thunder, the great Plumed Serpent. Why was his symbol here? Abbott's eagerness grew.

The block suddenly gave way and slid out onto the wet clay. The lantern showed them a yawning black cavity.

Quivering with excitement, Abbott squirmed through the square opening. In the darkness within, he lowered himself to a stone floor. Yanez passed through the lantern, and Abbott stared.

"Good God, what a find!"

The interior of the vault was a brilliant little treasure-chamber of mystery.

Its chief object was a wonderful stone sarcophagus, over which reared the coils and grotesque head of the Plumed Serpent.

"The serpent of Kukulcan! This is early Mayan, all right. But the Mayans never entombed anyone like this!"

He stared incredulously around the chamber. Its walls were a brilliant pageant of painted sculptures.

Not two thousand years had dimmed the cunning color of those marching figures. They were Mayan of the Old Empire's earliest period, those columns of priests, warriors and captains.

The pictured pageant represented a great migration. Above the marching columns of stiff figures extended a queer running chart that showed mountains, ranges and passes, a great river—

"That river's the Usumacinta itself!" ejaculated Abbott. "The configuration is the same. Why, this is a picture-history of the first great Mayan migration!"

He realized the vast importance of his discovery. This long-buried vault was key to the greatest mystery of Mayan archaeology, the riddle of the people's origin.

Eagerly, holding the lantern high, Garth Abbott followed the story back around the walls. The painted migration marched back, up the Usumacinta and then northwestward between two ranges that he knew must be the Ollones and Chistango.

Its beginning was in a place represented as a long, straight valley at the foot of a square black mountain. Here was the representation of a city. And here the glyphs again spelled the magic name.

"Xibalba!" Abbott exclaimed. "The Mayan valley of the gods! Why, with this chart, I could *find* that valley!"

His excitement soared. On that painted chart, in the valley of fabled Xibalba, he perceived two curious dominating symbols.

One was the rearing, fiery plumed snake of the god Kukulcan. The other was the dark, bat-winged figure of Zotzilha, the Mayan lord of evil. Black bat and plumed snake were pictured in deadly battle there in the valley!

Yanez had lifted the stone lid of the sarcophagus. "Senor, there is something in this stone coffin!"

Abbott's lantern spilled light into the coffin. There was dust in it, dust that had once been a man. But there was also the gleam of gold ornaments jeweled with jade.

A sword lay in the dust. It was a weapon of the most ancient Mayan pattern, a short, heavy copper sword edged with brilliant saw-teeth of green obsidian. The hilt was a miraculous carving of the plumed serpent, whose eyes were two big blazing emeralds.

Abbott eagerly picked the sword from the dust. "Whoever was buried here must have been a king, a great leader—"

He stiffened, his voice trailing off. For as his hand closed around the sword hilt, his senses suddenly swam from shock.

Power, tangible and tingling force, seemed rushing up into his arm and body from the ancient sword!

A roar like the thunder of waves dinned in Abbott's ears. He seemed encompassed by whirling mists, seemed to feel a vast and *alien* personality somehow seize upon his brain.

The mists abruptly darkened and before him flashed a face! A dark, smooth, handsome face with heavy-lidded eyes, which in spite of its unearthly beauty was somehow—hideous.

Repulsion, horror and a bitter hatred shook Abbott. Something in his mind, or in that alien mind that had weirdly gripped him, seemed to recognize that hovering face in the darkness.

"Zotzilha Chimalman!" Abbott heard a voice inside his brain flaring. "So you have watched, evil one?"

Silver-sweet, mocking laughter chimed from the handsome face before him. Its heavy-lidded eyes were taunting, malicious.

"Aye, I have watched for I knew that you would seek someday to return, Kukulcan. But it is too late now!"

"Not while I live!" Abbott heard that mental voice raging. "And I *do* live now, and soon I will—"

"Senor!"

Yanez' cry had such horror in it that it brought Garth Abbott back to awareness. He found that he had dropped the sword.

He looked a little dazedly around the low, lantern-lit tomb, and then at the Guatemalan's scared face.

"Senor, your face was strange," shivered Yanez. "It was like one of *those!*"

And he pointed at the fierce-faced warrior-priests pictured on the wall.

"I must have been dizzy, delirious, for a moment," stammered Abbott. "The air in this place is bad."

He was still quivering from the weirdness of that momentary delusion, but he forced it from his mind.

What the hell, Kukulcan and Zotzilha were mere phantoms, the forgotten gods of a people perished a thousand years ago! The influences of this place had been too much for his nerves, for a moment.

"Come on, Jose—we'll make our photographs and get out of here."

When they squirmed out of the vault a half-hour later, Abbott brought with him that strange sword.

Yanez looked wonderingly, almost fearfully, at him after they had replaced the block.

"And now, senor?"

Abbott's voice rang with excitement. "Now I've got a clue archaeologists have hunted for years—a clue to the lost heartland of the Mayas. We're going to charter a plane and search for Xibalba!"

But why was it, he wondered, that the name of the fabled valley was no longer golden and luring in his ears? Why was it that the very name of Xibalba was now somehow freighted with *dread?*

II

The plane was a stout little two-place job which Abbott had chartered from an air-express line in Barrios. It manfully bucked the tricky currents which swirled low over these blue scarps and ranges of the vast hinterland.

Abbott had been a war pilot in the Pacific, and hunting out an objective in unknown terrain was nothing new to him. But after hours of quartering the tumbled mountains northeast of the Usumacinta, he had to admit himself baffled.

"The valley I'm hunting should be right down there," he said impatiently, pointing. "But it just isn't."

Yanez looked skeptical. "The chart in that tomb was made a very long time ago."

"Mountains and valleys don't shift around," Abbott retorted. "It should be here. We'll circle around again."

He had carefully traced back the route designated by the pictured chart in the tomb—the route from Xibalba that had been followed by the Mayans of long ago. He had gone up beyond the Usumacinta, northeast between the Ollones and Chistango ranges, then on until he had spotted the stark, square black mountain of the pictures.

And the long, straight, narrow valley he sought should be somehow in sight south of that black mountain, but wasn't. There was nothing but a tumbled wilderness of blue peaks and green forest.

Yanez was obviously uneasy. This hinterland was nearly all Lacandone country, and those wild tribes weren't hospitable to fliers who make forced landings in their forests.

The Guatemalan presently uttered a warning. "The sky is getting queer."

Abbott abruptly realized that a strange change had come over the heavens. All around him the sky was growing strangely *dark*.

It was not the darkness of gathering clouds. It was as though the light of the sky was being conquered and submerged by a surging darkness from nowhere.

It was like the weird vibrant darkness that had momentarily enveloped his mind in his strange experience in the tomb!

"Better get out of here!" Abbott exclaimed, banking around sharply. "It's some queer freak of weather—"

Next moment, he realized their imminent danger. The unnatural gloom had deepened to such degree that he could barely make out the stupendous peaks that rose about them.

With a startled exclamation, Abbott opened the throttle. There was absolutely no wind, nothing but an unholy stillness in which the shadowy darkness gloomed and thickened.

He took a course to avoid the great square peak which he could no longer see. Then things happened swiftly.

A blinding flash of lightning seared across the heavens and revealed the black peak looming up just ahead of the plane!

Yanez yelled wildly, and Abbott jerked hard at the controls. The plane started to curve sharply about, but he had a sickening realization that he was too late to avoid crashing into the cliffs.

But a howling gust of storm-wind suddenly smote the little ship and flung it bodily back from the looming cliffs.

"Good God!" he cried, as he fought the controls. "If it hadn't been for that storm-gust—"

Thunder crashed to drown his voice. Sudden storm was unloosing its fury, spears of terrific lightning tearing the unnatural darkness to shreds, an inferno of winds raging around the little plane.

Again and again, that strange darkness closed in and left Abbott flying blind amid those threatening peaks. And again and again the lightning of the thunderstorm ripped through the gloom.

Lightning that was like fiery serpents writhing across the heavens, struggled titanically with the black-winged darkness that strove to annihilate them! So seemed that infernal battle of the heavens to Abbott, as he hunched over the controls.

A thin wail of terror came from the Guatemalan as the plane sank sickeningly. "The storm carries us downward!"

Abbott saw the altimeter needle rushing back. The plane was helpless in the grip of the howling storm.

Again the fire-snakes uncoiled across the sky.

By their flare, Abbott glimpsed the earth below rushing wildly up at them.

Then he glimpsed something else—a long, straight black line that looked like a mere crack in the earth. It was a narrow canyon, of unguessable depth, invisible from ordinary altitudes.

"That's the valley below!" he yelled. "That long canyon must be Xibalba!"

"We fall!" yelled Yanez, eyes popping from his head.

Invisible giant hands of the thunderstorm were dragging the laboring plane down toward that canyon, down *into* it!

"Bail out!" he yelled to the Guatemalan. "We're going to crash!"

He grabbed up his pack, scrambled to the cabin door. He pushed Yanez out ahead of him and then they were turning over and over in the air as they plunged downward.

Their parachutes puffed out.

As they fell amid lightning-torn wind and blackness and thunder, Abbott had dazed glimpses of lightning-illumined scenes below.

He glimpsed forests, gardens, the walls and terraces of a white stone city. Then with a ripping of silk, the parachute let him down through trees and brush. He felt a shock, and then knew nothing.

When he recovered consciousness, Yanez was bending anxiously over him. The Guatemalan's swarthy face was scratched, and looked wild.

"Senor, I feared you dead!" he stuttered. "This place—"

Abbott sat up. Awe and wonder fell upon him as he looked around.

There was no storm now. Quiet peace reigned here in a green forest of fairylike beauty. Tall ceibas, cedars and willows waved in the balmy breeze, in a curiously golden daylight.

Abbott looked up. The softened light fell from the crack of sky high above, the mouth of the canyon. Two miles above his head it yawned, and the canyon itself was only a mile in width.

"The merest crack in the surface of earth!" he marveled. "No wonder it's never been spotted by any plane."

Sudden remembrance increased his excitement. "I saw a city as we fell! A city, here in Xibalba—"

Yanez gripped his arm. "There are men around us in the forest, senor. I have heard them gathering."

Abbott scrambled to his feet. As he did so, from the trees around them stepped a score of fantastic figures!

To the young archaeologist, it was as though the remote past had suddenly come to life. These were warriors of the ancient Maya!

Copper-red, fierce-eyed men, their garb and weapons matched the sculptures on the walls of Chichen Itza and Uxmal and Copan.

They wore wonderful headdresses of brilliant red and green feathers, built upon light wooden frameworks; short kirtles of jaguar skin and sandals of the same hide; belts of leather gemmed with jade and emerald. Their arms were spears and swords tipped with obsidian, like that ancient sword in his pack.

"Mayans, of the oldest period!" whispered Abbott, his brain rocking. "By Heaven, the fabled valley, the city—is *living!*"

Abbott felt a thrill only an archaeologist could understand. For years, scholars had dreamed of finding a lost, living remnant of the old Mayan civilization.

Many a search had been made, in vain. But the clue of the old tomb, and the thunderstorm that had swept them down into this hidden canyon, had brought him into the heart of such a survival.

Abbott spoke to the advancing warriors, in the Mayan tongue that has remained almost unchanged through the centuries.

"We are—friends! We come from above, from outside this valley!"

The warriors stopped, swords raised. Upon the fierce face of their magnificently attired captain came a look of incredulity.

"From outside? You are lying, stranger! No man could descend the walls!"

"It is truth!" Abbott persisted. "Thunderstorm swept us down here—"

The captain's face stiffened. "You say that thunderstorm brought you? That is strange—that is very strange."

Abbott could not understand what the other meant. He watched the play of doubt on that dark red face.

The captain finally spoke. "This matter is not for my judgment. I, Vipal, am but a captain in the guards of Ummax, the king. You will come with us to Xibalba for his judgment."

"This *is* Xibalba, then?" cried Abbott eagerly. "The valley of the gods, of Zotzilha and Kukulcan?"

His question had an amazing effect. The Mayan warriors seemed to start, and into Vipal's yellow eyes leaped a fierce light.

"What do *you* know of Kukulcan, strangers?" he cried menacingly.

Abbott sensed that he had somehow blundered badly. He should have known better than to start asking questions so soon.

"I meant no harm," he said earnestly. "I thought that Kukulcan, the Plumed Serpent, the lord of thunder, was the greatest of your gods."

"Repeat that blasphemy and you'll not live to reach Xibalba!" hissed

Vipal. "Come!"

Abbott, wondering, picked up his pack. More and more, this whole experience seemed dreamlike to him.

Two thousand years might have rolled back for him, he thought. This buried valley hidden in the mountain-guarded wilderness lay untouched by time and change.

But if these Mayans held true to the ancient civilization, why had his mention of Kukulcan so enraged them? Kukulcan *had* been the most worshipped of the old gods in the Mayan cities of long ago, had been the thunder god, the enemy of dark Zotzilha and his evil powers.

Yanez trudged beside him, the tall, somber-eyed Mayan warriors marching on each side of them. Before they had gone far through the forest, they struck a broad trail that ran northward up the valley.

The forests were green and lovely. A small river flowed down the valley and the trail kept beside it. Looking up, Abbott glimpsed at the north end of the canyon the giant square black peak that blocked its end. Its frowning cliffs loomed stark and brutal.

He thought he could descry a massive flight of stairs leading up the cliff to the portaled entrance of a black-mouthed cavern.

"What is that cavern in the distant mountain?" he ventured to ask Vipal.

The captain looked at him stonily. "It is a place which I think you will soon see, stranger."

The menace in the answer was clear, if the meaning was not. Abbott felt more and more enmeshed in mystery and danger.

The trail led them past a giant, ancient stone pyramid-temple that rose in the forest. It looked crumbling, neglected, a terraced pyramid like the great temple at Chichen Itza.

Abbott glimpsed stone heads of gigantic plumed serpents rearing from its terraces, and realized it was the temple of Kukulcan. Why was it so neglected, forsaken, abandoned to the forest?

Then that riddle passed from his mind in a shock of wonder. The trail had emerged from the forest. Before them, beyond gardens and orchards, rose the fantastic white mass of the city Xibalba.

III

Golden light of the dying day struck across the city. It was a mass of low, flat-roofed white stucco structures which were grouped around a central cluster of sculptured stone palaces and pyramidal shrines. Biggest of the palaces was a massive, oblong pile surrounded by porticoes of giant columns, rich with grotesque carving.

Toward that barbarically magnificent structure, Abbott and Yanez were led by their fierce-eyed guards. As they entered the paved streets, the American's fascinated eyes beheld a vista of ancient Mayan life such as he had never expected to witness.

Copper-skinned men and women of the lower class were here in great numbers, thronging to stare in wonder at the two strangers. Farmers, potters, weavers, all these were dressed both sexes alike in short kirtles that left their bodies bare above the waist. Here and there brilliant plumed captains and dark-robed priests stood out in the throng.

They crossed wonderful gardens and paved ball-courts to enter the massive palace. Abbott guessed that a runner had gone ahead of them, when they stepped into the long, torchlit main hall.

For Ummax the king sat upon his throne of carven wood awaiting them, and warriors, priests and women crowded the room.

"Now, how came you into Xibalba, strangers?" demanded the king of Abbott. "Long has entrance to our valley been blocked by the great landslides of long ago."

Ummax was a giant of a man, his huge limbs wrapped in magnificent jaguar skins and jeweled leather trappings, the brilliant plumes of his fantastic headdress falling halfway to the floor. He sat with a massive black stone mace across his knees.

His dark red face was gross but stark in its strength, with brutality and cunning in his eyes as he glared at Abbott.

The captain Vipal spoke before Abbott could answer. "They say that they were brought down into the valley by thunderstorm."

A big warrior beside the throne, a grizzled, one-eyed, scarred-faced captain in white plumes, uttered a loud exclamation.

"By thunderstorm? And this stranger is fair of hair, as legend tells of—"

The king Ummax interrupted fiercely. "What you hint at is impossible, Huroc! The man is lying!"

A girl beyond the grizzled, scarred warrior spoke quietly. "The man cannot be lying when he has not yet spoken for himself."

Abbott looked at her in wonder and quick admiration. This Mayan princess was a figure of wild, barbaric loveliness.

Her slim copper body had for garment but a richly embroidered white linen kirtle, fringed with jade beads. Her soft shoulders and proud little breasts bare, her dark hair crowned by an elaborate headdress, her chiseled features and dark eyes had a compelling allure.

Ummax had turned on her furiously. "You, Shuima, are supporting Huroc in hinting blasphemy! I tell you to beware!"

Abbott found his voice. "I do not understand all this. It is true that storm brought me here, yet I was searching for this valley of Xibalba. I found a clue to its location in a tomb far away."

"A tomb?" mocked Ummax. "A tomb that led you to Xibalba? All lies!"

He raised his hand. "Vipal, you will take these two strangers to—"

"I'm telling the truth!" Abbott broke in desperately. And then he bethought himself of a half-proof he could show.

He stooped swiftly and tore open the pack he had dropped at his feet. From it, he drew that ancient, short, heavy sword.

"See, I found this sword in the tomb! And there was an inscription, telling—"

Abbott's voice trailed off. A strange and sudden change had come over every human being in the barbaric, torchlit hall.

Ummax, the big one-eyed captain Huroc, the girl Shuima—they and everyone else seemed stricken by a strange paralysis as they stared at the ancient, heavy weapon in Abbott's hand.

"The sword of Kukulcan!" whispered Huroc, his single eye wild, flaming with excitement. "Then the Plumed One after all these ages has returned!"

Ummax bounded to his feet, towering gigantic, clutching his great black mace as he glared at Abbott.

"So it *was* the lord of thunder who brought you here!" he hissed.

And then, abruptly, Abbott saw a strange and awful change take place in Ummax's face.

It suddenly distorted into a wholly different face, into the handsome, heavy-lidded, evil countenance that Abbott had confronted in that strange vision in the tomb.

Darkness seemed to gloom and thicken in the torchlit hall! Unearthly darkness, something cold, alien, terrifying—

And then swiftly the handsome, evil face was gone, and it was Ummax' own brutal, raging countenance that looked down at him.

Ummax seemed to struggle for control over himself before he spoke.

"Stranger, that sword is—known, here," he said finally. "Your tale may be true. At least, we welcome you as a guest until we can speak further of these things.

"Conduct them to fitting quarters," he told Vipal jerkily. And then he added fiercely, glaring around the awe-stricken throng, "And let no blasphemous talk of these things go abroad!"

Abbott, stunned and mystified, put the sword back into his pack and with Yanez followed the captain Vipal from the room.

The face of the tigerish Mayan warrior looked ashen in the torchlight of the sculptured corridors through which he led. He bowed low as he ushered them into a long, white-walled chamber.

"Food and drink will be brought you, lords," he said huskily, and withdrew.

Abbott looked wonderingly around the torch-illumined room. Brilliant feather tapestries woven with familiar Mayan designs hung from the walls. Low stools of carven wood and bright woven mats were the only furniture. Small barred windows looked out into the night.

Quickly, serving-maids appeared with colorful pottery trays and bowls and flagons. The copper-skinned girls, fair bodies bare to the waist, looked with extreme awe at Abbott and Yanez as they set down their burdens.

One, bowing low before him, seized his hand and pressed it to her lips.

"Many in Xibalba have waited long for Kukulcan's return, lord!" she whispered.

Abbott stared after them when they had gone. "I'll be damned! Because of that sword and the thunderstorm, these people have identified me somehow with their god Kukulcan!"

"Gods of thunder and gods of evil—this place is unholy, accursed!" exclaimed Yanez, crossing himself.

The Guatemalan's swarthy face was pale, his hands shaking. Abbott slapped him reassuringly on the shoulder.

"Buck up, Jose. Just because they're superstitious is no reason why it should affect us."

"It is not just superstition, no!" said Yanez feverishly. "You saw that devil-king call hell's demons to him there in the throne-room! You saw his face, saw the darkness that gathered—"

"Hell, will you let a few grimaces and a chance shadow scare you?" Abbott demanded impatiently. "We've found a wonderful place, a place that will make us famous. Forget all this nonsense of gods and devils."

But later, after they had eaten and were stretched on soft mats in the darkened chamber, Abbott found it not easy to forget.

He lay, watching the flickering gleam of torchlight that came through the windows from somewhere outside the palace, and turning over and over in his mind the weird situation into which he had stumbled.

Why had the chance identification of himself with Kukulcan roused in these people such deep and opposed emotions, of rage on the part of Ummax, of awe in others, of fervent hope in some? What *had* happened there in the throne-room when it had so strangely darkened?

Abbott did not realize that he had fallen into exhausted slumber until he suddenly awoke, alert and quivering. Then he heard a slight, stealthy sound.

A dark shadow was stealing toward him, bending over him. Instantly Abbott bounded upward and fiercely gripped the intruder.

He was thunderstruck to find himself gripping slim, soft naked shoulders, with perfumed hair against his face.

"Lord, it is I, Shuima!" whispered a throbbing voice. "Strike not for I am not your enemy!"

"Shuima? The princess in the throne-room?" whispered Abbott, stunned. "What the devil—"

A bigger, dark figure crossed the torchlight gleam from the window, and Yanez awoke to utter a startled squawk.

"Quiet your friend or all is lost!" warned Shuima swiftly. "It is Huroc, who has come with me on this mission."

Huroc? The grizzled one-eyed captain? Abbott felt more and more mystified but in a hasty whisper he silenced the Guatemalan.

Shuima's soft hand pulled him down to the floor beside the window. By the dim glimmer of light from outside, he could descry her chiseled face and the scarred mask of Huroc.

The girl was speaking quickly. "Lord, Huroc and I have come thus by secret stealth to your chamber, to warn you that at this very moment Ummax gathers the powers of the Bat-winged one against you!"

"The Bat-winged? You mean Zotzilha, your bat-god of darkness? Just what do you mean by that?" Abbott asked incredulously.

Huroc's deep voice throbbed. "Surely you know well. Have you not returned as we have long prayed you would, to crush that evil one? Is it not why you have come, lord Kukulcan?"

Abbott gasped. "You call *me* Kukulcan? This is all madness. I am no god."

"No, but you are the chosen of the god," Shuima said quickly. "You are the Holder of Kukulcan, as Ummax is Holder of dark Zotzilha."

Abbott mentally damned all superstition. Before he could protest, the girl was rapidly whispering on.

"It is strange that you do not realize these things yourself! For Kukulcan brought you here, his thunders sweeping you down into our valley as you told. And Kukulcan will surely manifest himself in you, for the final struggle that even now impends."

"Struggle? With what? With whom?" Abbott wanted to know.

"With the Bat-winged!" Huroc growled fiercely, his huge figure shaking with hatred. "With the dark lord of evil who for generations has fed and fattened upon our helpless race!"

IV

Shuima's soft fingers gripped Abbott's hand passionately as she whispered swiftly.

"Twenty centuries have passed since *both* Kukulcan and Zotzilha manifested themselves through living men in our valley. Zotzilha, the Bat-winged, to batten upon the life-force of the sacrifices offered him. But Kukulcan, the Plumed Serpent, to teach and help us!

"Kukulcan, through his Holder, blessed our people then. He drove the Bat-winged back into his lair in the black mountain, and he taught us ways of peace and happiness. Then, in a fateful day, the prince of Iltzlan who was then the Holder of Kukulcan led a tribe of our folk into the outer world when this valley became too small for our numbers.

"Iltzlan never returned! And the sword of Kukulcan by which a man could alone become Holder of the god, was lost with him in the outer world. So dark Zotzilha came forth from his lair and dominated our people, and since then has reigned in wickedness over them through such instruments as that Ummax who is now his Holder.

"But now you have come back with the sword, and now we know that Kukulcan means to manifest himself through you and to end the tyranny of the Bat-winged and his creatures in Xibalba forever!"

Abbott was appalled. The superstitious dualism of this lost people's faith had involved his own person.

His possession of that sword which he had taken from the tomb which he now knew was Iltzlan's, had made them think him a chosen instrument of their god Kukulcan.

"I know nothing of gods!" he protested. "By my people, Kukulcan is considered a mere myth."

"Kukulcan is no myth!" Huroc exclaimed. "He is force, invisible but tangible, real, mighty—aye, as Zotzilha is real and mighty. The Plumed Serpent is but the symbol of his lightnings. The *real* Kukulcan is not of this world."

It sounded almost convincing. But Abbott forced himself to dismiss superstition from his mind. He must keep his head clear.

"Just what do you expect me to do to unseat Ummax-Zotzilha's tyranny? You have some plan?"

Shuima's answer stunned him. "You go with us now to the neglected Temple of the Plumed Serpent. There have already gathered a host of those in Xibalba who still are secretly devoted to Kukulcan—like the two guards at your doorway who let us into your chamber.

"There in his temple, Kukulcan will manifest himself in you as his Holder. And when our people see that, they will follow you to the death against Ummax and his warriors!"

Abbott was appalled. They expected some kind of supernatural possession to manifest itself in him.

It was insane. Yet he had to fall in with the idea, to humor their belief, if he were not to be murdered in this palace-trap.

"All right, I'll go," he said quickly. "But remember that I claim none of the kinship with Kukulcan that you credit!"

He turned to the Guatemalan. "Yanez, it might be safer for you to get clear of this whole tangle once we're out of the palace. I don't want to drag you into further danger."

"I think there is danger everywhere in this valley tonight, senor," whispered Yanez. "And I go where you go."

Huroc opened the door, torchlight from the corridor outside outlining his massive figure. He had a heavy sword in his hand.

"Let us be quick! And forget not the consecrated sword, lord Kukulcan!"

Abbott took the heavy, ancient sword from his pack and followed the huge one-eyed warrior and the slim girl into the hallway.

The two guards on duty outside it bowed to him with deep reverence. "We are of the faith, Lord Kukulcan!"

"Come! This way!" whispered Shuima.

They had taken but ten steps toward the angle of the corridor when there suddenly came around it the captain, Vipal.

The Mayan was not three feet in front of them, and his tigerish face stiffened as he struck with the drawn sword in his hand.

"I *guessed* there might be treachery!" he hissed, as the obsidian-edged blade drove at Abbott's heart.

With a low, warning cry, Yanez shoved Abbott violently aside. As Abbott reeled, he heard a choking gasp.

"Senor—"

He regained footing, whirled with the ancient sword uplifted. But in that brief moment, it was already over.

Big Huroc's giant arm had whipped around Vipal's throat. There was a dull, cracking sound, and the tigerish warrior went limp with eyes rolling horribly.

"Quieter that way!" panted the one-eyed giant.

"Lord, your friend is hurt!" exclaimed Shuima.

Yanez lay, clutching the ghastly wound made in his side by that swift, saw-toothed sword. His face drained of color.

He whispered a word to Abbott bending frantically over him. The word and his life ended together.

"Damn it, I brought the man to death!" choked Abbott. "He took that sword-blow meant for me—"

"Death is close for all of us unless we get out of the palace at once," warned Huroc. He swung to the two guards who had come racing along the corridor. "Hide these bodies! We go!"

Abbott's brain was whipped with grief, remorse, doubt, as he followed the giant and the girl hastily out of the palace.

Deep black brooded the night over Xibalba, only a thin scimitar of stars across the heavens marking the mouth of the canyon high overhead. He stumbled with his guides across gardens, along unlighted and deserted narrow streets of the low city.

The torchlit mass of the palace fell behind and presently they were in the forest and pressing along a narrow trail. Birds screamed in the dark trees as they passed, branches whipped their faces.

Huroc looked back and uttered a low exclamation. Abbott descried, far back at the north end of the valley, torches made tiny by distance coming down the stair in that massive mountain-cliff.

"Ummax returns from the Temple of the Bat-winged!" rasped the one-eyed giant. "He will miss you, and then—"

He did not finish, but quickened his pace, Shuima's hand on Abbott's arm urging him ever faster.

Then through the forest filtered red torchlight. There rose before them the looming white terraces of the great pyramidal Temple of the Plumed Serpent.

Men and women numbering many hundreds waited with flaring torches on the terraces, a tense and silent host. Many were warriors fully armed, and the eyes of all fastened on Abbott's face as he went between his two companions up the first massive stairway.

"The sword! It *is* Kukulcan's sword!" he heard them whisper excitedly as they glimpsed the ancient weapon he carried.

"The lord of thunder! The Plumed Serpent!" swelled the cry.

Abbott felt dazed when he reached the flat shrine atop the pyramid. Here reared two enormous stone effigies of the plumed snake, great bodies coiled, mighty heads challengingly upthrust. Between them was a stone chair around which their coils writhed protectingly.

He turned and looked down at the hosts on the torchlit terraces. A deep, taut silence had now fallen upon them, and their faces were like graven masks of utter expectation turned up to him.

"You must sit in the chair of the Holder, and grasp the sword while we make the invocation to Kukulcan," Huroc told him.

"Huroc! Shuima! This is all crazy!" Abbott protested. "What you expect cannot happen."

"We *know* that you are the chosen Holder or you would not have found the sword!" exclaimed Huroc. "Take your place! The invocation begins."

They were chanting, those hosts down on the terraces. Chanting words that were familiar to Abbott from the old inscriptions.

"Bright One, Lord of the Thunder,

Plumed Serpent of living lightning —"

Sitting there above them, gripping the ancient sword, Abbott heard a low roll of thunder up the canyon and groaned inwardly.

"They'll think it the answer to their invocation! And when nothing else happens—"

"Lord of the storm-swept sky—"

The thunder rolled louder as the chant swelled. And Abbott stiffened suddenly on his stone seat.

Force again was rushing up from the sword into his arm and body, as it had seemed to in the tomb. But now more powerfully, his whole body tingling and quivering from its impact!

"Electric influences of that coming storm," Abbott tried to tell himself, his throat dry.

The torchlit throng below seemed to dissolve in bright mists, the swell of the chant and the roll of thunder to merge into a steady roaring in his ears.

He whirled, spun, was engulfed by shining mist. And again, but more completely now, he felt the impact upon his brain of a mind cool, vast and alien.

"I am he whom these folk call Kukulcan. But I am no god."

He *heard* that cool, quiet voice, in the whirling mists. Yet it spoke inside his own brain!

"You live in a universe that has infinitely many dimensions unknown to you. In those dimensional abysses dwell entities such as you have not imagined, formless, bodiless, yet powerful. And some of them are—evil.

"Long ago, one of those evil ones escaped our watch and penetrated through to the dimension of your Earth. He laired in this valley, became worshipped and dreaded as the Bat-winged, as a god of evil, by these ignorant folk.

"I, whose fault allowed his escape, was sent to force him back into his own dark dimensional gulfs. But he had grown too strong! He has maintained himself here, feeding on the life-force of sacrifices and utilizing men as his instruments, for centuries.

"And for centuries I have been unable to interfere, because the sword you hold was lost by chance in the outer world. That sword is a cunningly contrived key which can open the way between dimensions and allow me to manifest myself through the man who holds it. Your finding it enabled me to use you as my instrument against the Bat-winged.

"He must be destroyed, now or never, lest he grow too great for this valley and reach dark arms out over your earth. The black mace of Ummax is the key by which *he* can reach into this world. You must secure and destroy that mace, at all costs!"

Crash of thunder shook the mists that shrouded Garth Abbott's mind, and suddenly those bright mists were fading.

He opened dazed eyes upon the faces and windblown torches beneath him, and saw awe in Huroc's burning eye and Shuima's face. He knew that his own face must have been strange, unhuman.

Down from the gathering storm smote lightning that seemed to dance upon the temple top and outline the great Plumed Serpents of stone beside him, like coiling snakes of living fire.

"Kukulcan!" roared the throng beneath, frantically acclaiming the dazed Abbott. "Kukulcan returns!"

Abbott, brain reeling from that weird mental possession that still seemed partly to grip him, found himself crying out.

"I *am* the Holder of the Plumed Serpent! Kukulcan returns in me! And I say that we march on Xibalba now, to pull down dark Zotzilha's tyranny forever!"

V

Delusion, hallucination born of waking nightmare that the rush and strangeness of events had brought him? He could not wholly believe that, with that supernal wrath and purpose still possessing his mind.

If an unearthly, evil thing *had* reached into earth from alien abysses, if he himself was really the human instrument by which it must be driven back, he must not linger now to doubt!

"Huroc, gather our warriors!" he cried. "We march back on the city at once."

"We're ready now!" shouted the giant. "Our one chance is to surprise Ummax and—"

Shrill wail from the forest interrupted him, and up onto the torchlit terraces of the temple staggered a Mayan warrior covered with blood and dust.

"The city's people have risen against Ummax!" he cried. "When the king returned from the Bat-winged's temple and gathered his guards to follow you here, the people rose for Kukulcan!"

"No chance of surprise now! It's started!" yelled Abbott. "Come on!"

Huroc and Shuima were beside him as his host poured through the forest in a torrent of torches and swords.

"The people can't stand long against Ummax' guards!" Huroc was shouting as they ran. "But with you to lead them, all things are possible!"

Thunder of the oncoming tempest rolled behind them as they burst out of the forest into sight of the city.

Xibalba writhed in the throes of battle! Wildly shaken torches revealed the clashing combat in its streets as Ummax' solid masses of guards cut through the seething mob of rebel citizens.

Abbott saw that the raging revolt wavered already on the brink of defeat, that the disciplined warriors were cutting swiftly through the wild mob.

"Slay all with arms in their hands!" roared Ummax' bull voice across the din. "Stamp out these traitors, once and for all!"

Abbott glimpsed the towering figure of the king, his wonderful plumes nodding above the heads of his guards as he brandished and struck with the great black mace that was his weapon.

That black mace was more than a weapon! In Abbott's fevered brain, as he charged beside Huroc, rang remembrance of that mental voice that had seemed to speak to him in the temple.

"The black mace of Ummax is the key by which Zotzilha can reach into this world. You must destroy it, at all costs!"

"Kukulcan! Kukulcan!" rose the wavering cry of the rebels, even as they fell back before the swords and spears of the guards.

"Kukulcan is *here!*" roared Huroc, as he and Abbott with their warriors crashed into the melee. "The Plumed Serpent leads us!"

At sight of Abbott's figure, of the heavy, ancient sword he carried, a thunderous shout roared from the mob. They surged forward in mad new charge.

Abbott felt himself carried as on the crest of a human wave against the solid ranks of Ummax' guards. Saw-edged swords and spears gleamed in the shaken torchlight before his eyes.

He struck blindly with his sword, felt it bite into flesh and bone. He glimpsed awe on the faces of Ummax' men as they fell back, a superstitious dread.

"We're breaking them!" shouted Huroc close beside him, the giant exultant. "On, Kukulcan!"

"Hold firm!" roared Ummax to his men. "The Bat-winged is with us. See!"

Ummax had raised his black mace high in the torchlight. A swift, subtle change was coming over the raging scene.

Cold, malefic darkness seemed rolling down in an awesome wave upon Abbott and Huroc and their advancing horde, smothering their torches, dazing and blinding them.

"The wings of our master fall upon them! Strike and spare not!" howled Ummax, exultant. "But take the false Kukulcan and the traitors Huroc and Shuima alive!"

Abbott felt the pulse of dismay, of dawning terror, through his forces as that chill, rolling darkness deepened over them.

They were giving back, crying aloud in fear! And he too felt a strange dread of that gathering gloom.

He told himself fiercely that he was letting superstition affect him, that it was only a blast of chill air from the storm rolling up the valley that was smothering the torches. And yet—

Ummax' guards were breaking among his shaken forces, swords were striking fiercely at him now, Huroc fighting madly beside him.

"Shuima is taken, our men give way!" the giant cried hoarsely. "Lord Kukulcan, unless you lift the Bat-winged's darkness—"

Shuima captured? Ummax roaring in triumph as he urged his triumphant warriors on? Steady, wrathful anger that was not his own mind's rage seemed to possess Abbott's brain fully now.

"Fear not!" he heard himself shouting. "Zotzilha's dark forces cannot stand against *these!*"

And he flung his hand to point skyward, at blinding lightning uncoiling and searing through the chill darkness.

The hellish crash of thunder that followed those first lightnings of the breaking storm was punctuated by Huroc's cry.

"The fire-serpents of Kukulcan strike across the sky! The lord of thunder leads us!"

And as the full fury of the tempest crashed upon Xibalba, the warriors behind Abbott surged resistlessly forward.

"Kukulcan leads us!" shrilled the wild, exultant cry.

To Abbot, that battle in the storm-lashed streets became a mad chaos of swords and shouts and ghastly faces, of blinding lightning flaring in battle against sullen darkness.

Battle of gods as well as men? Or not of gods, but of entities from far beyond Earth's dimensions now in death-grapple here?

He could not speculate upon that now. He had but one objective in his mind, and that was to cut his way to Ummax and seize that mighty black mace which the towering king wielded.

But Ummax disappeared from view as the battle lost form and changed into a staggering, swirling melee. His guards were being split up, attacked in groups, overwhelmed by weight of raging numbers.

Abbott found Huroc grasping his arm, leaning to shout to him above the roll of thunder and hiss of rain.

"We've won the city! It's the end of Ummax' tyranny!"

"Not the end until he is dead and his black weapon in my hands!" cried Abbott. "Quick, to the palace! We must find him!"

Wolfishly-shouting, battle-fevered men poured after them over the last remnants of resistance to the massive palace.

In the torchlit corridors of the great pile they found no one but scared servants who gave them news of Ummax.

"The king and his last warriors fled past here to the Temple of the Bat-winged! They had the princess Shuima with them!"

Huroc uttered a hoarse exclamation. "We must catch them before they enter Zotzilha's dark cavern! For no man but Ummax himself can enter the Bat-winged's lair!"

Abbott whirled. "Quick, then! We can't wait for the others!"

With the hundred men who had followed them into the palace, he and Huroc plunged out into the tempest and hastened northward up the valley.

VI

Abbott could have imagined no spectacle of such awesome grandeur as the thunderstorm that was moving with them up the great canyon. Confined between those lofty rock walls, its thunders were deafening and each lightning-flash appeared to rive the universe.

Wind and rain were wildly rocking the forest along whose trails they pressed. They had no torches and only by light of the recurrent flashes could they finally make out the black, looming bulk of the square mountain that headed the valley.

"See, they climb the stairs to the Bat-winged's temple!" yelled Huroc, pointing with his sword. "After them!"

"We follow, Kukulcan!" cried the maddened Mayan warriors behind them.

By the lightning-flashes, Abbott saw the stair as a great flight of broad steps cut from the black living rock and leading right up the steep slope of the mountain.

Black stone statues of bat-winged Zotzilha guarded the landing halfway up the stair, and here Ummax' two-score guards had turned desperately with raised swords.

"They seek to hold us while Ummax escapes with Shuima into the Bat-winged's lair!" raged Huroc.

Abbott, by a blinding flash, himself saw Ummax climbing on up the stair and dragging the senseless form of the Mayan girl.

"Crush them down! See, Kukulcan's lightnings assault the evil one's lair!" Huroc encouraged.

The flashes of incessant lightning were indeed striking the face of the black mountain, riving away great masses of rock.

Reason told Abbott that metallic ores in the mountain must be attracting the lightning. But the stunning spectacle seemed to transcend such logic by its supernatural power.

Swords clashed and rang across the stair as they readied the landing and Ummax' guards. Abbott, staggering on the slippery wet stone, ducked one vicious blow and hacked at the distorted face beyond.

The lightning showed six men already cut down when the rest of Ummax' men, unnerved by the appalling flashes, gave up.

"Spare our lives, Kukulcan!" they cried, dropping their weapons. "The king forced us to stand against you!"

"Take them prisoner!" Abbott cried to his shouting warriors. "Now up the stair, Huroc!"

They raced with a score of their men up the last flight of massive steps. The whole mountain seemed rocking and quivering to the continuous lightning-blasts as they reached the top landing.

This broad stone platform was a mere shelf cut in the side of the cliff.

From it, a high, dark tunnel ran into the solid rock of the mountain. And over that dark portal spread the stone wings of Zotzilha, guarding, warding the lair within.

Abbott gripped his sword and started into the dark passage, and Huroc and the others hesitantly started to follow him.

They stepped into a deep darkness that was utterly cold. A freezing chill smote to Abbott's bones, a feeling of iciness and suffocation as the sullen darkness in the tunnel swiftly thickened.

"The Bat-winged's power is upon us!" choked Huroc. "I cannot move!"

He and the other Mayans seemed actually petrified, either by superstitious terror or by the malign grip of that icy darkness.

But though Abbott himself felt the smothering grasp of the frigid gloom, he was still able to struggle forward along the somber tunnel.

Flash on flash of lightning sent a momentary blinding glare down the passageway ahead of him, and for that moment he found himself able to pitch forward at increased speed.

"Kukulcan goes to slay the Bat-winged in his lair!" he heard Huroc shouting, behind him.

Abbott felt himself two utterly divergent beings as he pressed unsteadily forward through those gloomy cavern tunnels, sword gripped in his hand.

He was Garth Abbott, American and archaeologist, seeking to save the girl Shuima from the brutal savage tyrant who had dragged her here with murderous purpose.

But he was also the unearthly being who was using him as instrument, he was also that bright being from other-world dimensions whose century-old struggle with a thing of evil had now reached climax.

"Zotzilha, I come!" he seemed to hear himself shouting fiercely down the tunnels. "Will you meet me, spawn of darkness?"

The part of him that was Garth Abbott rejected that fierce challenge as mere mental aberration born of the influence of storm and battle on his fevered mind.

But the part of him that was Kukulcan drove him forward with raging eagerness against the rolling, turbid darkness.

The tunnel debouched into a mighty cavern. And here darkness seemed enthroned and supreme, a swirling blackness as of extraterrestrial abysses that blinded and staggered Abbott.

Hoarse, bellowing laughter like banterings in hell broke echoing around Abbott as he swayed irresolute.

"So you came to meet me, Kukulcan? Then be it so!" it mocked.

A titan thunderclap rocked the mountain as bright lightning flashed from outside along the tunnels into this buried cavern.

The throbbing flare of fiery radiance for a moment illumined the whole interior of the cavernous space to Abbott's eyes.

He saw, across the cavern, the gigantic, looming stone image of a huge bat with outspread wings, whose red jewel-eyes glared down at him and at whose feet Shuima's slim body lay unmoving.

And he saw also Ummax towering beside him, black mace already raised to dash down upon his head!

The lightning-flash died—and Abbott whirled away and heard the whistle of the mace as it grazed past him in falling.

Wrapped again in the suffocating cold darkness, Abbott lunged and stabbed with his sword—but stabbed empty air.

"This darkness is *my* realm!" mocked Ummax' voice. "You cannot escape—"

The lightning flared in the tunnels again, and in time to show Abbott that the towering Mayan was charging him.

Abbott struck savagely before the flare should fade, and felt his sword bite into his antagonist's shoulder. But the whirling mace struck his head a glancing blow, this time.

He staggered, felt himself falling, heard Ummax' hoarse shout of triumph. Desperately, as he fell, Abbott caught at the Mayan's legs and brought him down before he could swing the mace again.

They grappled on the rock floor of the cavern, Ummax ferociously choking him into helplessness. And the dancing flares of lightning that were now continuous in the outer tunnels showed Abbott the distorted face of Ummax as the supreme horror.

For it was the handsome, evil *alien* face he had twice before glimpsed that now had usurped Ummax' features.

Face of Zotzilha glaring down at him from the human body it used as instrument? Was his own face in this terrible moment the countenance of Garth Abbott or of Kukulcan?

His shaken senses were fading as Ummax' great hands throttled him. The towering Mayan leaped up, snatching up the black mace to bring it down on Abbott in a final death-blow.

Ummax' wounded shoulder checked him for a moment, forced him to shift his grip upon the mace. And in that moment, with desperate upsurge of last strength, Abbott bounded up and whirled his sword and struck.

He felt the sword crash *through* the uplifted mace, shattering it to fragments! He felt it tear deep into the towering Mayan's breast!

"Beaten, driven, by the Bright One!" howled Ummax as he staggered. "Forever exiled—"

Thunder rocked the mountain wildly, and the fiery serpents of lightning in the tunnels showed Abbott that as Ummax fell it was the Mayan's own gross face that now was stiffening in death.

And Abbott felt, at the same moment, release from the strange tension of possession that had seemed to grip him all this night.

Gone dark Zotzilha, forced back into the black abysses from which he had long ago crept into earth? And gone too Kukulcan, his mission finished?

Abbott heard the grind and roll of shifting rock, and by the fading flare his dazed eyes saw the giant bat-winged image rocking forward on its base.

He sprang unsteadily and snatched Shuima's slim figure aside as the statue raised of old by Zotzilha's worshipers ponderously leaned and fell and crashed to ruin.

"The Bat-winged!" choked the Mayan girl fearfully when he had carried her into the outer tunnel, and had revived her.

"It has perished, and there is no more to fear," he told her hoarsely.

Shuima clung to him, quivering. "Ummax would have sacrificed me to it, as he has sacrificed many others. Yes, for ages, dark Zotzilha has drunk the life of victims in that dread cavern."

Had it been so? Had, for centuries, some dark and alien being from beyond fed upon the life-force of men and women in monstrous vampirism? Or was that only superstition masking brutal murder?

"You have set Xibalba free from that horror, Lord Kukulcan!"

"Kukulcan no more," he told her. "Whatever I was tonight, possessed or mad, I am so no longer."

Possession or momentary madness? He would never know which, for certain. He might come more and more to believe that only the influence of time and place and superstition had given him those queer delusions of having been an instrument in a struggle transcending earth.

But, remembering the strange chain of fate that had brought him from a chance-found tomb to lead the fight against evil tyranny of this lost, forgotten race, he would never be too sure!

He walked unsteadily with Shuima out through the tunnels to the stone landing, and stood there with her in the flare of the dying storm as he faced the frantic acclaim of Huroc and his warriors.

"The Plumed Serpent is victor! Hail the Holder of Kukulcan, the new lord of Xibalba!"

Abbott knew then that whatever had brought him to Xibalba, he would stay here. He could bring these people the best of the outside world, could in time reveal them to that world.

But all that lay in future years. For now, standing with his arm tightening around Shuima, he was content.

The King of Shadows

John Fallon knew that he was going to have trouble with his Kirghiz guides, when he saw the little leather drums they had beside them as they sat around the campfire.

Shaman drums, those! And that meant that the four Kirghiz were afraid—afraid of something that wasn't human.

"I should have known it," Fallon muttered to himself. "They've been getting jumpier every mile nearer the mountains."

The mountains loomed northward, a black, giant barrier, shouldering the stars. They were an unexplored spur of the Kunlun Range that sprawled half a thousand miles across this high, lonely roof of the world where Tibet, India and China met.

The moon was rising, and from its direction blew a keenly chill wind that grabbled at the little campfire and then screeched on eerily through the narrow pass that split the range. Fallon had wanted to camp inside that pass, but the Kirghiz had demurred.

The hobbled pack-ponies stirred nervously as Fallon strode toward the fire. In the shifting red light, the flat, swart faces of the four natives looked up sullenly from under their sheepskin caps.

Fallon spoke casually in the Altaic language he had learned during his weeks of search.

"We had better sleep now. We'll want to start early through that pass tomorrow."

The four swart faces darkened. Then Mursul, the wrinkled, wizened oldest of the Kirghiz, spoke for them.

"Fallon-khan, we cannot go there! The land inside those mountains is forbidden, accursed! The lair of Erlik!"

As he pronounced that supremely dreaded name, old Mursul made a curious, swift gesture drawn from the antiquity of shaman religion. The other Kirghiz hastily repeated the sign.

Fallon kept his voice even. "Listen, I hired you in Khotan for this job. I told you that I was hunting for a man, and that I would hunt until I found him. And we haven't found him yet.

"His plane fell in this region—I know that from the direction of his last radio call. We've narrowed it down to this particular sector, and he's got to be here."

"Dead," muttered one of the younger Kirghiz. "You said it was a year ago. The man would be dead, by now."

"Or worse, if he fell in forbidden Santahar!" added old Mursul.

"He isn't dead to me till I find his body," Fallon said grimly. "Rick Carnaby was my friend. We flew from India to China together for two war years. When the war ended I swore I'd come back here and find him, and I'm going to. And you're going to help me."

Mursul stood up, a shapeless figure in his sheepskins, his withered face earnest in the firelight.

"Fallon-khan, you think us frightened children. It is not so! I have ridden from the Altai snows to the sands of the Kizil Kum, in my time! These old hands have killed Mongols!

"But we know that no sword or gun can avail against what lies within these peaks. In there dwell they who lived before the world—the Lord of Shadows and his ghostly people. Dark Erlik, who is older than the Earth!"

Fallon felt the impact of the other's fanaticism. He began to realize the hopelessness of combating it.

He remembered now what Martillette, the old French missionary up in Khotan, had told him of the ancient shaman beliefs of all these Central Asian peoples.

"They don't worship any gods," Martilette had said. "They think the gods are too far away to bother about us. But they say that the great rebel against the gods, the lord of evil, whose name is Erlik, is right here on Earth.

"Erlik is a type—perhaps a prototype—of Lucifer the rebel angel, of Satan, of Ahriman. But to them he's real. They call him the King of Shadows and say that he and his weird brood still dwell in a hidden mountain fastness called Santahar."

Fallon, looking down at the half-sullen, half-scared swart faces in the firelight, made one last attempt to conquer that superstition.

"Let it be so, then," he sneered. "I will go through the pass to search while you wait outside. That will make a pretty tale for the girls of Khotan—that four Men of the Sword were afraid of—shadows!"

He laughed scornfully. " *'Tokta, shungru!'* they'll call when you ride back through the Silver Gate. 'Run, sheep-men!' "

The youngest of the Kirghiz leaped to his feet, eyes glittering passion as his hand went instinctively to his yataghan hilt.

"I fear neither man nor demon!" he spat. "No one will ever call me—"

He broke off. His eyes, looking beyond Fallon, lost all their fiery passion and suddenly dilated.

"Hala an Erlik!" he yelled hoarsely, and wildly pointed.

Fallon spun around, and was momentarily frozen by an inexplicable sight.

A vertical scimitar of milky light clove the moonlit heavens above the shadowy, looming range. It wavered, twitched, like the beam of a colossal aurora streaming up the sky.

But this was no aurora, no fan of quivering pale rays. This was a single slash of milky light, from the inner ranges to the stars, pulsing up in wild, flaring beauty.

"The road of Erlik!" the Kirghiz was hoarsely repeating. "And see, Erlik's shadow-demons come down it from the sky!"

Fallon *did* glimpse a flicker of movement down that incredible banner-beam of light! A movement the eye could not clearly distinguish, as of shadowy things racing headlong earthward down the beam.

The racing rush of shadowy movement ceased, as he detected it. The great sword of light wavered, twitched—and was gone.

"It was only a queer aurora!" he said hastily as he turned. "There's nothing—"

Chuck-a-boom! Chuck-a-boom! The little shaman drums were throbbing under the frantic hands of old Mursul and one of the other Kirghiz.

"Erlik's shadows come for us now!" screeched Mursul. "Only the *tiungur* drums will save us!"

Shadows? There *were* little shadows gliding over the moonlit plain between them and the nearby pass! It was at them that Mursul and the others were staring in horrible fright.

Frenziedly louder throbbed the little shaman drums above the keen of the rising wind.

"Hell, it's only cloud-shadows!" Fallon swore. "Can't you see—"

Fallon stiffened as he looked up, his voice trailing into shocked silence. There were no clouds across the moon!

Yet the shadows out there on the dim plain were still gliding, swirling, advancing—

"Dwar Erlik!" sobbed Mursul's shrill voice over the frantic drumming. "The shadows of Erlik!"

The horses plunged wildly away from the camp, trying to break their hobbles, squealing in terror.

Fallon ran after them. "Your damned drums are scaring the ponies! Stop it!"

The drumming, the hoarse incantations, didn't stop. Fallon got the bridles of two of the ponies and tried to quiet their wild plunging.

They dragged him farther from the campfire and the rattling drums, away from the direction of the looming range. Fallon yelled for help that didn't come, and mentally damned all superstition.

Hanging to the bridles of the maddened ponies, he glimpsed an incredible scene at the campfire back there. The shadows were swirling around it!

Like dusky man-shapes those shadows glided around the red fire and the little knot of huddled men, as though questing—

Chuck-a-boom! Boom!

The hovering shadows there seemed oddly to recoil from that storm of dissonant vibration from the shaman drums!

The two ponies Fallon held broke their hobbles with an almost human scream of terror, and tore free from his grasp.

"Fallon-khan!" screeched Mursul's voice from over the crazy clatter of drums.

Fallon whirled, and froze motionless. One of the gliding shadows was close to him in the silver moonlight!

There were others behind it. And they were not flat shadows on the ground. They were erect, manlike shadow-shapes—like dark ghosts gliding toward him.

Fallon's heart hammered as that nearest shadow-shape approached him. This couldn't be real—it couldn't—

It was a girl-shape, this approaching shadow. A dark wraith slim and youthful, so sharply outlined beneath the moon that he could *see* its silhouette of lithe body and shapely little head, and reaching arms—

Those shadow-arms touched him! Fallon felt an icy, numbing shock in which the moonlit plain, the firelight and the thump of the shaman drums, seemed to recede to an immeasurable remoteness.

Shadow-face, girl's face, was close to his as his senses reeled into the abyss! Like the silhouette of a sweet, strange face he saw it, as unconsciousness pressed upon his brain.

Fallon was dimly aware that with an unsubstantial shadow-arm leading him, he was walking stiffly and without volition. Walking toward the moonlit mountain-range, toward the dark split of the pass!

He heard Mursul's screech of terror as though from far away in time and space. "Fallon-khan!"

Then unconsciousness possessed him completely.

II

Fallon awoke slowly. He seemed to struggle back to consciousness through numbing mists. He lay looking dazedly around him.

He was lying in a dusky stone room, a small chamber with high groined ceiling. One tall, unglazed window framed an erect oblong of moonlight. Wind whispered into the moonlit chamber from the opening.

"Why, what—" Fallon muttered numbly. And then suddenly crashing waves of memory rocked his mind.

"The Kirghiz! The shadows they were afraid of—good God!"

Fallon sprang erect, trembling and wild, clutching for support the ancient-looking bronze couch on which he had been lying.

It and two equally ancient bronze chairs were the only furniture of the dusky stone chamber. The corrosion of the bronze pieces, the thick dust in corners, spoke of ages of non-use…

"A shadow—a girl-shadow—that gripped my arm and led me away! Led me *where?*"

He stumbled toward the open window and stared wildly out into the moonshot darkness. And he looked out on a dark, fantastic city.

Domed, massive buildings of dark stone bulked somber in the silver moonlight. He was himself high in one of these round buildings.

Some distance away bulked the biggest mass—a domed, dark citadel that loomed starkly above all else, but there was no light or sound there, nor anywhere else in this weirdly unmodern metropolis.

"A dead city," Fallon whispered. "Like those whose ruins Stein found up by Khotan. But this one, hidden here inside the mountains—"

He had glimpsed the ring of frowning peaks and scarps that surrounded the silent, moonlit city on all sides.

He had come through the pass into this mountain-guarded land, without his own volition! Had come, led by—shadows!

Fallon fought rising terror. This was delirium, surely. He'd had some kind of mental lapse, had wandered into this dead city—

But was the city dead? His heart jumped suddenly. He had glimpsed movement down in those dark, silent streets.

He leaned from the window, straining his eyes. Yes, there was something stirring vaguely in the streets below.

Shadows moved in those streets! Dark, erect human shapes that were like the shadowy wraiths of men and women!

"The land of Erlik, King of Shadows, whose city is forbidden Santahar—" The old Kirghiz' warning echoed now in his mind.

With a strangled cry, Fallon recoiled from the window and stumbled panically toward the door of the room. Then he stopped short.

In the doorway poised a human-figured thing of darkness, a shadow that poised, watching him!

A shadow? No, it was more like a human figure composed of opaque dark gasses, now that he saw it clearly.

He recognized the dark silhouette as a girl's slim figure, and remembered at once the high-cheekboned little profile of the face.

"You—whoever, whatever you are—you brought me here!" Fallon said aloud, hoarsely. "I remember, now."

She—he could not think of that slim shadow by any other pronoun—glided toward him. Fallon recoiled, his skin crawling. But the gliding girl-shadow swiftly reached out a shadowy arm to touch him.

At the intangible touch, something of the paralysis of his former experience went through Fallon like an icy shock. But this time it did not numb his brain as before.

He seemed suddenly to see the girl-shadow before him more clearly—the sweet planes of her face, the watching eyes, the coils of dusky hair knotted behind her shapely little head.

"You are from the outer lands—the lands of Earth that lie beyond the mountains?" he heard her voice.

Her voice? No, he was not *hearing* her speak. He felt her speech, received it in his brain as a direct electric transmission of thought-currents, a clear, mental voice.

Some contact, some circuit between his mind and this girl of shadow, had been established by the touch of her hand.

"Who—what—are you?" Fallon whispered, staring wildly.

The answer came quickly. "Do not fear me! I am Valain of the First Race—the race that still dwells here in Santahar."

"Santahar?" He husked the name. "Then the Kirghiz told truth—this is the city of Erlik?"

"So you know of our Lord?" Valain said quickly. "Then legends still persist in the outer lands. But the other did not know—"

"The other?" For a moment, sudden excitement made Fallon almost forget the uncanny terror of this incredible experience. "The other? Do you mean a man like myself? Do you mean Rick Carnaby?"

The girl-shadow started. "Then you know the man Carnaby?"

"I'm John Fallon, his best friend, and I came here after him!" Fallon cried. "Then his plane did crash here? Where is he?"

"You shall see him soon," Valain assured. "But first, you go before Erlik. I am to bring you now."

Erlik? Devil-god of all Central Asia, dreaded rebel against heaven who was King of Shadows?

The momentary excitement at his discovery that Rick Carnaby was here, sucked out of Fallon's mind and left him prey again to the horror of incredible realization.

This girl Valain who touched him, whose mind spoke so clearly into his—she was *shadow!* Not real! And Erlik—

"Fallon, do not fear me!" came her quick mental plea. "I *am* real, and I was once human like yourself!

"Here is no magic!" she added. "It is but the science of the First Race that has made us so. Erlik will explain."

Something in her reassurance, some deep earnestness in the mind that so strangely touched his, lessened Fallon's horror a little. He could not feel that this girl—this shadow—meant him harm.

Valain's shadowy arm led Fallon from the dusky room, down dark stone corridors and crumbling stairs to the street.

And here in the moonlit street came and went the shadowy people of Santahar! Like Valain they were, human figures of dark non-solidity, gliding the ancient avenues, meeting and greeting silently.

Fallon moved unsteadily with Valain down that silent street of dark, thronging shadow-shapes. And the wraith-like men and women seemed to halt and look at him in wonder, as he passed.

"There's nothing supernatural!" he told himself frantically. "These shadow-people are natural, somehow."

They approached the looming dome of the central citadel. As they passed through its high, open portals, Fallon stopped. With a wonder transcending fear, he gazed into the great fane within.

In the lofty dome of this vast room was a wide, round opening through which the moonlight poured in a silver flood. It was reflected dazzlingly by a great circle of crystal set in the center of the floor.

Fallon saw shadow-shapes in here too—some just inside the portals, and others at the other side of the great room where rose a low stone dais that bore a massive bronze throne.

Valain's shadowy arm was urging him forward. "Lord Erlik awaits you! Come!" Fallon took a few mechanical steps inside the portals, and then something happened that he would never forget.

A shadow-shape glided suddenly from the little group inside the doors—a big, bulky male shape of darkness that seemed oddly familiar. It grasped Fallon's arm in that unsubstantial contact, and then—

"Johnny! Johnny Fallon!"

Fallon didn't hear that cry, other than mentally by the same strange telepathic contact as with Valain.

But though it was not auditory, something in its fiber triggered his memories so that instantly he recognized that oddly familiar silhouette that towered beside him.

"Rick Carnaby!" he cried. "Changed into—good God!"

It was the ultimate horror, to Fallon's rocking mind. Not even the shadowy hosts of Santahar had assaulted him with equal horror.

For Valain and those other people of the First Race, he had seen as shadow-shapes from the first. But big, grinning Rick Carnaby, transformed by hell-born magic into an unreal shadow of himself—

He fought for control, as he heard Rick's alarmed, agonized thoughts. "Johnny, you followed me here? You shouldn't have come!"

The big, wide-shouldered figure, the battered, button-nosed face, they were utterly familiar even in dark silhouette. He could even see the tautness in Rick's face, his clenched hands.

"What did they *do* to you?" ripped Fallon's cry. "It's horrible—"

"Johnny, listen, you don't understand!" Rick Carnaby began swiftly.

Then that nightmare scene was interrupted by Valain's clear, utterly urgent mental voice.

"Lord Erlik is watching. You *must* come now!"

Fallon felt himself tugged forward by that paralyzing force the girl-shadow could wield. He stumbled unseeingly in his horror.

Valain did not lead across that brilliant circle of crystal in the center, but around the edge of the room to the dais.

Fallon found himself standing before the dais, looking up dazedly at the massive, tarnished bronze throne that stood upon it.

On that throne, looking down at him, there sat—a shadow. A dark, living silhouette of a young man whose profile was cleanly handsome.

"Lord Erlik!" whispered Valain's thought to him.

Erlik! The legended King of Shadows dreaded for ages by half of Asia! The Fallen One, the foe of heaven!

Fallon felt blind hatred rage up in his mind. The brooding, unhuman shadow up there might be the prototype of Satan and Ahriman, but he was not afraid. Hatred swept fear from his brain.

"You're the one who did that to Rick Carnaby!" Fallon husked, glaring up at the shadowy shape. "Made him unhuman!"

Erlik's clear mental voice, calm and silvery, came into Fallon's mind telepathically without need even of shadowy contact.

"Yes, Fallon, I did that, just as I did it to my own people of Santahar long ago."

Fallon's trembling rage exploded. He bounded forward onto the dais, and his hand ripped his automatic from his belt. He fired a stream of shots into the shadowy shape on the throne.

Simultaneous with the thunderous echoes of the gunfire came a telepathic cry from Rick Carnaby, just behind him.

"Johnny, *don't!* Wait—"

The shots had not harmed Erlik. It had been madness to think they could harm one whose body was not of solidity.

But as the last bullet crashed harmlessly against the back of the throne, Erlik's shadowy arm reached swiftly forward. It touched Fallon's face.

The terrific shock of that energy-laden contact seemed to sweep Fallon violently into roaring blackness.

III

It seemed to Fallon that he was a shadow like Erlik, and that with Erlik he moved through a blackness vast and immeasurable.

He was clearly conscious of the strange quality of his new body. For it was a body that his mind inhabited, and not mere shadow. A body that was of discrete particles of force, instead of matter!

He and Erlik glided together through that awesome abyss, moving without hindrance across spatial dimensions at velocities beyond the leap of thought. And they were rushing toward a vast, lenticular shower of sparks that blazed in the dark.

"Now behold, John Fallon!" came Erlik's silver voice. "You see beneath you the galaxy of stars that is Earth's home!"

Fallon *did* see. He saw, as he heard, not by ordinary sensory organs but by vastly more flexible and subtle senses that pulsed inside his new, strange body of shadowy force.

He saw that burning host of stars from a dozen different points of view at the same time, from far away and from very close—and all these segments of vision were unconfused in his mind.

Erlik's voice rang again into his mind, as he stared wonderingly.

"You see our galaxy as it was long ago when the First Race ruled all of its starry spaces, before the Aliens came!"

Fallon's strange new vision leaped across a spectacle of wonder. He saw human-peopled worlds, in thousands on tens of thousands. He saw their ships flash through space from star to star.

He knew that this was the First Race, his own human race, which was not child of Earth as he had supposed but long ago had merely colonized Earth as an incident in its glorious expansion through the universe.

"Yes, the First Race of which Earth's peoples are the unknowing descendants," murmured Erlik. "You have seen their ancient glory. And now see how that glory ended."

Fallon saw that out of the shoreless abyss outside the galaxy came strange, brooding bulks of blackness without form or figure. And these alien entities could combine and recombine in great groups.

They were outsiders, life evolved in the unimaginably remote abyss. They invaded the galaxy in hosts, settled upon worlds like brooding vampires. The weapons of the First Race could not harm them.

"They are the Aliens!" rang Erlik's somber thought. "Creatures not of matter but of energy evolved in the gulfs outside our cosmos. They invaded our worlds, enslaved us by billions. They drove us back across the galaxy till this little Earth was our last free world.

"Then in the city Santahar on Earth, we scientists of the First Race took counsel. We could not resist the Aliens with ordinary weapons. Soon they would conquer and enslave the last free remnant of our race here, unless we found a way to match their powers.

"I, Prince Erlik, found the way! We must become like the Aliens, creatures of force rather than matter! Then we could meet them on equal terms. I devised the instruments that transformed each material particle of our bodies into a tiny vortex of undying energy, so that our new bodies of energy retained our mind-patterns and knowledge and will.

"Thus we of Santahar long ago became—undying shadows. The other peoples of Earth recoiled from our plan, would not follow us. And in time, we of Santahar became mere fearful legend to them.

"But *we,* in the ages since then, have lived on in our undying new bodies and have held off the Aliens from Earth! We have warded the unsuspecting Earth whose myths told of us as foes of heaven! Now see that war in far-off space we have waged to beat back the Aliens!"

John Fallon glimpsed that awful struggle. He saw the shadow-hosts of Santahar flash out into trackless space again and again, along that rushing beam of light they called the Road.

He saw the Aliens whose formless bulks ever and again glided toward Earth, each time met and driven back by Erlik's shadowy hosts. His mind reeled at the spectacle of incredible battle out there between Earth and Sirius—shadows fighting with weapons of their own vital energy that they could launch in blinding bolts.

"Ever we have pressed them a little farther back!" rang Erlik's cry. "Soon, we will free the enslaved humans of Sirius' worlds from them. And then, with an added strength, we shall press on until we have won back all the galaxy for the First Race!

"That is the struggle which unknown to Earth has gone on for ages, John Fallon! The struggle in which you too can play a part—as one of us!"

Fallon felt a wild throb of mingled excitement and dread. And then he felt his shadowy form changing back into his own solid body—

He opened his eyes. He was lying on the bronze couch in that dusky stone chamber where he had first awakened.

"Good God!" he cried. "Then all that was a dream—"

His voice trailed off. Over him bent a shadow—Valain!

"It was no dream, Fallon," came Valain's quick telepathic assurance. "Erlik held your mind for a little time, and what he showed you was true.

And then I led you back here, at his command."

Fallon looked up numbly at her sweet-profiled silhouette of darkness. "Then all you—shadows—were really human once?"

"Yes, Fallon." Valain's answer was faintly wistful. "But that was long ago. We became like this, so that we could match the Aliens."

Her thought was almost pleading. "Do we seem so horrible to you because of that?"

Fallon shook his head dazedly. "God, no! If all that was true, you of Erlik's people have guarded Earth from the Aliens for ages!"

Then sudden sharper remembrance made him sit up. "But Rick! You didn't have to make *him* one of you! Why did you do it?"

"Johnny, listen!"

It was Rick Carnaby's mental voice that echoed in Fallon's brain. He spun around.

The bulky, shadowy figure of Rick stood behind him, a hand on his shoulder. Again, Fallon felt passionate resentment at the sight.

"Rick, I've hunted for you and now I've found you like this! Isn't there some way you can be changed back to your own body?"

Rick Carnaby's thought came solemnly. "Johnny, I don't want to be changed back. It would only mean that I would die."

"You'd die?" repeated Fallon, bewildered. "But why—"

"Johnny, listen! My plane crashed here in Santahar and I was fatally hurt. I was dying when Erlik used the forces of which he is master, to transform me into this shadow-body of energy!

"They saved me from death by making me one of them. And I *am* one of them now, helping in that great fight against the Aliens."

Incredulous amazement held John Fallon as he looked up into the shadowy face of his friend.

"Rick, you mean that *you* have gone out there beyond our Earth, too?"

"Many times, I've come and gone by the Road," Rick Carnaby answered simply. His thought rang eager. "And fighting the Aliens out there beats flying against Japs, Johnny! This is a fight for all Earth!"

Fallon remembered something out of that swift vision that Erlik had poured into his mind. He felt an icy chill.

"They're going to do the same thing to me?" he whispered. "Make *me* shadow, too?"

Valain answered troubledly. "Erlik says that you must not go back to carry news of us to outer Earth. We would have hordes of your folk coming here, attempting to enter Santahar.

"Therefore, says Erlik, you must stay in Santahar! You can stay as one of us, letting Erlik's science transform you. Or if you refuse, he will cast you into mindless sleep from which you will not awaken."

Fallon felt a shrinking horror at that dreadful choice offered him.

"I couldn't give up my real body, become a shadow!"

"You must decide by tomorrow night," Valain said troubledly. "For then the Road will be opened to send more of us out to Sirius. And Erlik himself is to lead those of us who go this time."

Rick Carnaby's thought broke in tautly. "Johnny, I won't let them do it to you! You came here after me—it's my fault—"

"What can you do to save him?" murmured Valain to Rick. "Erlik has set me to watch him. Even if he evaded me and escaped outside the mountains, we could follow and seize him as we did last night."

Fallon looked at her dazedly. "You were sent to seize me because I was too near the mountains? Why didn't you take the Kirghiz too?"

"Their drums held us back," Valain told him. "The vibrations prevent our seizing their minds. But you were not near the drums."

"A trick of vibration, Johnny," nodded Rick. "The Central Asian shaman cult evolved it out of superstition but it has sound scientific basis. The drums produce a pattern of sonic vibrations which by self-hypnosis defends the shamans against mental attack."

Bright morning sunlight had crept into the stone chamber. And Rick Carnaby, a fantastic shadow-figure in the light, turned away.

"Tomorrow is already here," his thought came swiftly. "I'm going to see Erlik now! I'll make him let you go, Johnny!"

"It is useless," murmured Valain. "Erlik will not change his decree."

But Rick's thought beat confidently into Fallon's mind. "Keep your nerve, Johnny! I'll be back!"

As his big, shadowy figure glided out of the room, Fallon looked numbly after him. His stunned mind still could not realize the dread fact that this might be his last day of human life.

He to become a shadow-shape of energy? Impossible, an unreal nightmare! It could not happen—

From Valain's slim, shadowy figure came a questioning thought. "Are you hungry? I had almost forgotten that you might be."

Fallon had forgotten too, but now he numbly realized that he had not eaten for many hours and that his throat was dry with thirst.

"There is still food of a sort here in Santahar," Valain told him. "Come!"

He followed her mechanically down crumbling stairs and out the back of the massive building, into what had once been a gracious garden.

Trees shaped like conifers but bearing pale yellow and rosy fruit had run wild here. They grew amid brush and weeds, clustering thickest around a mined stone spring that still gushed icy water.

As he ate the pulpy, insipid fruits, Fallon felt that dazing horror lift a little from his brain. Valain watched him curiously.

"*We* drink energy from vortexes of force here in Santahar, so that when we return to the struggle we can be strong," she said.

Her slim, dark silhouette poised in the bright sunlight, as she looked around the ruined garden.

"In the old days, this was the loveliest spot in Santahar," she murmured. I remember walking here on moonlit nights, long ago."

It struck Fallon suddenly, the realization that she had once been as humanly real as himself.

He could picture Santahar as it had been then—a splendid city of fair men and women. Men and women who now were undying shadows!

IV

"Yes, Santahar was beautiful then but the shadow of the Aliens was over it," said Valain. "We knew that soon they would come to Earth as they had invaded all our other worlds.

"Thus, when Erlik's science opened the way for us to change and resist the Aliens, we did not hesitate. We stepped willingly out of our former life, into the age-long struggle.

"But yet"—her thought had a poignant quality—"yet I cannot forget that other life. I wish that for a little time, for a very little time, I could be human once again."

"I wish so too, Valain!" Fallon said impulsively. "I've never met a girl like you."

She looked down at him, and in the tilt of her shadowy little head, in the tone of her thought, was a touch of diablerie.

"Is it possible that you would waste soft words upon—a shadow?"

"I can't think of you as that, Valain," he said slowly. "Any more than I can think of Rick so."

The little flash of gay mockery vanished as she put her shadowy hand in an intangible touch against his.

"I am glad you said that, Fallon, I am glad that you do not think of me with horror."

"Valain, couldn't the process that changed you be reversed?" Fallon asked suddenly. "Couldn't you become real again and leave here?"

Her shadowy figure started. "I could not do that! It is true the change can be reversed, but I couldn't leave Erlik and the others."

"You don't want to live human life again?" he asked, puzzled.

There was the quality of a sob in Valain's telepathic cry. "I would give centuries of this immortal shadow-existence for one year of real human life again! But I could not desert Erlik and our host now when our age-long battle nears a crisis. For in the struggle with the Aliens out there, a crisis is near at hand."

Fallon was silent a moment. "I understand, Valain. I've been a soldier. And if I *do* have to join you and share your fight—"

Emotion seemed to quiver through her shadowy figure as she interrupted. "Let us not speak of what may come tonight! Tell me of your world and people, Fallon."

He talked, sitting there in the silent, ruined garden while the sun wheeled overhead. Telling of Earth's lands and peoples, of their wars and ways, he forgot that it was a shadow-shape who listened.

He could not think of the slim, silhouetted figure beside him as other than a real and living girl. And it seemed to Fallon that in their quick and complete mental rapport he found a kinship of spirit he had found in no other woman.

"I wish I could see those cities," Valain murmured. "For so long, I have known nothing but dead Santahar and the Road that takes us out to the struggle in the great abyss."

"Do none of you ever perish in that struggle with the Aliens?" he asked her.

"Many have perished," she answered soberly. "But we have recruited our numbers from those who strayed in here, as you and Rick did. And once Sirius' worlds are liberated, we shall have great hosts to help."

Then her shadowy arm made a quick gesture toward the sky. "The day is dying, already. Rick should have returned."

Fallon felt a cold thrill along his nerves as he realized that hours had passed and that night was not far away.

"I hope that he has won Erlik to let you go," Valain murmured. "But I am afraid—"

When they went back into the dusky building, Rick Carnaby was just returning. And in the way the big, shadowy figure approached them, Fallon read defeat.

Rick's thought was desperate. "For hours, Erlik wouldn't see me. And when he did, he rejected my plea. He says that in this crisis we can't risk Fallon going away and bringing outsiders back to Santahar!"

Fallon tried to keep his face unmoved. "You did your best, Rick. It seems that I've no choice but to become—one of you."

"I won't let it happen!" stormed Rick desperately. "I'll do something—"

Valain's clear thought interrupted. "There is nothing you can do. But I could get Fallon away."

Fallon stared at her shadowy face in amazement. And Rick's thought was incredulous. "You, Valain? But why should you—"

She interrupted passionately. "Because today I have remembered our old human life, and I do not want to rob another of that life! Because I do not want Fallon to share our shadowy immortality!"

Her thoughts raced swiftly. "Soon all our people will be gathering in the citadel for the opening of the Road. I can guide Fallon out of Santahar to the pass. Before night ends, he can be far outside the mountains."

"But Erlik set you as his guard!" Rick Carnaby exclaimed. "When he learns what you have done—"

"I'll not let you help me if it brings danger to you, Valain!" cried Fallon.

"There is no danger!" retorted the shadow-girl. "Lord Erlik will be very angry, but that is all. For the great crisis of our struggle is too near for him to think long of this matter."

She turned back to Rick Carnaby. "But you must not go with us. If you are not there when the Road opens, Erlik would suspect."

Rick's shadowy form bent nearer the haggard Fallon. "Then—then this is good-bye, Johnny. I wish we could shake hands!"

Fallon felt a lump in his throat. "'Good-bye, Rick."

And then the other was gone, gliding out of the dusky room. Rick Carnaby, gusty, swearing war-pilot of the old days, now a shadow-warrior on his way to greater struggle than any Earthly war!

Night had come, down upon Santahar, and the moon already cast slanting silver beams over the dark domes. And through the window, Fallon saw the shadow-hosts converging through the streets upon the looming citadel of Erlik.

Valain's shadowy hand touched him, with that little tingling shock that the contact always brought.

"We must start now!" she told him. "For a little time, the way is clear."

Her intangible touch was still upon his arm, leading him, as he went down with her into the street.

Valain led swiftly through the moon-bright city. They met no shadow-shapes as they traversed its silent ways. But as they neared the edge of Santahar, there came a sound from behind them.

It was a sharp, twanging sound as of forces suddenly released. And looking back, Fallon saw that now a tremendous beam of milky light stabbed up from Erlik's citadel toward the stars of Canis Major.

"The Road has been opened!" Valain's thought came swiftly. "Now those who bring report to Erlik from the struggle will come down it. And soon then we will be missed! We must hurry!"

Fallon started to run, with Valain gliding effortlessly beside him. As he ran, he looked back again.

He saw now that strange flicker of shadowy things, racing down the flaring Road! Shadow-warriors, couriers from the great struggle out there by Sirius, racing back to Santahar with report for Erlik!

"Faster, Fallon!" begged Valain. "The pass is still far away—"

It seemed to Fallon that he was running faster than any man normally could, that Valain's shadowy touch on his arm was pouring vital energy into him to spur him forward!

The mountain-wall loomed ever vaster before them. Now amid its moon-silvered cliffs he could make out the dark crack of the pass.

"We are near, now!" Valain encouraged. "Once you are far outside, you will be safe."

And then suddenly, swifter than the eye could follow, something flashed through the moonlight from behind them.

And abruptly, in the very mouth of the narrow pass, there stood a dark shadow-shape confronting them.

"Lord Erlik!" cried Valain, despair ringing in her thought.

Fallon felt an iciness grip him. For the dark silhouetted figure that stood before was clearly recognizable.

Erlik, indeed! And the Lord of Shadows was advancing toward them, gliding nearer until his handsome profile was clear in the moonlight.

"Did you think so easily to deceive me, Valain?" came his calm thought.

"There is no escape now, John Fallon!" sobbed Valain's mental cry. "I hoped for you—"

Her despair triggered a rage in Fallon, equal to that hot passion with which once before he had faced Erlik. His fists clenched despite his awareness of the futility of the gesture.

"It's all right, Valain," he said huskily. "I'm not afraid."

Erlik was looking curiously at the shadow-girl as Fallon tried to comfort her.

His silvery mental question was wondering. "So even a shadow can love, Valain? After all these ages?"

"It is so," Valain answered hopelessly. "But I didn't want to keep him with me as a shadow. I wanted him to live his human life."

Erlik's thought was musing. "I had almost forgotten our human emotions of long ago. Almost—"

Then his mental voice came decisively. "Fallon can go free. It matters not now if he brings the outside world to Santahar. For tonight we, *all* of us, leave Santahar by the Road!"

Exaltation throbbed from him. "Yes, tonight word has come that at last we have liberated the enslaved First Race of Sirius' worlds! Now we go out to lead their hosts in the final struggle that will drive the Aliens completely from our galaxy!"

Valain started. And then her shadowy figure turned toward Fallon. "Then this is farewell, Fallon!"

In Fallon's rioting mind, one thing stood out with passionate intensity. He leaned toward her sweet, shadowy face.

"Valain, you said you loved me! And I know now I love you, shadow or girl or both!"

Her thought yearned. "Fallon, you cannot love a shadow!"

"I do!" he cried. "I can't let you go!"

Erlik broke in calmly. "She must go, for this is the great hour for which we have lived our shadow-life for ages. But some day, she may return and change."

"I *will* return!" cried Valain. "I will come back to you and become human again for you, Fallon!"

For a moment, Fallon felt shadowy arms around him, shadowy face against his own—a bitter-sweet, intangible touch.

And then she and Erlik were gone—shadow-king and shadow-girl gliding away beneath the moon toward the domes of Santahar and the flaring Road.

Fallon looked back with tears in his eyes, at the somber city. Minutes passed, and then he saw it—a great rush of hosts of shadowy figures racing up the shining Road. And then slowly the great beam faded, and the city of Santahar lay dark and empty even of shadow-life.

Gone, the King of Shadows and his shadow-host! Gone Rick Carnaby, out to fight his dog-fights now amid the stars! Gone, Valain—

But she would return. In his mind was the certainty, the knowledge that some day she would return and that a strange science would again make real the shadow-girl he loved and would always love.

Fallon turned and started into the pass. It was a long way to the outer world. And it would be a long way back, with the supplies that he would bring.

For he would come back, and here in Santahar he would be waiting when at last Valain returned.

Serpent Princess

Hugh Macklin told himself that he was acting more like an imaginative boy than a serious, thirty-year-old archaeologist. But that couldn't stop the vague, meaningless dread that oppressed him.

He had lain awake for hours, on his narrow camp-cot. And it was not the hot closeness of the air inside the little tent, nor the solemn boom of surf from the nearby Persian Gulf, that had prevented him from sleeping.

"The wrath of Anu, lord of the sky; of Enlil, lord of the wind; of Adad, lord of the lightning; be on him who again opens this temple and uses its instrument to awaken evil Tiamat and her folk!"

That terrific invocation ran through Macklin's mind now, as it had ever since morning when they had first uncovered the blocked, sealed entrance of their great find, the temple of Tiamat.

De Ferdey, head of the expedition, had translated the crumbling columns of age-old cuneiform, his high-pitched voice shrill with excitement. The elderly little scholar had almost babbled, when Macklin and Thorpe confirmed his reading by independent translation.

"A temple dedicated to the serpent-goddess Tiamat! This proves that it's the oldest find in Babylonian archaeology! It makes Woolley's work at Ur, and de Morgan's at Elam, look modern!"

Roos, the hulking, fat Dutch artist who was sketcher for the De Ferdey Expedition, was the only one who had looked troubled then.

He had stood with them in the sandy excavation on the very shore of the blue Gulf, staring with puzzled eyes at the square, massive little stone building and the inscribed blocks that sealed its doorway.

"But why?" he had asked. "Why should they have put so terrific a curse on their own temple?"

"Enki wither his body, Nergal freeze his soul, Shamash burn him in fire, who awakens again those of the abyss whom I, Marduk, have bound!"

"Tiamat was the serpent-goddess of the sea-deeps, in ancient Babylonian legend," De Ferdey had explained. "She and her evil race were supposed to have been chained somehow by Marduk, ancient hero-king."

The little scholar's eyes had kindled. "It's always been supposed Marduk was only a solar myth—but this inscription proves he really lived! A ruler of the world's dawn who suppressed the worship of Tiamat!

"We'll know more of this when we open the temple tomorrow!"

Tomorrow was only hours away, now. And still Macklin had not been able to sleep, because of that vague oppression.

It was ridiculous, he told himself in renewed self-disgust. The people who had carved that inscription had been dust six thousand years and more. They and their invocations and curses were merely material now for a scholarly monograph.

Macklin knew an old trick of sleep he had learned from an Asian shaman. He used it now, willing his feet, his limbs, his body, to relax.

He slept. And, it seemed instantly, the vague oppression that he had felt leaped suddenly into horror.

The sound came first. Faint and distant, the mere echo of a memory of a sound. It crept to him through the night and touched him with delicate cold fingers, and somehow he knew what the sound was. Someone, long ago in another world, had struck a great crystal bell. Hugh Macklin could hear it speaking still, clear and sweet and wicked, like the pulsing of an alien heart.

In his dream, Macklin saw himself rise and go out of the tent, because the bell-note called him and he knew that he must go.

He stood on the shore of the dark sea, looking outward, and now the crystal singing of the bell blended with the voices of the waves and the sea wind, but was strengthened rather than lost. It called him still, and Hugh Macklin followed, out into the sea.

The black water closed over his head. He was not afraid of the water. He was not conscious of cold or the need to breathe. He felt himself gliding swiftly downward, deeper and deeper into the gulf, and still the bell sang to him.

He was afraid of the bell. Terribly afraid. And yet as he plunged downward into the utter blackness of the ocean bed he was aware of a growing excitement, an eagerness that ran through him like sudden fire.

Then a strange knowledge came to him, though in his dream it did not seem strange. The lovely crystalline voice of the bell was only the stronger echo of another voice, more delicate, more beautiful, more evil.

The voice of a woman, calling from the long night shadows of the sea.

Pale phosphorescence, pale spreading light like the silver radiance of stars. Macklin knew that he was almost *there.* He saw the great cliffs rising sheer behind their veils of water, and the long clean stretch of sand and whitened shells that was the ocean floor. He saw—the city.

Crystal towers, cut from the clear green-white crests of breaking waves. Walls of coral and floors of the shining silver sand. He passed over the clustered roofs, where they lay between the two folding arms of the black cliffs. He looked down, and saw the blurred, still shapes that slept in the crystal chambers, dreaming dreams as old as the sea.

But he did not pause. He rushed on, with a terrible hungry eagerness.

Above the city, apart from it, like a diamond on some great primal altar, a crystal palace stood on a ledge of rock. And the woman's voice spoke in Hugh Macklin's soul, and it was glad, and full of power.

The bright walls flowed past him like a broken star, and he was in the palace.

Upward through the silent gleaming halls, moving with the floating smoothness of a dream. Upward past vaulted chambers where the great golden doors stood open, swinging with the stately breathing of the sea. Upward to the highest tower, and the stillness was deeper than death.

She waited for him, there.

No one barred the way. No guard was at the door but a flight of little fish like a shower of butterflies. She had no handmaids, no courtiers, no one to attend her. But even now she had worshippers. Great shadowy creatures hung in the clear water around her as she slept, their fins moving slowly, slowly, and a long coiling shape curled lovingly around her, its shining head upon her shoulder, watching with cold strange eyes.

Macklin saw these things vaguely, as he saw the high clear vault of the roof and the couch whereon she lay, that was like an open shell and glowed like mother of pearl. But they did not matter. *She* was all that mattered.

Her voice would be like a faery bell, ringing silver in his heart. If she moved, her body would have the grace of all the sea's bright children, sinuous strength, wonderful ease and quickness. Her limbs were smooth, shaped out of the joyous whiteness of foam, and it seemed a pity that they should be so still.

She was human and yet she was not human. She was more beautiful than any human woman Macklin had ever seen. She was beautiful like the morning of the world, when the gods were born out of sunlight and sea waves and the strength of the wind. There was no weakness in her, no fear, no change. The heavy trampling feet of the ages of mankind had never touched her, and somehow Macklin knew that to her there was no such thing as death.

It was a pity that she slept. A pity that such wondrous life must be so still.

He looked into her face, her lovely face that had in it a shining wickedness so far beyond the petty evils of human life that it ceased to have the meaning of wrong as Macklin knew it. Her shadowed eyelids brushed her cheeks with gleaming lashes, and Macklin's heart was wrung with the pain of it, that she slept and he could not look into her eyes.

But she could speak to him! Macklin heard the singing crystal voice clearly in his mind now, and knew that it was her mind that spoke to his.

"Yes, my mind," came her sweet whisper of thought. "*It* is not chained in sleep, like my body. It can reach out and draw other minds to me—as it has drawn yours."

In his dream, Macklin's thought was awed, his hungry eagerness tempered by dread.

"You are—the goddess Tiamat?" he murmured.

"The *princess* Tiamat!" rang the answer. "Yes, princess of the older human race—the race who went back to the sea from the land, as the great sea-reptiles and the great whales went back."

Her speech, her thought, rushed swift and shining now through Macklin's dazed and dreaming mind.

"We of the sea were older—and wiser—than the men of land. That is why we sought to teach the brutish, barbarous land-folk our arts and wisdom. And we taught them much."

Macklin felt the heavy weight of ages of time in Tiamat's brooding thought.

"The land-folk called us, by a great bell whose sound was power. They called and we answered, rising from the sea to instruct them. We gave them the first elements of civilization. We even brought many of them by our arts to this sea-city, land men who dwelt with us here in the sea! And they worshipped us as gods.

"All except Marduk, their king. He was jealous of us. He hid his hatred until he had learned our arts of magic science from us. And then Marduk proclaimed us as evil, and used our own arts against us to bind us in this paralyzed, death-like sleep!"

Like silver flame blazed the bitter wrath in Tiamat's thought, and then Macklin felt it sink back to dull despair.

"Sleeping, sleeping, as age on age has rolled across the earth—but only our bodies! And that was the horror of the fate that treacherous Marduk fastened on us, that our minds should remain wakeful!"

In his dream, Macklin's heart wrung to pity for her.

"Tiamat, can you never be awakened? Can you never live again?"

Swift came her answer. "There is one way! The great bell in the temple on the shore—the bell by which long ago the land-folk called to us! Its vibration can shatter the paralysis in which Marduk bound us! It would awaken us!

"The bell still exists! Marduk dared not *destroy* it, for the very act of destruction would have sounded the bell and awakened us! He could but seal it up, with a curse upon it. You have but to open the sealed temple. First break the inscription on the outer block—"

"First break the inscription," Macklin murmured mechanically.

"—and then pull the center blocks aside," prompted Tiamat's silver whisper.

"The center blocks—" Macklin repeated, again.

Suddenly, in his dream, it seemed to him that the whole undersea world about him heaved and rocked to a violent shock.

And then it was all wavering and fading, the weird sea-city below and the crystal tower in which he was, and the pearly couch on which Tiamat's sleeping, unhumanly-human body lay.

"Macklin! Macklin!" a thunderous voice seemed roaring through the waters as all darkened and faded. *"Wake up!"*

Macklin opened dazed eyes. It was Thorpe's voice he heard, and Thorpe's square, aggressive face was close to his as the other shook his shoulders violently.

"Macklin, what are you doing?"

Macklin looked dazedly around. He was not now in his tent. He stood in the moonlight at the sealed entrance of the temple of Tiamat.

But that entrance was no longer sealed! Hands had torn aside the blocks inscribed with Marduk's curse and warning!

His hands, Macklin suddenly realized! His fingers were bruised and bloody where they had torn at the blocks. In his sleep, in his dream, he had opened the long-sealed temple of Tiamat!

In the moonlight, Thorpe's aggressive face showed his astonishment and bewilderment.

"Why did you open the temple secretly? Why not wait till morning as we planned?"

"I didn't know what I was doing," Macklin stammered. "I was sleep-walking, dreaming—"

Dreaming? Of a sudden, he felt an aching sorrow that Tiamat's unearthly beauty had only been a dream.

He saw her again as he had seen her in that weird vision, sleeping in her crystal palace tower down deep beneath the sea, her loveliness warded and watched by grotesque creatures of the deep.

But had it been only—dream? Had not her mind urged him to open the temple and sound the mysterious bell that could awaken her again to life? And had he not, at the very moment he dreamed that, been blindly tearing aside the inscribed blocks to enter the temple?

Fear settled upon Macklin's mind like thin ice forming on a pool. A dream that could take possession of a man's mind and body like that, was more than dreaming!

New voices aroused him from his brooding.

De Ferdey and Roos had been awakened by Thorpe's shouting, and were approaching.

De Ferdey, his scrawny little figure ridiculous in a brilliant dressing-gown, had anger on his pinched face.

"Thorpe, what are you and Macklin doing? You had no right to open the temple without me!"

Thorpe shrugged. "I found Macklin doing it. He says it was somnambulism, a dream."

Jan Roos' hulking, obese figure stiffened, his moon face and round blue eyes showing how much he was startled.

"A dream?" rumbled the fat Dutch artist. "I too was having one when I awoke—a *verdommt* nightmare about *that.*"

He gestured with his flabby hand across the little strip of beach toward the moonlit, heaving expanse of the Gulf.

Macklin looked at him swiftly. Had the Dutchman too dreamed of—Tiamat?

Unreasoning, hot jealousy flared for an instant in Macklin's mind, at the thought that his strange dream-tryst with that sleeping princess beneath the sea had been shared by Roos.

Next moment, he was appalled by his own reaction. Was he cracking up mentally, to harbor such crazy ideas?

He got a grip on himself. "I'm sorry about the temple, sir," he told De Ferdey. "I guess I've been so eager about opening it, that when I started sleepwalking I went and did it."

The little scholar looked placated. "I suppose there's no harm done, Macklin. But if some of our Arab workers sneaked inside before morning, they might loot it."

"I'll stand guard," Thorpe offered. De Ferdey nodded assent and turned away. "I suggest we go back to bed."

Jan Roos looked at Macklin a little furtively as they parted outside the tents. "Macklin, this dream of yours—" he began.

Again, Macklin felt the prick of senseless jealousy, and it made his answer curt.

"There's no point in discussing nightmares. Good night, Jan."

In his tent, he did not go back to his cot. He lit his gasoline lantern and sat sprawled in a camp-chair, smoking mechanically as his mind churned.

Never before had he experienced the unpleasant sensation of losing control even briefly of his own body's action. And it had shaken him.

He told himself that he had to reason it out or it would leave a scar of fear on his subconscious.

"It's easy enough to explain," he assured himself. "The inscription on the temple, cursing anyone who might want to 'awaken Tiamat,' was what triggered off my mind."

Macklin had been steeped for a half-score of years in Babylonian archaeology, in the faith and thought of those men of ancient Sumer who had first of all men reared a civilization.

And their great legend of how Marduk, the warrior magician-king, had conquered and bound evil Tiamat and her serpent-folk of the sea, was so familiar to him that it had sprung alive in his dreaming mind.

"Yet there were some things in the dream that are *not* in the legend," Macklin thought, puzzledly.

He got out his reference books and leafed through the pages of transliteration from ancient cuneiform which told the epic story of that primal conflict.

"Evil and beautiful was Tiamat, of the serpent people of the sea. Evil taught she from the waters to the sons of men, luring them by her bright beauty to deathly life beneath the sea. Spirit of heaven remember! Spirit of earth remember!"

Like a stern voice out of dim ages spoke to Macklin this saga of an ancient and awful conflict.

"By their own tricks of force did Marduk conquer the serpent folk, binding Tiamat and her horde in sleep, to waken not till the world dies. Spirit of heaven remember! Spirit of earth remember!"

Macklin went through the pages twice, seeking reference to that part of his dream in which Tiamat had spoken of a great bell that had been used to summon her, and that now could awaken her.

He found no such reference. But that, he reasoned, must have been a fictive detail supplied by his own imagination. For all the rest of his dream obviously came from his own memory of the ancient legend.

The assurance quieted his shaken nerves. Even so, he was reluctant to sleep again. But when he did sleep, no further dreams came.

In the glare of morning sunlight, Hugh Macklin felt a little foolish as he recalled the night.

"Just nerves," he muttered as he shaved. "Too much of ancient Babylon. I need a dose of New York, night-clubs, subways."

Thorpe, yawning and stretching, greeted them when they went to the temple on the sandy shore.

Their white-robed Arab workmen, curious to see the result of their long digging, stood in the background as De Ferdey, twitching with eagerness, directed the removal of the rest of the blocks that filled the massive door.

"The most ancient type of Sumerian masonry!" burbled the little scholar. "Careful not to crack those blocks! Now we'll have a look inside!"

De Ferdey could walk in upright, but the rest of them had to stoop in the low doorway.

The angling beams of their heavy flashlights showed the interior of the temple as a single dark, oblong, windowless room. Directly in front of them rose a low stone pier four feet high.

It was inscribed, but it was not the inscription but the thing that lay upon the pier that first caught their eyes.

"Why, it's a sistrum!" De Ferdey exclaimed, amazed. "But not like the Egyptian or any other known type."

The thing was a thick, foot-long bar of gold, with a handle midway by which it could be held. Projecting from the bar were seven little sistra on whose golden wires were strung tiny crystal spheres.

Thorpe was excitedly translating the inscription graven deep in the pier.

"The power of Marduk, the wisdom of Marduk, the scepter of Marduk, whose force can freeze and bind!"

Macklin picked it up, shook it slightly. The little crystal spheres chimed together on their golden wires.

Faint as was the note, it seemed for an instant to pierce his ears and brain. He felt himself reeling—

"Put it down!" ordered De Ferdey. "That sound is excruciating in this confined space."

An exclamation from Jan Roos made them swing around. The obese Dutch artist was playing his flashlight beam upon the walls of the room.

His fat face was suddenly strange. And as Hugh Macklin looked up, he felt an equal impact of emotion.

"Those mural paintings—they're odd," De Ferdey was saying puzzledly, behind Macklin.

The ancient murals of Tiamat's temple were more than odd, to Macklin. They were stunning.

For they showed a city beneath the sea—a city of crystal towers and walls of coral, and doors of silver sand. Above the city on a great ledge glittered a crystal palace, and about palace and city swam serpentine humans who were not quite human.

"The same scene, exactly the same scene, that I saw in my dream last night!" gasped Macklin.

De Ferdey looked startled, for a moment. But then he said, "You must have squirmed in and had a look, while you were sleepwalking."

"But I too—" Roos began, and then, fell silent.

Macklin noticed now that in the pictured undersea city, beside the swimming serpentine sea-folk, there walked ordinary men—men in ancient Sumerian dress, men with blind-staring eyes and strange faces.

He remembered that in his dream, Tiamat had said the sea-folk brought land-men somehow living to their city. And he remembered also a phrase of the ancient legend he had read during the night.

"Evil taught Tiamat to the sons of men, luring them by her bright beauty to deathly life beneath the sea."

"Look what I've found back here!" called Thorpe, his voice pitched high with excitement.

At the back of the temple room, a well eight feet across yawned in the stone paving. It was a black mouth of water, obviously connecting by a passage with the sea that boomed on the nearby shore.

On either side of the well rose a stone pillar, and the two pillars supported a massive stone cross-bar from which hung a bell.

The bell was of shimmering crystal, flaring out six feet from the ring at its top to its curving lip. It was inscribed with characters that were not Sumerian nor any other human language. And it hung with its lower third submerged in the black water.

Macklin felt a deadly tightness close upon his heart. "The bell of Tiamat!" he whispered. "The bell by which long ago they summoned her, and that now can awaken her!"

He knew, now. He knew that his strange vision of the night could not have been mere dream built of memory.

For in the ancient legends, in his memory of them, was no mention of such a bell. But the bell, the bell that Marduk could not destroy without reawakening Tiamat's folk, was here!

Then Hugh Macklin suddenly shouted. "Roos, *don't!*"

Beside the crystal bell, there hung from the stone cross-bar a massive crystal mace, a striker. Nobody but Jan Roos had noticed it.

Roos had seen and grasped it, and was lifting it to strike the crystal bell. And a terror born in dream suddenly brought that cry of dread from Macklin's lips.

Roos paused, glaring at Macklin with eyes that at this moment were not the Dutch artist's naive blue eyes at all.

"And why not?" he asked thickly. "Why not sound the bell?"

Macklin, seeing the glazed, strange look in the other's eyes, knew beyond all doubt that Roos *knew.*

"You can't!" he cried. "It means—"

Thorpe was staring at them, puzzledly, but De Ferdey's shrill voice intervened.

"Macklin is right—do you want to take a chance of cracking this bell?" he sputtered at Roos. "It's an invaluable relic!"

Slowly, Roos let the mace fall. It swung like a heavy crystal pendulum by the heavy gold wire that held it to the cross-bar.

"This place is unprecedented!" De Ferdey was babbling joyfully, now. "I'd like to see their faces in Philadelphia when we publish this!"

The little scholar peremptorily motioned them out of the dark stone room.

"Don't touch a thing until we can photograph everything *in situ!*"

Macklin was the photographer of the expedition. He was glad of that, for the pressure of excited work that day kept him from thinking. And he dreaded to think.

He wanted not even to consider the implications of a dream that anticipated reality—a dream of beauty and horror that had wrenched his heart with a great throb of mixed fear and desire when Roos had almost struck the bell.

He had wanted that bell to sound. He had wanted it because something deep in his mind knew that its sounding would awaken that dream-visioned sleeping sea-princess whose beauty was still an ache in his heart.

But even more deeply he had dreaded the sounding of the bell, for there was that in him which knew it was a tocsin for unutterable evil.

"We've made the find of the century!" De Ferdey exulted at dinner that night. "There must be other incalculably ancient relics in this region. We'll comb this whole coast!"

He told them that he had sent up to Basra for boats and diving equipment.

"There has probably been subsidence here—we may find much more under the shallow waters along shore."

Hugh Macklin hardly listened. He was watching Roos across the table. The big Dutchman was unusually silent.

But his moonlike face was colorless, strange. Time and again, Macklin saw the man's eyes shift through the open door of the tent to the dark, tumbling sea.

Macklin could no longer doubt that the Dutchman too had dreamed, that a strange call from the sea had come to him too, that—

He clenched his fist beneath the table and silently told himself, "I am Hugh Macklin of Ardmore, Pennsylvania, and I am a scientist, and I blindly believe no thing that can't be proved."

It didn't work. It didn't take the shadow of that incredible memory out of his brain.

Lying on his back in his dark tent later, he felt that his defenses against the impossible were weakening. For now it seemed to him that in the breathlessness of the night there was something hushed and fearfully expectant, in the shout of the surf something *joyously* expectant.

"I am Hugh Macklin—"

Clang!

Earth and sea and sky seemed suddenly vibrating to that distant, muted silvery sound.

It was not loud to his ears. It was a ghost-sound, touching octaves of sonic vibration that his hearing could barely attain.

Clang!

Again, the ringing note, its swelling pulse making complex counterpoint with the first note's echoes, moving fast and far—

Macklin found himself on his feet, sinking. "Roos! He's sounding the bell of Tiamat!"

Fear flung Macklin out of his tent like a giant hand, and urged him in a stumbling run along the moonlit shore.

It was not fear for himself. It was a quaking dread that that summoning bell might cause an impossible thing to happen—a thing that would forever shatter for him the solid-seeming surface of the ordinary world.

"It couldn't happen!" he told himself prayerfully. "It couldn't! But if it did—"

The intolerable ringing sweetness of the bell had died away. But on his right, as he ran, the black sea boomed hoarsely jubilant on the beach.

Tiamat's temple came into sight, low, squat and gray in the moonlight, its open door staring out to sea like a blind eye.

"Roos!" yelled Macklin, as he pitched forward.

Then he had his answer. But not from Roos. It came from far out on the heaving black ocean, out where great billows leaning toward land flung white spray-lace at the moon.

Over the sound of wind and wave there came from far seaward, a silver, singing cry. A high, sweet shout, throbbing with superhuman exultation.

Hugh Macklin stopped dead, seized by a cold breathlessness. He strained his eyes seaward.

"Tiamat!" he choked.

Like a hoarse, loud echo, from nearer in the sea came the sobbing howl of a great voice.

"Tiamat!"

It was Jan Roos' voice that uttered that hoarse and eager cry. And now Macklin saw him.

The hulking Dutchman was floundering out through the shallows, half-stumbling and half-swimming, clumsily flailing his great arms.

He was going out to answer that silver, singing call, and already only his massive head was above the billows.

"Roos, wait! Wait!" yelled Macklin, breaking the spell and running out into the surf.

Roos never turned. He floundered madly on, toward—

Toward what? Was it a glistening, coiling white woman-shape that swam those distant wave-crests with lithesome ease? Was it that, or curling foam?

Then Hugh Macklin glimpsed white arms flung up from the waves toward the moon, glimpsed an exultant face, heard again the joyous, pulsing cry. And again, Roos shouted as he plunged on.

For a moment, Macklin glimpsed the two heads together—then saw white arms like supple serpents coil around Roos' neck, and heard the Dutchman's wild shout of *joy* as he sank beneath the billows.

And then, there was only the wind, and the surf on the shore, and Hugh Macklin crying out across an empty, moonlit sea.

"Roos! Roos!"

Yet not horror for Roos' fate shook him most deeply, in this moment. The horror was there, but with it was blind jealousy.

Another had awakened Tiamat, another had answered her call and gone down with her into the sleeping city beneath the sea! He, Hugh Macklin, should have been her chosen—

Macklin knew later that he must have been very close to the brink of sanity at this moment, very close to hurling himself seaward in answer to that blind, aching impulse.

It was the voices that held him—first the excited shouts of Arab laborers running toward the shore, and then the alarmed exclamations of Thorpe and De Ferdey as they dragged him back out of the surf.

"Macklin, what's happened?"

Hugh Macklin pointed seaward with a shaking hand. "Roos! He sounded the bell to awaken Tiamat, and she came and called him! And he went!"

He heard Thorpe swear and tell De Ferdey, "He's out of his head. Stay with him and quiet him down, while I find Roos."

Macklin sat on the sand with his head in his hands, hardly conscious of De Ferdey's nervous voice or the low voices of the scared Arabs.

Then Thorpe came back.

"Roos isn't here anywhere, sir! Macklin, exactly what happened?"

Macklin told them. And he saw the growing incredulity on their faces as he told.

"It's *true!"* he finished desperately.

Thorpe spoke swiftly to De Ferdey. "I don't doubt that Roos did throw himself in, sir. He and Macklin have both been acting queerly. I'll take Macklin back to his tent and give him some luminal."

The drug drew a thick, wooly blanket over Macklin's mind, with merciful quickness.

When he awoke, the late afternoon sun was slanting through the door of the tent. Thorpe sat in a camp-chair watching him, his square brown face thoughtful.

"Feeling better?" he asked Macklin casually. "Here, have some coffee."

The hot coffee from the thermos was black and bitter. Thorpe waited until he had drunk it, and lighted a cigarette.

"Now tell me all about last night, Macklin," he said quietly.

Hugh Macklin laughed mirthlessly. "I see. You're trying to humor the madman."

"Bosh!" retorted Thorpe. "You're not crazy. Roos may have been, a little. He was a high-strung, nervous type, for all his fat. But you've just had a little too much work, heat and flies."

Macklin shrugged. "It's a good explanation. Only it isn't so. Now listen."

He forced himself to talk carefully and coolly. Thorpe listened without attempt to interrupt, till he had finished.

Then he spoke deliberately. "You really believe, then, that the sounding of that bell awakened a sleeping woman in the sea?"

Macklin hesitated. "Not a woman—not as we know women. They're a different kind of humanity, a species of man that split off long ago and went back to the sea. This is perhaps the last remnant of that offshoot human species.

"And Tiamat was not just sleeping. It must have been a queer form of suspended animation, the vital nervous centers paralyzed by some application of force. It's been done with animals in the labs."

"I see," said Thorpe. "And you think that Marduk did that to Tiamat long ago? And that the bell's vibration could break that paralysis and thus awaken her from suspended animation?"

Macklin flushed. "I know it sounds fantastic. But what other explanation is there?"

"The common sense one," Thorpe said forcefully. "You and Roos were both tired, nervous, excited by our finding of the temple. The temple of Tiamat suggested a weird dream to your tired mind—"

"A dream in which I heard the bell, remember!" Macklin interrupted. "And at that time we didn't know there was such a bell inside the temple."

"You were sleepwalking—you must have squirmed inside and seen those mural paintings and the bell," Thorpe insisted. "It's the only logical explanation."

"But I *saw* Tiamat out there on the waves, calling to Roos!" exclaimed Macklin.

"By your own account, you saw something vague and white," Thorpe retorted. "Sea-foam in the moonlight—your overwrought imagination supplied the rest."

Hugh Macklin hesitated. The part of his mind that clung desperately to the common sense, everyday world wanted to believe Thorpe.

But he couldn't believe. He knew that Tiamat lived, and had awakened. And, most frightening of all, that belief brought him a strange, singing joy.

Thorpe pressed his argument. "Look, Macklin—I want you to get this feverish fancy out of your mind. There's one sure way to do it. That's to sound the bell tonight and let you see for yourself that nothing really happens."

Instantly, again, Hugh Macklin felt that powerful throb of mixed fear and desire. If the bell were sounded, would Tiamat come again?

Or was it as Thorpe said, mere delusion born of an overtired mind? He had to know, one way or another. He had to know.

"All right," he said, keeping his voice carefully even. "We'll do it."

When he and Thorpe went out of the tent into the gathering twilight a little later, they met De Ferdey. The little scholar was too upset to give Macklin much attention.

"The Arabs are threatening to leave!" he shrilled. "What happened last night aroused their superstitions. You know—the usual talk about the ruins of the ancients being accursed. And right when we may be on the verge of further discoveries!"

He pointed toward the flat boats and heaps of equipment that now lay drawn up on the beach nearby.

"The boats and the diving suits came this afternoon—we could maybe find a whole city in this shallow water. But if they leave—"

"I'll talk to them, later," soothed Thorpe. "A little higher wages should fix it. Right now, we're going to the temple."

De Ferdey stared, seeming to notice Macklin for the first time. "To the temple? For what? Macklin, have you got over your delirium?"

"Of course he has," Thorpe said hastily. "Come along, Macklin."

In the deepening darkness, the little oblong temple brooded still as though watching with its blind eye the eager, reaching hands of wave-foam that grabbled up the beach toward it.

The moon was rising but it was very dark inside—so dark that Macklin could at first discern only the glimmer of the sistrum on the stone pier, and the vague, shimmering outline of the great crystal bell back in the deeper shadow.

His uncanny feeling of mingled hope and dread was getting stronger by the minute. He had a wild impulse to turn and flee, but knew that to do so would be to prove to Thorpe that his wits were tottering.

Thorpe turned, at the bell, and his voice was embarrassed. "Macklin, don't take offense. But you haven't been normal. And I don't want to take a chance of anything happening to you when I sound this bell."

Hugh Macklin was puzzled for a moment. "What do you mean?"

The other took a pair of leather straps from his pocket. "I want to secure you before I sound this bell. Sounds can have queer effects. I don't want you throwing yourself into the sea, too."

It took Macklin aback. He knew now that despite Thorpe's calm manner, the other thought him at least partly insane.

But he forced himself to nod assent. "All right. I quite understand."

Thorpe tied him around the shoulders with the straps to one of the two stone pillars that supported the bell.

Then the other grasped and raised the heavy mace. "A sound is just a vibration of the air. Keep remembering that, Macklin."

Thorpe struck the bell.

It wasn't as Macklin had expected. It wasn't a faint, ringing pulse of sound such as he had heard the night before.

He had been at a distance, then. But now he was right beside the crystal bell, inside the confined space of the little temple. The sound was different.

It was not like a sound at all. It was like an explosion of immaterial force that threatened to rive heaven and earth. A god might signal the end of a universe by such a mighty note.

Macklin, half-stunned, saw the water in the black well quivering wildly around the submerged bottom of the bell. The sound was going out through the water to the sea, out even faster and farther than it could go through air.

Thunderously drowning the ringing echoes came Thorpe's second stroke upon the bell. Another stroke followed, and another, until the dark little temple seemed crowded with raging, silvery sound.

Thorpe let the mace fall, and stood panting. "That was loud enough, wasn't it? And you see, nothing has happened."

Nothing? The last ringing reverberations were dying away, and Macklin's ears could now again detect the sound of the sea-wind and the boom of the dark surf out there beyond the open door.

Nothing? Why was it that the murmur of the wind suddenly strengthened, grew louder and keener, grew to a high, sweet singing cry outracing the leaping billows toward the land?

Macklin uttered a cry. "Thorpe, she *is* coming! Tiamat! I can hear her—"

Thorpe's voice broke in, taut with anxiety. "Macklin, get a grip on yourself! You have to conquer this thing in your mind right now!"

He pointed at the moonlit ocean out there beyond the open door and the beach.

"Can't you see that there's nothing there, that—"

Thorpe broke off. His shadowy figure became rigid as he stared.

For there was something out there on the moonlit sea. A slim shape, swimming with seal-smoothness toward the shore.

A serpentine white arm broke from the water, and dark hair swept back like wind-driven seaweed as a delicate, triangular face tilted moonward to utter that singing silver cry.

"Tiamat!" Macklin yelled again. "Thorpe, I told you—"

But Thorpe didn't hear him. Thorpe was striding out of the temple, toward the beach and the breaking waves.

"It's a woman, only a woman!" Thorpe's thick voice came back. "I'll prove it!"

Macklin knew that the man's matter-of-fact world was shattering beneath his feet, and that it was the supreme need for reassurance that drove him.

He saw Thorpe walk out until the breaking waves clasped his waist, staring fixedly ahead toward that white woman-shape that was swimming swiftly, swiftly, in toward him.

Macklin suddenly strained against the straps that bound him to the pillar, and yelled an incoherent warning.

He knew that Thorpe could not hear him. But Thorpe's own sudden dread spun the man around to start toward shore.

Swiftly, smoothly, flashed the lithesome swimming shape of Tiamat after him. In the moonlight, Thorpe's pallid face became suddenly ghastly as white arms *coiled* round his neck from behind.

Macklin heard a cry of horror that mingled weirdly with a joyous silver shout. And then two heads went down.

He guessed afterward that for a time he hung half-conscious in his straps. For his next clear sensation was of hands nervously unbinding him, and De Ferdey's shrill voice.

"I *saw!*" De Ferdey was shrilling, over and over. "I saw that—something—come in and drag Thorpe down!"

The little scholar was shaking, his hands quivering violently as he tried to unbuckle the straps.

"And the Arabs saw too! They've gone, fled! Macklin, what are we to do?"

A queer, cold calm had come upon Hugh Macklin's soul. He answered evenly.

"I am going out there, after them. After Tiamat. She will have no more victims."

De Ferdey recoiled from him a little. "Are you mad? Go out into the sea—drown yourself?"

"There are the diving suits," Macklin answered. "They're tank-suits, self-contained, strong enough for any reasonable depth. I'm going in one of them."

His voice suddenly shouted. "What else can I do? We've wakened something ancient and evil, by our blundering disregard of Marduk's warning! As though our modern science was the only science that ever had existed!"

The little scholar wrung his hands. "It's mad, what you say! And yet—I saw!"

Macklin disregarded him in the next feverish hours. He assembled one of the diving suits. It was a simple affair with duralumin oxygen-tank between the shoulders, devised for amateur divers in shallow waters.

He fastened the lead-weights to his belt, and then as the sun rose, clumped back on the lead-soled shoes toward the temple.

De Ferdey followed him fearfully. The little scholar watched wide-eyed as Macklin lifted the sistrum of Marduk from its inscribed pier and thrust it into his belt.

"Macklin, you're crazy!" he cried. "If you think that there is any power in that ancient magical instrument—"

Macklin's somber eyes traced the inscription on the stone. *"The power of Marduk, the wisdom of Marduk, the sceptre of Marduk, whose force can freeze and bind."*

Macklin said, "There was power in the bell."

He turned and went slowly toward the sea. The slow, swinging, ponderous tread of the heavy boots, the unhuman outlines of suit and helmet, gave him the look of some antediluvian god-thing striding toward judgment. With every movement the sistrum gave out a faint chime of sound, softer than a child's breathing, and yet Macklin thought that the waves shied from it like frightened horses in their landward rush.

He walked out into the surf, but this time there was no voice of singing crystal calling to him. The water closed over his head. He was afraid of the water. He was conscious of the cold, the crushing, numbing weight of it. This time he did not glide with the smooth bodiless ease of a dream. He walked, and his steps were slow and painful, and there was no joy in them.

Instinct, or the memory of his dream, led him toward the city, and it seemed to him that ages went by in the dark green depths of the sea, and his heart was heavier than the lead weights that held him down.

Pale phosphorescence, pale spreading light like the silver radiance of stars. The great cliffs rising sheer behind the veils of water, and the long clean stretch of sand. The crystal towers, carved from the crests of breaking waves. And above, on the black ledge of rock, the palace of Tiamat like a fallen star caught on the breast of a storm-cloud. And Hugh Macklin cried out in his heart, a broken, desperate shout of negation.

He had known that he would see it, as he had seen it all before. And yet it was a shock—to be awake, terribly awake, and see the country of a dream.

He knew that even after all that had happened he had still not quite believed. A man, if he were sane at all, could not quite believe. A man, if he were sane at all, could not help hoping that it had only been insubstantial dream.

He went on, across the sand and the crumbling shells, with the slow leaden tread of doom. The doom of all mankind, which had abdicated an ancient, alien glory for the sake of a human soul.

The sleepers no longer slept.

He saw them in the open spaces, bright beautiful shapes that sported with their cousins of the sea. Great gleaming fish went arrowing between the crystal towers, and the people of Tiamat played with them, more fleet, more graceful, than the perfect children of the sea. The game they played together was more than a frolic. It was a living hymn of joy because the long sleep was over, because the shackled bodies were free again. And the sea was glad, and her children welcomed back their gods.

Hugh Macklin walked between the coral walls of the city, and one by one the people of Tiamat stopped and watched him and drew back before him, and the fish ceased from their flashing play and watched him too, drifting motionless beside the white shoulders of their lords. It seemed to Macklin that the very motion of the sea had stopped, as though the water itself had life and were watching him.

His hand was on the shaft of the sistrum, and he could feel its chiming vibrant whisper as he moved.

Sceptre of Marduk, whose force can freeze and bind.

The people of Tiamat were afraid.

Macklin looked upward to the palace, and waited.

She came, as he had known she would. She came like a drift of pearly foam, bright as the morning sun, and her beauty was like a stabbing pain in Macklin's heart. Tears came hot and blinding to his eyes, and he shook them away because he must look at her, must see her clearly and for all time, because there would not again be light and loveliness in all the world for him.

Dark hair floating around the delicate face, the flesh like soft pearl, tender and radiant. The strong sweet shoulders and lifting breasts, the long line of the flanks and slender hips, the limbs that were all sinuous grace.

He tried to see where and how she differed from the human, and realized that the difference lay in inner structure. There was no stiffness, no awkward articulation of joints, no heaviness. Her bones were light and supple, and all the lines of her body and the motion of it were curving and perfect as the waves, without angularity or limitation. She was the original, the perfect creature, unmarred by the restricting shackles of evolution on the unfriendly land. She was the mold, and humanity was only the broken echo.

He wanted to fall down on his knees and worship her. More than that, he wanted to tear off the hampering suit that weighed his body and gather her loveliness into his arms and kiss her little curving mouth that had in it the laughter and the mocking joy of all the waters that ever danced in the morning of the world under a warm young sun.

He looked into her eyes.

He was sorry that he had. He was sorry that he had not been satisfied to remember her as he had seen her first, with her lids closed in sleep.

Dark mystic depths, and lighter shades like shallows over sand, and little errant glints of light like the touch of moonbeams. Knowledge long forgotten and visions half remembered were in her eyes.

They were eyes that had watched the banners of all the nations of man brighten and fade and go down into dust, and yet were not sad, but like the eyes of a child that watches an endless and fascinating play. Youth was in them, and joy, and above all they were the eyes of a woman and they smiled.

Hugh Macklin forgot the cold and crushing weight of the sea. He forgot the sceptre of Marduk, and the reason for his coming. Very softly he spoke her name—"Tiamat! Tiamat!"—and the sound of it inside his helmet was like the whisper of distant surf laughing at the shackled land.

The remembered voice of his dream spoke within his mind, like silver speech transformed to thought.

"Why have you come, Hugh Macklin?"

For a long time, he could not answer. The still sea waited, and the people of the city waited, and the great fish lay motionless and watching. The sistrum, too, was silent, unshaken by any motion of the water.

And Hugh Macklin could not answer Tiamat because her eyes were on him, and he knew that she had known the answer to that question before he had left the temple, and she was laughing at him.

She was not afraid. Her people might fear, but not Tiamat. He knew that even Marduk had not been able to teach her fear.

Finally he answered hoarsely, speaking the thought that he knew her mind could hear.

"You know why I've come."

She had floated closer to him, imperceptibly. Her flesh glowed with the warm soft lustre of pearl. Macklin's hands reached out, unconsciously, blindly, and she laughed, a little silver ripple in his mind.

"I know," she said. "But do you?"

He had to tell her. He had to look into her eyes and tell her. The words hurt him, each one separately as he dragged them out.

"You're evil, Tiamat. You killed my friends. You—"

He stopped. It was hard to speak. Her body was long and wonderfully slender and her shoulders were like white coral under her dark floating hair. He tried again.

"I came to—"

He could not say it. It was blasphemy.

It was worse even than if he said, *"I have come to kill you."* To chain that breathing vibrant loveliness in a living death—

Tiamat smiled and whispered, "You came because you love me."

And Hugh Macklin knew that she was right.

She stretched her white arms upward, lazily, and said, "I have taken lovers before from the world of men."

She drifted closer on the breath of the sea, and her eyes were merry and full of light.

"Would you like that, Hugh Macklin? To love me, to stay with me always?"

"Yes," he said. "Yes."

He was racked with longing, just to be near her, to watch her move among the crystal towers and listen to the singing music of her voice. Through her, a man might glimpse the wonder of eternal life, of youth and never-ending beauty.

"Take off your helmet, Hugh Macklin. That ugly thing that hides the beauty of the sea. Let the water touch you. Let me touch you, let me kiss your lips and set you free of the land forever."

Her hands, reaching out to him. Her mouth, tender and passionate and laughing—

"Take off your helmet, Hugh Macklin."

He wanted to, he hungered to, but one last memory of fear held him. The remembered picture of the temple walls, covered with paintings of other men who had answered the call of Tiamat.

"What of them?" he asked harshly, above the pounding of his heart. "Were they happy here, the dead who could not really die?"

"Why do you call them that? They had eternal life, until Marduk destroyed them because he was mortal and must die himself. Look around you. Could you be unhappy here?"

No, thought Macklin, not unless one could be unhappy in fairyland.

Tiamat said, "Could you be unhappy here—with me?"

Macklin slowly raised his hands, and began to fumble with the heavy bolts of the helmet.

It was then that Roos and Thorpe came, thrusting their clumsy way between the people of the sea. They had lost their goddess, and they had hunted for her, and now they had found her.

They scrambled toward her across the sand, floundering, their human bodies pitifully unsuited to the task. The huge Dutchman, the lean, hard-bitten Thorpe, men Macklin had known and worked with—but they were men no longer.

They were nothing, not beast nor fish nor anything that lives normally under the sun. They were not even alive. They did not breathe for they had no need of breath, now that their life was only a pseudo-life fanned within them by the magic of an ancient, evil science.

Their faces were the empty patient faces of the dead, and their eyes were without sight or soul or hope.

Until they saw Tiamat.

Then it was as though torches had been lighted in a dark cave. They scrambled toward her, dog-like, and fell at her feet and worshiped.

Hugh Macklin said heavily, "Are they, too, your lovers?"

Tiamat's eyes had narrowed as she sensed the sick, cold horror that struck him like a blow. But she only smiled.

"One is ugly, the other old. You are young, Hugh Macklin, and you are not ugly." Her face was lovely, tempting, eager, with lips that would be for him alone.

"Take off your helmet. Stay with me—and love me."

Roos reached out one water-wrinkled, flabby hand and touched her little foot, and ground his forehead in the sand.

Macklin took his hands away from his helmet and gripped the sistrum, and the golden haft of it seemed to burn his hand.

He saw dreadful anger flash into Tiamat's face.

He saw the waiting ranks of her people break into chaos, into movement, into attack.

He felt the fear that was greater than the fear of death run like a wave through the sea, and all the universe was full of rushing silver bodies like a rain of stars.

He felt himself go down under the attack, but still he gripped the sistrum and shook it, and the shock of his fall shook it harder.

More with his soul than with his hearing, Macklin heard the first piercing chiming of the sistrum swell into a terrible, rending sword of sonic vibration.

Sound could daze, sound could stun the nerve-centers. And this awful, poignant sound could stun them into—paralysis.

It seemed to him that all the torrent of living things rushing upon him was instantly shocked and frozen by that dread, piercing note that struck and stunned their more delicate brains. It seemed to him that all the waters and life of earth were stilled.

The awful voice of Marduk's sistrum commanded, and the world obeyed, and Hugh Macklin knelt on the floor of the sea, blinded with tears, as he shook the sceptre made of gold and crystal and living death.

After a time he dropped the sistrum, and he also lay still.

Hugh Macklin rose, like an old and broken man, from the floor of the sea. He lifted the sceptre of Marduk from the sand and thrust it into his belt again, and then he raised his eyes and looked at the thing he had done.

The crystal towers stood as they had before, but their domes were cracked and riven by the vibration-voice of the sistrum. The fish had fled before it. And on the sand between the broken towers, the people of Tiamat slept.

In all the city, only two things moved. Roos and Thorpe, whose human mechanism, like Macklin's, was too dull to be paralyzed by the subtle vibration. They crouched like two weeping children on the sand, and watched Tiamat.

Hugh Macklin raised her lovely body in his arms. Her eyes were closed now. No more memories, no more light, no more laughter. All the wonderful swiftness and grace of her body stilled, all the life and the joy. Macklin had ceased to weep. What he felt in his heart was too deep for tears.

He started off, toward the cliff where the shining palace waited. Thorpe and the Dutchman followed. They moaned for Tiamat, and they could not understand.

Hugh Macklin climbed a precarious path up the black cliff to the ledge, bearing the sleeping Tiamat in his arms. He entered the palace.

Upward through the silent gleaming halls, slowly, heavily, sadly. Upward past vaulted chambers where the great golden doors stood open, swinging with the stately breathing of the sea. Upward to the highest tower, and the stillness was deeper than death.

When he entered Tiamat's chamber, he saw that already the fish were coming back, slipping like shadows into the room.

He laid Tiamat on her couch, gently, tenderly, straightening her limbs so that she might be comfortable, stroking the dark hair back from her face. Roos and Thorpe crept to the foot of the couch and knelt there, and Macklin knew that they would stay, beyond the end of the world if need be, waiting for Tiamat to awake.

He leaned over her, wishing that he might kiss her lips, and the slow tears fell and blurred the glass window of his helmet.

Just at the last she spoke to him, very faintly because her mind was still stunned. She spoke his name, and the singing, crystal sweetness of her voice was far off and infinitely sad.

"You will come back, Hugh Macklin."

Macklin closed his eyes. He said, "I love you, Tiamat. But I will not come back."

He turned and went out of the room. At the door he paused and looked back, once, and saw that again that great coiling creature of the deep had looped itself around the still shape of beauty, and that its head was once more pillowed on her shoulder.

Roos and Thorpe crouched unmoving at Tiamat's feet, and he knew that they would never move from there.

He went away from the palace, down through the crystal city, and still the chiming echo of her voice followed him.

You will come back. You will come back.

He was full of a terrible weakness. The ocean floor was dark, and empty, and very cold.

He knew that the land, when he reached it, would be no better. He knew that he could not bear to live where he could not hear the sea, and yet also that the sound of every breaking wave would break his heart again.

You will come back, Hugh Macklin.

"Perhaps, Tiamat," he whispered. "Perhaps some day I will."

The Daughter of Thor

From far in the north, colossal banners of cold radiance streamed up across the brooding night sky. They pulsated in a shifting glory of red and green, waving stronger and reaching higher toward the zenith. Beneath that weird, quivering glow of the Northern Lights, the snow-clad mountains were like cowled white giants guarding the black reaches of Narvik Fjord.

Mart Fallon watched from the barred window of his dark prison. His lean, tired faced, haggard and unshaven, showed deep lines of fatigue in the shifting glow. His black eyes were dull and somber, and his shoulders sagged inside his torn RAF uniform jacket. He was feeling a bitterness of despair that was not his alone in these first fateful weeks of the Nazi invasion of Norway.

The heavy, rumbling voice of his fellow-prisoner came out of the darkness behind him.

"There will be battle and death tonight," Helverson muttered. "When those lights flame in the sky, the Valkyries are riding."

Fallon turned to peer at the other. "What are you talking about, Nels?"

He spoke, a little haltingly, in the Norwegian that his fellow-prisoner had taught him during the weary time of their confinement.

Nels Helverson had risen to his feet. More clearly even than Fallon, he showed the effects of terrible ordeal. A Norwegian soldier of giant frame, beneath his shock of yellow hair his massive face was gaunt, his blue eyes wild and burning.

"The Valkyries," Helverson repeated, staring out fixedly at the unearthly flare of light. "The warrior-maids, the messengers of Odin, who bear those slain in battle to Valhalla."

Fallon looked at him a little uneasily. "You surely don't believe those old superstitions."

"They are not superstitions," rumbled the Norwegian gutturally. "The old hero-gods of my people still live! They will come to our aid—Odin the one-eyed, Thor of the lightnings, and all the others. They will sweep these treacherous invaders into the sea."

Helverson's eyes were blazing, his gaunt face wild with passion. He towered huge in the quivering glow of the shifting rays outside.

The young American pilot felt deepened dismay. His big fellow-prisoner had been increasingly strange and moody of late. Dazed by the hammer-shocks of sudden invasion, exhausting battle and disastrous defeat, Helverson's half-crazed mind was turning now to the ancient beliefs of his race.

It was not to be wondered at. All Norway was dazed and reeling. Without warning the Nazis had struck, sweeping in from the sea and in a single night seizing nearly a thousand miles of coastline from Oslo to this far northern port of Narvik. Their tanks, planes and guns had shattered the bewildered defenders, and now the invaders were ruthlessly and rapidly marching up the valleys to complete their conquest.

Britain had been equally unprepared for the audacious Nazi stroke, but had rallied to counter it. Big patrol bombers of the Royal Air Force had roared northward to reconnoiter the invaded Norwegian ports and ascertain at which ones an Allied counter-invasion could best succeed. Mart Fallon, American volunteer pilot, had flown one of those bombers to this Nazi-held port of Narvik, far north of the Arctic Circle.

He had not flown it back. He had been shot down over Narvik Fjord, and ever since had been caged in this improvised prison which the Nazis had established on the heights above the town. And here, for day after day, he had been mercilessly questioned about British preparations by Victor Heysing, the wolf-like young Gestapo officer in charge.

"I know how you feel, Nels," he told the Norwegian. "Heysing's prodding has nearly driven me crazy myself. But don't let it get you."

Helverson's bull neck corded, and his eyes were fanatic as he glared out at the witchery of the Northern Lights above the snows.

"Comes soon the time when the old gods rise against these spawn of Hel," he muttered. "The sword of Odin and the lightnings of Thor will blast them." He pointed a quivering hand at the shifting rays. "Already the sign is in the sky! The Aesir are awake, and shield-maidens ride this night! Blood and vengeance are near!"

Fallon saw the madness in the giant Norseman's flaming eyes. The ancient faith of a race had awakened to life in him. The young American groaned inwardly. This monomania of his friend was almost the last straw.

"Nels, get a grip on yourself and forget those myths," he begged. "The Northern Lights aren't any omen. They're nothing but—"

Boom—*crash!* Like a burst of sudden thunder, the nearby sound struck Fallon silent. It was followed by more thunderous reverberations.

"By Heaven, that's guns!" the American yelled. "Big guns, too! It's from down in the fjord!"

He ran to the window. But it faced away from the fjord. He could see nothing but the eerie light upon the snow outside, and the stockade of barbed wire that enclosed this makeshift warehouse-prison.

Nazi soldiers were running out there, dark figures against the snow. The thudding of guns from the west was rising to a crescendo. A siren began its warning scream at the Nazi airfield near the prison.

"Those are British ships that are shelling the town!" Fallon yelled excitedly. "Twelve-inchers, too! There must be a battleship in the squadron!"

He and Helverson, pressing against the barred window, saw searchlights stab into the heavens from the nearby airfield. Anti-aircraft guns coughed frantically out there, at planes swooping from overhead.

Then came a sound of a gigantic door slamming, and a great gout of red flame exploded at the edge of the airdrome. Another British bomb exploded two seconds later, much nearer the prison. Fallon, from his experience as bomber-pilot, knew the third bomb of the stick was coming.

"Down, Nels!" he yelled, throwing himself and the big Norwegian to the floor.

As they hit the cement, the whole world seemed to go up in the explosion of the third bomb. The floor heaved and rocked under them, there was a shattering crash of falling masonry, a clang of iron on stone.

Wounded Nazis were yelling thinly somewhere nearby, when Fallon dragged himself groggily back to his feet. The stone outer wall of their cell was cracked above and below the barred window. The bomb had evidently hit one end of the prison, or near it.

Nazi fighter-planes were roaring up from the neighboring field, into the swinging sweep of the Northern Lights. Machine-guns stuttered up there in the sky, hardly audible over the thunder of the distant shelling.

"Did I not say that blood and vengeance were near?" shouted Helverson. "The sign in the sky was true!"

Fallon was scrabbling with sudden furious hope at the bars of the window. The bomb-blast had blown in the glass, and the split of the stone wall had wrenched half the bars loose in their sockets.

"Nels, help me! If we can get out of here before Heysing and his devils get over their surprise—"

Helverson's fanatic excitement did not prevent him from grasping immediately the opportunity of escape. The giant Norwegian brushed Fallon aside, and exerted his great strength to bend the loosened bars. His hunched back cracked audibly—but the bars gave inward.

In a second, Fallon and he were outside the window. They crouched a moment in the shadow of the wall, knee-deep in snow and shivering to the icy wind. They could see now that the whole western end of the long, low stone building had been smashed in.

Beyond it, they glimpsed the battle going on down in the fjord. The darkness down there was constantly torn by red gun-flashes. By that uncertain illumination, Fallon glimpsed a British battleship and a half-dozen destroyers pouring shells into moored Nazi destroyers and into the Nazi batteries that were fiercely answering from the town.

The British planes were now swooping down to spot and bomb those batteries, hampered by a savage swarm of Messerschmitts. The battle was nerve-chilling in this uncanny setting of snowy peaks and dark sea lit by the flaring Northern Lights.

Fallon perceived that a section of the stockade had been levelled by the bomb. He dragged Helverson with him through the snow, in a run.

"Can we reach the British ships?" gasped the Norwegian as they ran.

"No chance of that," Fallon panted. "This is just a raid, not a landing party, for there's no transports. But that airfield is near, and if we can get our hands on a Nazi plane—"

A rifle *blam-blammed* behind them and a hoarse German voice shouted the alarm. The prison guards, recovering from the demoralization caused by the bomb-hit, had sighted the two fugitives.

Fallon and Helverson flung themselves behind a snowy hillock as more rifles went off. As they stumbled on through the hip-high snow, the American heard Victor Heysing's clear voice blaring orders.

He judged from the sound of voices that the Nazi guards were making for the fjord, assuming that the escaped men would try to reach the British ships still shelling the town. Fallon breathed a prayer of thanks for that, as he and the Norwegian pitched on toward the airfield.

There were only three or four Nazi planes left on the snowy field, he saw when they reached its edge. But they were in luck, for one of those planes was near them. It was a Messerschmitt whose pilot was hastily hammering and cursing at something in the cockpit. The motor idled.

"I'll take him," Helverson rumbled as they crept out across the field, keeping that nearest plane between them and the Nazis farther away.

The Norwegian's great hands reached in and clamped the neck of the Nazi pilot, before he knew they were behind him. In terrible silence, Helverson drew the squirming man out of the ship. There was a dull cracking sound. The Nazi's choking utterances ceased, and Helverson dropped him.

"There's one of Hel's children who will blast no more of our villages!" flamed the giant.

Fallon had scrambled into the cockpit. "Quick, Nels—squeeze in here! Unless we—"

The clean crack of a pistol punctuated his words, and Helverson staggered with blood suddenly spouting from his shoulder.

The American turned, and saw a single man racing from the direction they themselves had come, his pistol raised for another shot. In the eery rays that painted sky and snow, there was no mistaking that slender, black-uniformed figure, that blond, wolf-handsome face.

Victor Heysing had not made the same mistake as the Nazi prison guards who had taken it for granted they would head for the fjord. The Gestapo officer had trailed them through the snow.

Helverson's right arm hung useless. With a frantic movement, Fallon tugged the staggering Norwegian into the cockpit, jamming the narrow space. A second bullet from Heysing's pistol slammed into the thin armor around the pilot's seat, as Fallon gunned the idling motor.

The Messerschmitt roared down the field and took off so heavily that it barely cleared the hillocks beyond. Almost instantly, Fallon found himself flying out over the deep fjord. Down there the battle was drawing to a close. The British warships, their guns still thundering, were steaming out to sea. Two Nazi destroyers and a half-dozen transports had been reduced to flaming wreckage.

Fallon banked around and headed northward, into the full flare of the Northern Lights. Fighting for altitude, he won over the nearby snowy peaks and laid a course slightly east of north.

"We can't make Scotland in this fighter—not half enough fuel," he jerked over his shoulder to Helverson. "And even if the Allies have counter-invaded in the south, we can't reach those ports either. We'll have to make for the fishing villages on the far northern coast, that are still in Norwegian hands."

Helverson, holding his hand over his wounded shoulder, nodded his great head. His blue eyes still held that fanatic glare.

"We go toward Odin's land—the north. That is well!"

Fallon glanced around worriedly at his half-crazed comrade. He stiffened as he glimpsed a black speck far behind them in the aurora sky.

"That's a Nazi fighter following us!" he cried. "That devil Heysing! He didn't have time to get word to other pilots to follow us. He must be in that plane himself!"

Fallon knew the young Gestapo officer was a pilot—Heysing's technical questions during that long torment of inquisition had shown that. And he knew that Heysing thought he possessed valuable information, and was determined at any risk to prevent their escape.

The relentless singlemindedness of the Nazi in his pursuit woke new rage in Fallon. Remembering those days when Heysing had bullied, slapped and hectored him for hours on end, Fallon was tempted to turn back and meet his pursuer in combat.

But he knew that his chances in such a fight would be slim, for his overloaded plane could not maneuver to match the other. And it was his duty to make good his escape to those far Arctic coastal villages beyond the northern wilderness, for from them he could reach England with information on Narvik's defenses that would be vital to the Allied cause.

He opened the throttle to the limit. But the plane behind crept closer. At a roaring pace of miles a minute, pursued and pursuer rushed above the vast, almost uninhabited wilderness that is north Norway.

Fallon saw it as a forbidding vista of towering, jagged white mountains and somber shadowed valleys, and great glaciers creeping like glittering serpents toward the distant sea. Nowhere was there a light of house or village. Not even the wild Lapps who herded their reindeer on the barren plains far eastward would come into this lifeless, icy land.

And over snow-clad peak and glacier shot and shimmered the stupendous brilliance of the Northern Lights. The whole sky ahead was a palisade of luminous splendor, from which the wheeling rays stabbed south across the frosty heavens. He had never seen such an aurora.

Helverson made an archaic gesture of reverence toward that blazing sky, his eyes burning.

"The old gods have awakened this night! And we go toward them."

Fallon could not find utterance for disbelief, this time. He felt hypnotized by the aurora. Its fierce rays were still growing in intensity. It was as though they were flying into the sun.

Tingling forces seemed thrilling through his exhausted body. He felt somehow on the edge of tremendous revelation that made him forget the relentless pursuer behind. Like the fanatic Norseman, he too was feeling a strange, wild eagerness of superhuman expectation as they flew on.

CHAPTER II
The Valkyries

Brutal interruption drove all uncanny feelings from Fallon's mind. Machine guns yammered behind him, and a stream of tracer screamed past the left wing of his plane.

Instant awareness that Heysing had overtaken them tripped the trained reflexes in the American pilot's brain. Without a second for thought, he slammed over the stick and kicked the rudder to bank sharply around. He caught just a glimpse of Heysing's plane, leaping around after him with relentless swiftness.

"The Nazi devil!" he thought ragingly. "He'd follow us to hell rather than see us escape."

Helverson was bellowing in stark fury. But Fallon's mind became ice-cold and clear as he tensely maneuvered for position.

He knew this battle was to the death. His overloaded plane could not escape Heysing. One or the other of them had to go down. The Nazi's lighter ship had superior maneuverability. But Fallon was hoping that the Gestapo officer might be rusty as a combat pilot.

Like two circling hawks, they clawed for position in the supernatural splendor of that incredible aurora. Down below, the howling wilderness of snowy ranges and creeping glaciers sheened in the wheeling rays. They must be far, far north, Fallon thought fleetingly, far up over the wild, unvisited Finmark mountains and near the Arctic Ocean coast and its few fishing villages. If he could down Heysing, they could—

No time to think of the future now! There wouldn't *be* any future if he let Heysing get on his tail as the Nazi had now almost succeeded in doing. Fallon gunned his heavy ship into a bewildering corkscrew, screamed steeply upward until his plane was almost hanging on its prop, and then looped back and down and found himself roaring a hundred yards behind the baffled Nazi.

In a split-second he had Heysing's plane in his sights, silhouetted blackly against the tremendous aurora. His finger savagely triggered. But there came no answering roar from the machine guns of his ship. The fire-control of this Messerschmitt was jammed and dead.

Appalled, Fallon suddenly remembered the Nazi pilot of this plane had been hammering and cursing in the cockpit when they seized it. He knew now why that pilot hadn't been up in the fight over the fjord. But the knowledge came too late.

"No guns, Nels!" he shouted to Helverson. "We can't fight, and I don't think we can get away."

Heysing had already discovered their presence behind him and had banked startledly away. But now the Nazi came rushing back in from a rear quarter, with all guns spitting.

"He cannot kill us," Helverson's great voice was booming with fanatic confidence. "The old gods fight with us tonight."

Fallon had no such confidence, and his heart was cold with foreknowledge of doom as he flung the plane all over the sky to escape the Nazi. Seeming to sense their helplessness, Heysing was boring in recklessly at every opportunity, flinging bursts at them from every possible range.

Up into the mad dance of dazzling rays in the aurora-painted heavens they thundered, and down again toward the wild, snowy peaks and valleys. It was only a question of time, Fallon knew. But the time ran out even sooner than he had expected.

A gust of rising wind smacked him as he zoomed steeply. As he fought frantically to avoid stalling, Heysing swooped from above. The Nazi's machine guns flung a whiplash of lead that tore across Fallon's motor. His engine choked, coughed and died. His instruments showed him that at least two oil-lines were gone.

"Got us!" Fallon cried, his raging shout loud now that the motor was dead. "Hang on, Nels—we're going down."

A dead-stick landing down in the snowy mountains below was a hundred-to-one chance, he knew. But it was the only chance left.

Rising winds screamed past his wings and buffeted the crippled ship as he rushed down through the twitching auroral glare. Heysing came down over them and loosed another burst that tore through their fuselage. Fallon knew bitterness at not being able to take the Nazi with him.

He was aiming for a long, snowy gorge walled by marching ridges of icy peaks. Keeping the nose of the plane as far up as he dared, he craned tensely to estimate distances in the unreal illumination. Now the wind was a whistling shriek, and the floor of the gorge was slamming up toward him with appalling speed.

Fallon felt the wheels hit the snow and the frozen ground close beneath it. The plane, traveling at express-train speed, bounced crazily back up from the floor of the gorge. Then it smacked down again, hit deeper snow, and heeled over on its nose with a crash that stunned him.

He did not know exactly how long he had been unconscious, when he awoke. Dazedly, he felt around and found Helverson still unconscious. He squirmed weakly until he got the door of the jammed cockpit open. Then he hauled the senseless Norwegian out with him into the snow.

Freezing winds hit him in the face, blowing up the gorge from the west with increasing violence. To north and south rose sheer, icy cliffs. The sky above still flamed awesomely with that supernatural splendor of Northern Lights.

"Nels, wake up!" he cried hoarsely, slapping the unconscious giant's face. He could see now that Helverson had lost much blood.

The Norwegian stirred weakly, opened dazed blue eyes. He seemed not to see Fallon bending above him.

"Listen, they come!" he exclaimed huskily. "I hear them above the wind, riding toward us."

His eyes flared in exaltation. "The Valkyries come! We are dead and the messengers of Odin ride to bear us to Valhalla!"

So wild and eery their surroundings, that the staggering Fallon himself seemed to hear thunder of rushing hoofbeats and a stabbing of silver-clear cries above the screeching wind.

Snow suddenly kicked up a yard from the American, and a shot rang through the uproar of tempest. He whirled, and stared unbelievingly.

Victor Heysing was coming up the gorge toward them, his black figure clear against the aurora-lit snow. The Nazi triggered his pistol again and the slug whistled past Fallon and hit the Norwegian's lower arm.

Fallon could have admired the Nazi's relentless devotion to duty, at another time. It was clear that Heysing had watched their plane land, had seen that they could have escaped injury, and had himself landed down the gorge and come on foot to finish them while they lay unconscious.

Blind rage at the merciless pursuit exploded in Mart Fallon's brain. He flung himself with a crazy access of strength toward the other.

Heysing's gun kicked twice and searing flame grazed the American's temple. He was upon the Nazi before he could trigger again. He tore at the man's gun, his other fists weakly smashing at Heysing's face.

"You weak fool!" snarled the Nazi, contemptuous of the strengthless blows as he sought to free his gun-hand.

Heysing's blond, devilishly handsome young face had not a trace of apprehension in it. The superbly muscled officer had a wolf's tough strength, and Fallon knew that he himself was going fast.

That knowledge, and the red sting of hate, convulsed his body for a final effort. He jabbed both hands savagely into Heysing's chin. As the Nazi struggled to keep his balance, Fallon snatched fiercely at the gun.

He got it. But before he could use it, Heysing was charging back in at him with a snarl of fury. His cap had been knocked off and his blond hair and contorted, handsome face were clear in the spectral brilliance. Fallon's arms felt like lead as he struck clumsily with the clubbed gun.

The weapon rang on the Nazi's head, and he pitched into the snow. Fallon turned back toward the Norwegian, and as he did so, fell forward on hands and knees. He knew consciousness was running out of him but he crawled blindly forward through the snow.

But why, above the shriek and whistle of the winds, did he still seem to hear the thunder of nearing hoofbeats and the squalling cry of a hunting beast? Why did the unearthly flare of the aurora seem waxing in brilliance all along the gorge?

Helverson was on his knees in the snow, his massive face flaming wildly as he pointed back down the gorge.

"The Valkyr-maidens!" he was shouting in a hoarse cry against the wind. "They come!"

Fallon tried to turn to look behind him, but everything seemed spinning around him now. His brain refused to credit what his eyes saw.

Rushing up the gorge was thundering a wild troop of riders. They *were* Valkyries, warrior-maids of ancient legend, mailed and armed and with their pale gold hair flowing from beneath their winged helmets. Their silver cry streamed out on the shrieking wind.

"Yo to ho! Yo to ho!"

The messengers of Odin, the choosers of the slain, riding fast toward him through night and wind and flaming Northern Lights!

Fallon knew it was delirium as those incredible riders rushed upon him. In their lead, upon a black stallion, rode a mailed girl who wore no helmet and whose gold hair streamed back in the wind like flame. And by her knee, like a hunting dog, loped a huge white lynx.

This Valkyr-leader had seen the little group—the prostrate Nazi, the raving Norwegian, the drunkenly swaying American. Her voice pealed in a cry of command as she drew rein beside Fallon.

An incredibly beautiful white face looked down through the dark mists that were closing over Fallon's mind. It was a face fearless and dynamic, whose most wonderful feature was the stormy blue eyes in which little lightnings seemed to flash.

Her red lips uttered a ringing order. The white lynx padding toward Fallon snarled and stopped. A Valkyr-maid spurred to the senseless Heysing and stooped low and pulled him across her saddle-bow. Another took the Norwegian in similar fashion. And Fallon felt the unbelievably strong arm of a third girl hook his shoulder and pull him onto her horse.

The unhelmed girl leader shouted another command and spurred forward. And the whole troop galloped on up the snowy gorge, with the wind at their backs and their silver cry pealing in the Northern Lights.

"Yo to ho!"

Fallon knew that all this must be the delirium before death, yet he struggled to remain conscious as he jounced on the galloping steed.

He could dimly hear Helverson's voice raving near him. "I told you the old gods lived! We are dead, and they bear us to Valhalla!"

Fallon's darkening mind wondered if the Norseman could be right. He might, indeed, be dead for his body seemed now to have lost almost all sensation.

He opened his eyes for a last time. They had galloped up the gorge to a narrow, snowy pass. Beyond its crest lay a great valley cupped by towering, icy peaks.

But he could not see down into that valley. Was it his dimming vision or was it magic that made the whole valley seem an unseeable blind spot?

His sight seemed to curve *around* it. The entrance to it was an uncanny blank in his vision.

Yet the girl leader was riding fearlessly forward, and the other Valkyries followed. Fallon felt a sudden sharp, wrenching shock as though he had fallen from a great height. He was now inside the blind-spot valley.

And now, he could see its interior. It stretched miles away, a dim vista of forests and fields and stone castles, toward a distant sheer cliff against which bulked the frowning mass of the biggest stone citadel.

He could no longer sustain consciousness. As he sank into darkness, his last sensation was hearing Helverson's mad, exultant cry.

"Valhalla! Valhalla!"

CHAPTER III
Daughter of the Gods

Fallon woke from heavy sleep, with a feeling of extraordinary lightness and well-being. He looked around bewilderedly. He was lying upon a bed made of hides stretched on a massive wooden frame whose four posts were carved into wolfsheads. It occupied a corner of a dusky stone room that had no other furniture except some hide chairs.

There were two windows, tall, narrow and slit-like. They were wholly unglazed and unshuttered, and admitted air so sharply chill that it set Fallon to shivering. At one window bulked the massive figure of Helverson, gazing eagerly forth into the gray daylight.

"Nels!" exclaimed the American, sitting up. "I thought you were nearly dead. Those two wounds you got—"

Helverson turned. His blue eyes gleamed with a curious exaltation as he approached.

"Why, I *am* dead," said the Norwegian simply. "So are you."

Fallon felt a gust of impatience. "What are you talking about? You're as alive as I am."

"We are dead," Helverson repeated with firm conviction. "We died in that snowy gorge, and the Valkyries came and bore us here to Valhalla."

Fallon suddenly remembered. The crash of their plane, the fight with Heysing—and then that incredible troop of wild Valkyr-maids who had galloped up the gorge and had carried all three of them into an uncanny hidden valley that could not be seen from outside.

Surely that had all been delirium? Yet if so, where were they now and how had they come here? Fallon stumbled hastily to one of the narrow windows. Astonishment and awe fell upon him as he looked forth.

His window was high in that massive, square stone castle which hugged the looming cliff at the head of the valley. He could look straight down into paved courts and smaller stone buildings. Down there were mounted men and men afoot. But they wore armor and horned helmets and short fur jerkins. And they carried swords and shields and axes!

Fallon's dazed eyes lifted to search the distance. The gray daylight had a curiously pale, cloudy quality but by it he could see far back down the valley. Dark forests of shaggy pine and fir clothed its floor and the lower slopes of the bounding precipices. He glimpsed other, smaller stone castles out there, miles away. Most upsetting of all, he could nowhere see out of the valley, now that he was in it.

"I don't understand this," Fallon gasped. "There's no one at all lives in the wilderness of north Norway. What is this place?"

"It is Valhalla, the home of the old gods," Helverson said with absolute faith. "The paradise to which are borne all who die in battle.

"Was it not the Valkyries who brought us here?" the Norwegian continued. "Was their leader not Thor's daughter, the warrior-goddess Brynhild herself, she who is magic mistress of lightning, wind, and storm as her father was?"

"Thor's daughter?" Fallon remembered now the beautiful girl who had ridden unhelmed at the head of those wild warrior-maids, with a great lynx loping at her knee.

"Aye, the daughter of Thor, the god of lightnings," affirmed Helverson. "She it is who always leads the messengers of Odin."

The American exploded. "Thor and Odin and the other old Norse gods are only myths! You must be out of your head from those wounds. Here, let me look at them."

He opened Helverson's bloodstained jacket. A chill amazement shocked him to find that the Norwegian's two bullet-wounds had disappeared. There were only two livid scars to mark their place.

Stunned, Fallon raised his hand to his own temple. The furrow that Heysing's grazing bullet had cut there was gone. He could feel nothing but a healed scar.

"This is insane," he choked. "Our wounds couldn't have vanished like that. It's magic!"

"Aye, magic of the Aesir, of the old gods," rumbled Helverson devoutly. "Now that we are dead and in Valhalla, no wounds can harm us."

Fallon's Twentieth Century mind shook beneath the impact of unexplainable mystery. His skepticism wavered. What if they really *had* died back in that gorge?

He knew the legends of the old Norse gods. Legends of their fabulous home in Asgard, the castle Valhalla to which were borne all warriors who died in battle and who there lived immortally on. Legends that for thousands of years had been firmly believed by the fierce Vikings of the North. What if those stories were not legend, but *truth?*

"I won't believe it!" Fallon shouted, seeking to prop up tottering reason. "This is the year 1940, not the dark ages. And I'm not dead—I'm living. If I weren't living, would I feel cold?"

He was, indeed, shivering from the sharp chill of the air from the open windows. Looking around, he noticed fur jackets hanging from pegs in a corner of the stone room. With relief, he donned one of the short, jerkin-like garments.

In doing so, Fallon discovered inside his own uniform the heavy pistol he had wrenched from Heysing in the fight. Its magazine was still half full, and it gave him a sudden new feeling of confidence.

"Listen, I want you to get over that crazy notion that this is Valhalla, and get down to earth," he told Helverson urgently. "We're going to go out and find out where we are and how we got here, and what the shortest route to the northern coast villages is."

The Norwegian shook his yellow head. "We can't leave here. Those whom the Valkyr-maids bear to Asgard never return to men."

"*We'll* return to men," Fallon promised grimly. "The information I have about the Nazi defenses at Narvik will be vital if I can get it back to England, and I'm going to get it there."

He tucked the pistol inside his fur jacket and started toward the heavy plank door of the chamber. It opened suddenly before he reached it, and two men strode in.

They were figures out of history and romance. For they were Vikings, big, burly men whose yellow hair flowed to their shoulders and whose pale eyes were bleak as the northern ice. Each was armed with a heavy sword and round shield. Each wore a horned helmet, and a fur jacket over a mail shirt and tight breeches of soft leather.

One of the two Vikings, a man of over middle age with iron-hard, weather-seamed face, spoke curtly to Fallon and Helverson. He spoke in an archaic form of the Norse tongue, strange but comprehensible.

"The princess Brynhild commands your presence, strangers," he barked. "We will lead you."

"Brynhild! Thor's daughter!" cried Helverson. He turned excitedly to the American. "Said I not that it was so?"

Fallon was staring bewilderedly at the two Vikings. "You two are not men of the outer world!"

The older warrior shrugged. "We were of the outer world once. I am Tyr, captain of the Aesir, and this is Heimdall,"

Helverson gasped, his eyes dilating with awe. "Tyr, the god of war? And Heimdall, the watcher of the gods?"

Fallon looked incredulously from the one warrior to the other, from the iron-hard face of the man who called himself Tyr to the alert, keen, middle-aged face of Heimdall.

The young American felt caught in a nightmare of unrealities. These men were as real as himself. Yet they claimed to be of the Aesir, the ancient Norse gods who had been legend for thousands of years.

Fallon struggled against the crumbling of his skepticism. "Then this *is* Valhalla?"

Tyr stared at him. "You stand in Valhalla castle, citadel of the Aesir and stronghold of Asgard."

He and Heimdall led the way out of the door, and the American pilot followed with Helverson as numbly as in a dream.

They went along a shadowy stone corridor and then down massive stairs. Fallon glimpsed men and women in the chambers and passageways of the castle. They seemed all of the same big, fair-haired race as his escort. The warriors wore armor, and carried sword or axe. Some of the lithe young girls were in glittering mail also. Others wore white gowns.

He and Helverson were conducted to a long stone hall of giant dimensions. Its only occupants were a group of towering chieftains of the Aesir who were gathered near a raised stone dais at the farther end.

As they neared that group, Fallon went tense with recognition and reawakened hatred. For Victor Heysing stood there. The handsome, blond young Nazi officer, looking oddly out of place in his black uniform, was watching Fallon's approach with narrowed eyes.

"So that devil was brought here too," Fallon muttered tautly. "Then I'm not dreaming. *He's* real, anyway."

"Thor's daughter!" Helverson was gasping. "I told you that it was she!"

Fallon followed the Norwegian's eager, reverent stare, his eyes lifting to the girl who sat on the dais in a black marble chair.

He thrilled to a shock as of tangible force. All thought of his bitter enemy was swept away by the tumult of his emotions. His first thought was that this girl who was looking down at him *was* a goddess.

She did not now wear the shining mail that she had worn as leader of the wild Valkyries. That had been put aside, and almost her only garment was a short black kirtle held by a jeweled girdle, and high-laced sandals of soft leather. Her only upper garment was the long hair that fell like a torrent of golden flame around her high, white breasts. A queer, lambent light seemed to glow from her body.

It was the unearthly, dynamic beauty of the face that held Fallon's eyes. The royal beauty of perfectly chiseled features and sweet red lips was a frame for eyes whose blue gaze met his like a sword-shock. Those eyes, clear azure depths in which tiny lightnings seemed constantly to flash and play, held him hypnotized.

A low snarl woke him from the spell. Beside the marble chair of Thor's daughter, crouched the white lynx. The beast was huge beyond the custom of its kind. And it was showing menacing fangs and talons as its slant green eyes blazed at the American.

Brynhild's voice rang impatient, silver command to the animal. "Be silent!"

The lynx settled back upon its belly obediently, but it continued to glare at Fallon.

The eyes of Brynhild ran over Fallon's tall, lean figure and black hair, glanced at the eager, massive face of Helverson, and then returned to the American.

"*You* do not look like one of our northern races, dark one," she said to Fallon with musing interest. "What is your name?"

Unsteadily, he told her. Brynhild repeated it, her sweet red lips forming it oddly. Suddenly she asked, "Why were you and this other outlander battling in the gorge?"

Fallon shot a bitter glance at Heysing. "He is our enemy. Our peoples are at war."

The result of his statement amazed him. A flash lit Brynhild's blue eyes. And from the towering Aesir chieftains came chorus of eager and excited exclamations.

"War?" cried the fierce-eyed Tyr. "War in the northland again? You bring good news, outlander!"

A murmur of exultant agreement came from the other Aesir chieftains. The fact of war in the outer world seemed to stir them like a trumpet-blast.

"It has been long that the outer peoples have slumbered in soft, fat peace," Brynhild declared. "Tell me of this war, stranger."

Fallon pointed accusingly at Victor Heysing. "His people, the Germans, began the war. They have invaded the northland and attacked its people without reason, and my own outland countries seek to help the Norse defenders resist."

Heysing took a step forward, speaking hastily to the listening daughter of Thor.

"It is not so, princess!" denied the Nazi. "My people are of the north themselves, blood-cousins of the Norse. We came into the northland only to protect our Norse friends from the degenerate outlanders who would have used them as tools for their own purposes."

Helverson uttered a roar of anger. "The German lies! We Norse wished none of his protection!"

Fallon spoke earnestly to the girl, whose brilliant blue eyes were searching their faces during this hot dispute.

"Is it possible to leave this valley?" Fallon asked. "I have information that would help my people drive the invaders out of the northland, if I can get it to them."

He waited tensely for the answer. He could not, in spite of everything, believe that he and Helverson were really dead. If they were not, it deepened the mystery of this unearthly fulfillment of the ancient legends of the gods. But it also meant that he was duty-bound to escape this uncanny place and get his information back to his commanders.

Brynhild spoke decisively. "You cannot leave the valley of Asgard, outlander. At least not until we have learned all the truth about this war of which you speak."

She brooded, her chin upon her white hand. "We Aesir are tired of peace. Now that war has come again to the northland, it may be that once again we shall know the joy of battle!"

That electric flash came and went again in her eyes, fleeting revelation of a wild, fierce, untamed spirit.

Fallon protested. "But I must get out of here and get back to my own people!"

Brynhild's blue gaze darkened stormily. Her silver voice flared. "No one here in Asgard says 'must' to the daughter of Thor, outlander!"

Helverson plucked at Fallon's sleeve and whispered frantically. "Do not anger the goddess!"

Brynhild was continuing haughtily. "It is not often now that I ride forth into the outer snows with my Valkyr-maids. It has been our custom, when we do so, to bring back wounded men we happened to find, and give them life here. But none of them leaves this valley thereafter!"

Victor Heysing gave Fallon a taunting smile, as the German understood that the young American could not get away with his information.

The triumph in that smile infuriated Fallon. He felt desperate. He must somehow get out of this mysterious valley of ancient gods. The fate of an Allied attack on Narvik depended on his doing so.

His hand slipped inside his fur jacket and grasped the butt of his pistol. He suddenly flashed out the weapon and covered Brynhild with it. His lean face was dark and tense.

"This is an outland weapon," he told her harshly. "It can kill you in an instant. You are going to allow me to leave this place."

A roar of rage broke from the Aesir chieftains, and their swords rasped from their sheaths. The white lynx crouched and snarled, gathering itself to spring upon the American. Helverson, appalled by his action, seemed petrified by superstitious horror.

"Keep back, all of you!" Fallon shouted. "Your princess will die before you can touch me."

It was bluff on Fallon's part—wild, desperate bluff.

Brynhild was laughing! Sheer amusement rippled in her silver laughter as she looked down at Fallon. With a gesture, she had restrained the crouching lynx and the furious Aesir.

"Do you really think you could kill the daughter of Thor with that toy?" she mocked. "Why, stranger, you are mad, I think. Watch!"

And she levelled her hand in a swift, thrusting gesture. What followed was almost beyond Fallon's comprehension.

Lightning seemed to leap from her hand, a flashing bolt of electric flame that struck his pistol and sent it flying through the air.

Fallon staggered, his whole arm suddenly numb from shock. He felt half-stunned, wholly unable as yet to *believe* that the girl above had actually wielded such force. He saw the awe on Helverson's face, the amazement and sudden calculation on Heysing's. But clearest in his dazed vision were the contemptuous blue eyes of Brynhild.

Magic-mistress of lightnings she might be, but that cool contempt in her face swept Fallon to a climax of unreasoning rage and despair. Heedless of consequences, he rushed forward at the girl on the dais.

CHAPTER IV
Magic Menace

Brynhild instantly moved her white hands faster than the eye could follow, in a curious weaving gesture. Her whole body seemed to *flame.*

Dancing brands of lightning blazed from her hands to form an awful, dazzling curtain of electric fire in front of her. Crashing thunder shook the great stone hall. Fallon recoiled staggeringly from that curtain of lightning—and swiftly, it was gone.

"Good God!" husked the American, staring at the girl with unbelieving eyes.

Roars of anger came from the Aesir captains. One of them, a tall, fair, sullen-faced chieftain, raised his sword to lunge at Fallon.

"Wait, Thialfi!" rang Brynhild's silver command. "I said not that the man was to be killed."

The chieftain called Thialfi halted, but protested angrily. "And why should he not be killed, when he has dared threaten one of us Aesir?"

"*I* rule the Aesir, cousin Thialfi," she reminded imperiously. "You grow too presumptuous, I think—too much as your father Loki was."

She laughed softly, eyeing Fallon. "This outlander has courage, even though he is not of the northern folk. He shall not die—yet."

Fallon stood, still literally stunned by the incredible phenomenon that had almost cost his life. Was this wildly beautiful girl human? Could any human have evoked that crashing blaze of lightning?

Could any but a goddess have loosed such forces? A goddess who could control the very elements of nature? Magic of superhuman powers clung about this girl like a tangible and terrible aura.

Helverson's awed whisper echoed his whirling thoughts. "She is, indeed, daughter of Thor, the storm-god of lightnings."

Brynhild heard the Norwegian, and nodded her fair head. "Yes, Norseman. I am daughter of Thor and granddaughter of Odin, and though Thor and Odin are gone now, I hold their wisdom and their power."

Victor Heysing stepped forward. The amazement on the Nazi's blond, handsome face had now been replaced by a breathless eagerness and excitement.

"Princess, *I* never doubted your power," the German said quickly. "Yet I am bewildered by all these things. My own people have for three thousand years reverenced the names of Odin and Thor and the other Aesir, yet we dreamed not that any of you still existed. Are you really the ancient gods?"

Brynhild mused. "Are we gods? You of the outer world always thought so. I remember how your world hailed me and my Valkyr-maids as goddesses when we rode forth, a thousand of your years ago."

"A thousand years ago?" gasped Heysing. "Your pardon, princess—I do not presume to doubt. But if you Aesir are immortal—"

"I said not that we were immortal," Brynhild answered impatiently. "A thousand of your outside world's years equals but ten of *our* years. Time is slower in this valley—a hundred times slower."

The shock of that revelation woke Mart Fallon's numbed mind to life. Was it possible that that was what underlay all the awesome mystery of this valley of the gods?

"You would not understand if I were to explain to you," Brynhild was continuing, half-contemptuously. "Your outland wisdom is only a practical science of matter and machines. You have nothing of the deeper wisdom of cosmic powers and forces which we Aesir learned here."

Her brilliant blue eyes brooded. "This much, I will tell you. Time is an attribute or dimension of space. And space, as you may be beginning to learn by now, is not static but is a curved, expanding sphere. The strain of expansion causes faults or weak spots in that space-time sphere—spots where time is foreshortened. This valley is such a spot. A year in our valley equals a hundred years outside it.

"It was three thousand of your years ago that my people, the Aesir, found this magic valley. They were but one of the Norse races of that time, warlike Vikings who followed their chieftain Odin through the northern wilderness in search of a new home. They came upon this valley and settled in it, and named it Asgard.

"Three thousand of your years ago that was—but only thirty of *our* years! Here, under the wise leadership of Odin, my people built their homes. And here Odin and his son Thor delved deep into the cosmic forces that are brought to a focus in this fault of the space-time sphere, and won for themselves such powers as your outer world knows not."

Brynhild's face was dreaming. "I was born in this valley Asgard, twenty years ago by my time—two thousand years ago by yours. I was but a little child when my grandfather Odin and my father Thor taught me the first rudiments of their wisdom. We Aesir were great, then. Rumor of our powers and our superhuman length of life drifted to the outer world, and the northland races out there worshipped us as gods."

Bitterness came into her voice. "But pride and ambition brought tragedy among us, when I was still but a child. My own father's cousin, the brilliant and evil Loki, aspired to replace my house as ruler of the Aesir. Dreadful battle came from Loki's rebellion—battle in which not only he but Odin and my father Thor also met their deaths."

The Aesir chieftain named Thialfi made angry protest to Brynhild. "Can you never forget my father's rebellion? All that is dead and past now."

The girl's eyes flared at him momentarily, but then she relaxed. "Yes, all that is of the dead past now," she admitted. "You know that I have never held your father's evildoing against you, Thialfi. You were but a child then, as I was a child."

Her golden head lifted in pride. "But even as a child, I succeeded to the rulership of the Aesir, and inherited the powers of Odin and my father Thor over natural forces."

"And you have ruled us with wisdom, niece Brynhild," the stern-faced Tyr declared loyally. "It is not your fault that life has grown tame and wearisome for us in this peaceful valley."

"This flat and featureless peace wearies *me,* too!" Brynhild exclaimed almost fiercely. "We Aesir were made for war, not for soft living. We rust and rot away our lives here, without the joy of battle."

She made a scornful gesture. "But it would have been no use for us to have left our valley for the outer world. Until now, tame and ignoble peace has reigned out there in the northland for hundreds of their years."

Mart Fallon had listened in deepening bewilderment and dismay. So this was the incredible reality behind the age-old legends of the Norse gods and their immortality and superhuman powers over nature?

It was logical enough, his dazed mind admitted. Granted that this secret valley in the northern wilderness was really a fault or weak spot in the space-time continuum, it followed that time here *could* be foreshortened so that a hundred days outside were but a day here. It followed, too, that this spot could well be the focus of tremendous natural forces whose mastery had been won by the rulers of these Aesir.

But, and this was what dismayed Fallon in his first realization, if that were true, then the hours he had already spent in this valley amounted to weeks or months in the outer world! By this time, the battle of Narvik would have been decided long ago. His plan to take his vital information back to his commanders was now hopelessly obsolete and useless.

Fallon became aware that Victor Heysing was speaking to the Aesir princess. The young Nazi officer seemed possessed by excitement.

"Princess, not all the outland peoples are tame and soft," Heysing affirmed. "My own German people, who are blood-kin to you Norse, reject like yourselves the soft blandishments of peace in favor of the stern ideals of war."

The Nazi's voice had a ring of fanaticism. "We have a Leader, the greatest in the outside world. He has brought war back to the world, though the cowardly southern and western nations pleaded for peace. He has made of us a race of warriors who stride to conquest of all the world."

Heysing leaned forward, his eyes glowing. "You Aesir could join us in that mighty battle, princess. A battle whose loot will be the world itself! You are a northern race like us. If you joined us, your powers over natural forces would sweep the soft peoples of the world before us!"

Fallon was thunderstruck. The Nazi, like himself, had realized that this valley was the focus of cosmic natural forces which somehow the daughter of Thor knew how to harness and use.

With characteristic opportunism, Heysing was seeking to enlist the unguessable power of those weapons upon the side of Hitler's legions! He had proposed flattering alliance to the Aesir princess, meaning without doubt to use her and her powers as the tool of his conquest-minded country.

Brynhild's eyes had flashed as she listened. "It is good to hear that one race of the outer world has remained hard and warlike!"

And the Aesir chieftains had become suddenly tense with fierce excitement.

"Princess Brynhild, I favor this man's plan!" exclaimed Thialfi, a savage light on his sullen face now. "With you and your powers to lead us, and the hordes of his German race to follow us, we *could* loot the world!"

"At least, it would mean battle and action again instead of rotting away in this valley," muttered the tall Aesir captain, Heimdall.

Appalled, Fallon burst into interruption. "Do you realize what this German would have you do?" he cried to Thor's daughter. "He would have you join a leader whose hands are red with the blood of slaughtered nations, a nation that without pretext has attacked unoffending peoples."

Brynhild looked down at the American with an expression of disdain. "I thought you were a warrior, outlander. Yet you talk as though war was horrible."

"It *is* horrible," Fallon declared from the depths of his feelings. "It is to end war forever that my people are fighting the German race."

The daughter of Thor and the Aesir chieftains stared at him with a cold, biting contempt, as though he had said something shameful.

"By the Norns, the German spoke truth when he said that the other outland races are degenerate!" exclaimed Thialfi scornfully. "This fellow is fit only to be a thrall."

"*My* people do not hold such cowardly beliefs," put in Heysing proudly. "We exalt war and the warrior above all else."

He looked up eagerly at Brynhild. "Will you join us, princess? Will you ally your powers to the only true warrior race of the outer world?"

"I say, let us join these Germans," Thialfi declared, and there was a quick chorus of agreement from many of the Aesir lords.

"I remind you again that *I* rule the Aesir," Brynhild flared at Loki's son.

Until now, Helverson had stood beside Fallon, bewilderedly listening to the excited discussion. Now, for the first time, the big Norwegian spoke in his rumbling voice to the girl on the marble seat.

"You would not join the Germans?" he asked incredulously. "You are the Aesir, the ancient hero-gods of our Norse race. And the Germans are our enemies."

Heysing hastily intervened. "We are not enemies of the Norse people," he denied. "As I told you, we seek only to protect them from the cowardly western nations who would trick them for selfish purposes."

The Nazi added quickly to Brynhild, "Once you Aesir appeared and joined us, all the northern peoples would fall in behind us. For your names have an ancient power in the hearts of the north."

Fallon knew that the Nazi was right in that last claim. The appearance of the Aesir of ancient legend, led by Thor's daughter herself, *would* swing age-old Scandinavian beliefs toward the side of the Germans.

Before the American could protest Heysing's other falsehoods, Brynhild rose to her feet. Her blue eyes were brooding and thoughtful as she looked down at them.

"Lords of the Aesir, the decision on this matter is not to be made lightly," she told them. "Before I decide, I shall take counsel of all the chieftains of our people. Summon them here for council tonight."

Thialfi pointed to the Nazi. "With your permission, I'll keep this man with me today. I wish to hear more of his plan."

Brynhild nodded curtly. "But bring him to the council here in Valhalla tonight."

Her eyes rested a moment on Fallon's dark, desperate face. "See that this man and his comrade make no attempt to leave the valley," she ordered. "I make you responsible for them, Tyr."

Her slim figure disappeared through a curtained doorway beside the dais, the white lynx padding silently at her side.

Heysing went with Thialfi, glancing back with covert triumph at the American. Fallon found Helverson plucking at his sleeve.

"I cannot understand," the Norwegian said, his massive face anxious and puzzled. "These are the old gods of my people. Surely they would not join with the invaders who now devastate our land?"

"They won't join the Nazis if I can help it," Fallon said tautly. "Nels, we've got to stop that somehow! My God, that girl can control the lightning and forces of nature itself! If the Nazis get hold of her powers—"

The dreadful possibilities unreeled in his mind. They held disaster for the Allied cause. That disaster would not come from the mere addition of a few thousand fierce warriors to the Nazi legions. Not even though the appearance of the legended Aesir as allies of the Axis might well superstitiously influence the northern peoples into following Hitler also.

The real menace was in those tremendous and mysterious powers of which Brynhild was mistress. This unique fault in the continuum of space-time was the focus of cosmic forces unknown to the outer world. The ruling house of the Aesir had learned how to wield those forces. If Germany learned that also, its scientists would be able to forge weapons that would blast the armies of the democracies from existence.

"Heysing must not persuade Brynhild to join the Nazis!" he said feverishly. "They'll use her and her warriors as tools, and as soon as they have learned the secret of her powers, will throw her aside."

Helverson groaned. "How can *we* stop it? These Aesir long for war and battle. They are tempted by the German's promise of fighting."

"They're a race with the Viking warlike traditions of centuries ago," Fallon agreed. "They think war is all that is manly and admirable."

"Thor's daughter seemed to like you, Fallon," the Norwegian said doubtfully. "I could see that you interested her. Maybe if you made love to her, you could turn her against Heysing's proposal?"

"Don't be a fool," the American retorted. "She and all the rest of these people think I'm a coward now because I said I hated war. We've got to find some better plan than that to beat that damned Nazi—"

He broke off. The chieftain Tyr was approaching them, for now the great hall of Valhalla was almost empty except for themselves.

Tyr had a half-disgusted expression on his hard, grizzled face. "Now I have you on my hands to guard," he growled. "Let me give you fair warning—at the slightest attempt to escape, you'll be killed."

"That's clear enough," Fallon admitted. "But you don't have to lock us up in that chamber again, do you?"

Tyr shrugged wide shoulders. "You can come out with me to watch our warriors at their games, if you wish. Or perhaps the sight of even friendly fighting would sicken a lover of peace like yourself?"

Fallon flushed at the gibe, but answered evenly. "We'll go out with you and watch."

As they accompanied the armored Aesir chieftain down a long stone hall, the American asked him a question. "Is that fellow Thialfi very close to the princess Brynhild?"

Tyr looked at him quizzically. "He hopes to be her bridegroom. Though I do not know why that should interest you, outlander."

Fallon was dismayed by the information. He knew the sulky-faced Thialfi strongly favored Heysing's proposal. If the man were that close to Thor's daughter, he would surely influence her toward the plan.

The situation seemed more and more hopeless, but the American refused to surrender hope. Somehow, he told himself desperately, he *must* find a way to defeat the Nazi's evil scheme.

They emerged from the massive face of Valhalla castle into the chill day. Looking back upward, he was struck by the way in which the citadel hugged the sheer, frowning rock cliff that rose far overhead.

Helverson was staring puzzledly at the gray sky. "I cannot understand why there is day and night in this valley," he muttered. "If the time here is a hundred times faster than outside, there should be daylight and night every few minutes."

"You're forgetting that this is the midnight sun country, far north of the Arctic Circle," Fallon reminded him. "The day and night are each months long, outside here. In here, they're only hours long."

"Then it's already been months since we entered here!" gasped the Norwegian. "What has happened out in my country since then?"

Horsemen were galloping away down the valley toward the other distant castles, spurring along narrow roads through the dark forest.

"They go to summon all our chieftains to the council tonight," grunted Tyr. "Niord and Bragi and Hermod and all the rest will be here."

The grizzled captain led the way to a small natural amphitheater near Valhalla castle, in which a crowd was gathering. Tall Viking warriors, lithe Valkyr-girls in glittering mail, older women in long white linen gowns, even children—all had come to watch the games.

Fallon was astonished by the character of the contests. Aesir warriors fought with padded battle-axes that were still highly dangerous to skulls. They wrestled furiously, with many bruising falls until one or the other was senseless. They sparred with sword and shield until both contestants were bleeding from serious wounds. The crowd applauded wildly.

"You Aesir have rough sports," the American commented in amazement. "I'd think that you would all kill each other in these games."

"Now and then a man gets killed but not often," Tyr answered casually. "Many are wounded, but Brynhild's magic makes them whole again."

He added discontentedly, "But we're tired of this mock fighting. There's nothing else to do—nothing but hunt occasionally in the forests and supervise the thralls who till our fields. We'll be joyful if Brynhild leads us forth to taste real war again!"

From nearby, the chieftain Heimdall launched an ironical invitation at Fallon. "Would you care to join in the sword-contests, outlander?"

A roar of insulting laughter went up from all the Aesir. Fallon turned dull red, knowing what these fierce, warlike men now thought of him.

He rose to his feet, determined to accept the satirical invitation and prove that he was no coward. He remembered enough of sabre-fencing from military-school days to make at least a showing.

But a sudden inspiration crossed his brain. It was the idea for which he had been seeking to defeat Victor Heysing's plans. It might work, and if it did, it would crush the Nazi's scheme.

Fallon sat down again, slowly and unwillingly. He hated doing so, but he dared take no chances until he could carry out his idea tonight.

"I thought that you would think twice before entering the games," Heimdall said scathingly to him.

Tyr turned and glared at the American. "By the Norns, you love peace indeed. The one who calls himself a German was right about the softness of your race."

Fallon ventured no reply. But on the way back to the castle later with their disgusted guard, he found a chance to whisper to Helverson.

"I've an idea for ending Heysing's devilish plans," he said rapidly. "If that Nazi *dies* tonight, his scheme will die too!"

Darkness came softly and slowly down on the valley Asgard. It was strange to think that this slow nightfall was really the coming of the long months of Arctic night to the lands outside.

Torches flared in Valhalla's halls and passageways. Chieftains of the Aesir were constantly riding up from the castles farther down the valley, by now. Each brought with him retinue of excited fighting-men.

Tyr conducted Fallon and the Norwegian into the great council-hall. In its red torchlight, hundreds of the Aesir lords were gathered. Thialfi was there, near the throne-dais, and Victor Heysing was with him.

"Homage to the princess!" roared the shout of fierce throats as Brynhild entered and faced them from the dais.

Pride and consciousness of power were brilliant in her blue eyes as she faced them. The white lynx crouched beside her, whining softly.

Before she or anyone else could speak, Mart Fallon put his desperate idea into execution. He took a step toward the dais and raised his voice loudly.

"Princess Brynhild, hear me before your council opens!" he demanded. He pointed at Victor Heysing. "That man has said that I lied when I told you his Leader and his purposes are evil. I maintain that he lies. That forms blood-feud between us, by your own Viking traditions."

His voice rose louder. "I claim warrior's right to settle that feud here and now. By tradition, you are bound to give swords to my enemy and myself and let us fight to the death!"

CHAPTER V
Storm Sorcery

It was Fallon's desperate inspiration. He had dimly remembered that ancient Viking custom of permitting a warrior to settle a personal feud by public single combat. And he had seen in that a hazardous chance to avert Heysing's evil schemes by ending the Nazi's life.

How hazardous the chance was, he fully realized. Heysing, like most German officers of his class, would in all probability possess more skill with the saber than Fallon's own rusty practice. But the American's desperation was such that he would almost have welcomed death for himself if he could be sure of taking the Nazi with him.

The torchlit hall was in an uproar. The fierce Aesir chieftains had instantly warmed to the prospect of a death-duel.

But Thialfi was on his feet, glaring at Fallon. "It is a trick!" he accused. "The dark outlander is a coward who has no wish to fight."

Victor Heysing himself spoke up confidently. "I am ready to meet him," affirmed the Nazi loudly. "We Germans do not dodge battle."

A roar of applause greeted his boast. In this brief interval, Brynhild had been staring down at Fallon with a puzzled light in her eyes.

"I cannot understand—" she murmured perplexedly, but then broke off, and spoke in clear, chill tones to the American. "You have claimed Viking right and you shall have it, outlander. Heimdall, give them helmets, shields and swords."

A wide space was hastily cleared for the duel, in front of the dais on which Brynhild sat. Expectant excitement pervaded the throng of Aesir warriors as the preparations were made.

Helverson was expostulating with Fallon. He paid little attention, for Heimdall now had brought him the gleaming horned helmet, the small, heavy metal shield and long sword he was to use in the combat.

Tyr showed him how to hold the shield upon his left arm. "You'd best handle a sword better than a shield or you're dead now," he grunted.

The helmet felt heavy on Fallon's head, and the shield was an awkward encumbrance as he gripped his sword and stepped to meet Heysing.

Brynhild's voice rang clearly. "The fight is to the death, or until one combatant shall admit himself vanquished," she told them.

Victor Heysing had a thin, triumphant smile on his handsome blond face as he turned to face the American.

"It is too bad," he mocked Fallon, "that when you got this crazy idea, you did not know I was saber-champion at Heidelberg."

Fallon set his teeth and said nothing. The daughter of Thor, leaning forward, spoke sharply. "Begin!"

It was almost death for Fallon in the first minute. Heysing had not lied when he had boasted of his skill with the saber. The Nazi came in with a rush, his pale eyes gleaming behind his lunging blade. He was obviously determined to finish the fight as quickly as possible.

Fallon tried to parry that blow with the shield, and nearly lost his life. For his clumsy use of the unaccustomed shield merely caused it to deflect the lunging blade toward his heart. Only a frantic sidestep saved him, but the sword of his enemy slashed his sleeve as it grazed him.

Fallon stabbed back, uncertainly at first and then with rapidly increasing sureness as his rusty skill came back to him. But Heysing deftly parried the thrusts, and came back with wicked, slicing sweeps before which the American had to give ground.

Heysing knew himself the superior swordsman for certain now, and exultant satisfaction shone in his eyes.

"I am glad you challenged me, Fallon," he said mockingly under his breath as they fenced. "It will greatly increase my prestige with these people when I kill you."

Fallon made no answer. Cold premonition of imminent failure and death were chilling him. He could not get through the German's guard for a moment, and the other's sword seemed thrusting from everywhere.

As they circled and struck, blade ringing against blade or against a clanging shield, he glimpsed the torchlit, fierce faces of the Aesir throng watching the fight in delighted silence. And he had momentary vision of Brynhild's white, beautiful face and widened blue eyes.

"Take it!" hissed Heysing suddenly, and his sword-point came in like the head of a striking snake toward Fallon's heart.

Fallon frantically tried to raise the heavy shield but was only able to deflect the thrust. He felt the white-hot sting of steel searing along his left shoulder, and sprang back with blood wetting his jacket.

Roar of excitement came from the watching Aesir throng at the sight. And now Heysing was coming in with wolf-savageness, thrusting, lunging, slicing, using all his skill to beat down Fallon's guard.

Another roar from the crowd, as steel whizzed past Fallon's head and inflicted a grazing cut on his cheek.

"Finish him, now!" the voice of Thialfi was shouting in adjuration to the German.

And Fallon, red with blood and dazedly fighting off the Nazi's savage attack, glimpsed Brynhild's eyes looking at him in *pity*.

Crimson rage exploded in the American's brain. He'd be dead in a minute and this damned crowd of wolves would yell with glee. By Heaven, he'd do his best to take the Nazi with him!

Furiously, he flung away the encumbering shield and helmet. Bareheaded and with his lean, dark face raging, he flung himself forward and struck like a madman at the German.

"The outlander is berserk!" rose a yell from the watching Aesir crowd.

Fallon hardly heard it. He saw Heysing through red mists. The German's face was startled. He recoiled from the crazy attack.

No fencing or scientific swordsmanship now! Fallon was possessed by the rage to kill. And the furious sweeps of his sword were an unpredictable attack against which Heysing had no immediate defense.

The convulsive strength of his strokes beat down the Nazi's parrying blade. As Heysing staggered, Fallon slashed fiercely in again. The German tried to raise his shield. It caught the first impact of the American's sword, but the sword flashed off it and bit into Heysing's side.

The Nazi swayed, dropping his sword and then falling heavily. His helmet hit the stone floor with a resounding clang. He lay still.

"The outland berserk has conquered!" cried Heimdall incredulously.

Thialfi rushed out, his sullen face furious. "The outlander did not conquer cleanly! The German slipped in the blood on the floor."

Voices disputed that assertion of Thialfi's, but other voices supported it. The uproar in the torchlit hall of Valhalla was tumultuous.

Thialfi was appealing to Brynhild. "Let the duel be fought again when the German's wound is healed! That is but justice."

Fallon leaned on his bloody sword, panting for breath and with those red mists only now dissolving from his brain. Brynhild, Tyr, all the Aesir, were eyeing him now with a perplexed respect.

They knew he was no coward now, he thought with grim satisfaction. For they thought him a "berserk," most dreaded of Viking warriors, a man who flung away his armor when possessed by blood-madness in battle.

Brynhild raised her hand imperiously to still the clamorous dispute about the fairness of Fallon's triumph.

"*I* did not see the German slip, cousin Thialfi," she said curtly. "But since you claim he did, he shall be allowed the chance to repeat the duel when he is fit to fight again."

Fallon, standing a little weak and dizzy from loss of blood of his own wounds, made no objection to that decision.

"It's all right," he told Helverson, who had sprung to his side anxiously. "Heysing will be unable to hatch his scheme until he recovers, and that will give us time to figure a way of beating him."

But he was soon to discover that his calculations had reckoned without the fantastic powers of which Brynhild was mistress.

Thor's daughter had come down from the dais toward him. That new, puzzled respect was strong in her dynamic face as she spoke.

"Outlander, I shall soon heal those wounds of yours," she told him. "I see now that we misjudged you. Come with me."

"And the German?" Thialfi interjected urgently, gesturing to the prostrate man.

Brynhild nodded her golden head. "He, too. Bring him, Tyr."

She raised her clear voice to the Aesir throng. "We cannot hold council now, chieftains. It must wait until the morrow."

Brynhild moved through the curtained doorway beside the throne-dais, with the white lynx padding softly at her side. Fallon unsteadily followed her, and Tyr came after them, carrying the unconscious Nazi.

Fallon found himself with the daughter of Thor in a torchlit stone corridor that led toward the rear of Valhalla castle. It ended in a heavy door of massive bronze, beyond which was a spiral stairway tunneled out of the solid rock of the cliff.

"Where do we go?" Fallon asked doubtfully, as they entered the dark stairway.

"To heal your wounds," Brynhild answered impatiently. "I have the power to do so. Come!"

She grasped his wrist, leading up the twisting rock steps. It was the first time Fallon had experienced her touch. It sent a thrilling, faintly electric shock through him, as though life and energy flowed into him from the contact.

And Brynhild's slim white body glowed in the darkness of the stair with that dim lambency that had been only barely noticeable in the lighted hall. It made her seem more eerily unhuman—and yet the warm, tingling clasp of her fingers was far from that.

The lynx snarled from the darkness above them, and Brynhild laughed softly. "Inro is jealous of you, outlander."

Fallon felt a queer thudding of his pulses. He could hear Tyr grunting below them as he climbed with his senseless burden.

They went higher and higher inside the cliff. Fallon estimated vaguely that they must be near its top. A dim uproar of winds came to his ears from above, and gusty currents of freezing air smote his face.

They emerged suddenly into darkness and cold, buffeting winds. Fallon stopped short, momentarily appalled by the giddiness and danger of their situation.

This was a small, flat platform hewn out of the solid rock at the very peak of the lofty cliff. It was only a dozen feet across, and completely unrailed and open to the winds. Far, far below gleamed the torchlit windows of Valhalla castle. Overhead pressed the dull black canopy of the magic valley's night sky.

Poised above the solid rock floor of this dizzy perch was a massive silver ring nine feet in diameter, carved with strange runic symbols. It hung mysteriously in midair. Moving with fearless lightness, Brynhild led him inside this queer circle.

"Put the German down here, Tyr," she bade, and the old Aesir obeyed and laid the senseless German inside the silver runic circle.

Then Tyr hastily stepped back out of the circle. He muttered, "I'll wait down inside the stair. I do not much like your healing magic, niece Brynhild."

Fallon found himself swaying on his feet, partly from the dizziness of his precarious situation and partly from the wounds that were slowly draining his strength. Brynhild touched him steadyingly, and again, tingling strength seemed to flow into him from the touch.

At her direction, he stripped off his jacket and stood with bare, bloodstained torso shivering in the freezing wind. He also removed Heysing's jacket, exposing the deep wound in the senseless Nazi's side. The white lynx had retreated to the stair, snarling uneasily.

"Now stand close beside me, outlander, and move not out of the rune-circle for your life," Brynhild warned him. "The forces I am about to summon can heal swiftly—but they can kill swiftly too."

Standing just outside the circle, Thor's daughter raised her naked white arms toward the night sky. Her blue eyes shone brilliant through the wind-swirled torrent of her pale gold hair. And the uncanny lambency that invested her fair body deepened to a glow.

Great gusts of wind suddenly buffeted them furiously, howling and shrieking in their ears as though seeking to tear them from the lofty cliff. The chill night was suddenly roaringly alive with rising storm-voices. Fallon felt a shivering not wholly born of the cold.

Brynhild's silver, ringing laughter pealed out on the raging wind. Her face was turned toward the zenith, and from her upstretched fingertips seemed to dart tiny threads of light. The American's hair rose on his head. He sensed the ominous gathering of vast forces.

Crash! He staggered, dazed and blinded by the terrific bolt of lightning that stabbed down at them. That flaring bolt seemed to strike down toward Brynhild's upstretched hands, and then to be deflected toward the silver ring. Another awful bolt followed it, and another and another. Electric flames danced dazzlingly on the silver rune-ring.

Fallon shouted hoarsely to the girl, his voice thin and puny against the rocking thunderclaps. "If that lightning strikes us—"

"It will not, for I am its mistress," pealed Brynhild's voice. "But keep here within the ring!"

The scene was mind-shattering, to the American. The almost continuous bolts of lightning striking all around the ring, each sheeted flare throwing into wild illumination Brynhild's glowing figure; the deafening thunder; the shrieking winds that swept their dizzy perch.

Electric flame now completely encircled them in a slowly rising wall. Fallon felt the thrilling shock of electrical or other forces that pervaded every cell of his body. His brain spun with vertigo.

"Stand fast!" warned Thor's daughter over the crashing tumult. "It will be but a moment."

It seemed more like a timeless eternity to Fallon's stunned brain that he stood with the Aesir girl and the unconscious German in the heart of a blazing, inconceivably powerful sphere of electric force.

The thrilling tingle in his body was almost unbearable. He looked down and saw violet electric brush spraying from his own body. He heard Brynhild laugh above the smash of crashing lightning.

"It is enough," she seemed to be saying. And she lowered her arms.

Magically, the bolts of lightning ceased. And as the rocking reverberations of thunder ebbed away, the wall of flaming force around the silver rune-ring sank and died.

Fallon, coming slowly out of his daze, found himself standing with Brynhild in the windy darkness. Her body still shone uncannily bright, and her brilliant, laughing blue eyes mocked his stupefaction.

"Look at your wounds now, outlander," she told him.

Fallon did so, and felt the shock of increased amazement. The stab in his left shoulder and the cut upon his cheek were both incredibly healed, as though by weeks of time. No trace of the wounds was left except two faint scars. And he felt none of his former weakness, now.

He looked down at Heysing. The Nazi still lay unconscious, but that deep sword-slash in his side was healed to a smooth scar too. And his breathing now seemed easy and normal.

"He is completely healed, as you are," Brynhild nodded to the unbelieving American. "He will wake in a few hours, as well as ever."

She raised her voice. "Ho, Tyr! Come and take the German—my magic is ended."

Tyr came reluctantly up onto the windy place, with the white lynx bounding ahead of him to rub its fierce head against Brynhild.

"I heard you at it," growled the old Aesir chieftain. "Hel take me if I ever liked it, niece. I thought the lightnings would split the whole cliff this time."

He shouldered Heysing's senseless weight as though the man was a straw, and returned with him to the stair inside the cliff.

Fallon looked earnestly at the radiant face of Thor's daughter. "Brynhild, is this how Helverson and I were healed of our wounds when we were first brought here by you?"

She nodded. "Yes, by the healing magic of the lightning. I have so healed more than one wounded or dying warrior whom my Valkyries and I found outside and brought here, in past years."

His dazed mind groped for possible explanations. He could understand that the terrific bombardment of electric radiation to which he had been subjected might by concentrated therapeutic power cause unprecedented acceleration of the processes of cell-regeneration. But how was it that Brynhild was able to summon lightning at will?

She smiled cryptically at that question. "Can you not guess an answer? You have heard that this valley represents a fault or weak spot in the fabric of space-time. Is it not possible that the vast electric forces outside our universe could easily be admitted here? And could not Odin, and Thor, and I, use those forces to convert our living bodies into powerful electric accumulators which could attract the lightning?"

Her smile deepened as she continued teasingly, "Or perhaps that is only dust that I throw into your eyes. Perhaps there are strange spirits of force inherent in the elements of nature, and maybe I can control those elementals. What think you to be the truth, outlander?"

"I can't guess," Fallon confessed. "Helverson, my comrade, thinks that you are a goddess and he explains all so."

"Then you do not think I am a goddess?" she exclaimed, with mock indignation in her voice but with taunting humor in her eyes.

"I thought you were a goddess when you called down that blaze of lightning just now," Fallon admitted. "But right at this moment, you look like a girl, the most beautiful I've ever seen."

Brynhild looked up at him demurely. "Are there no fair girls in your outer world, then?"

Her brilliant blue eyes were provocative, challenging, more than a little amused and yet a little breathless too. The royal beauty of her perfect young face stood out in the darkness with that uncanny faint radiance that was inherent in her body.

The American's throat tightened with emotion. He had lost all awareness of time or place or of anything else except those wonderful eyes in which the little lightning-sparks were now all muffled by new softness. He told himself desperately that he was losing his head, that Brynhild was only flirting with him because he was new and different to her, that he must not—

His hand went out and touched her bare shoulder, unsteadily. The tingling energy that thrilled through him from that touch completed the demoralization of his will. Fallon's arms went around the daughter of Thor and he bent and kissed her parted red lips.

The dizzily sweet shock of it set the blood roaring in his ears. He felt the torrent of golden hair against his cheek like soft flame. And Brynhild did not draw back from his clasp. When he breathlessly raised his head, she looked up at him with a strangely youthful and shy eagerness in her shining eyes.

"This is crazy," Fallon gasped. "I didn't mean to do it, but—"

"I am glad you did," Brynhild said softly. "Outlander, I was drawn to you when first I found you. But until tonight, I thought you a coward as we all did. I ask pardon for misjudging."

"You ask *my* pardon?" Fallon choked, still holding her. "It should be the other way around. I'm only a man, and you're a goddess or something near it "

There was sudden interruption—a voice speaking in fierce anger.

They both turned. Old Tyr had come back up the stair and had emerged onto the dark, windy crest of the cliff to see them in each other's arms. The Aesir's chieftain's iron face was suddenly raging.

"You lying outland dog!" he spat at Fallon. "You dared lay your vile hands on the princess of the Aesir!"

"Tyr, be silent!" ordered Brynhild imperiously. "You know not what you are saying. This outlander loves me, and you may as well learn now that I love him."

The frank avowal set Fallon's pulses racing wildly. But it seemed to increase the fury of Tyr to a point at which the chieftain's weathered face crimsoned.

"He loves you?" Tyr repeated furiously to the imperious daughter of Thor. "He has told you that? Now I see that it was well I came back up here to keep watch upon him."

The old Aesir levelled an accusing finger at Fallon. "He does not love you. He only seeks by professing love to influence you against becoming an ally of his enemies, the Germans. I overheard his comrade today, advising him to make love to you for that purpose!"

Appalled, Fallon suddenly remembered what until now he had entirely forgotten—Helverson's naive advice to make love to the Aesir princess.

And he remembered now too that Tyr had been close to them when the Norwegian had proffered that advice. It was only too evident that the old Aesir chieftain had overheard.

Brynhild saw that sudden dismay on Fallon's face, and her own white face stiffened.

"Is this true that Tyr tells me?" she asked the American with dangerous softness.

"Let him deny it if he can," Tyr bellowed.

Fallon's voice was hoarse. "It's true that Helverson said something foolish like that. But I paid no attention to him. Brynhild, you can't believe that I had that in mind just now—"

Brynhild's small hand flashed and the stinging slap stopped the words in Fallon's throat. He stared at her unbelievingly.

Wild anger blazed in the face of Thor's daughter. The little lightnings in her blue eyes flashed out ragingly. As though sensing its mistress' mood, the crouching white lynx sprang up and snarled horribly.

"I see that I did *not* misjudge you, and that the German was right!" flared Brynhild. "Coward you may not be, but false-hearted trickster you *are!*"

"Brynhild, listen!" he pleaded desperately, but the white-hot flame of her anger brooked no defense.

"Now I see that the German spoke the truth when he said that all your outland western nations are treacherous and evil!" she blazed. "Nations whose men hate honest war, and seek to gain their cause by whispering lying words of love."

She made a furious gesture. "Tyr, my decision is made. We Aesir ally ourselves to the Germans. They, at least, fight by clean war and battle and not by trickery. With them, we'll shatter the western peoples and all their evil!"

Fallon stepped forward, in frantic appeal. "Brynhild, you *can't* do that! If you let the Germans use your powers—"

A swordpoint pricking his back checked his advance, and the harsh voice of Tyr grated a question.

"Shall I kill the dog now, niece Brynhild?"

"No, he shall see the doom of his degenerate race begin, for his greater punishment," choked the raging daughter of Thor. "He and his comrade shall ride forth with us when we Aesir go to join the Germans."

Her voice flared like a silver bugle. "Lock them up until then, Tyr. And send riders down the valley with orders to gather every warrior of the Aesir here at Valhalla tomorrow night. Tell them we go forth at last to war, that we ride forth then to join the Germans in the great battle for the outer world!"

CHAPTER VI
Wrath of a Goddess

Darkness was creeping again across the valley Asgard, like a slow, stealthy tide. During all the long day, there had been ceaseless bustle of feverish activity around Valhalla. The clang of hammers on weapons and armor, the excited shouts of hurrying men, the rattling hoofs of horsemen hastily coming and going, now faded into a tense silence with the coming of night.

Fallon looked sickly down from the narrow window at the swarms of tossing red torches in front of the castle. The torchlight glinted off the gleaming helmets and armor of hosts of horsemen who were gathering down there. There was something ominous and unnerving about the quietness of that warlike host.

His face was haggard as he turned to Helverson. The big Norwegian sat somberly in a corner of the locked room, his wrists bound behind him by hide thongs as Fallon's were. He did not raise his leonine yellow head as the American came toward him.

"We've got to *do* something!" Fallon exclaimed, his voice raw. "They're gathering down there now."

"There is nothing we can do," rumbled Helverson. "All now is in the hands of the Norns."

"Damn such fatalism!" raged Fallon. "If I'd killed Heysing as I intended, things would have been different. And even though I failed there, Brynhild still wouldn't have turned toward the Germans if it hadn't been for your cursed fool's advice that came to her ears—"

He stopped, suddenly. He looked shamefacedly at the somber, stolid Norwegian.

"I'm sorry, Nels—you know I didn't mean that," he muttered. "My nerve must be cracking.

"But we can't let Brynhild lead the Aesir out to join the Nazis," he repeated tautly. "It's not just the Aesir warriors I'm most fearful about, though their appearance will have a superstitious effect that may swing the whole north behind the Axis. It's Brynhild and her terrific powers over natural forces. I saw her call down storm and lightning, last night. If Hitler's men get the secret of powers like that—"

He left it unfinished, for his agonized mind had swung to his other and deeper torment.

"And she thinks that I made love to her only as a trick! I couldn't convince her that I do love her and always will, whether she is girl or goddess."

Helverson's thoughts had shifted, for the big Norwegian rumbled: "Many months must have passed in the outside world during the couple of days we've been in this valley. What has happened in the war out there during that time?"

Both men jumped to their feet as the lock of their door grated. Red torchlight spilled into the dusky room. Tyr and Heimdall, in full armor, entered with two warriors.

"Are you ready to ride, outlanders?" spat Tyr. "Are you ready to go forth with us and see us join the Germans to smash your lying race?"

"Tyr, let me talk with Brynhild," pleaded Fallon. "If she'll only listen to me—"

"She's listened to too many of your honeyed lies!" roared the old Aesir chieftain.

Tall Heimdall, glaring at the two comrades, added: "If we had had our way, you'd have been dead hours ago."

For a moment, Fallon's mind lit to a vague gleam of desperate hope. Perhaps the fact that Brynhild had prevented their deaths so far meant that despite her anger she had not completely conquered the love for him which she had admitted.

Then he saw the falsity of that hope. She was sparing them this long only that they might taste the bitterness of seeing the defeat and disaster of their country's forces.

Tyr shoved him roughly toward the door. "Get started, outland dog. The Aesir are ready now to ride."

Hands still bound behind them, Fallon and Helverson walked in heavy silence down the massive stairs ahead of their stalking escort. They emerged from Valhalla castle into cold, windy darkness splashed by the quivering light of many red torches.

Out here in the torchlit night, a great host of fierce-faced Aesir warriors in full armor silently sat their horses. The crimson rays glinted and gleamed from horned helmets and battered breastplates, from huge battle-axes and sword-hilts. A superhuman tension of expectation seemed brooding over the two thousand mounted men.

Thralls held the bridles of a score of unmounted horses. Fallon and the Norwegian were roughly thrust into the saddles of two of these steeds. Their hands were not unbound, and glaring Aesir warriors took the bridles of their horses to lead them.

At that moment, the tense silence of the great host was broken suddenly by a tremendous shout.

"The princess!" crashed the chorus of yelling voices.

Fallon twisted in the saddle. His heart thudded as he saw Brynhild striding lithely out of the castle into the torchlight. She wore the supple, glittering mail, but her pale golden head was unhelmed. Her light sword swung at her belt, and the white lynx loped beside her.

A little behind her came the sullen-eyed Thialfi, and the trim, handsome black figure of Victor Heysing. They were followed by the slim, mailed Valkyries.

Fallon's heart contracted with impotent rage at sight of the Nazi. Heysing showed no sign of ill effects from his wound now, and his pale eyes had a glitter of triumph in them.

"The princess! Homage to Thor's daughter!" crashed the shouts of the hosts, and a forest of swords and axes flashed up in salute.

Brynhild flung up her white hand in acknowledgment of that wild greeting. Her royal beauty was like a thing of leaping flame tonight. Her brilliant eyes swept the fierce host, ignoring Fallon.

"Lords and captains of the Aesir, this night we go forth again to that which you all have longed for—to war!" her voice rang. "Yes, to clean, honest war, man to man, sword to sword, a fair, fierce combat such as we knew and loved before we came to this valley."

"War! Good, clean war again!" yelled the eager host in fierce delight.

"Before this night passes, you shall know battle again," Brynhild promised. She gestured toward Victor Heysing. "This man tells me that the valiant Germans, who are to be our allies, are less than a night's ride from here."

"It is true!" Heysing exclaimed loudly to the host. "I went forth from this valley just now, and communicated by certain means with an army of my countrymen that is not far from here."

Fallon understood. The Nazi had gone out of the valley to his plane in the gorge, and had used its radio to communicate with the nearest German forces.

Heysing's face was flaming with excitement. "I learned that almost two years have passed in the two of your days that I've been in this valley! And during that time, our German forces have conquered all the northland except for one large guerilla band that still resists.

"A German force is even now moving to attack that band. It and the British tricksters who have deluded it into resisting us are holding a coastal village on the shore of the Arctic Ocean, only some hours' ride from here through the mountains."

Brynhild's clear voice concluded. "We ride over the mountains to join that valiant German force in its attack! We shall be their allies henceforth against the traitorous outland peoples. This very night, we Aesir awake from sluggish peace and strike again in clean, manly war!"

Deafening roar of acclamation greeted her fierce promise. As it reverberated, the daughter of Thor vaulted lightly into the saddle of her black stallion. The others were mounting hastily too.

Fallon called desperately to her. "Brynhild, you must listen to me! This purpose upon which you start is evil! You have been tricked into it by lies—"

"*You* are the one who deals in tricks!" she flamed at him. "Now you go forth with us to see the fruits of your cunning treachery."

She spurred with her Valkyries, and Heysing and Thialfi, to the front of the great host. Her glittering mailed arm flashed up into the torchlight in signal.

"Lords of the Aesir, we ride!"

Trumpeters instantly sounded their brazen horns in a long, thrilling blast. The ground shook from the tread of thousands of hoofs. The Aesir host moved forward, fierce warriors galloping knee to knee as they streamed down the valley.

Fallon, jolting in the saddle as the mounts of himself and Helverson were led by their guards just behind the Valkyries, plumbed a nadir of black despair. And the same emotion throbbed in the hoarse voice of the Norwegian.

"Fallon, did you understand what the cursed German said?" cried Helverson over the roar of rushing hoofs. "It's 1942 by now out in our own world! The Nazis have conquered all Norway except the far northern wilderness, and now they've sent an army to conquer that!"

"And Brynhild's Aesir are riding to help the Nazis do that, and crush the last Norwegian guerillas," Fallon agonized.

"They *can't* do it," Helverson asserted dazedly. "Thor's daughter will surely never use her powers against us Norse."

But Fallon had no hope left. He had lost the game to Heysing, from first to last. The German riding ahead there was on his way to a supreme triumph. It would not be long before the Nazis would penetrate the secret of Brynhild's powers. Their scientists would come to this hidden valley, would pry into the cosmic forces focused here, and forge irresistible weapons.

And Hitler's lieutenants would find a way to dispose of Brynhild, once she had served their purpose. It was maddening—the thought of how she and her clean love of combat were about to be used as a tool against the embattled democracies.

They were riding on down the dark valley, in perfect silence except for the throbbing thunder of thousands of hoofs. It did not seem long to Fallon's overstrained nerves before they were approaching the western end of the valley.

Nothing was visible ahead except a wall of blankness in the dark. It was impossible to see out of this uncanny blind-spot. When Brynhild and her Valkyries, at the head of the host, vanished magically into that blankness, Fallon knew they had emerged into the outer world.

The weird blank barrier loomed in front of his own led horse. Tyr and Heimdall and all the other Aesir chieftains were riding fearlessly on. They reached the barrier. And as he passed through it, the American felt again that sharp, wrenching shock through every atom of his body.

He was outside Asgard valley—back again in his own world of faster time.

"It is winter again, out here," Helverson was muttering, staring incredulously. "*Two* winters, since we crashed here two days ago."

That was hard for Fallon to believe too, that two years could have passed out here. For the snowy white gorge looked just the same.

The sky overhead was ablaze with the brilliant winter stars. But already the first bars and banners of the Northern Lights were wheeling across the nighted heavens as Brynhild led her host of warriors in a rapid trot down the long gorge.

Fallon, looking up haggardly at that quickening dance of the aurora across the heavens, wondered fleetingly if it could be true that Brynhild called forth those spectral lights to illuminate their way. He had little room to doubt it, knowing her mastery of storm and sky.

For hours, the Aesir host moved through the snowy mountains. Brynhild led the way ever northward, through gorges and narrow passes. They were close, Fallon knew, to the Norwegian villages on the wild Arctic coast which he himself had been making for when his plane crashed.

In silence that had a quality of gathering fierce tension, the warriors of Asgard urged their mounts over the ranges in the teeth of a bitter wind. At last the daughter of Thor halted their host beneath the slope of a last, long snowy ridge.

"Just over this ridge lies the coastland where we shall join the Germans!" she called. "Now give your horses breathing and see to your swords and axes, for soon we clash blades with our enemies."

The blazing excitement in her eyes was reflected by the fierce battle-light in the faces of all the Aesir host.

Fallon tried despairing final appeal.

"Brynhild, you can't do this thing—"

He was interrupted. Heimdall had been alertly listening and now uttered a sharp exclamation.

"Listen! There is battle now over the ridge!"

Dimly to their ears there came dull roar of distant explosions, and a lurid red light paled the aurora just north of the ridge.

Victor Heysing shouted exultantly. "It is my German comrades whom we came to join! Already they are attacking the enemy down there!"

"Then we wait here no longer!" flared Brynhild's silver voice. "Up to the ridge, men of the Aesir! We ride into battle."

"We follow, princess!" came Tyr's deep, eager shout. "Oh, that your father Thor were with us as again we sweep to war!"

Up the snowy slope spurred the whole great host, led by Brynhild's slim, shining figure and the loping lynx. And the wild war lust of the Aesir thousands broke forth in ringing battle-cries.

Fallon, gripping the saddle with his knees as his own mount was swept along by his guards, saw that Nels Helverson's face was crimson with emotion. The big Norwegian was making mad efforts to burst his bonds, as he heard the roar of battle from over the ridge.

"My countrymen and yours are fighting over there!" he cried hoarsely to Fallon. "I will fight and die with them if I can get free, even against Thor's daughter and the Aesir!"

Spread out in a long mass, the excited Aesir host reached the flattened crest of this last ridge. And there they suddenly stopped.

Brynhild had abruptly drawn rein, and so had all her fierce followers. They seemed stricken into stupefaction by the spectacle which lay before them, and whose ear-splitting uproar now clearly reached them.

Fallon, close behind her, saw the blazing excitement fade from the face of Thor's daughter. He saw it replaced by a stunned, bewildered expression.

"Why, what is this that takes place?" she exclaimed bewilderedly.

Under the Northern Lights, the scene before them was appalling. From the ridge on which they sat their horses, the snowy terrain sloped downward for two miles to the ice-fringed shore of the heaving black Arctic Ocean. Out on the sea, two small steamers were struggling bravely through the ice toward the docks of the little village on the shore.

Half the wooden houses in that Norwegian village were burning fiercely. Dive-bombers with the black swastika on their wings were swooping continually down through that lurid glare, and the shattering explosion of bombs was constant. Gouts of bursting flame seemed to engulf houses, streets, and women and children who were fleeing toward the docks.

The land side of the village was protected by low barricades of frozen earth. Behind those flimsy defenses, scattered handfuls of men with rifles were resisting the advance of a mass of several thousand Nazi infantry pressing toward them from the west. The Nazis were preceded by light tanks that already were riding roughshod over the barricades.

"What is this that we see?" exclaimed Brynhild again, seeming stunned like her followers by the hellish uproar.

"It is my countrymen who attack!" cried Victor Heysing triumphantly. "Look, they seek to conquer before those British ships can reach the harbor to take the defenders away. This is how we Germans make war."

"But *this* is not war!" burst out Brynhild. "Not clean, man-to-man war by sword and spear in equal combat, such as we Aesir knew and loved! This is a massacre by machines of iron and fire!"

A dazed cry of agreement rose from her stunned Viking followers all along the ridge.

Tyr's iron-like face was raging as he watched. "Why, these Germans are not warriors! They are butchers who slay women and children by dropping flame upon them from the sky."

"And those whom they massacre are of our own Norse blood!" cried Heimdall furiously. "The German said that his countrymen sought only to protect the Norse."

Brynhild's face was a white flame of anger and loathing. "We Aesir will never ally ourselves with a race who fight like that!"

She swung toward Fallon. "*Now* I understand at last why you said you hated war. This war *is* hateful, and so are those who unloose it upon the world."

She spurred close, and her dagger flashed and cut the bonds of the American and Norwegian. Her blue eyes appealed to Fallon.

"Outlander, I beg forgiveness! You spoke truth from first to last. It was the German who lied—"

She swung back suddenly, her voice flaring. "Where *is* the German? Seize that lying plotter!"

The mounted Aesir warriors milled upon the snowy ridge in a confusion of swift searching.

"The cursed German is gone!" yelled Tyr. "He must have seen the way the wind was blowing, and slipped back down over the ridge. And Thialfi is gone too."

"Find and seize them!" cried Thor's daughter. "If Thialfi has turned traitor and deserter—"

But the Aesir warriors who rode furiously back down behind the ridge soon returned—with Thialfi, but not with Heysing.

Loki's son was dying. A gaping slash in his throat bubbled horribly as he looked up at them from the snow in which they had laid him, and tried to speak.

"The German—slipped away from beside me when he saw your horror and rage," Thialfi choked to the princess. "I galloped after to halt him—but he turned and pretended surrender, then struck suddenly with a dagger—"

Thialfi's head rolled slack. Whatever else he had been, Loki's son had been no traitor.

Fallon saw white, terrible rage gather in Brynhild's face and stormy eyes. And that rage was reflected in the faces of all the Aesir.

"Look!" shouted Heimdall, pointing down toward the roaring battle by the village. "The Germans come toward *us!*"

It was true. The advancing Nazi force had suddenly wheeled away from the barricades it had been attacking, and was starting up the slope toward the crest on which the Aesir horsemen were.

The tanks already led the way, rumbling up the snowy slope with their snouted guns swung forward ready for action. Behind them came the masses of the infantry, in quick, rapid march.

Fallon understood instantly. "Heysing escaped to them and told them of our presence here! They're after *you,* Brynhild. If they can capture or kill you and shatter your Aesir, Heysing knows they can invade your valley and gain the key to great powers there."

"That's been the lying devil's plan all along!" cried Helverson.

A cry of rage went up from the Aesir host as all understood the duplicity with which Heysing had planned to trick them.

"They would invade Asgard, would they?" roared Tyr. He flashed his heavy sword in the air. "It seems that we shall have the fighting we hoped for, after all."

Brynhild's blue eyes were blazing. Her voice rang along the raging host on the ridge.

"From henceforth, the German butchers are our blood-enemies and the Norse and their allies our friends. Make ready, children of Asgard, for the battle is near."

Wild shouts of exultation answered her. Swords and axes flashed out in readiness. Helverson had secured Thialfi's axe, and handed the dead man's sword to Fallon.

"Brynhild, what are you going to do?" cried Fallon to the daughter of Thor. "You can't stand against those Germans. No matter how brave your warriors, swords and axes are no good against planes and tanks and guns!"

The Nazi forces were already streaming up the lower slopes. The tanks rumbling ahead in the snow would be spitting death from their machine guns within a few minutes. They and the automatic-riflemen behind them were almost within range.

And the dive-bombers that had been attacking the burning village had turned from it and were banking around in answer to radio commands. Those planes, Fallon knew, would quickly spot the Aesir host and come down upon it.

Brynhild answered Fallon's expostulation with a ringing laugh. "I tell you that despite their machines of iron, we shall shatter them this night. Now keep back from me, and await my signal."

Thor's daughter rode forward, out onto a little promontory of the snowy ridge. Her slim mailed figure and unhelmed head were silhouetted against the wild glare of burning village and flaring Northern Lights.

She raised her hands toward the sky in a fierce gesture. The Nazis charging up the slope had glimpsed her, and the machine guns of their rushing tanks spat a hail of missiles toward her. But Brynhild remained unmoving upon her steed, hands still reaching upward.

Fallon felt a great throb of fear as he saw the distant Nazi planes now roaring toward them. In a few moments, those planes would be overhead and would be diving to release their bombs and shatter the Aesir host before tanks and gunners arrived. In a few moments the girl he loved beyond life would be blasted—

The flaring sky suddenly darkened. Clouds like vast black wings closed down upon a moaning wind to blot out the aurora's rays.

"It is the storm-magic," muttered Tyr in a voice suddenly hoarse. "See—"

Fallon felt the hackles rising on his neck. Those vast black cloud-wings that had appeared so suddenly were sweeping with incredible swiftness lower and lower toward the crest of this ridge.

The moaning wind was rising to a whistling, screaming gale that smote from overhead toward the north. The throbbing planes out there were batted like leaves by the raging tempest.

"I am afraid, Fallon," husked Helverson, his eyes dilated in the ghastly dusk. "It is the wrath of the goddess—"

Heaven and earth leaped into blinding light as titanic bolts of lightning seared down out of the descending blackness. The lambent, gleaming figure of Brynhild was revealed, wild hands still raised skyward.

The American glimpsed those dazzling lightning bolts hitting the rumbling tanks down on the slope, fusing them to scorched metal. He saw the masses of Nazi infantry pause confusedly.

"The hammer of Thor's magic power falls upon them!" yelled Heimdall. "Make ready, comrades!"

Unceasing detonations of thunder rolled across the blackened sky. Torrents of raging hail were sweeping the lower slopes, and still the dancing brands of lightning struck and struck down there.

Fallon saw the struggling Nazi planes swept from the sky by that appalling storm. Continuous sheeted flares of lightning showed the German troops milling wildly down there in the snow. Out of the infernal tempest, Brynhild appeared suddenly at his side.

She was goddess indeed, now—her figure shining with that eery lambency and her wild white face transfigured in the lightning.

"Sons of the Aesir, *we ride!*" stabbed her silvery voice.

Three thousand voices crashed answer through the thunderous din, and the trumpets clamored as the yelling host spurred forward.

Fallon felt lifted out of himself by superhuman emotion as he galloped beside Brynhild down the snowy slope toward the milling enemy. He heard the blood-chilling, squalling scream of the white lynx as it leaped ahead of the racing steed of Thor's daughter.

His sword was in his hand and he was leaning far out over the neck of his mount as they rushed down through the lightning and hail and darkness. And over all the uproar rose the stabbing cry of Brynhild and the Valkyries.

"Yo to ho!"

They smashed down into the hosts of Nazi infantry like a thunderbolt. Fallon, seeking to spur ahead of Brynhild for her protection, glimpsed scared, desperate German faces and striking bayonets everywhere.

He hacked furiously down with his sword at men who sought to swing up their rifles to shoot. He saw Nazi soldiers recoiling with screams of horror from the leaping white lynx, and glimpsed Tyr shouting fiercely as he struck. And close by in the press, Helverson rode and whirled his heavy axe, blood-mad with heat of battle.

But try as he might, Fallon could not spur ahead of Brynhild. The slim sword of the daughter of Thor leaped in blurringly swift and deadly stabs. And always, it seemed, the sheeted lightning struck just ahead of her galloping horse, and advanced with her.

Out of the phantasmagoric, lightning-lit battle, a furious and wolfish face rushed toward Fallon. All Victor Heysing's handsomeness was gone as he came riding toward the American with a levelled automatic spitting fire from his hand.

Fallon felt the tug of the bullets at his jacket and through the uproar heard Heysing's raging shout.

"Gott, I'll at least take you—"

Lightning rocked the crazy scene as Fallon spurred into the spitting pistol with his sword extended straight toward the German.

He felt the stinging sear of one bullet along his thigh, and then his outstretched blade tore into Heysing's body and he felt its hilt smack hard against the German's ribs. The onward rush of his steed tore loose his sword, and he looked back to see the Nazi fall from the saddle.

The Nazi troops were everywhere fleeing in confusion, now. And after them rode the raging Aesir warriors. Within the half hour, it was all over. The storm was muttering away, and Fallon was almost glad that darkness veiled the scattered hosts of German dead on the snowy slope.

He sat his horse beside Brynhild on the crest as the Aesir host regathered and came riding back up the slope. A wild shout crashed from them as they raised red swords and axes in salute to Thor's daughter.

"Homage, princess! Thanks to your storm-magic, we have left no German living here!"

"Aye, but there are others of the butchers in the northland," Brynhild reminded them. "And now we Aesir shall not rest until they are driven back from whence they came. We shall ride forth again and again from our valley and strike them wherever we find them, until the land is clean of them."

"We hear and we will follow you, princess!" came the fierce answer.

"And *I* will follow you, if you let me," Helverson rumbled, his face flaming.

But Fallon was silent. And Brynhild looked at him in sudden anxious earnestness. "I know that you come with us, too."

He shook his head heavily, and pointed down at the distant village where the two ships had now reached dock and were embarking the refugees.

"Those ships go to England, Brynhild," he said slowly. "And I must go with them."

"But you cannot!" she cried. Her brilliant eyes burned into his. "Outlander, you know that I love you. Even when I was angry for what I thought your deception, I still loved you and was sure that you loved me."

He leaned in the saddle to put his arms close around her and to feel the thrilling contact of her lips.

"Girl or goddess, I do love you, Brynhild," he said hoarsely. "But I swore an oath of duty that I must keep. I must go back to England to take up again my part in the war in the sky."

Her white face yearned toward him. "But you will come back, Outlander?"

"I'll come back, Brynhild. Nothing can keep me from coming back."

Fallon stood at the rail of the crowded little British freighter as it and its sister ship struggled doggedly out through the ice to open sea. He stood looking back achingly at the wilderness of snowy mountains that stretched awesome and forbidding beyond the shore.

The joyful Norwegian refugees who crowded the deck behind him were still excitedly discussing the mystery of their salvation. All they knew was that some terrific battle had taken place on the distant slopes which had destroyed the Nazis who had been on the point of conquering them. Storm had veiled that battle, and the mystery of their saviors' identity was unsolved.

"They must have been a large force of Norwegian guerillas, who went back into the mountains after they destroyed the Nazis," said a man.

A tall Norse woman, her eyes glowing with a strange light, shook her head.

"They were the old gods, come back from Asgard to help our people. Only Thor or his daughter could have blasted the invaders by storm like that."

Fallon, in the months to follow, was to hear that half-eager, half-doubtful assertion time and again, in the strange stories that were to drift out of embattled Norway.

Stories were to come of the old gods reappearing to aid their invaded land, of the mighty Aesir coming down again and again in night and storm in raids upon German posts; stories of the mystification and anger and fear of the Nazis, of the whisper of hope running through that northern land that Thor's daughter and her Valkyries were riding again, a whisper and hope that would keep Norway's people fighting until the tyrants could be overthrown.

Some day, Fallon knew, that overthrow would come. And some day, he would come back again to that wild, weird northern land, and would ride up into the mountains to the valley where the daughter of Thor would be waiting.

ALSO AVAILABLE

Want to get an e-book for free? *The Infernal Bargain and Other Stories* is available exclusively for DMR Books mailing list subscribers. Go to www.DMRBooks.com and get your copy now!

Cahena by Manly Wade Wellman - The brave and beautiful warrior queen known as the Cahena was believed to be a sorceress and prophetess. Her glorious reign over the Berbers in the seventh century was marked by passionate romance, stirring battles, and bold mystical deeds. Rich in historical detail and dramatic action, this is a story to rival the great war epics of all time. DMR Books is proud to bring Manly Wade Wellman's final novel back into print for the first time since 1986.

Renegade Swords – This anthology contains eight fantastic tales, each of them obscure or overlooked in some way. Includes stories by Robert E. Howard, Clark Ashton Smith, Manly Wade Wellman, and more!

Swordsmen from the Stars by Poul Anderson – Three classic novellas from the pages of *Planet Stories*. Heroic science fantasy at its best!

Lands of the Earthquake by Henry Kuttner/Under a Dim Blue Sun by Howie K. Bentley – The first split release from DMR Books in the tradition of the Ace Double series! *Lands of the Earthquake* is a classic science-fantasy adventure from the pulp era that has never been published in book form before. On the flip side you'll find a brand new sword-and-planet tale. A US soldier hijacks a Nazi spaceship and lands on a planet threatened by snake-men!

The Thief of Forthe and Other Stories by Clifford Ball – After the death of Robert E. Howard, Clifford Ball was the first writer to follow in his footsteps and pen sword and sorcery stories for *Weird Tales.* For the first time ever, all of Ball's stories are collected into one volume. A must-have for pulp historians and fans of fantasy, horror, and weird fiction!

The Sapphire Goddess: The Fantasies of Nictzin Dyalhis – At last, the stories of one of the most unusual writers of weird fiction are collected! This volume contains all of Nictzin Dyalhis' works of fantasy and science fiction, many of which have never before been reprinted. Those who love the wild imagination and masterful prose of authors such as Clark Ashton Smith and C.L. Moore are sure to enjoy this collection.

A Million Years in the Future by Thomas P. Kelley - For countless millennia, Earth has been ravaged by the Black Raiders from the distant planet Capara. The last surviving Earthman, Prince Jan, is captured by the Raiders and taken to their home planet. Will Jan learn the secret to destroy Capara, or will he perish? *A Million Years in the Future* was originally serialized in *Weird Tales* in 1940, and has never been published in book form before.

Necromancy in Nilztiria by D.M. Ritzlin - The world of Nilztiria is an ancient one. Beneath its brilliant crimson sun and demon-haunted moons wondrous treasures lay buried, waiting to be uncovered by intrepid adventurers. Yet peril abounds as well, in the form of nefarious sorcerers, grotesque beasts, and inexplicable phenomena. If you crave stories of adventure and wonder with a touch of gallows humor, look no further than these thirteen tales of Nilztiria!

Printed in Great Britain
by Amazon

10907436R10139